A Skirt in the Ranks

daughter of Er + Joyce Georges

Kathleen Gasior

Copyright © 2017 Kathleen Gasior
All rights reserved.

ISBN: 1512175889
ISBN 13: 9781512175882

DEDICATION

For the men in my life: For my Dad, Elvin, who loved a good story. For my brother Peter, who always has my back. For my husband, Luke, who simply kept whispering, "Write the book." And for my son, Evan, who reminds me that all things are possible.
K.

1

2001

Julianna Petersen wakes as she does every morning, with her husband Chris gently squeezing her toe. Jules is a light sleeper and the squeeze is all it takes to rouse her to consciousness. It is five-thirty a.m. and Chris is leaving to catch the six-fifteen train into Manhattan. An attorney working for Cantor Fitzgerald, he has repeated this routine every weekday for the past four years.

"Hey, babe, I'm going."

She looks squint-eyed at the clock. "It's early, isn't it?"

"Yeah, but it's beautiful out, I'm going to walk, grab a cup of coffee." Their house is fifteen minutes from the train station, an easy walk when the weather is right.

She looks out the bedroom window, open and letting in a crisp breeze. The sun is just up, promising one of those crystalline late-summer days.

"How's your day look today?" she asks.

"Brutal. Two depositions before lunch and then I get to spend the afternoon writing motions for the Dellaventura trial."

She wrinkles her nose, "That sucks. Regular time tonight?"

"Even if I have to bring work home." He sits on the edge of the bed and slides his hand under the covers, relishing the feel of her warm, soft skin. This is part of their routine too. "Maybe we could go to bed early," he says, nuzzling her neck, "work on that project."

'That project' is getting trying to get Jules pregnant, something they have been doing for the past two months. She laughs and puts her arms around his neck, loving the soapy, male smell of him in the morning.

"Maybe we could work on it now and you could be just a little bit late," she offers. "What time is your deposition?"

He kisses her. "Eight-thirty. I gotta go, baby, can't be late today. I'll take a rain check, though. See you tonight?"

She smiles ruefully, not wanting to let him go. "Okay, tonight. Have a good day; don't let the bastards get you down."

He grins—the handsome, wolfish smile that captured her from the first day they met, nine years ago. "Not a chance. They don't know who they're dealing with. Besides, I got my secret side project, so now I'm really motivated."

"Go get 'em, baby." She slides back under the covers, seduced by the warmth of the bed.

"Hey, Jules."

She peers out from under the comforter; he has one hand on the door jamb, poking his head back into the bedroom.

"Mmm?"

"I love you."

"You too."

It is eight-fifty-five a.m. and Jules is in court, working as a victim advocate for the domestic violence unit of the county prosecutor's office. Her first case is a twenty-four-year-old whose husband tried to strangle her when she was four months pregnant. The municipal prosecutor is reading the charges aloud when a bailiff approaches the bench and leans in to whisper to the judge.

Damn, what now? A delay at this time could throw her whole day off. She's guessing it's some tactic from the defense attorney; introducing a new witness or asking for another postponement. The judge nods to the bailiff, who exits briskly. The judge clears his throat and hesitates before speaking.

"We're going to take a short recess....it ah, it appears there's something happening in New York." There is whispering among those assembled in the courtroom. "The attorneys may join me in chambers. Please make sure that your clients remain separate for safety reasons."

Jules quietly instructs her client to wait in the municipal prosecutor's office with one of the cops who's working the case.

She and the defense attorney, McCormick, file into the judge's chambers, along with the municipal prosecutor, the bailiff, and the court administrator. The judge looks just as confused as they are. He is turning on a small TV behind his desk. The first channel that appears shows a female reporter standing in front of the World Trade Center in New York, the North Tower dissected by a gigantic plume of smoke and flame marring blue sky. The reporter is talking in a pressured voice, posing unanswered questions about the accident: Small plane? Commercial airliner?

They catch her in mid-sentence: "... limited information from the FAA at this time." At that moment a second plane flies directly over the reporter's head, imploding into the South Tower.

Jules feels time slow down, people in the room are gasping and crying out. She is counting floors. Cantor Fitzgerald offices occupy 101 and 103 to 105 of the North Tower. Chris could be either on 104 or 105 today. The fire is below those floors; Jules knows this but doesn't want to know it. There have been problems in the towers before and they've gotten the occupants out. The matronly court administrator, Rose, is whispering to her assistant, discreetly inclining her head towards Jules. Rose knows that Chris works at World Trade. Everyone in the rooms stares at the television as the judge flips channels looking for more information. Jules watches the buildings burn for what feels like hours.

The reporter is talking faster now, improvising in the absence of actual facts. "...Clearly some kind of terrorist attack. We know now that this is not just an accident."

Jules feels someone pushing a chair against the back of her knees. It is McCormick, who has been informed that she has someone in the towers. "Sit down, Jules." She sits, completely focused on her own thoughts. They'll bring helicopters in above the burning floors; land them on the roof to evacuate the employees. *They must have the capability to do that, right?*

Time passes as Jules tries to puzzle it out logically, trying desperately not to let the rising panic overtake her. She racks her brain. *What time did he say the deposition was?* She is having trouble believing Chris is actually there, that this is happening.

The news cuts back to a pair of bewildered-looking news anchors who stutter out the fact that yet another plane has crashed, this time into the Pentagon in Washington, D.C. Rose comes and kneels beside Julianna, gently touching her hand. Jules flinches as if she's been cut.

"Jules, honey, do you want to hold my hand?"

Being touched will make it real.

"No, Rose, thank you. I just, I just….." she trails off, not knowing what she needs. She needs to wake up from this dream. She will wake up under the comforter on their bed and Chris will be there next to her, warm and still sleeping. She'll wake him and tell him she had a horrible dream about the towers.

One of the clerks lets out a stifled scream; Jules lifts her eyes to the screen in time to see the south tower come down. She feels a crushing weight in her chest, a rise of bile as a clammy film of fear coats her skin. She doesn't realize she's stopped breathing until she hears herself gasping for air.

Jules is going away, her mind protecting her from the moment. She feels vaporous, a ghost watching papers flutter against the brilliant blue sky. She is unaware of anything but her own breathing. Time—minutes? hours?—crawls by. The room is filled with people who've pushed in from the courtroom, clutching each other's arms, unable to tear their eyes from screen.

An affiliate station cuts in, reporting another plane crash in Shanksville, Pennsylvania. Jules is losing her grip on the situation.

The world has gone mad, it seems, with planes simply falling out of the sky. One of her friends, Trooper Riddick, leans in over her shoulder. "Jules, do you want me to drive you home?" A chivalrous but ludicrous question; she doesn't even live in this county. She turns to face him. "No, thank you, John," her voice is oddly formal.

She begins to hear the police radios crackle with new dispatches. John looks at her, appearing torn between duty and her obvious, immediate need. "Okay, Jules, I'll talk to you soon. Call me if you need anything." The cops push their way toward the door and he joins them.

Jules hears sound bites of whispered conversations around her. She closes her eyes and tries to quell the nausea, but the world tilts dangerously so she opens them again. She looks reluctantly at the television. There is a sudden collective scream as the North tower collapses, lightly, like a house of cards. Everyone in the room is frozen, the women crying. The judge stands, zipping his robe back up and trying gamely to compose himself. He turns to Jules, his eyes locking with hers. They have known each other for years. He knows the truth of her situation, but will not speak it yet.

He makes an announcement to the room. "We'll recess court for the day. Mrs. Johnson, cancel everything. People need to get home." He leaves the room, squeezing Jules' shoulder on the way out.

The squeeze jars something in her brain. *Chris squeezed her toe this morning, just like every morning.* Her cell phone is in the car, as it always is when she's in court. He will call her. He may be calling her now. She races from the room, fumbling her keys from her briefcase. She gets the car open and retrieves her cell from the console. She flips it open. The message icon is on.

Julianna freezes. He has already called; she missed him. She looks at the time stamp: nine-ten a.m. He could have gotten out, could have been out of the building for some reason.

She hesitates, understanding that she can never take this moment back; the moment before knowing.

She dials the voice mail with a shaking hand and punches in her password. She closes her eyes. *Please God, please God, please.*

"Jules, it's me." Chris' voice sounds shaky. "Look, honey, I guess you're watching or something; or you're in court, maybe you haven't seen, but there's this fire below us." There is a long pause. "It's bad, Jules, really bad. The thing is Jules….I don't think…we're not getting out of here. I know that's not what you want to hear, it's not what I want to say, but it's true. They're not even evacuating us." She can hear screaming and crying in the background. "Some people are…they're jumping…I'm not going to do that, I can't do that. I'm going to help for as long as I can. The girls here, they're really scared. Shit, we're all really scared." A longer pause. "Anyway, I guess I should have stayed home and worked on that project with you." He barks a short, ironic laugh. "I know this wasn't part of the plan Jules, I'm so fuckin' sorry. I love you so much; I just want you to know that. And there's nothing unsaid between us, okay? I know how much you love me." She hears the exploding glass. "I have to hang up now. I don't want to, but it's getting pretty crazy here and I don't want to get cut off. So, I love you, Julianna. Everything's going to be okay. I know you'll be okay. You're the strongest person I know. So, I need you to be strong now for both of us, okay?" His voice cracks. He is crying. "All right, baby. I love you so much. I'll be with you, Jules. I'll always be with you."

She holds the phone to her ear for a long time, rocking quietly. Scared to let go of his voice, she finally presses the Save button.

2

Three years later

The sleek blonde secretary nods to her. "Ms. Petersen, Mr. Williamson will see you now."

Julianna stands, smoothing her skirt and glancing down once more to make sure she has no spots on her suit. She follows the secretary to a heavy set of oak doors and is ushered in.

Robert Williamson, CEO of RSW Geological, Inc., looks exactly as she expected: early fifties, blankly handsome, full head of silver hair. He carries himself with the ease of bearing that only generations of spectacular wealth can give. Crossing the room to her, Williamson offers his hand and then gestures to a man seated on the left side of the desk. The man, a rangy Latino with an annoyed look on his face, stands slowly. He reaches out to shake her hand.

Williamson makes the introduction, "This is my lieutenant, Ramon Ramirez. Lieutenant, Julianna Petersen." She takes his hand, her grip firm and measured. Ramirez nods curtly.

"Good to meet you, Lieutenant," she says.

Shit, this guy is the real deal. Lieutenant Ramon Ramirez, according to the information she could find on the corporate website, leads Williamson's in-house security detail. Everything else is a guess. Early forties maybe, Puerto Rican or Cubano. Definitely ex-military, definitely hardcore. Handsome in an intimidating way. Brown eyes, black hair cut short, graying in front and at the temples. No smile, no warmth, only assessment: measuring her value to the organization, to him. It is obvious to her that he will be the real interviewer.

"Please, Ms. Petersen, sit down," Williamson offers. He leans back in his chair and gets comfortable before he begins. "So, the lieutenant and I have reviewed your resume and completed your background checks. While it appears that your prior performance is exemplary, when it comes to experience in *this* field, you have nothing to speak of. Quite frankly, the only reason we're seeing you today is on the recommendation of your instructors. They seem to believe that you're a natural. Would you care to elaborate?"

After losing Chris she'd been floundering, looking for a way to start over. Needing a way to channel her anger, she'd turned to her previous passion for martial arts. After she and Chris had been married and settled into their home life, she'd spent years taking boxing and kickboxing classes, loving the combination of tough physical exertion and mental focus required for the sports.

Six months after 9/11, when it was clear that Jules was struggling emotionally, one of her instructors had suggested she try a hand-to-hand combat technique called Krav Maga.

As she explored the new discipline, she found it was an antidote to the creeping depression and hopelessness that pervaded her waking hours. As she trained harder, she felt stronger and was finally able to sleep properly. Even her appetite came back. She was still working but needed to make a change. A year after losing Chris, she quit her job at the prosecutor's office, finished her black belt in Krav and became a certified instructor, teaching four days a week. Spurred on by her newfound confidence, she started to research other careers. She'd looked into Homeland Security, but quickly realized that because of her status as a victim of 9/11 she'd never pass the vetting process.

Trolling websites, she saw an ad for the Executive Protection Academy. When her heart started pounding as she read the curriculum, she knew she had found something to work towards. If she could train, fight and learn to protect others, she wouldn't have to spend the rest of her life being a victim.

Facing her interviewers, Julianna takes a breath and tries to speak without letting her nerves show. "Sir, I'm fully aware that I have zero experience in the field. I know that your firm employs the best security detail in the country. I know that applying here is a bit of a reach, but I've given this a lot of thought. I'd rather start with any assignment here than a better position with a less reputable team. I'm a quick study and a hard worker. I've been training and studying full-time for almost two years. This is what I want to do and I'd love to do it here." She turns to Ramirez for a reaction. He is completely impassive.

"You're qualified expert on pistol and rifle?" Ramirez is reading from her training file.

"Yes, Lieutenant."

"What's your preferred weapon for carrying?"

"I prefer a nine-millimeter Glock. I realize a forty-five has more stopping power, but the Glock is more comfortable for me."

He nods.

She is getting the distinct impression that this interview is merely an exercise on his part, designed to pacify Williamson, who had decided he wanted to bring a woman onto the detail. On the phone last week, Williamson blathered on about "updating our image to keep in step with the new diversity."

The RSW crew is entirely male. Julianna understands that Williamson's impulse to hire a woman for his security detail is spurred only by a desire to be politically correct, but intends to use that desire to get her foot in the door of one of the most highly regarded teams in the field of executive protection.

Williamson launches into the standard line of questioning. He covers her resume, which includes a degree in social work, her long tenure at the county prosecutor's office, and a certification in executive protection, roughly one-hundred hours earned over a seven-day period.

Julianna emphasizes her expertise in martial arts: five years of training in boxing and kickboxing and two in Krav Maga.

Just as she's starting to feel confident, things get personal.

Williamson begins, "Of course you know that we've done an extensive background check, Ms. Petersen. There are some things we'll need to explore."

"Of course," she replies evenly. She knows what's coming.

"Forgive me for being indelicate, but you're a widow, quite a young one at that."

"Yes." Best not to give them anything they're not asking for. She is pretty sure no one in this room cares about her feelings.

"You were married for nine years. May I ask how your husband died?"

She waits a beat, thinking. If he knows Chris is dead, then of course he knows what happened. He is simply testing her ability to keep her composure. She feels Ramirez watching her like a predator. She tells the story, condensed after hundreds of recitations. "He died on September eleventh. He was in the North Tower, at Cantor Fitzgerald, when it came down." She takes a soft, deep breath, trying to quiet her hammering heart.

Ramirez cuts in, and she feels herself being positioned for a vital strike. "These last few years must have been stressful for you. What makes you think you're ready to take on a completely new career at this point?"

She takes her time, choosing her words carefully. *No mistakes now, Jules.*

> "Well, I spent about a year really struggling. Of course, others were grieving too; I was just one of thousands. I had my friends and family around, and they took great care of me. Unfortunately, grief is something you go through alone. I finally decided I had to grab hold of a goal, something that was just mine. I wanted to do homeland security, but the first people I spoke to about it made it clear that my personal experience with 9/11 would be seen as a liability. My research led me to personal protection, a way to help one person at a

time. So I started training; that was how I got through losing him." *Honest, direct, but not a sob story. Ramirez is looking for weakness, she won't hand it to him on a platter.*

He frowns at her, unmoved. "We've seen a lot of candidates over the past few weeks, most who were completely incompetent and didn't last more than ten minutes. This isn't the kind of job you get by answering a couple of interview questions."

"Understood, Lieutenant."

"The first issue is you're too attractive. We don't need our crew drawing attention. You'd have to blend in better."

"Okay …any suggestions?" She can play this game.

He looks her up and down with a critical eye. Jules has never felt so exposed. She'd spent days deciding on the outfit, a plain navy suit, modest but confident. She has her dark hair pulled back into a sleek chignon and is wearing only mascara and nude lipstick. Her only jewelry is a watch and pearl stud earrings.

"No skirts, except for formal occasions or business overseas. No heels over two inches, no visible makeup and no flashy jewelry. No visible lingerie, hair pulled back except for dress occasions."

No visible lingerie? What is she, a stripper? Perhaps he'd like her to visit his barber and get a crew cut.

"That all seems perfectly reasonable."

"We attend a lot of social events, dinners, charity balls, weddings. The attendees are very well-lubricated men and their extremely influential women. However, these men are VIPs, who can never be embarrassed or lose face. Understood?"

"Yes."

"Stand up."

She complies immediately, trying to appear relaxed and assured.

"Over here." He gestures for her to take a position against a blank wall covered in some kind of expensive-looking fabric. She stands as if she were on post, eyes ahead, hands clasped loosely in front of her.

"Now, I'm an inebriated male, who happens to be one of Mr. Williamson's associates. Deflect me without drawing attention to the situation."

"Of course."

The lieutenant approaches her in an unsteady line, doing a damn good impersonation of a drunk. When he reaches her, he puts one hand on the wall next to her head, the other on her waist and leans in way too close for comfort. He begins whispering in her ear.

"You're way too pretty to be stuck in a job like this. I happen to be looking for a personal assistant. I'll pay you more and make sure you get regular bonuses," Ramirez hisses as he aggressively presses his hip into hers.

He is convincing enough to make Jules' skin crawl. She has already had enough. "I appreciate your interest, Mr. Jones, but I'm quite happily employed," she replies in a conversational tone. She takes his hand off her hip delicately and exerts enough backward pressure on his pinkie finger to make him move away from her in pain and surprise. She deftly maneuvers him so that *his* back is now against the wall. Jules brings her thigh up into his pelvic bone—just hard enough to make him squirm, but not scream. "I really need to go check on my partner. You have a pleasant evening now, Mr. Jones," she says sweetly, releasing him and walking away.

"Brava!" cries Williamson. "Well done!"

Ramirez composes himself, looking at her without amusement.

Jules can see she won't be getting any Brownie points for their little skit.

"Wait outside while we talk," he growls, dismissing her.

Williamson nods and smiles encouragingly.

She takes her previous seat in the waiting area, lush with potted plants and silky wall coverings. The secretary looks at her sympathetically. "Well, you've been in there a lot longer than any of the others," she whispers.

Jules smiles, shrugging. "It's anybody's guess at this point."

Twenty excruciating minutes pass, during which she is sure the lieutenant is enumerating an endless list of flaws and inadequacies, including her emotional instability and barely visible lip color.

Finally the door opens and only Ramirez emerges — not a good sign, she's sure. He barks, "Do you have PT gear with you?"

"Yes, I have a gear bag in my vehicle." Thank God, she always carries her training gear in the car, just in case she ends up running late for a class.

"Get it and meet me in the gym. I'll show you where to change."

She hustles to her car and grabs the bag, abruptly realizing that he did not give her directions to the gym. She is positive, though, that this is not an oversight, but part of the testing. Protection agents have to be able to find their way through strange buildings and locations. She heads back in, showing her visitor's pass to the two men on duty at the reception desk. "Can you direct me to the gym?"

"Sorry, *amiga*," the taller man says. "We have instructions not to give you any information from this point on. Part of the drill." He shrugs.

She nods and then notices that he is emphatically tapping the point of his pen on the desk. Jules grins. *Downstairs.* "*Gracias.*"

She takes the stairs, grateful for the chance to stretch her legs at last. She follows the scent of bleach and male sweat to a set of double doors down the corridor. Gathering her courage, she steps through the doors and pauses at the threshold.

The gym is large and hard-used, but very clean. Five speed bag stations along one wall, six heavy bags of good quality, nothing fancy. The entire floor is covered in thick blue mats and in the far left-hand corner is a full-size boxing ring. *A good sign*, she thinks. It means these men take their fitness and combat skills seriously. There are only two sets of free weights, something that encourages her further.

A lot of guys think bulk equals badass, but it's a misconception. In her experience, cardiovascular endurance is everything. A real fight may last only a minute or two, but if you have poor conditioning, it will be the longest two minutes of your life. In hand-to-hand combat training, she learned that the big guys go down easy, but the smaller, more compact ones give you a run for your money. They're faster and get winded far less quickly.

As a sign of respect and deference to the trainer, Jules slips her dress shoes off at the door. One never walks onto the mats in street shoes; mats are expensive and a pain in the ass to keep clean. She spots the lieutenant across the gym, perched on bleachers next to the boxing ring. He is accompanied by a short, beefy Latino of indeterminate age with close-cropped, curly black hair. As she gets closer, she sees that his nose, a sculpture of cartilage and flesh, appears to have been broken several times.

Okay Jules, here we go. Don't lose your nerve now. She squares her shoulders and approaches the pair.

Ramirez makes a point of looking at his watch when she arrives in front of them, implying that she is late for some unmentioned arrival time.

"This is our trainer, Jorgé Suarez. He runs this place."

"Hola. ¿Como esta?" She puts out her hand.

"*Esta bien. Mucho gusto.*" He nearly crushes her hand with his huge paw. She tries not to flinch. Where did they find this guy? Now that he's in front of her she can see that he's in his twenties, but his face looks like it's been dragged behind a truck.

Ramirez cuts in, impatient with the social niceties. "We don't have a women's locker room. There's a storage closet next to the office. You can change in there. Make it quick, though. You're cutting into lunch."

"Yes sir." As if she were the one who made the interview stretch out for an hour and a half. *He's a real charmer. Unfortunate that he doesn't have a personality to go with that amazing body.*

She finds the storage closet; it is surprisingly orderly. Jorgé clearly takes his job seriously. She struggles out of her business attire and into workout clothes, a black racer-back sport top that hits at her waist and loose, knee-length judo pants. Realizing that the top will expose the tattoo on her shoulder, she throws on a large white t-shirt over the outfit. She pulls on socks and laces up clean gym sneakers. She grabs a pair of rolled hand wraps, unsure of what tasks she'll be asked to perform. Better to be prepared than not. She takes a couple of deep breaths and looks skyward for spiritual support. Finding only water stains, she exits her VIP locker room.

Jorgé is warming up, doing some light stretching and shadowboxing.

Jules watches him. *Great, I'm going to get my ass kicked by a guy who's built like a cinderblock.*

Ramirez approaches, "Jorgé will put you through a series of PT tests. Afterward you'll do some light sparring and then you can show us some of that Krav voodoo."

"Yes, sir."

Jorgé instructs her to stretch first, and as she complies, Ramirez barks at her again. "Take the t-shirt off, I want to see what kind of shape you're actually in."

She strips the shirt off, wondering if he is deliberately trying to embarrass her. *I'm in great fucking shape, thank you very much.* Jules has worked her ass off to get in the best possible condition. She realized early on that a woman breaking into a man's field needed to be as strong, fit, and fast as anyone they could put her up against. Training six days a week for the past two years she'd carved out a lean, curvy body most women would trade their bank accounts for.

As she tosses the shirt aside, she braces herself for their evaluation. *So much for covering the tattoo.* It's a rendering of a thistle in flower, in a graceful *S*-shape across her shoulder blade. Entwined in the thorny stalks are the words, BREATHE, FIGHT, TRUST, BE. She loves the piece and is not ashamed to show it, but the personal nature of it makes her want to keep it from Ramirez's scrutiny.

His gaze rakes over her body, a lift of an eyebrow showing he's not unimpressed, and despite her best intentions, she drops her gaze from him, feeling a flush in her cheeks. She swallows hard. *Focus, dammit. You'd better get your head on straight or Jorgé's going to "lightly spar" you into next week.*

Jorgé puts her through a series of timed physical training tests: military pushups, pull-ups, sit-ups and triceps dips, all with a minimum number which must be completed for her to pass. The tests are standard—things every law enforcement and military class in the world endures in order to achieve the highest levels of fitness. All are exercises Jules does in every class with her students. She tackles them easily.

Jorgé nods every time he hits the stopwatch, pleased with her strength and perfect form. Jules is sweating and just starting to breathe hard, but after the tedium of the previous hours, it is blissful to work out the tension in her muscles.

Although she'd prefer not to have the commandant watching her every move, she finds it a welcome change from the verbal grilling. After about twenty minutes of PT, Jorgé motions her to move into the ring, asking if she wants hand wraps. She holds hers up, indicating that she'll use her own gear.

Jules winds the cloth wraps in figure-eights around her wrists, knuckles, and palms, using the time to make a game plan for sparring with Jorgé. He is shorter than her, so reach will not be a problem, but those bricks of his that pass for hands mean she'll have to protect herself at all times, especially her torso.

She will wear a sparring helmet, and they will be "going light," but she has no illusions that one 'light' shot could leave her with a broken rib or rattle her brains to the point of incoherence. If that happens, the application process will undoubtedly come to a screeching halt, and she'll end up working for some hack company doing mall security.

She pulls on the helmet, inserts a mouth guard, and works her hands into a pair of well-worn leather boxing gloves. Ramirez looks suddenly very happy and alert. Julianna's sure he wishes he could do the job himself, if that were possible without messing up his expensive suit.

She pulls herself up into the ring and approaches Jorgé.

"All right, Ms. Petersen, we'll do a three-minute round at seventy percent. You don't have chest protection, so I won't hit your upper torso. Keep those hands up and show me what you got. Nice and easy."

She nods and goes to her corner.

Her boxing experience is limited; she's never competed; only sparred for conditioning and to learn the sport. Boxing is called the "sweet science" for a reason. It truly is both an art and a science. Just to make it more complex, nearly every boxer and trainer in the world has a slightly different style.

In her corner, Jules waits for the bell that will signal the beginning of the round. When it goes off, she moves to the center of the ring and touches gloves with Jorgé. They move clockwise, sizing each other up. In a real fight it might pay to move in aggressively, but she needs to be careful and methodical. If he lands a surprise shot, Jules may well be finished before she begins. She moves in, closing the distance between them. She forgets about Ramirez. Now the universe consists only of her and the man in front of her.

She curls her body in, abs tight, hands up, chin down, leading all movement with her left foot in a classic boxer's stance. Julianna gauges her reach to him with a quick left jab. About an inch short if she wants to follow all the way through, she adjusts her proximity, all the while circling away from him. He is good: he slipped her jab easily, good reflexes.

Jorgé brings his own jab now, moving in close because his arms are shorter than hers. She counters with a right, pulling the punch slightly to meet the seventy percent rule he's set for the round. From there, they get into it.

Jules employs classic left, right, left-hook combinations, nothing fancy, just showing him her basic skills. Jorgé seems fond of the jab, right-uppercut combination, so she learns quickly to protect her jaw at all times with her left hand. There is a spot on every human being, along the jawline, about an inch from the center of the chin. Fighters call it 'the button' because if you're able to push it, your adversary crumples nicely to the floor and you win.

Jorgé lands a nice right hand in combination, and it rocks her a little. She moves back to regain her equilibrium, and he pursues her.

Jules is getting winded, breathing improperly from her own nervousness and his increasing aggression. Now that he has seen what she's capable of, Jorgé's increasing the pace and the intensity. She glances at the round timer. It reads one-fifty-five. More than halfway there, but miles to go before she rests.

As she turns her head, she is surprised to see that Ramirez has been joined on the bleachers by Williamson and several other spectators. Jules breathes deeply in through her nose, keeping her eyes locked on Jorgé. He may be the trainer, but she suspects from the way he's sucking air that he doesn't do a lot of cardio work.

She realizes that he is tired too. She uses this as an opportunity, moving suddenly and aggressively to him, landing a nice right to the jaw and a decent left hook to his body. Jorgé breaks his own rule, momentarily dropping his hands due to fatigue. She presses the issue with a flurry of jabs, driving him back nearly to the ropes. He counters by taking a loopy swing to her head, catching her on the temple. A little more than seventy percent, but so sloppy that she saw it coming and was pulling back even as he connected. Jules feels a dull pain in her head, but shakes it off.

They part again, circling each other once more. Jules is exhausted, but as she tells her students, now is the time to dig deep. She feints left and then drives in with a hard right, catching him on his unprotected chin.

Jorgé feels it, but it seems to piss him off more than slow him down, and he comes back hard. She has to move backward, weaving away from a barrage of punches. The good news is that nothing connects, and this last burst of aggression cost him all his wind. Thankfully, the round timer rings while they are both trying to figure out what to do next.

Jules pulls off the sparring helmet and spits out the mouth guard to facilitate breathing. Jorgé does the same and they stand there, panting and grinning.

He concedes, "Nice job. You made me work. Got a couple nice shots in, too. You box a lot?"

"Just for cardio, not in competition, but I love it. I watch a lot of fights and read a lot about boxing." She realizes too late what a geek she sounds like. *How many women sit around reading about boxing?*

"Hey, Ramon, whatcha think? Girl made me work, she got a bad right, too," he yells to the bleachers.

Jules turns her attention to Ramirez. He is nodding assent if not approval. He turns and says something to Williamson, who smiles. One of the spectators is climbing into the ring bearing two water bottles. He tosses one to Jorgé and brings the other to her. Another Latino, slight and handsome, with glossy black hair and an intriguing intensity. His brown eyes seem to gleam with some private joke.

He grins at her. "Hi, I'm Gi, Lieutenant's second. That was nice! Jorgé's slow, but if he catches you right, you're going down. You know how to take a punch, girl."

"Thanks. I'm Julianna. My friends call me Jules."

"Well, Jules, none of the other *chicas* made it into the gym; you must be doing something right." He leans in, making a show of helping her pull off the gloves. Softly he says, "Ramon can be a real ballbuster, but he's the best in the business. Do what he tells you and maybe we'll see you on the other side. You're doing good, drink that water."

She smiles at the floor, aware that she is being watched closely. "Thanks. I will."

Jules sighs, flexing her aching hands. She sips the water, realizing she has had nothing to eat since breakfast.

Ramirez is ringside, motioning her over. "We're taking lunch now. There's a vending machine in the gym office if you need something to eat. We'll be back in an hour and then you'll demo some of your Krav with Matthew."

"Yes Lieutenant. Thank you."

She retreats to the safety of the storage closet, immensely grateful for its utility sink. Jules unwraps her hands and holds them under icy running water for a few minutes. Splashing her face, she dries it with a rough brown paper towel from the dispenser on the wall. Feeling better, she digs out some change from the bottom of her gear bag and goes to the gym office to peruse the contents of the vending machine. She selects a granola bar and some salted peanuts. Anything more and she'll just end up puking during the next round.

The next round. *Come to think of it, who the hell is Matthew?*

Jules gets comfortable on the floor of the closet, closing the heavy metal door for privacy. She digs her watch out of the bag and checks it: one-thirty p.m. Her interview began at nine a.m. She has been incarcerated with Ramirez for four and a half hours and she's not close to being finished. Good thing she hadn't scheduled anything else for the day, she could be here 'til midnight at this rate. She eats her food and then refills the now-empty water bottle from the sink.

Jules yanks the elastic off her hair, which is now hanging in wisps and damp curls on her neck. She wets it down and pulls it back into a more utilitarian ponytail. So much for her polished interview look; now she looks like some sweaty gym rat. *Oh well, screw it.* She guesses that at this point it's not really about the look anymore. She is afraid to get her hopes up. She thinks she's done okay, though it's hard to tell with Ramirez continuously scowling at her. *Ballbuster is not the word.*

Jules stretches out on the floor, cracks her back and sits up in a half-lotus position; legs crossed over knees. She closes her eyes and focuses on her breathing for a while, trying to calm her nerves. She begins to visualize the Krav combatives she'll use in the demo.

For her, Krav Maga had been a perfect fit. Developed by an Israeli police officer, Krav is a self-defense system for street fighting. After the officer had been on a street detail and engaged in real close-quarters combat, he realized that the combatives he'd learned during his military training weren't helpful in a down-and-out fight. Krav training employs a 'whatever works' philosophy, which supports the assumption that if you're being assaulted by someone who's trying to inflict harm, any tactic is a fair response. The instructors teach the basic elbow strikes, punches and kicks used in kickboxing and mixed martial arts, but students also learn groin slaps, eye gouging and painful pressure-point techniques.

As a student of the discipline, Jules first learned to master confusion and fatigue by enduring brutal cardio sessions and defensive training. She was then taught to put together a series of combative moves that felt comfortable and natural to her. In combat, during her testing and later instructor certification, she'd learned to be fast and accurate.

She had discovered, as all martial artists do, that thinking gets in the way of efficacy. Once you've performed endless repetitions of a technique, your body remembers what to do. Then all you need to do is figure out how to get your mind out of the way so your body can react instinctively.

Jules finishes her visualization exercise and retrieves her hand wraps. She re-wraps her hands more carefully, as this time there will be no boxing gloves to protect them. The assumption with a 'demo' is that you show your skills without hurting the opponent, merely indicating how pain would be inflicted if it were an actual fight.

The knock on the door comes all too soon, but Jules is so keyed up that she just wants to get it over with. She opens the door to an Asian man in his twenties, lithe and graceful-looking.

"Hi. I'm Matthew Lee; I'll be your partner for the demo. Lieutenant said Krav Maga, yes?"

"Yes. Nice to meet you, I'm Julianna Petersen. Have you studied Krav?"

"No I'm a student of Tae Kwon Do."

"Oh, that's such a beautiful discipline." Jules doesn't miss Matthew's humble reference to being a student. In Tae Kwon Do, respect and humility are all, so Mr. Lee is probably a third or fourth-degree black belt.

He is friendly and polite, dressed in black athletic pants and a spotless white t-shirt, bearing the RSW logo. He leads her back out to the gym floor, where Ramirez and the rest of the men are looking well-fed and cynical. Williamson is now absent; obviously he has better things to do with his time. Ramirez stands, stretching, making them wait. He approaches, nodding to Matthew.

"All right let's get this done. Give us a ten-minute demo. I want to see at least three different scenarios, one on the ground. Matthew is our Tae Kwon Do instructor, so you'd best be fast or you're going to find yourself lying on the mat wondering what happened."

Jules nods. As Ramirez walks back to the bleachers, she and Matthew face each other, bowing at the waist. Jules instructs him, "Approach me from behind, do whatever you want to try to take me down and I'll respond."

As he passes from her line of vision she readies herself, relaxing her body and clearing her mind. Her hands are loose at her sides, her feet planted at shoulder-width. Suddenly Matthew grabs her from behind in a headlock, pulling her down and to the left. He is incredibly strong, but Jules doesn't need strength to oppose him. She moves with him, swinging her right foot wide and planting it, knees bent for stability. Her right hand moves in an arc to Matthew's groin, delivering a cupping, one-handed slap, stopping just shy of actual contact. She hears every man in the room cry, "Ohhh!"

At the same moment, she brings her left hand in front of Matthew's face and with her left index finger stiffly extended, presses in and upwards at the base of his nose. As he instinctively moves backward to evade the pain, Jules pursues her advantage, forcing Matthew backwards until he is off-balance. As he falls onto his back, she releases the pressure-point and feints a roundhouse kick to his head. She then steps back into a ready fighting stance, hands curled in front of her face, leg poised to kick again.

Matthew is on the floor, smiling delightedly, the skin around his eyes crinkling. "Sweet!"

The spectators hoot and cheer, mostly in Spanish.

Jules extends a hand to help him up. She avoids looking to Ramirez for approval, knowing she won't find it. She continues with Matthew.

"Okay," she says. "So choke me any way you want, from the front, side or pushing me towards the wall. Make it real."

Matthew complies instantly, grabbing her throat from the front with both hands, squeezing hard enough to take her breath. Jules shoots both arms upwards over her head bringing them back down to use her hands in a plucking motion. She exerts pressure on his thumbs, momentarily breaking his grip. She then curls her right hand around the front of his neck, gripping him hard and forcing his face to the side with her forearm. Left hand gripping his bicep, she pulls him down and in to her, bringing her knee up into his diaphragm. As he doubles over, she makes a fist with her right hand and brings it down in a hammer blow to the vulnerable base of his neck. He is now on his knees defending himself, when Jules feints a vertical kick to his face. Matthew falls back, hands up in surrender.

"Okay, Julianna!"

She helps him to his feet again. More encouragement from the crowd which has again increased in size.

"Okay Matthew, last one. You put me down on the ground and we'll go from there."

As she finishes the instruction, he politely responds by sweeping her feet out from under her with his leg. She lands backwards on the mat with a graceless thud. She curls up like an overturned turtle, hands protecting her face. She plants one leg on the ground and lifts the other, poised to kick. Matthew circles quickly, looking for an opening to kick her. Jules pushes with her grounded leg and follows his movement, spinning on her back, keeping her eyes on him at all times.

Matthew shifts his weight to his left leg to deliver a right kick to Jules' head. She counters with a right-leg kick just above his left knee. If it had been fully delivered, the kick would have broken Matthew's femur or blown out the knee. He jumps back, shaking his head, realizing that Jules has just effectively taken him out of the fight.

She springs to her feet. They bow formally to each other and she thanks him. She turns to the bleachers. Ramirez is sitting back, elbows resting on the riser behind him. He looks neither displeased nor moved. Jules stands at ease, saying nothing. He takes his time getting up and coming to her. The other men are talking and laughing, replaying the combat through hand gestures.

"Interesting," Ramirez says. "You held your own with Mr. Lee. That, in itself, is an accomplishment. Change back into your business attire and return to Williamson's outer office upstairs. I need to speak with him. We'll meet with you later."

"Thank you sir." *Later. What does later mean? Twenty minutes? Three hours? Christ, who knows with these two. Probably send her out for a little DNA testing next.* Jules heads back to her now-beloved storage closet. She guzzles some water and rinses off again. Rummaging in her bag, she locates a small towel, which she uses to mop off the sweat. She peels off the soaked gym clothes and reapplies her deodorant, hoping for the least offensive presentation she can muster.

So much for dressing to impress. She's guessing she now looks like she swam a river, though there is no mirror in the closet for her to confirm this. She peers into the blurry surface of the stainless steel paper towel dispenser and reworks her hair for the second time. She rubs a wet finger under her eyes, trying to make sure her mascara hasn't migrated southward. She has lipstick in her bag, but hesitates, hearing Ramirez growling about make up. *Oh, fuck it.* He's already decided about her one way or another. At least she'll feel better. She pulls out the tube, a discreet nude shade. Applying it carefully, she then kisses the back of her hand to take half of it off. She digs for a piece of mint gum, chews it vigorously for a moment and then spits it out into the garbage.

As she wriggles back into her business suit she feels almost human again. Oh well, it's the best she can do. She hurries outside and stores the gear bag in her vehicle then walks back into the building as if heading to an executioner.

She can't imagine that Ramirez is going to let some chick past the imaginary razor-wire fence he's keeping around his all-male crew. Jules is quite sure he'd rather eat broken glass than admit a woman into the fraternity. She is holding onto a tiny glimmer of hope that Williamson could turn the tide, except she's not sure he's actually in charge.

Jules wearily returns to Williamson's waiting room, feeling like a stray cat next to the coolly beautiful secretary, who tilts her head at her, "Oh Ms. Petersen! You're still here? Oh my gosh, can I get you some coffee, a soft drink?"

Although Jules cannot imagine anything better than a cold can of soda at this moment, she declines, opting for coffee instead, black, no sugar. It certainly won't do to have the lieutenant come to retrieve her, only to find her guzzling soda like a teenager. From the look of him, he probably lives on wheatgrass juice and whiskey.

Jules waits. She finishes her coffee, her empty cup instantly whisked away by the secretary, who seems to have no other duties than staring into her computer monitor, though she never hits a key. A half-hour, then an hour passes. After an hour and ten minutes, the door to Williamson's office opens.

"Ms. Petersen." Ramirez sticks his head out and gestures for her to enter. She stands, her legs shaky after the workouts and caffeine. She holds her head up as she passes Ramirez, not allowing him to think she's been defeated. It has been more than six hours and all she wants to do is go home, take a shower and lie down. Staring at the ceiling suddenly seems like an appropriate career path. Julianna enters the quiet office, lit with tasteful brass lamps. She greets Williamson once again, offering her hand. He bids her to sit and she does so gratefully.

Ramirez leans against the wall, arms crossed over his chest. She takes a deep breath and makes eye contact with him. He stares sullenly at her. She turns back to Williamson, all hope extinguished. She steadies herself for the polite letdown to follow.

"Well Julianna! All reports are that you did very well today."

Reports? Surely not the lieutenant's reports. She perks up a little.

"In fact," he shuffles some papers on his desk, "I believe the language from both Mr. Suarez and Mr. Lee said 'exceeded applicant expectations.'"

Ah yes, those reports.

"Now Lieutenant Ramirez is, of course, very protective of both his crew and the quality of our personnel. My life depends on it, as you know. And though he does have a few reservations in regard to adding a female agent, I believe I was able to convince him to give it a try."

Startled, she looks at Ramirez. Nothing new there. She turns again to Williamson, not quite sure of what he's saying. "Sir?"

"If you're still game, we'd like to offer you a position, Julianna."

She sits stunned for a moment and then quickly finds her voice. "Yes! Yes, absolutely still game. I'd love to accept." She hears Ramirez shifting uneasily against the wall. Jules rises to shake Williamson's hand vigorously. "Thank you so much sir, you won't be disappointed."

"Of course not."

Julianna approaches Ramirez tentatively, offering her hand. "Thank you, Lieutenant. I'm very grateful." He nods as he shakes her hand.

Williamson chimes in again. "You can go with the lieutenant to his office and hammer out all the details and I'll see you when you report for duty."

"Yes sir. That will be fine. Thank you again." Jules wishes she could hug Williamson.

She follows Ramirez out through the waiting area and down a long, tastefully appointed corridor. His office is at the end of the hall, the last door on the right. He uses a card key to open another heavy oak door and waves her in.

As she steps in, she feels a mixture of elation and anxiety. The space is masculine; dark wood, low lighting and heavy upholstered chairs. She is enveloped by the scent of his domain, a mixture of sweet cigar smoke and subtle, spicy cologne; a warm, comforting smell that improves her opinion of him. She notices his coffee cup, a big black mug that reads,

> *"Treat your men as you would your own beloved sons. And they will follow you into the deepest valley."*
>
> *— Sun Tzu, The Art of War*

"Sit please. We have a lot to go over."

"Yes sir." No rest for the weary. She sits in a large, brown velvet chair. She swallows, worried about what's next.

He leans forward in his heavy leather chair, elbows planted on his immaculate desk, hands clasped, shoulders squared. His dark eyes lock on hers. "So, Ms. Petersen. You're with us, for a time at least. Let me speak plainly. The training period is five months long. For those five months, your ass is mine. Every day, all day. You'll train with various members of the crew, but everyone reports to me and nothing happens without my approval. It's no secret I don't want a woman on this crew. I think it's dangerous, inappropriate and cumbersome. That being said, Williamson wants you here, provided you can pass muster. My job is to learn everything I can about your abilities, or lack thereof, during the training period. If you have a weakness I will find it and exploit it. Now, it was clear today that you've built some physical discipline for yourself, so hopefully that won't be an issue. However, this job is about mental acuity. No amount of muscle is going to help you if you haven't planned properly for your principal's security. That means checking and re-checking every last detail, as well as having the flexibility to rewire the plan at any moment. Williamson is no investment banker. He is the CEO of the largest petroleum brokerage firm in the U.S. I hope I don't need to explain to you the current sentiment toward oil executives in this economic and political environment."

"Of course not, sir." She agrees with Ramirez's assessment; a lot of average Joes would like to see Williamson dead or somewhere in the vicinity of dead. This is where RSW Geological Inc.'s own private security detail comes in. Ramirez and his team are no parking-garage attendants. They are an elite squad, each hand-picked for their expertise in specific areas: evasive driving, weapons and various hand-to-hand combat methods. Most are ex-military, some ex-con, though no ex-law enforcement as is customary. Likely because the lieutenant doesn't want anyone with their own pre-conceived ideas about how to provide protection.

"Okay, some ground rules, which I expect you to commit to memory. First, we follow a military chain of command here. I am your superior officer; you do nothing without my permission. That includes eating, going to the head or taking breaks of any kind. The only phone you will carry while on duty is the one we provide you with. All phones and vehicles are equipped with GPS units, which means that I know where you are at all times. There are no personal calls made or received while you are on duty. Any emergency calls go through dispatch and are screened by me. That means if you get a personal call, someone better be dead or in the hospital. If your boyfriend wants you to pick up a quart of milk, he can leave a message on your personal cell, which you can retrieve when you are off-duty. Are you reading me so far?"

"Yes."

"Second. Every man on this crew currently outranks you. You are a probationary agent. If someone tells you to do something, you follow instructions under the assumption that they come directly from me. All instructions are to be carried out without hesitation. Attitude, argument or insubordination: each is grounds for immediate dismissal. If you receive an instruction you don't understand, you are to speak up immediately. We do not improvise, we do not second-guess or mind read. If you fuck up in any way, you are to own up to it immediately. If I find you covering up a mistake, I will dismiss you without discussion."

Jules is nodding her understanding, maintaining direct eye contact. As rigid as the rules are, they make sense to her. After all, someone's life and the life of his family are at stake. In this job, a mistake is not a typo, it is a window of opportunity for someone to do harm.

Despite his harsh demeanor, she respects Ramirez and what he's built. He has a huge responsibility and the weight of a fourteen-man detail on his shoulders all day, every day. Personal security is twenty-four-seven, 365 days a year. The scheduling alone would make her weep. She can almost sympathize with the fact that he's not excited about training a girl. *Lucky for him he got this girl.* She plans to ensure that he changes his mind about her.

Ramirez slides two pieces of paper across the desk to her. The first is an offer letter for her employment during the probationary period and the second, a training waiver. The training waiver spells out the fact that if she's hurt or mutilated during training it's her own damn fault. She signs them both happily and passes them back.

Ramirez is finally finished. "I'll see you at zero-six-hundred on Monday morning. Report to the front desk and they'll let you know where to find me."

"Thank you Lieutenant." She shakes his hand again and turns to leave.

"Rest up, Ms. Petersen," he says in his quiet, gruff voice.

She looks back at him. There is the smallest sparkle of amusement in his eyes.

3

Ramirez glances at the brass clock on his office bookshelf: 1845 hours. He turns off the overhead lighting. He settles in the desk chair with a glass of Glenfiddich single malt and a slim, sweet cigar. On his desk is a file, the one he has compiled on Julianna Petersen over the past few months.

Out of twenty-two female applicants, she'd been the only one who'd seemed even remotely promising on paper. Still, they'd seen them all, mostly to pacify Williamson, who had convinced himself that adding a female agent would make the firm look modern and expansive. His men had done cursory investigations on the entire batch of applicants; standard criminal, legal and financial checks.

However, Petersen's file had seemed to merit some of Ramirez's valuable time. Ramon had personally spoken to a senior detective from her unit at the county prosecutor's office, as well as an assistant prosecutor who'd worked a lot of cases with Petersen.

The phrases that came up repeatedly were 'great kid' and 'very well-liked.' The detective, a gruff, old-school type had made reference to Julianna's 'rough time' after the loss of her husband. Ramirez had used that opening to dig deeper with the detective.

"Alcohol problem?"

"No, that would be me."

"Drugs?"

"No way. You know, insomnia, nightmares, typical post-traumatic stress stuff."

Somewhat disappointed, Ramirez probed further with the assistant prosecutor, a cocky, young up-and-comer. "Ever hear any rumors about her; financial problems, personal stuff?"

The AP laughed, "Hey man, this is gossip central up here. If there was something going on, believe me, I'd have heard about it; true or not. I do know a bunch of our guys started hitting on her after Chris died, but it was only like six months later, way too soon for her. She just kept turning them down and eventually they left her alone."

Ramirez tried one last tack. "She ever screw up on a case, piss off anybody important?'

"I've worked probably fifty, sixty cases with her; all family and domestic violence stuff. Of course the defendants and their attorneys are always pissed off at us, we're prosecuting them. But Jules is very cool under pressure, she knows how to back people down without getting too aggressive. It's a fine line, you know, because some of these abusers are volatile guys, very dangerous. But Jules never let them intimidate her; she had no trouble just laying it out for the defendants. 'Here are your options: take the plea or have a trial: your choice.'"

The AP was on a roll, enjoying the sound of his own voice, as all attorneys do. "The only time I ever saw her piss off a judge was when we had this nasty D.V. case; three kids, all under the age of ten. Dad had a habit of working mom over and finally went too far, put her in the hospital. Dad decided he wanted a trial; wanted to drag his wife through the mud, make a case that she was unfit. For some reason the kids were in court that day, they weren't allowed to testify but maybe there was no babysitter, I can't remember. Anyway things got ugly with the defense attorney questioning the mom and the seven-year-old was crying, really shook up. Jules picked her up and took her out of the courtroom, along with the rest of the kids. Judge reamed Jules out later in chambers, said it was disruptive and over-dramatic. It didn't rattle Jules, she apologized formally, but everyone knew she'd done the right thing by the kids."

Ramirez sighs wearily, "All right. Thank you, you've been very helpful."

"No problem. You guys should definitely hire her; she's a really good kid."

"Yeah, I've heard that about her."

Ramon was dissatisfied. He'd been hoping to find something that would disqualify Petersen from the application process.

Her training file from the Executive Protection Academy in Virginia had not proven any more helpful. It contained glowing reports from Petersen's instructors regarding her physical fitness, firearms skills and 'natural aptitude for advance work.'

Her senior instructor had made an emphatic recommendation. 'The ratio of female-to-male students at the academy is quite low. Most females wash out in the first two days, due to the rigorous nature of the coursework. However, Recruit Petersen stood out among the class of seventeen for her stamina, ability to focus under pressure and natural leadership qualities. She was able to complete the assigned tasks efficiently, as well as to motivate other individuals who were struggling. As the scenarios became more difficult, Recruit Petersen was able to adapt, refocus and complete the original directives.'

Yeah, and she's cute too. Shit. He can't imagine that all of these guys are wrong about her, but maybe she just knows how to play them. If that's the case, she's got a real wake-up call coming. He doesn't give a damn about charming; you can either do the job efficiently or you can't. He is notorious for his ability to ruthlessly cut probies from the training program. Five months is a long time; if Petersen has a weak area, eventually it will show up.

He has to admit, he'd been surprised by her today. He'd watched her as she walked into the interview. Tall, attractive brunette; well-dressed and well-groomed in her navy-blue suit. Outstanding legs, nice hips, small breasts. As she'd shaken his hand and made eye contact, he'd noticed the eyes; gray-green and alive with intelligence and curiosity. They lit up when she smiled. The smile was wary and a little crooked.

As he'd observed her during the PT testing and interacting with the men, she'd been confident and fairly relaxed. She seemed to carry her sexuality easily. It was obvious that she was comfortable around men. Petersen had also lapsed casually in and out of Spanish with the Latino crew members, a point in her favor.

In her interactions with him, Petersen had been formal and respectful, never familiar. No attitude that he could detect, and he'd been watching for it. The day had been a long one, she'd arrived at 0900 and left at nearly 1730. He'd had made sure she was hungry, tired and uncomfortable. He'd deliberately isolated her in between tests and had made her wait for each subsequent task to measure her patience and composure.

Williamson had eventually called an end to it, forcing him to concede that Petersen had performed well enough to warrant a probationary offer. Ramon had vehemently defended his original position; that adding a female agent would prove disruptive and inefficient.

He'd lost the argument. It seemed his boss had made up his mind about Julianna as soon as she'd pinned Ramirez to the wall and submitted him like a teenage boy.

Jules lets herself into the house; her gear bag slung over one shoulder. Flipping on the kitchen light, she drops the bag on the floor with a thud. She pulls off the suit jacket and kicks off her shoes simultaneously. She stands guzzling a bottle of water, emptying half the bottle in one gulp. She forages inside the fridge again and finds a large tub of Greek yogurt. She grabs a spoon and the bear-shaped squeeze bottle of honey, squirts the honey directly into the container, and attacks the whole mess with the spoon, ravenous.

"Oh my God," she sighs, mouth still full. She has never been so hungry. She makes audible noises of pleasure as she leans against the kitchen counter and finishes the food. She tosses the container in the garbage and the spoon in the sink, unbuttoning her blouse with one hand. She stands in her bra, skirt and stocking feet. Jules wants to burn her interview suit. She feels as though she's been held hostage all day.

But she got it! Well, a probationary offer; but still, a foot in the door. She thinks about the five months; about Ramirez's warning words, 'Your ass is mine.' *Could be interesting, Jules. Yeah, could be hell on earth too.*

She gathers up her clothes and heads to the master bedroom; her space. The room is inhabited by a king-sized oak bed, leftover from the days when she had someone to share it with. After Chris died, she'd spent a good six months in that bed crying, in between working and attempting to function like a normal person.

The other half of the room is a small boxing gym; speed bag station mounted on one wall, hundred-pound heavy bag hanging from a chain in the ceiling. Metal hooks on the wall hold assorted pairs of boxing gloves, handwraps and jump ropes. Completing the collection is a round timer, CD player and yoga mat.

Jules' private sanctuary is rounded out by an eclectic collection of books and a vanity full of makeup, perfume and jewelry.

She strips off everything and puts on a huge t-shirt that reads 'Ringside Boxing: Kansas City.' She flops on the bed. Everything hurts: her back, hands, and head. She rolls over and digs in the nightstand drawer for a bottle of ibuprofen. Since she began training, physical pain has been her constant companion. She takes three tablets with the rest of the water.

Jules wants to tell someone her news. This is when Chris' absence hits her hardest; when she has something to share about her day and no one to share it with. She picks up the bedside phone and dials her brother in Maryland. No answer. She doesn't leave a message. She looks at the clock and hesitates, her best friend, Lily, will be putting her kids to bed, no point in even trying now. Jules lies back on the bed; thank God she doesn't have a class to teach tonight. It's Friday, so she has the entire weekend to recover from the interview and get ready for the coming week. She stares at the ceiling, wondering idly about Lieutenant Ramon Ramirez. Is he really that much of a hardass or is it just her? His men seem to like and respect him, so maybe it's just a façade, an act he puts on when he's interviewing.

She ponders his past: married, kids? She hadn't noticed a ring on his finger and can't imagine that he'd have time for a family with a job like his.

He must have been unbelievably handsome as a young man. *What is he? Early forties?* Even now, there's definitely something disquieting about his looks. When he'd had her pinned to the wall during the exercise, she'd reacted to the proximity of that body.

Julianna had only been with one man since Chris, late this past summer, a young landscaper she'd hired to clean up the property. It had been casual, and she'd ended it when he'd seemed to be growing too attached. She'd had plenty of opportunities before that, but her broken heart had always overridden her body's needs.

A few weeks after Chris had died, Jules had gotten her period. She had wept inconsolably, knowing that she'd lost her last chance at keeping a part of him with her. As he'd said in his voice mail message from the tower that horrible day, she was going to have to revise their project, making a baby. She had honestly tried to be strong as he'd asked her to. Though there wasn't much Jules couldn't do on her own, she sometimes longed for the safe feeling she'd had as a child with her father and later with her husband.

Despite an innate ability to be aggressive, Jules was a very feminine female. She loved the trappings of a being a woman, all of them: clothes, makeup, perfume, lingerie. She'd learned, during her years of working around law enforcement types, how to 'tone it down' as Ramirez had instructed, though also she knew how and when to use 'it' to her advantage.

Jules understood how to blend, though not disappear, into a roomful of men, never entirely masking her femininity. She believed that though men had their physical power, women had sensitivity, social skills and grace; giving them an edge which rivaled any man's strength.

Jules is not naïve, she sees that Ramirez is an immoveable object. She has no doubt he will put her through her paces physically, emotionally and intellectually. She sighs, picturing his face scowling at her, his deep voice lecturing her. It could be a long ride or a short one, but Jules is determined to savor every second.

There is a knock at Ramirez's office door, a soft double-tap he recognizes as Williamson's. Ramirez rises and admits him.

"You're here late tonight, Ramon."

"Just reviewing the Petersen file to make sure I didn't miss anything significant."

"And?"

"Everything seems to be in order. She'll start training Monday at zero six-hundred".

"Ramon, I know you're opposed to this, but I truly believe it's what's best for the firm. We have to be forward-thinking. Female agents are being utilized now, even head-hunted from other professions. There can be distinct advantages to having a female agent in-house. On family trips, she can be a low-profile addition to the team. In some types of foreign business, a woman can provide a welcome distraction from the tension of aggressive negotiations. We have a lot of that coming up next year: Tokyo, Buenos Aires, and San Juan."

"I'm aware of that. However, you've got to understand my position. You have an expectation for this team. We are the best in the business. Bottom line is Petersen will have to achieve that standard. She's got zero experience. She may have some specific talents, but if she can't execute under pressure, she's not going to make the cut. This is by no means a done deal, Robert."

"I have every confidence you'll get it done, Lieutenant. That's why I pay you so handsomely."

"It's up to her. She's got five months."

4

Jules is up Monday morning at four a.m., though she knows she'd better get aligned with the military time that the team uses, so it's actually 0400. She has coffee, stretches a bit, and showers. After eating, she dresses: black pants, a fitted white shirt (nude lingerie), and black jacket. She does a mostly bare face: mascara, lip balm and the sheerest blush she can find. Her hair is pulled back into a sleek ponytail, with extra gel to make sure it doesn't work its way loose during the course of the day.

She peers into the mirror. "You are crazy," she tells her reflection. "You could have had some nice, easy job working as a security guard." She is so nervous she feels physically sick. Putting her elbows on her knees, she cradles her head in her hands and concentrates on breathing. She can't help feeling that she has made a terrible mistake, but there is no pulling out now. She lifts her head and once again regards herself, lips pressed together in thought.

She pictures Ramirez getting a phone call from her saying she's reconsidered. Then she sees him laughing his ass off. *Fuck that.*

She addresses the pale girl in the mirror, "Okay, time to man up. You only have to remember three things: no crying, no talking back and no quitting. You are a fighter, you will gut it out. Now move your ass or you're going to be late."

Spurred out of inertia by her little pep talk, she leaves the house at 0500.

When Jules drives up to the front gate to the RSW Geological complex, she is greeted warmly by the security guard in the booth.

"First day, Ms. Petersen. Welcome. I'm Victor. This here is your probie pass; wear it all times, don't even think about losing it, they'll fire you for that. This pass expires on May twenty-second. If I don't get the employee badge day after that, I can't even let you in the gate. How's that for cold?"

"Pretty cold. Course if they don't hire me after probation, I probably won't be coming back to visit."

Victor laughs loudly, "Damn straight. Good luck to you Ms. Petersen, you're gonna need it."

"Thanks." She looks at the pass before she slips the breakaway lanyard around her neck. It reads 'Probationary Agent Julianna Petersen.' Below are the expiration date and a picture of her from the day of the interview, looking pale and terrified. That seems about right, since she's probably going to have the same expression on her face for the next five months. She drives her pickup truck into the parking garage and makes her way to her fate.

Jules approaches the front desk, where two muscular men in very nice suits nod at her. She glances at her watch, it is 0545.

"I'm supposed to meet with Lieutenant Ramirez at 0600."

"Yeah he's expecting you. They're in conference room B, second floor. I'm Xavier. Me and Leonard here, we do mostly travel gigs, extra muscle; but Lieutenant wanted all the guys on the regular detail to meet you, so we're filling in this morning."

Xavier is a short guy, no neck, well-groomed. His dark hair is cut to about a quarter-inch, his clean scalp shining through. He has the smile of an angel, except for a gold tooth with the initial *X* engraved on it. Leonard is tall and thin, with a shaved head and deep acne scars on his beautiful espresso skin.

"Nice to meet you, I'm Julianna." She sticks out her hand and is rewarded with a pair of crushing handshakes.

"All right, Julianna, you'd better hustle on up. Don't want to piss him off this early in the day. He ain't even had his second cup of coffee yet."

"Right." She hustles. There are motion-activated cameras everywhere—corridors, elevators and every room in the building except the offices of Ramirez and Williamson.

God, she hopes they're not all in front of a monitor somewhere, watching her approach. The thought makes her stand up straighter. She takes off her overcoat and drapes it over her arm. Exiting the elevator, she finds conference room B clearly marked. Pausing just before entering, she breathes. *God please don't let me screw this up.* She knocks once and enters.

The room is filled with men. Well-dressed, good-looking men of all races and sizes. Twelve of them, to be exact, including Ramirez. They all stand simultaneously as she enters, as if they'd rehearsed; chairs scraping back, throats clearing. Ramirez heads towards her, glancing at his watch.

Again with the watch! She is seven minutes early.

"Ms. Petersen, I thought you should meet the detail as a whole," he says, looking her frankly up and down. He doesn't twitch or frown, so she guesses she has passed the 'blending in' test.

"Thank you sir."

The men are standing around the long table at parade rest, hands clasped loosely behind their backs, knees slightly bent, feet shoulder-length apart, posture perfect. Jules has no doubt that they would stand that way all day if the lieutenant told them to. Their collective demeanor is formal, their eyes curious, taking her in.

The lieutenant walks around the table, introducing each man by name and special duties. Jules stays where she is. She does not plan to do anything she is not specifically told to do, today or ever.

Ramirez pauses behind the first man. "You've already met Guillermo Sanchez, my second in command."

Guillermo is 'Gi', the kind soul from the boxing ring who'd given her the bottle of water and the helpful advice.

"Gi is our blade expert. He'll be instructing you on blade work and defense at a later date." Gi nods at her, throwing in a quick wink. Jules nods back.

Next Ramirez stops behind a wiry Asian man with black eyes and a terrible scar on his chin. "Tam Bok, automatic weapons specialist and our driving instructor. These men, Junior White and Solomon Johnson are also weapons specialists."

Junior and Solomon are wide, tall African-American men, nearly identical except for their skin tones. Junior's is the color of coffee ice cream and he has amazing light green eyes. Solomon's skin is a shiny blue-black, and his right eye wanders slightly. She smiles at both of them. They start to smile and then apparently think better of it, nodding gravely.

Ramirez continues: "You met Jorgé Suarez, our trainer, in the ring on Friday. He and this man will be your new best friends; after me, of course. This is Eduardo, our boxing coach, former Golden Gloves Eastern Division champ, 1981, '82 and '83."

Eduardo is a lean, scary-looking guy with a gray buzz cut, sporting a thin, neatly trimmed goatee. His gaze is unflinching as he appraises Jules.

Must be one of the lieutenant's pals, she thinks. She nods, meeting his gaze.

"You know Matthew, of course, from the Krav demo, our Tae Kwon Do instructor." Ramirez then stops behind a young, olive-skinned man. "This is Bruno Gianoni. Bruno is our medic. He'll be patching you up."

Jules notes that the lieutenant didn't say, 'if you get hurt.' It seems to be a foregone conclusion that she'll be injured during training. *Great.*

"And these three men are part of our travel detail. Yoji Sun, fluent in Japanese. Saul Guzman; and Henry Taylor, they're with us when we're on the road."

Yoji is an innocent-looking young man; he smiles broadly at her and makes a slight bow. She responds in kind. Saul is another Latino fireplug, whose eyebrow is dissected by a half-inch scar. Jules imagines his very presence would be a deterrent to the criminal element. Henry Taylor is a short, wiry African-American man missing his two front teeth. Jules figures by the cords standing out in his neck that he is either a boxer or a steelworker, maybe both. He nods continually, as if once he's started, he can't stop. She smiles, suddenly grateful for the money her parents spent on braces.

"All right. Let's get started," Ramirez barks. An empty seat suddenly appears in front of her as the men shuffle into their seats. She hears a low voice from a couple of seats away, "*Hijo de puta. Una falda en las filas, eh?*" Jules can't help it, her head swivels to place the speaker. It was Eduardo and if she had her Spanish right he'd said, 'Son of a bitch. A skirt in the ranks, eh?'

They spend the next three hours reviewing her five-month training schedule. Every hour of each day is accounted for: a dizzying mix of classroom time and one-on-one training with every member of the detail. She'll be spending at least two hours each week learning the specialty of each crew member, from weapons to advance planning for travel. There are two hours of daily gym time with Jorgé and Eduardo. Jules also has a daily half-hour of supervision with Ramirez. *Really looking forward to that.* She is stunned by the amount of time that Ramirez must have spent creating the schedule. She'd like to believe that it is simply an adaptation of any probationary agent's course of study, but suspects that Ramirez has created this little slice of suffering especially for her.

As the morning drags on, Jules feels the men watching her, scrutinizing her for any signs of stupidity, craziness, or inappropriate behavior. She realizes that for the next twenty weeks she'll have to keep her guard up at all times. They'll all be looking for her shortcomings, and of course they'll find them. However, Jules is determined not to give them anything substantial enough to warrant a dismissal. Though she has no idea how she'll manage it, she has never yet backed out of a commitment and is not about to start now.

At the conclusion of the meeting, the men file past, each nodding at her, some shaking her hand and welcoming her. She stands straight and makes eye contact with each of them. She gets a pretty good idea from their reciprocation or the lack of it which ones are in her corner and which ones are hoping she'll disappear.

Ramirez directs her to follow him to his office. She studies the back of his head as they make their way down the long corridor. Over the weekend, she'd asked a law enforcement friend to run a background check on Ramirez. Jules figured if they were going to spend the next five months getting up close and personal, she'd better know who she was dealing with. Her friend had faxed her some handwritten notes, so the lookup couldn't be traced back to him. It was slightly illegal to run a criminal check on a non-suspect. The notes read:

> Ramón Miguel Ramírez: Born: October 10, 1961, Bayamón, Puerto Rico, Santa Olaya district. Father: unknown; mother: Teresa Aña Ramirez. As a boy, Ramirez primarily resided with his grandmother, Rosarita Maria Ramirez.
>
> Attended school sporadically when he was not needed to help his grandmother earn money for food and living expenses. Grandmother took in laundry for well-to-do city dwellers, and Ramirez was enlisted to haul the clothes back and forth. At thirteen, he began to run with a crowd of feral boys. They spent their days stealing and working on cars. At seventeen, Ramirez was arrested and charged with auto theft. The car he'd stolen turned out to belong to a wealthy local businessman. The judge, a friend of the businessman, sentenced Ramirez as an adult to serve eighteen months at Rios Pedras State Penitentiary. He did nine months of 'good time' and was released early, due to overcrowding of the prison.
>
> Upon his release, Ramirez found his way to Miami, Florida, where he spent approximately eighteen months working in a garage and learning English.

At nineteen, he joined the U.S. Navy, working as an engineman. He was a quick study and distinguished himself as a relentlessly hard worker. After completing his required four years active duty, he applied for and was accepted into nearly a year of Navy SEAL training in Coronado, California. After graduation from Basic Underwater Demolition (BUDS) training, he went to jump school in San Diego and was then assigned to his SEAL platoon (location classified). After a six-month 'work-up' period, he was deployed overseas (location classified), where he spent the next three years in active rotation.

Ramirez was head-hunted directly from SEAL duty by Robert S. Williamson, a fledgling oil broker, who had parlayed his third-generation trust fund into a burgeoning empire. Williamson, after receiving several credible death and kidnapping threats from third-world competitors, decided he needed someone with 'special skills' to form an in-house security detail. Williamson reached out to his Harvard roommate, who'd made a career in the Secret Service. Williamson asked him to come up with a short list of exceptional soldiers, pulling one name each from the Army, Navy and Marine Corps. Williamson used his considerable resources to procure a file on each name and after some discreet inquiries, he'd decided that he admired Ramirez's climb from poverty and hardship to elite military service. Contact was made while Ramirez was home on a brief leave. Ramirez attended the proffered meeting chiefly out of curiosity. The twenty-eight-year-old, lured by the extravagant salary and a promise of the freedom to assemble his own detail, accepted the job at RSW Geological. The base of operations was to be in Bedminster, New Jersey, a wealthy bedroom community to New York City. Ramon's next move was to install his grandmother, Rosarita, in a two-bedroom condo nearby. Though the fate of Ramon's mother was unclear, it was rumored that Teresa, a known prostitute, had been beaten to death by one of her johns in the late seventies.

Jules had been completely intimidated by the information she received. She'd guessed that Ramirez was ex-military, but SEALS were unbelievably hardcore. What it told her was that the lieutenant had already endured the most brutal physical and mental training the military had to offer and come out of it unscathed. Although the title 'lieutenant' was honorary, bestowed by Williamson because he liked the impression it gave to civilians, Ramirez had earned everything else the hard way.

Now she understood that even the slightest complaint of physical or emotional discomfort during her own training would not be tolerated. What she was about to undergo was a picnic to Ramirez.

Sure enough, as soon as they were seated in his office, he began.

"So, Recruit Petersen. Here we are. First, some house rules and housekeeping issues. If you are inside the gate, you are on duty. On duty means no alcohol, no nicotine, no unauthorized breaks or phone calls. All our personnel are subject to periodic physical training tests and random urine testing for drugs. If you are in house, you are on task as directed by your superior officer, me. The only one who supersedes my authority is Williamson. If, for some reason, I am unavailable to you, you are to direct any and all inquiries to Gi. No one else. Understood?"

"Of course."

"Now, there is the issue of a locker room for you. If you make it through probation, Williamson will contract to have a suitable space constructed in the gym, adjacent to the men's locker room, but in the meantime; you'll use the storage closet as you did previously. I've asked Jorgé to make it workable for you. If you are called to work a double shift or need to leave early on a travel day, there are dormitory rooms on the third floor. There are three shared bathrooms on that floor, each with two showers. One of those bathrooms will be designated solely for your use when you are in residence." He shoots her a chagrined look, letting her know he considers her employment to be a logistical nightmare.

"There are four private dorm rooms, normally designated for me, Gi, Eduardo and Jorgé, as the senior men on the detail. However, Gi has a girlfriend who lives nearby, so he's volunteered to give you his room. Dorm rooms are to be kept in pristine condition, all gear stowed away, bed made, etcetera. There is also a laundry room on the dormitory floor. The housekeeping staff performs basic cleaning on the weekends, but daily upkeep is your responsibility. That goes for the bathroom also. There is a full kitchen in the basement. It has a fully stocked pantry, refrigerator, commercial range, microwave, blender and coffeemakers, again to be kept in pristine condition. Any questions so far?"

"No sir." She hopes there are schematics of the building somewhere with those red dots that read 'You are here.'

"All right." He goes on to tell her about the indoor range, the vehicles, the closed-circuit cameras and card-key coded doors. Jules is starting to feel as though she's wandered onto the set of *Mission: Impossible*. They probably require a retinal scan to get a cup of coffee. She cannot imagine how much it costs to run the physical plant of the complex, let alone salaries, benefits, vehicles, weapons and travel expenses for all of them.

Jules is the daughter of a mechanic and an elementary school teacher; she has never been exposed to this kind of wealth. Chris had been an attorney, but as an associate, between his starting salary and student loans, they'd been in the red more than the black for most of their married life. As a 9/11 widow, she'd been compensated by both the federal government and Cantor Fitzgerald. As a result, she has health insurance for life and the house is paid off, with a substantial amount of savings in the bank. However, she still lives simply, as she always has.

Ramirez is peering at her. "Are you with me, recruit?"

"Yes sir, of course."

"All right, that covers the house. Now, there is one thing for which I have zero tolerance. That is, you never, ever, discuss your personal life in front of the principal or his family. I don't care if your boyfriend just dumped you for a hooker, your cat died or you have your period. If I ever hear you complain, gossip, whine or joke within his earshot, you are done. You will know the location of your principal at all times. Therefore, there should be no reason for you to be gossiping in the break room with one of the men and have the principal come walking in. I will accept no excuses on this point. We are a security detail, which means we are locked and loaded twenty-four hours a day. In-house, you are ready to go at all times. *Comprende?*"

"Si, tieñente."

He looks at his watch. "You're scheduled to get your equipment from Gi. Go."

Jules takes the elevator downstairs to the basement. She finds the equipment room next to the kitchen. The room occupies a large space, dominated on two walls by two weapon safes and a separate ammunition safe. The center of the room is taken up by a rectangular stainless-steel table, used for the cleaning of equipment. The room smells of solvent, leather, and gun oil. Gi looks up from a clipboard and bounds across the room to her.

"*Amiga!* Congratulations, Jules, you made it. Welcome to hell."

She laughs. "Thanks! Lieutenant said you have some equipment for me."

"Sure we've got lots of junk for you and you have to sign for every bit of it. That way, if it gets lost, sold, or stolen, I don't know nothing."

"Sounds fair."

"Okay. First thing is your work cell. They all have GPS on 'em, so don't be anyplace you're not supposed to be or you're totally busted. Anyway, I got a feeling Lieutenant's gonna be tracking your ass. Oh and he told you no personal calls on duty, right?"

"Right."

"Okay, sign here."

She scrawls a signature on the clipboard's checklist.

"Okay, next you got your key card. All the doors in the building are locked and wired to the alarm system. Every time a door gets opened, it comes up on our monitors and gives us the information on who is coming in. The doors also lock automatically after you, just like in a hotel room. Now, 'cause you're just a probie, this card gives you limited access to certain areas, main entrance, all main doors inside, stairwells, and parking garage. Also this card is keyed to your dorm room. Restricted areas, you have to be buzzed in by someone with access. That's anybody's personal office, this room and the range. Got it?"

"Got it. Hey, thanks for giving up your dorm room. I really appreciate it."

"No problem. My girl lives right down the road. She was happy about it. Except she ain't so happy I'm working with a girl now."

"Well, no threat here. I sort of keep to myself."

"Oh yeah? You gay or something, chica?"

Jules laughs, shaking her head. "No, I like men. I just don't date much. Too much of a hassle."

"Naw. I didn't think you was a lesbian. Course, there's a few of 'em in this biz."

"Yeah, I've seen the type."

"Anyway, you don't have that vibe."

"Oh yeah? What's my vibe? Do I want to know?"

"Nothing bad. You know, cool girl, comfortable hanging out with a bunch of guys. Like that."

Jules smiles conspiratorially. "I'll let you in on a little secret, Gi."

"Ooh, I like this." He leans in closer.

"I actually prefer to hang out with guys. Women talk too much."

"Hah! You can say that again sister. *Es' verdad.* You speak the truth."

"Okay, enough confessing. What else do you have for me?"

"Okay. Your practice weapon. Lieutenant said you prefer a Glock. Now, probies aren't allowed to carry, so you'll have to sign this in and out when you go to the range, should be at least every other day. The only people got keys to the safes are me, the range master, that's Junior; lieutenant and the designated detail officer for the shift. You have to clean your weapon every time you shoot, that's before and after. The lieutenant's a fanatic about that, and he checks, so don't ever skip it." Gi lifts a brand new Glock nine-millimeter out of its pristine aluminum case. Facing away from her, he carefully slides the barrel back and locks it open so she can inspect it and see that it's completely empty. He hands the weapon to her and then gives her a full clip of ammo.

Jules takes the weapon reverently. It gives her a jolt of pleasure that Ramirez had requested her preferred weapon. Jules turns slightly away from Gi, inserts the clip and releases the slide. She takes a Weaver grip, pointing the weapon to the far corner of the room, getting a feel for it, though she will not be at the range until tomorrow. She lowers the weapon, unloads it and hand it back to Gi. "*Perfecto. Gracias.*"

"*De nada.* Oh and you don't get any protective gear yet, Kevlar or nothing like that. As long as you're on probation, if you're out on a detail, you're just a spectator. So if any bad shit happens, your job is to get the fuck out of the way. *Comprende?*"

"*Si.*" She smiles. She likes Gi. He's to the point, but still manages to be friendly and decent about it.

"All right. One last thing." He sets aside the Glock and its clip and slides a narrow, five-inch leather sheath to her. He motions for her to open it. "Practice blade," he says like a proud father.

Jules carefully slides the blade out, revealing a stubby, gleaming, double-sided blade with a thick rubber grip. As she lifts the knife from its case, the oily sheen of the blade makes her stomach flutter. "We practice with real blades?"

"Course, girl, otherwise what's the point, right? Anyway, I'm the blade instructor, I ain't gonna let you get hurt. You might bleed a little, but nothing life threatening"

"Okay," she says, unconvinced. She really is going to need Bruno the medic. Gi cheerfully takes the case back from her.

"So Junior will get you started on the range tomorrow and you and me will get down to some blade work soon."

"*Gracias*, Gi."

"Hang in, sister. See you soon."

After meeting with Gi, she spends the rest of the day in a blur of instruction, from the vehicle guy to the computer guy and then back to Ramirez again. The good news is she hasn't pissed anyone off or been fired. Yet.

5

Jules' second day arrives much too early. Still in bed, she reviews her schedule for the day. A 0800 meeting with Williamson, 0900 range practice with Junior, and 1100 sparring practice in the gym. That's just the first half of her day. The afternoon is slated for the computer lab, where she'll be studying procedure and protocol.

After work, she has to teach an eight p.m. Krav class. Just the prospect of getting through the day makes her want to crawl back under the covers. Oh well, as they say in the military, 'The only easy day was yesterday.' "Get up, get up, get up," she mutters as she forces herself out of bed and into the shower.

At 0650, she finds herself again in front of Williamson's stunning secretary, Lauren.

"Oh hello, Ms. Petersen. Good to see you again. He's on a conference call at the moment. I'll let him know you're here the minute he's off the phone."

Jules sits, having an unpleasant moment of déja-vu. At least this time she's not sweating through her suit. Ten minutes pass and then Lauren ushers her in, closing the heavy doors as she exits. Williamson rises from his desk to greet her.

"Ah Julianna, welcome! Congratulations. You made it through your first day."

"Yes, sir."

"Everyone's been treating you well?" A question that supplies its own answer.

"Yes, of course."

"Wonderful. Well, I really just wanted to touch base with you to go over some of my special requirements, familiarize you with my domestic situation, etcetera. I know, of course, that the lieutenant is handling the house rules and policy with you, but I thought we'd have a little get-to-know-you chat. Do sit down."

Jules flinches inwardly, but smiles, "Excellent, sir."

Williamson hands her a heavy silver picture frame. She turns it to find a photo of Williamson, a glacially beautiful wife, two daughters and a Golden retriever. The wife looks seriously well-maintained, from her flaxen pageboy to her ballerina pink manicure. The girls are platinum blondes, glowing with rosy good health. They have their father's gray eyes and their mother's aristocratic nose. Even the retriever looks as though he's just won Best in Show.

"What a beautiful family, sir."

He takes the picture back, turning it to point each one out. "Thank you. This is Grace, my second wife. My first wife is, mercifully, dead. After ten years of account-draining alimony, may she rest in peace. Thank God, there were no children from that union. These are my two angels; Annalise, fourteen, a bit high-maintenance, as you might imagine, and my darling Hope, just turned ten. Hope is more driven, like her daddy, so I'm expecting she'll be somewhat accomplished. With Annalise, my only dream is that she'll marry well. And this sweet boy is Baron, lord of the manor." He laughs heartily, indicating the retriever.

Jules smiles politely. She can only imagine what kind of energy it takes to maintain that image of perfection.

"Now. You'll be spending time with the family during our vacations and little day trips and such, so we'll plan to have you get acquainted soon. Let me be quite candid, Julianna, so you will have all the information you need. My wife Grace, although a lovely woman, is somewhat, shall we say, high-strung. Grace and I became involved when I was still married to my first wife; so of course, she harbors some lingering doubts about my ability to be faithful to her. Of course as she ages, those doubts become more intense, and because of my constant traveling, it becomes harder for me to reassure her.

Now, being aware of that, you can imagine that she's not entirely pleased about the addition of a female agent. She has demanded that I let her meet you immediately, so I would appreciate it if you could, as the lieutenant had suggested, downplay your attractiveness. And if you could somehow reassure Grace, just by being your lovely self, that you have no designs on me. Do you think you could assist me in that way, Julianna?"

She finds it difficult not to smile. "You're my boss, sir. My job is to assist you in any way you deem necessary."

"Superb. Now, as I said, with Grace being a bit anxious, there are occasional domestic 'flare-ups,' if you will. The men on the detail are quite used to them by now. Ramon, excuse me, the lieutenant, has become quite efficient at handling them. However, I'm hoping that perhaps in the future a woman's touch may be more helpful."

Jules feels a blip on her professional radar. With her background in domestic violence, she is sensitized to 'family situations.' Usually when a man refers to his wife as 'hysterical' or 'nervous,' she has good reason to be. However, the largest part of executive protection is discretion, no matter what your principal is up to.

"Just for clarification, and so I can be truly helpful, when you say flare-ups . . . ?"

"Oh you know; nothing too awful. Grace gets to drinking, and if I've been away a lot, her imagination begins to run away with her. She'll make accusations and the like."

"And the accusations? Any basis in fact?" Jules is treading carefully here, trying not to imply any judgment. She is aware that men of Williamson's class step out on their wives as a rule, not an exception.

"Well Julianna, I'm not a *saint*. One does occasionally fall prey to temptation, but one never allows that to spill over into his home life. I'm extremely discreet, and of course I expect the same from my employees."

"Of course." He's not exactly taking the moral high ground. As long as he's not hurting his wife, she can tolerate it.

"Forgive me for asking sir, but when Grace begins making accusations, does it ever get physical?"

"Oh my goodness no, Julianna. We have children in the house; I'm not some stevedore throwing his wife into walls."

"My apologies, but you must understand, regardless of my loyalty to you as an employee, I couldn't be a party to that."

"Nor would I ask you to. You'll see; it's just Grace being dramatic. Sometimes when she feels she's not getting enough attention from me, she creates a situation. We let things cool down and I buy her a new car or some very expensive bauble, and she settles down."

"I understand. Well, I hope I can be of service next time." *That is a blatant lie.* She hopes she'll be as far away from their domestic flare-ups as possible.

"Excellent. I've got a meeting in three minutes. It was wonderful chatting with you. I think we accomplished quite a bit here."

"Yes, sir, thank you."

Ramirez is waiting for her out in the corridor when she leaves. His eyes travel over her, pausing at her cell phone, ID badge and face. Satisfied that she is carrying all her required equipment and not offending anyone with her face, he strides down the hallway toward the elevator. Jules assumes that he will be accompanying her to the range. She trots behind him. On the way down to the basement, he begins to quiz her on the meeting with Williamson. Somehow he seems to know the content of the entire meeting.

"You been briefed on the domestic issues?"

"Yes sir."

"You know the names of the wife, the children and the dog?"

"Grace, Annalise, Hope and Baron"

"The dog is the most important of the four. Keep it in mind."

She frowns to keep from smiling. "Of course."

"The only good thing about your presence here is that now *you'll* get to handle the 0300 hissy fits. You never take sides. You talk her down, give her a Valium, put her to bed and sit with her until she falls asleep. Then you check the kids to make sure they're not traumatized, read 'em a bedtime story, whatever."

"Do *you* read them bedtime stories Lieutenant?"

He shoots her a look. She sighs.

They exit the elevator and return to the equipment room. Gi is absent, but Ramirez uses his key card to access the weapons safe to retrieve her weapon and several boxes of ammo for her range practice. She notices that he also takes ammo for his Sigarms .45, which he is carrying in a shoulder holster. Jules ventures to create some goodwill.

"I wanted to thank you, Lieutenant, for the Glock. It's beautiful. I didn't expect to get a brand new weapon."

He looks at her, nonplussed. "We don't hand out used weapons here, Petersen. It's not a car dealership."

So much for goodwill.

They spend the next half-hour cleaning their weapons. He watches her every move, asking her questions about the weapon. She answers succinctly, beginning to realize that being friendly is not going to earn her any points. Finally geared up, they exit a fire door at the back of the room, which leads through a corridor to the indoor range.

Jules can hear the change in acoustics as they enter the range. It is state of the art, expensively appointed in black and chrome, every surface spotless and gleaming. She can hear the hum of heavy-duty filters, made to remove lead and gunpowder from the air. Ramirez sets her up in a shooting lane with ear and eye protection. "Load your weapon and Junior will give you instructions on range protocol."

She puts on her shooting glasses and slips the high-tech ear protection around her neck.

As she's loading the seventeen-round clip into the weapon, she senses Junior's bulk behind her. She lays the weapon down on the shelf and turns to him.

"Ms. Petersen, how are you? Wouldn't have figured on me being the rangemaster, right?"

"Actually, it makes perfect sense. You're the weapons expert; I'm guessing that makes you handy with pretty much anything that shoots."

Junior smiles, the skin around his beautiful green eyes crinkling. "Something like that. Spent a few years with the Marines; they take their shooting seriously and so do I."

She nods, suddenly nervous. *Oh man, ex-Marine.* The crew is probably made up of a bunch of other Marines; more SEALs and a few Rangers thrown in for good measure. *You are so far out of your league, it's ridiculous.*

"All right, Ms. Petersen. I know you've shot on a range before, but this is *my* range. First, eye and ear protection at all times. Second, you never bring a hot weapon out of the lane; always unload before you step out, even if someone calls you to another lane to have a conversation, always unload. Never come up unannounced behind an active shooter for obvious reasons. Also, when the range is cold, step back so everybody knows you aint messing with a loaded weapon. Got it?"

"Yes sir."

"Good. Ever shot in combat?"

"No, I'm not military."

"That's all right, Jules, the world needs civilians too. We're going to have you shooting a couple hours a day for the next few months. Once the weather warms up a bit, we'll drill you on an outside course, shoot-and-move scenarios, civilian recognition, and stuff like that. By the time you're on detail, we'll have you up to speed, even if I have to kick your ass a little."

She grins. "Thanks. I appreciate your time."

"All right, show me what you got, girl. We'll start stationary at three yards to get you warmed up."

The ninety-minute session passes in a blink. Ramirez does his own round of practice and then spends the rest of the time observing her. When she and Junior convey the target up to the front of the lane to inspect the shot groupings, Ramirez moves in behind them, but says nothing. As she prepares to start another round, he and Junior put their heads together. Jules is aware of Junior making large hand gestures and hears him say, "…..natural!" She hears nothing from Ramirez.

She shoots at three yards, five yards and seven yards. When Junior indicates time, Ramirez is already gone.

Junior praises her. "You did real well, Jules. Nice tight groupings, you were able to see your mistakes and make corrections, and most importantly you followed all my rules. You'll be shooting like a real agent in no time."

"Thanks. What did the lieutenant think? Did he say anything?"

Junior smiles at her naiveté. "Let me give you a little tip about Lieutenant, Jules. If he's not talking, consider that a good thing. When he starts talking, that means you fucked up. When that happens, you'll wish you were anywhere in the world but here."

"Got it, thanks."

"My advice, keep your mouth shut and your eyes open, Jules. He's just looking for a reason."

She nods gravely, Junior having confirmed her suspicions. She is on borrowed time here.

She looks at her watch and realizes that she has twenty-five minutes to clean and secure her weapon, get to the gym, change clothes and be in the ring for her 1100 sparring session.

Jules hustles, but makes sure she does everything by the book. Gi is in the equipment locker and puts the Glock away for her, reminding her not to be late.

She exits the equipment room and hurries across the hall to the gym. She already has her gear bag stashed in the storage closet, which has been gently renovated to serve as her temporary locker room. As she passes the gym office, she nods to Jorgé, lounging in his ancient chair, feet propped up.

The closet has been transformed into a thing of utilitarian beauty. Jorgé had cleared a space for her in one corner, adjacent to the sink. He'd thoughtfully hung an old, stained mirror and five metal hooks for her bag, gloves, handwraps and clothes. On a stool is a stack of clean white towels.

He'd also added a small stainless steel cabinet with a drawer. When Jules opens the drawer, she finds cotton swabs, peroxide, rubbing alcohol, petroleum jelly, gauze pads and hand tape; the beauty products of a fighter. It pleases her. There is also a five-gallon bucket for ice, puke or spit, depending on your mood.

Jules changes quickly into her workout gear. As she sits on the stool, wrapping her hands, she realizes that the schedule did not list her sparring partner. Likely Jorgé or Eduardo, since he's the boxing coach.

Finally ready, she grabs her gloves, mouthpiece and a towel, heading into the gym. There is no one there, so she climbs into the ring and begins to warm up; she looks at the clock, it is 1102. Eduardo materializes from inside the office, followed shortly by Jorgé. At the sight of Eduardo, she feels a wave of apprehension. *Please let it be Jorgé, at least he is familiar.* Eduardo climbs into the ring, but he has no gear on; Jules breathes a little easier. He crosses to her, looking her up and down. "You're on time, that's good. You ready to do some boxing, *gringa?*"

"I'm not really a boxer," she says uncertainly.

"Yeah, but you're a fighter, *chica*, I saw you the other day with Matthew. Don't worry about it."

"Who am I sparring with?"

Eduardo raises an eyebrow. "They didn't tell you?"

She shakes her head, no. Eduardo turns his, motioning in the direction of the locker room. Ramirez is coming out, hands wrapped, dressed in a t-shirt and athletic pants and holding a pair of well-used leather boxing gloves.

Jules' heart hammers so hard she feels as though it is choking her. She forces herself to look away from him, trying to get her composure back. Her mind is racing.

With a building full of men closer to her size and skill level, there is only one reason Ramirez would want to get into the ring with her: pure sport. And he's got his buddy Eduardo here as a spectator, pretending to be her corner man. *Fuck.* Julianna is panicking, close to tears. Ramirez is at least six-three, probably two-hundred pounds, that gives him seven inches of reach and about forty-five pounds on her.

Her only advantage is that he smokes and drinks and most likely does not work out with the intensity that she does. If they go two, two-minute rounds, it will only be a matter of protecting herself and waiting for him to lose his wind.

He is climbing into the ring. She can see prison and military tattoos snaking down his biceps and forearms. He is lean and cut, in very good shape for forty-six.

She straightens, squaring her shoulders. Eduardo is grinning, "Ramon, man, you shoulda' let her know it was gonna' be you. That ain't fair."

"If she's on a detail and something goes down, she's not going to know who her opponent is. Shouldn't make any difference, right Petersen? Besides, we're just sparring."

Jules nods, looking him squarely in the eyes. She puts her game face on. There's no point in letting him see her fear. Besides, he already knows she's terrified. That's the whole idea of the exercise, letting her know that he controls her fate.

Jorgé comes bustling out, swinging up into the ring. "Hang on Eduardo, let me corner Jules today." Jules breathes a little easier. At least now she's not alone in the ring with the two rattlesnakes.

She notices that a few men have assembled in the bleachers again. Word is apparently out.

"All right Jules, let's have a word." Jorgé takes her to her corner. Jules looks at him like a drowning person coming up for the last time. He lowers his voice. "Yeah I know, it's a lousy deal, but you drew the card, so let's focus. Just like with me, seventy percent; only Ramon is the real deal, so you watch yourself. Two, two-minute rounds; just pace yourself and keep those hands up. He's got a right cross that'll lift you off your feet. Deep breaths now." He pulls her head gear and gloves on. She bares her teeth to show him that she has her mouthpiece in. He swats her on the ass and sends her in.

Ramirez is already center ring, waiting. She looks at him and summons her will. *Screw you and your games. Let's go.*

They touch gloves and begin circling each other. He comes in suddenly, aggressively, with a jab-right combination. She slips the jab and narrowly escapes the right on the way back up, but he is open, so she gets him in the ribs with a left hook. He takes it with a huff of air, but she can see it has the desired effect. He backs off, rethinking his strategy of going all out. Jules suspects he wants to finish her in the first round so he won't have to deal with his lack of wind later.

He comes in again hard, surprising her with an uppercut after he feints a jab. She manages to block the shot and it catches her on the hard edge of her forearm.

From the resulting pain, she realizes that he is swinging hard, not pulling back to seventy percent as outlined by the rules. *Well, he's the boss; he gets to do whatever he wants.*

Jules moves in suddenly and feints another hook, knowing he'll drop his hand to protect that sore rib. When he does, she pops him with a solid right that snaps his head to the side. As he absorbs the hit, she feels how truly strong he is. He shakes it off and gives her a pleased look that says, 'you wanna' play?'

He comes around her to the right, crowding her, and she's backing up just to widen the distance between them. It is the worst possible position she could be in. She stops suddenly and bobs almost to a full squat, springing up with an uppercut that catches him hard under the jaw. It rocks him, but not enough. As she is regaining her position, he comes in with that right cross before she has her hand back up to her face.

The cross catches her, coming directly across the bridge of her nose. Jules hears the sickening crunch of cartilage as a spray of blood hits the mat. An excruciating, blinding pain follows and she is on her knees, trying to breathe. She yanks off the headgear as if it were causing her pain. She spits out her mouthpiece, aware of a flurry of activity around her. There is a river of tears, snot and blood dripping onto the mat. Jorgé is kneeling next to her, talking.

Jules wants only one thing. She lifts her head to find Ramirez. He is leaning against the ropes, hands on thighs, bending over, trying to recover his breath.

Ramirez is sucking air, keeping his eyes on the drama unfolding in front of him, when Petersen locks her gaze on him. The look in her eyes is one he has seen before: in combat, on the street, but never on the face of a woman. Her eyes are filled with a killing rage. She fixes him in her sights, and it makes Ramon rethink his relaxed position against the ropes. She looks as if she's going to hurl herself across the ring and rip his throat out.

He straightens up, suddenly mindful of her proximity. He has to admit, he's gone too far, hit her too hard. But he's found out what he needs to know. Someone has hurt her. And she's learned how to fight to make sure it never happens again. This is information he can use. Though it will likely cost him in flak from Williamson, it will be worth it.

Jorgé hauls Julianna up by her armpits, away from Ramirez and into her corner. She twists her head around to maintain eye contact with him. Some asshole rings the round bell. Eduardo is suddenly there, solicitously handing over an ice pack.

Jorgé is trying to hold her head still so he can check her nose. "*Esta bien*," she barks. She yanks away from him and slides through the ropes, heading for the storage closet. She cannot tolerate the attentions of the men, feeling like she's been played.

She enters the closet, slamming the door shut. Running the tap cold, she soaks a clean towel in the icy water. As she tries to hold it to her face, the pain makes her throw up into the sink. Her entire face is throbbing; an immense pressure behind her left eye is making her squint. When she is done being sick, she rinses her mouth. She wrings out the cold towel and lies down on the floor in a fetal position, letting the blood drip onto the towel. She cries silently.

The pain and rage make her thinking cloudy. *Focus, Jules.* What does it mean? Has she failed? Is she out because she let him hurt her? *No.* He thinks if he fucks her up badly enough, she'll quit on her own. Ramirez wants her to go home crying and to decide the job's not worth it. Then tomorrow he'll feign surprise when she says she wants out. She flashes back to the endless week of her Krav instructor certification, when she went to bed every night with ice packs, convinced she couldn't get up and make it through another day of fighting. But she had made it and, in doing so, had learned something about herself. That if they could dish it out, she could take it. *Game on, Lieutenant.* No way is she going out like this.

There is a harsh knock on the door. She doesn't answer, whoever it is can go fuck themselves. Jorgé comes in with Gianoni, the medic. As predicted, he will be patching her up. Now Jules sees the joke in Ramirez's introduction.

"All right Jules, sit up. I got Bruno here, he's gonna take a look."

She does as she's told. Bruno has his professional EMT demeanor on, but even he winces a little when he gets up close to her. He looks at Jorgé. "Jesus, I thought you said they were sparring. It looks like he stomped on her face. Sorry, Ms. Petersen."

"Don't worry about it. Does anyone have a Percocet?"

"Ms. Petersen, you have to go the ER. This is going to have to be set by a plastic surgeon."

"Oh come on, people get their noses broken all the time. You're an EMT, just straighten it out," she says more sharply than she had intended. The anger and frustration well up again.

Bruno looks at her, stunned. "Have you looked in the mirror?"

This gives her pause. She stands up and goes over to the ancient mirror Jorgé had installed. She peers into it with her good eye. *Damn.* Her left eye is blackened and swollen shut. Her once-straight nose is normal halfway down and then takes a decisive swerve to the right. Jules can actually see where the cartilage is broken. A mixture of blood and snot run from her nose to her chin. She looks like a dog that has been feeding on something dead. A tear trickles from her good eye.

She turns back to the men, even more pissed off. "I'm not going to the hospital. That means a workman's comp claim. You think Lieutenant is gonna sign off on that without making my life miserable? No way. Give me a painkiller, we'll ice it for a few minutes and then you put it back where it was."

She notices a bunch of guys loitering in the hallway outside, eavesdropping. Julianna walks over and viciously kicks the door closed.

Ramirez takes a hot shower, his conscience somewhat clean. All right, she got the short end of the stick, but she's the one who wants to play with a bunch of men. It is what it is. If she can't handle a broken nose, all she has to do is write him a short, sweet little note. Better yet, throw him an 'I quit' on the way out of the building. He, of course, will have to come up with something to tell Williamson, but it shouldn't be a problem.

'Irreconcilable differences.' That should be a term Williamson can relate to.

After an excruciating half-hour of holding ice to her face, Jules whimpers in pain as Bruno uses both his thumbs to return her nose to some semblance of its normal position. When the procedure is over, she promptly throws up into a bucket.

Eduardo sticks his head in the door, relaying orders from Ramirez: Go home immediately and report back for duty the next morning at 0900. Bruno offers to take her home, but Jules declines, just needing to end the humiliation. She gets to the house, washes the blood off in a cold shower and passes out with a bit of pharmaceutical assistance.

Now, awake at 0600, she sits up abruptly and feels as if she's getting slugged all over again. She has an instant, crushing headache and the pain behind her eye seems to pulse with every heartbeat. She cries a little, knowing that she could make a phone call; end all of it right now, go back to bed and call it a day. She lets herself fantasize about it for a few minutes.

As she lies there, she gets a flash of the lieutenant's face watching her from the ropes. She feels a flush of rage again, thinks of all the ways she could hurt him, damage him. She refuses to be defeated by some jarhead misogynist. If she ends this, it will be on her terms, not his.

She thinks of her husband. He'd once advised her, "*Don't let your fears hold you back from what you want.*" He would tell her she was stronger and smarter than some has-been warrior. The thought makes her cry harder.

She misses Chris so badly; he'd always known how to pull her back from the edge. Now, filled with doubt, there is only the unkind voice in her head: *You're on your own, tough girl.*

6

Ramirez sits in his office, drinking a double espresso. He checks his watch; 0750. Truthfully, he'd expected a call from Petersen by now. He'd steered clear of her after the fiasco in the ring, not wanting to get into any lengthy discussions. Figured he'd send her home; let her work it out on her own. He'd woken this morning feeling like a bully, ashamed of how brutal he'd been with her.

At the time, it had seemed a reasonable response to her aggression, but now he realizes that he lost his composure. It was unlike him. *What was it, just her presence here or something about her that made him react?* She's a scrapper; he'd seen it for the first time yesterday.

He'd grown up that way himself, it was something he could admire, but in a woman? The woman he knew were soft and domesticated; eager to please. Except of course, his grandmother, who'd ruled him with an iron fist. It had been exactly what he'd needed, though even that hadn't kept him out of prison.

Doing time had held many lessons, all of them brutal. There was no protection for a seventeen-year-old on his own. Within days of his arrival, he'd been inducted into Ñeta, a gang that operated under the guise of promoting rights for the incarcerated. He'd been jumped in, which meant he'd been beaten within an inch of his life by some of the members while the guards looked the other way.

He'd learned how to withstand abysmal levels of pain during daily beat-downs by senior members. Every time he broke a rule, his transgressions earned him a quick and violent correction. A short time later, he'd been coerced into stabbing an inmate who'd encroached on their underground drug dealing. Knowing that his fate depended on this debut act of violence, Ramon watched impassively while his twenty-year-old victim bled out in the baking sun of the yard. His remorseless demeanor secured his Ñeta membership and his safety for the rest of the sentence.

Perhaps that is what irks him now: watching a young recruit, eager to be admitted into the inner circle. A kid willing to take any kind of punishment in order to prove her worth. Maybe making Petersen bleed had made an old wound fresh, reminding him of what he'd hoped to forget.

At 0845, the phone buzzes. Ramon breathes a sigh of relief, this will undoubtedly be her. The voice is female, but it is Williamson's secretary. "Lieutenant, Mr. Williamson asked that you and Ms. Petersen see him in his office as soon as she arrives."

"I expect her at 0900. We'll be in then." *Fuck.* As he'd expected, a raft of shit from Williamson, who'd no doubt heard the story by now and received Ramon's incident report. However, Ramon had expected a private audience, not a meeting with the injured party. *Time to improvise.*

He barks down to the front desk to have Petersen report to his office upon arrival. Minutes later she knocks twice. He opens the door to find her perfectly dressed and looking like she's been using her face for a doorstop. It takes everything in him not to flinch at the sight of her. Streaked with purple-and-red bruising, her face is stomach-turning, one eye blackened and only partially open. Her nose is swollen to twice its normal size, with a ridge of broken cartilage horizontally seaming the middle. She hasn't bothered with makeup or a bandage, but her hair and clothes are impeccable.

He shakes his head slightly at her tenacity. "Williamson wants us in his office now."

She seems to have trouble meeting his eyes. "Yes sir."

As they walk to Williamson's office, it feels to Ramon as though too much has passed between them in that moment of violence. Trading blows had somehow created an intimacy, unwanted by both of them. They arrive in Williamson's outer office. At the sight of Petersen, Lauren's mouth drops open. She recovers admirably quickly and stands to open the door for them, never taking her eyes off Jules.

Williamson's face betrays an atypical flash of anger as his gaze flicks from Petersen to Ramirez. "Sit." There is a long silence and then he speaks in a clipped tone, "I have to say I am stunned. Had I known that this was a possibility, I would never have allowed anything of the kind to be part of the training schedule. Lieutenant, you are responsible for the well-being and safety of all of our recruits, but especially so for our first female. Is this some kind of hazing?"

Petersen jumps in. "Sir, it was my fault. Truly. I dropped my hands while we were sparring. I'm an experienced fighter and I know better. Lieutenant's skills rattled me and I forgot my training. It was simply an accident. I'm really fine."

"Fine? Have you taken a good look at your face? Perhaps that blow impaired your ability to see what others see, Julianna. Forgive me, but you look like a victim of a terrible crime. You're going to need a good plastic surgeon. At the company's expense," he adds, looking pointedly at Ramirez.

She tries again. "Actually sir, it looks much worse than it is. Once the swelling and bruising go away, it'll be just the tiniest bump. Bruno set it for me yesterday, he's very good. I don't even want it fixed. I always thought broken noses are kind of cool-looking, especially on a girl. They make you look tough."

"Well. You look *tough*, Julianna. *Hockey-player* tough. All you need are a couple of missing teeth. Do you wish to litigate?"

"Excuse me?"

"I said do you wish to litigate against Lieutenant Ramirez? It would certainly be your right. Of course we'll pay for any medical bills."

Petersen looks at Ramirez. She is horrified at Williamson's suggestion. *Sue her instructor? These people really live in a different universe.* "No, of course not. I wouldn't even consider it. I just want to keep training."

Now it is the lieutenant's turn. "Sir, I take full responsibility, as I stated in the incident report, I was responsible for recruit Petersen's safety in the ring and I dropped the ball. In fact, I'd gladly pay for her medical care out-of-pocket if you'll allow it."

He sees that Petersen is frowning, but she seems to think better of it. It probably hurts too much.

"That is ludicrous, Lieutenant. Here's what *is* going to happen. Ms. Petersen, you are going to take the rest of the week off. You may return to work on Monday morning, bearing a doctor's note that says you are fit for duty. You'll see my personal physician; Lauren will make the appointment for you. Lieutenant, you will personally follow up with Ms. Petersen each day until then. There will be no more sparring until further notice and never again between the two of you. Are we all in agreement?"

They reply in concert, "Yes sir."

"Very well."

Ramirez exits silently. He holds the outer office door for her like a gentleman. As it closes, he hisses "In my office now."

Once inside, Ramirez squares off with her. He begins, "Don't you ever cover up for me. First of all, you broke a cardinal rule; never lie to your principal. Second, I don't need your help. I've been with this firm for twenty-two years, he and I understand how things work. If I'm in trouble with him, I take the heat, not some fucking probie."

"It wasn't a lie, I did drop my hands. What did you want me to do? Agree to sue you? Jesus. What kind of a boss suggests that?"

"The kind who's worth billions and knows how to control an ugly situation."

"All right. You want to talk straight? Let's lay it all out. I'm not going anywhere. You and I both know you didn't break my nose by accident. Just the fact that you put me in the ring with you showed me that there was another agenda. You don't want me here. I get that. But I'm not some wannabe. I will take whatever you give out because I want this job. I don't want to be an accessory for some bored businessman. I want to work. I want to learn everything you and the crew have to teach me and I'll be here when the five months are up, you can bank on that. You know, Lieutenant, if you could get past whatever preconceptions you have about me, you might realize I could be an asset, not just a liability."

"You done, probie?"

She feels a flush of embarrassment flaming her cheeks. "Yes."

He is staring her down. There is something different in his eyes. *Resignation? Maybe even a little respect.* "You're done for the rest of the week. Check in with me by phone tonight and every night until you get the okay to return to duty. And by the way, whatever time you take off gets added to the probationary period."

Ramon spends the rest of the day holed up in his office, returning phone calls, completing paperwork and revising Petersen's training schedule. He sends an office-wide e-mail regarding her current absence and checks with Lauren to make sure the doctor's appointment has been made.

Petersen's words rattle around inside his head. He thinks of all the things he could have said, should have said. He cannot believe she had the balls to speak to him like that. 'Bank on it.' *We'll see about that.* He sighs, cracks his neck, and rubs his head. *Now he has to talk to her, even on the weekend. That should be a real treat. No rest for the weary.*

At 1400, he shuts it down and puts Gi in charge. Maybe he can get out of the building without going another round with Williamson. He was definitely pissed, more so than he'd ever seen him. Williamson seems to have decided that Petersen is his pet project. He definitely didn't like seeing her roughed up.

Williamson has a thing about appearances. Above everything else, the whole empire has to look effortlessly polished and under control, from the men all the way down to the dog. Ramirez has to work the house detail schedule around the fact that the retriever goes to a doggy salon once a week. Bath, haircut, manicure, tooth brushing, the whole nine yards. Unbelievable. Probably costs more than one of the men's salary.

Ramon leaves in his black Escalade, which is indistinguishable from the rest of the fleet, except that he reaps the benefits of having the SUV for his own personal use, all expenses picked up by RSW.

Instead of driving home, he drives into town, stopping at a bakery, *Sweet Dreams*. He buys a dozen of the tiny almond filled cookies that his *abuela* adores. At ninety-one, she is diabetic and has an insatiable sweet tooth. The caregiver who does her grocery shopping has been instructed by Ramon not to buy any sweets, but once a month he brings her the cookies. After all, what pleasures does she have left besides her Spanish soap operas and her cat Miaow?

Ramon knocks once to let her know it's him. He uses his key so she won't have to get up from her recliner, where she spends most of her time. Rosarita's wizened, beautiful face lights up when she sees him. She has a fashionable short haircut, which disconcerts him every time he sees her, though it's been years since she cut it. When he was a child, she was known for her shiny black hair, worn in a ropy braid down her back. His mother had possessed the same glorious mane, though his memory of her is fuzzy. He brushes the thought of his mother away, an insect waiting to sting him.

He kisses Rosarita's cheeks and she peers closely into his face, immediately recognizing that he is tired. She inquires, refusing to accept his answer that everything is fine. He brings her thick, smoky coffee and puts the cookies on a plate.

She turns off the television and prods him. He sits wearily and gives in to her questioning. *After all, isn't this why he came?* No one sees him the way she does. As always, he is soothed simply by being in her presence.

He tells her briefly of the issues at work: Petersen, the broken nose, Williamson's reaction. She regards him tenderly. She speaks in decent English; she likes to keep up on her 'Americano.'

"Always when there is trouble, a woman is in the story somewhere. Why do you hurt this girl, Ramon?"

"It was an accident."

"When a man hits a woman it is never an accident."

He feels deeply ashamed, thinking of Petersen's similar accusation.

"You want this girl, but she is taken?"

He flushes. "No. She's a recruit, *abuelita*. She's a widow. It's nothing like that." He hesitates. "I just don't want a woman on the crew."

She lifts her chin defiantly. "A woman cannot do this job? To protect a family?" She laughs creakily. "*Querido*, women do this since the beginning of time. This girl, she's a widow; already taking care of herself. You beat her up like a bully on a playground, but she fights back, yes? She stays when she could leave, *si?*"

He nods sullenly.

She leans forward, gesturing with her hands. "You give this girl a chance, *hijo*, same as a man. She will show you; better than a man. Just as strong, but with a softer heart."

Ramon frowns, nothing to say.

"*Abuela* knows. You have a heart too. You're a good man, Ramon. Don't be afraid of a good woman."

7

Jules is at home on the Saturday following her mandated 'vacation.' On Wednesday she saw Williamson's personal physician, who took her to task for the delay in seeking treatment. After ten minutes of reprimand, he informed her there was nothing to be done short of having the nose re-broken or going under the knife to have a plastic surgeon fix the damage. Not caring for either option, Jules politely declined any further treatment. She also said no to a prescription for additional painkillers, which she'd found made her too fuzzy to function. As ordered, she makes awkward, minute-long phone calls to Ramirez each evening. It is always the same; he asks if she is resting, inquires as to the state of her healing, replies 'good' and then hangs up on her.

It is a sunny, cold day in late February and Jules has had a cord of wood delivered to the house. With oil prices through the roof, she's been trying to keep up with the use of the wood furnace. What used to be Chris' job has now fallen to her, hustling the wood into the basement by wheelbarrow loads. Though she could pay someone to do it, it's good exercise and gets her out into the fresh air. Being in the dusty basement and feeding the wood burner reminds of her of Chris, who'd always relished the chore after sitting in offices and courtrooms all day.

After working for nearly an hour, she is sweating and has taken her jacket off, enjoying the cold air on her skin in just a T-shirt and jeans.

Jules hears a vehicle pulling down the long driveway and warily looks to see if she recognizes it.

The house is isolated and since she's been on her own, she doesn't like unannounced visitors. She shifts her posture, peering at the plates on a shiny black Escalade, but they're not familiar.

The SUV draws to a stop and Ramirez gets out. She relaxes, but only a little. *What the hell is he doing here?* On a Saturday, no less. She forces herself to smile and extend her hand. "Lieutenant, what a surprise, how did you find me?"

"Actually I've been here before. When we were doing the background check, I drove out to see what your place was like."

"Oh." She is completely taken aback. She has a mental picture of him wandering around the house, peering in windows. She shivers slightly. *How absolutely creepy.*

He studies her. "What are you doing?" It feels like an admonition.

She sweeps her hand to the woodpile, "I'm heating with wood, so on the weekends I stock the basement. Trying to save on oil. Kind of ironic, considering who we're employed by."

Ramon is struck by her use of 'we.' He is not used to familiarity from her, but of course, he's on her turf now. He hears Rosarita's voice in his head, reminding him to play nice. "Here, let me help you."

"No, that's okay. I mean thanks, but you must have come here for a reason, not to lug wood."

"Just came to check on you. Please, I can't stand around and watch you work," he says moving towards the wheelbarrow.

"Wait. You need gloves or you'll get splinters." Her own hands are cased in weathered calfskin, pulled snug around her wrists by a strip of adjustable rawhide. In ancient jeans, a T-shirt and work boots, she looks like some kind of forester. *A kind of very cute forester.*

She runs into the garage and returns with a pair of men's gloves. He pulls them on a little self-consciously; acutely aware of whom they must have belonged to.

He begins loading the wheelbarrow.

Jules notices that he eases into the manual labor naturally, balancing the load correctly and handling the task as though he's done it a thousand times. Having only ever seen him in a suit, she is slightly surprised by the way he looks now, in black cargo pants and an old cotton shirt, untucked, open at the neck. Over the shirt he wears a canvas jacket, faded, with the front breast pocket ripped off. He catches her scrutinizing him and she looks away.

"I'll get another cart."

They work in tandem, the only sound the thunk of the wood and crunching of leaves and sticks underfoot. It is harder work than he'd imagined and he's impressed that she keeps this up on her own. After a few minutes he takes off his jacket. He ventures a conversation. "So how's the nose?"

"Still broken, thanks for asking." She smiles at him.

The swelling has gone down and her eye is open again, though she has some spectacular yellow and violet bruising. He studies her profile; there is no way it's going to be as she'd reassured Williamson, 'just a little bump.' But she was right about one thing, it does make her look kind of cool. Somehow the flaw accentuates the prettiness of her face rather than detracting from it. "What did the doctor say?"

Jules wonders if that's why he's really here, to hear the doctor's verdict and find out if she's going to sue him. "He said it's hopeless and I might as well forget corporate security and become a bouncer."

He laughs, surprised that she is funny. "What did he really say? I have to write a follow-up report." As soon as the words are out, he regrets the way they sound, like he doesn't actually give a shit about how she is, just needs to finish the paperwork.

Jules looks at him, her smile fading. "He said I waited too long to get treated and now it would have to be re-broken or I'd have to get a nose job. I'm not going to do either one, it's fine the way it is. Oh, and I'm still not going to sue you, you can put that in your report too." She stalks away from him, moving to refill the cart.

He follows her with his empty wheelbarrow. "Look, that's not why I came; I actually did want to find out how you were." He doesn't like the way this is progressing.

She goes back to tossing wood into the cart and then turns to him. "Don't sweat it. The doc gave me a note to return to work on Monday. I'm good to go."

"I actually came to apologize." He lets the words hang in the air, trying to salvage the situation.

Jules turns again to face him, not sure she has heard him correctly. Speechless, she blinks at him.

He tries again. "The other day. I did have an agenda. I wasn't trying to hurt you, but I wasn't trying *not* to hurt you either. Things got a little out of hand, but it won't happen again. If I'm going to train you, there has to be some trust between us. I can't imagine that you trust me very much right now."

She snorts. "Boy, you really blow hot and cold, don't you?"

"Not usually."

"I'm tired. Do you want a beer?"

He heaves a sigh of relief. "Yeah, a beer would be great."

She strips her gloves off, grabbing her coat. "This way you can see the house from the inside." He notices the edge in her voice. He hears his grandmother's words in his head, 'She will show you; better than a man.'

He follows Jules into the house. He stops just inside to take it in. The place is warm and tasteful, vivid, deep colors, furniture with clean lines, somewhat expensive art on the walls. It's clean, too. He'd hoped to discover she was a secret slob.

She hangs her jacket on a hook and takes his too. An aging orange cat winds around his leg. "That's Helen. Don't worry if she bumps into you, she's blind. Are you allergic? I can put her in the other room."

"It's okay. My grandmother has a cat," he blurts out. He feels like a fourteen year-old, talking about his grandmother. Any dignity he'd had when he'd arrived here is slipping away. He takes the beer she offers, gratefully.

"C'mon, I'll give you the tour so you can write a more detailed report. 'Subject appears to live alone with a blind cat. Unannounced visit revealed no drug paraphernalia or obvious illicit activity, though subject's general mental health still remains in question.'"

He smiles. He admires her ease in ribbing him about the tension between them.

Jules shows him the kitchen, another living room and a spare and master bedroom. Ramon cocks his head at the heavy bag in the bedroom, but says nothing. She is an odd creature. He's seen lots of things, but never met a woman with a boxing gym in her bedroom. They return to the living room, filled with comfortable couches and a beautiful view overlooking a lake.

"This is a great place."

"Thanks. Of course, now it seems ridiculously big for one person, but Chris and I did a lot of entertaining…before." She looks wistfully at the view.

Ramon has a sudden awareness of her loss and the fact that she must still be struggling with loneliness. For him, it is something he's become accustomed to. "You must have a lot of memories here. Why do you stay, why not get a smaller place?"

She looks as if he'd woken her from a dream. *Her eyes are green today.*

"This is my home."

It is Sunday evening after the lieutenant's visit and Jules is making dinner for herself. She had always loved to cook and still forces herself to make nice meals on the weekend, as a way of taking care of herself. She whisks the dressing, thinking again about the lieutenant's visit. She's still unsure about his motives, but it had seemed to turn out all right. They'd had a couple of beers and talked lightly about their lives, easy topics like siblings and parents. They had something in common: both their parents were dead, though Ramon had no actual details about when or how either of his parents had died.

For the first time, Jules had felt lucky to have been at the funerals of those she'd loved most in the world. She'd spoken enthusiastically about her brother and his son Ryan, who lived in Maryland. Her brother was now the single parent of an eight year-old; his wife having left them both when she'd met a golf pro who'd whisked her off to a condo in Florida.

Jules explained that she saw them as often as possible, mostly holidays and during the summer.

Ramon had seemed interested in the details of her life, though when she'd carefully asked him about his personal life, he'd been terse and seemed anxious to shift the subject. He had let on that he'd been married 'very briefly' in his twenties, while serving in the SEALs, no children. When she'd asked about a girlfriend he'd mumbled something about having company when he wanted it. Jules had raised an eyebrow, wondering if that meant hookers or bar pickups. Didn't sound like anything too satisfying, but who the hell was she to pass judgment on relationships? It had been pretty much her and the cat for the past three years.

At Ramon's apartment, his late Sunday afternoon feels endless. He is deeply restless. Having had a whole day off, he'd gone grocery shopping early to avoid the after-church crowds, visited Rosarita, done some laundry and watched a football game. He thinks about going into the office to check on things but knows that there is no point in it. Gi makes sure everything runs like clockwork when he's away and if there were a problem Ramon would get an immediate phone call.

He lifts weights, does some push-ups and crunches and takes his second shower of the day. He tries to read, but cannot concentrate. He checks his watch again, 1730. Still early. He picks up his cell phone and speed-dials a number.

"*Marta, hola. Si. ¿Cómo estás? Esta bien. Si, si.* Do you want to come over? I'll get some takeout. I know. I know it's been a long time, work stuff. We've been hiring again. I'm training a new recruit, too. What time? Yeah, seven is perfect. I'll see you then."

He hangs up, sighing. Marta is one of two women Ramon keeps around. They are both in their early forties, divorced and eager for his company. He calls them sporadically; just enough to keep them interested but not enough to let them imagine they're in a real relationship with him. Occasionally Marta will rebuff him, complaining about lack of attention. Over the years Ramon has become accomplished at distracting her from her anger long enough to persuade her to come to his place for the evening.

The other woman, Anna, is a single mother who spends most evenings working as a bartender at a pricey restaurant. She will occasionally come over after a shift, depending on her mood and which babysitter is with the child. Only one of the sitters will stay late.

They were both spotty arrangements, but nicely suited Ramon's schedule of late nights and frequent travel. Both women knew not to count on him for anything but dinner and sex, but the sex was good and they didn't have to cook, so there were few complaints. Ramon was always a gentleman and never got rough or drunk. The deals worked just well enough for everyone to tolerate them.

Ramon tidies up his books and newspapers, puts clean sheets on the bed and orders Chinese takeout. As he waits, his mind drifts to Jules. The visit had gone well enough to salve some of his guilt over her injuries. She was easy to talk to, smarter and funnier than he'd expected, with a quick wit that caught him off guard. After he'd left, it had occurred to him that listening to someone say 'yes sir' and 'no sir' wasn't a very good way to get a feel for their personality. He'd have to spend more time observing her.

There is a brisk knock at the door and he answers it; Marta, windblown and slightly late. She explains that she'd had to stop to put gas in the car. Ramon peels off a twenty-dollar bill for the gas and tucks it into her purse, kissing her on both cheeks. Marta is short and voluptuous, thick in the hips and ass and fond of propping up her breasts in wildly colored bras that made the most of her cleavage.

She has frizzy, black hair that she sweeps up into one of those awful plastic clips with teeth, but beautiful skin and sparkling brown eyes. What she lacks in sexual talent, she makes up for in buoyant enthusiasm. She is crazy about him.

"Ramon!" she cries, planting a dramatic kiss on his lips, leaving a residue of sticky lip gloss. He backs up a little, taking her purse and coat and stowing them on a chair.

"Oh, you look so handsome. You should call me more *hijo*, I'm telling you. I'd take such good care of you." Tonight Marta is resplendent in skintight white jeans and a purple wrap blouse from which peeks a turquoise lace push-up bra. She puts her hands on her hips and does a graceless spin. "So, how do I look?"

Ramon smiles in spite of himself, "Delicious. Let's eat, I'm starving."

They both eat ravenously, watching a boring television show. As soon as they are done, she clicks the television off with the remote and straddles him on the couch, demanding his full attention. He lets her have her way, untying her blouse to enjoy her overwhelming décolletage. She wriggles happily on his lap, kissing him as if she's hoping to win a prize for most cinematic kiss. He succumbs for a few moments and then gently heaves her off, taking her by the hand into the bedroom, leaving the empty cartons of food on the coffee table.

She disrobes like a stripper, turning to make sure he notices that her too-small panties match her bra. He is already undressed and lying on the bed, waiting for her. Marta has her own routine, in which she is the star of her own fantasy.

She unclips her hair and it falls into a long frizzy wave. She shakes her head and all of her hair moves at once, molded into one piece by a heavy-handed application of hairspray. He glances at the clock, nearly 2200 hours. Impatient with the encore performance of a show he has seen too many times, he motions to her, "*Marta, venga aqui. Por favor,*" he adds as an afterthought.

She pouts a little, but complies, climbing onto the bed and taking her preferred position on top. Ramon leans back and lets her do the work. He grabs her substantial hips and closes his eyes, relaxing into her undulations. He breathes heavily, enjoying the familiar pleasure of her exertions. Suddenly an image of Julianna in her jeans and work boots is there. *Shit.* He shakes it away, opening his eyes to Marta, moaning dramatically, her frosty blush glowing in the darkness of the bedroom.

Furious to be interrupted by an image of his recruit, he rolls Marta over abruptly and finishes with a concentrated intensity that she believes is inspired by her talents. Ramon keeps his eyes open, feeling more comfortable with Marta's Technicolor splendor than with the disconcerting development of having Petersen in his head while he's fucking.

When he's done, Marta curls up next to him like a cat, breathing heavily. "Ramon, you must have missed me, eh? You never did it so good baby. I told you *papi*, I'll come over anytime you want."

Ramon grunts noncommittally, sitting up on the edge of the bed and guzzling from a bottle of water on the nightstand. Now, as always, his dilemma is to find the most graceful way to get Marta out the door. He turns to her, forcing an affectionate demeanor. "*Querida*, that was so nice, but I've got an early shift tomorrow, got to be up at four."

"So I'll stay and make you breakfast, *amor*."

"I'm not going to have time for breakfast, *novia*. I really need to get a good night's sleep, big day tomorrow."

She heaves a sigh. "*Si, si*, I know you want me to go. This is the problem, Ramon, you're so cold. You need to let a good woman love you, but you wouldn't know a good woman if she bit you on the ass." She is getting worked up, but is pulling her clothes on, so Ramon takes the verbal abuse in the hope that her anger will move her towards the door.

"Marta," he says in a soothing voice, "I know you're a good woman, but you know how my schedule is, *esta loco*." He pulls on a pair of boxers and leans in to kiss her on the top of her head.

She swats him away. "Always with your schedule. What about me Ramon? Don't you think I get lonely for a little company? You couldn't let me stay one night?" She is pulling out the big guns now, pouting and sighing. This is why he only sees her every other month.

"I know, *lo siento*." He heads into the living room to clean up the food. Lingering in the bedroom to continue the conversation would be a mistake. He is in the kitchen throwing out cartons when Marta appears fully dressed and re-clipped, standing in the doorway of the small, galley kitchen, hands on hips. "Well, are you going to kiss me good-bye?"

"Of course." He moves to her and lets her pull him into a crushing hug, her spicy perfume suddenly cloying to the point of nausea. *Why does he do this?*

He pulls away, planting a firm but perfunctory kiss on her lips. "I'll walk you out."

"Don't trouble yourself."

"It's no trouble."

"No, no, I'm parked right in front. Besides, I'm mad at you." She sticks out her tongue like a three-year-old.

Ramon can't help but laugh. He holds his hands up in surrender. "*Esta bien. Buenos noches*, call me when you get home."

She slams the door and is mercifully, gone at last. Ramon locks the door behind her. He gets a glass of Glenfiddich from the cabinet in the kitchen and sits in the living room, turning off all of the lights. He sighs, wondering again if an hour of sex is worth the two hours of drama that accompanies it. *Ah well, a man has needs.*

He closes his eyes, swirling the smoky liquor in his mouth. He finally feels relaxed. *Relaxed, except for the nagging reminder of Petersen's intrusion into his thoughts. Petersen in those faded jeans. That's what he gets for playing Good Samaritan and going to her house.* He decides: tomorrow it's back to business. He has one job for the next five months and that is to break her. No more distractions. Ramon goes to bed and sleeps like a child.

8

Monday morning at 0600, Jules is back on duty at the morning briefing. She ignores the stares of the men, who are checking out the aftermath of her bout with Ramirez. She holds her head up higher as she hears the whispers in Spanish about her renovated appearance. Ramirez enters the room and the men quiet; he takes them all in at a glance. Finding all present and accounted for, he begins.

"Good morning. As you know, the usual travel detail is leaving for Caracas today. We will be gone for five days. Those on base detail know how to reach me. As Gi is traveling with us, Eduardo will be in charge of recruit Petersen's training in my absence. He has her revised training agenda. Williamson has specified that there will be no sparring for recruit Petersen until further notice." He pauses, letting the statement hang in the air like an indictment of her disruptive influence.

Jules hears some low snickers among the men. Eduardo's mouth twitches from across the table; he looks like a snake waiting for his dinner of live mouse. She sits up straighter, looking defiantly at him, though she could not be more humiliated. Less than a week in and she has had her face rearranged by the boss. She's sure there is a betting pool on how long she'll last. Gi catches her eye and gives her a nod of encouragement; somehow it makes her feel worse.

Ramirez continues, "So; Gi, Tam, Bruno, Xavier, Leonard, Solomon, Henry, Williamson and I will depart on the corporate jet from Teterboro at 0800. Questions?"

Jorgé raises his hand. "Yeah Lieutenant, how come Eduardo gets to be in charge of Petersen? I think we should flip a coin. Winner should be the one gets to spend five days with the skirt."

There is a wave of laughter from the men. Solomon murmurs, "With that face, it should be the loser that gets her."

Jules forces a smile, any other response would just fuel the fire. She glances at Ramirez, he is not amused.

Ramirez replies, "The next man that calls Petersen 'skirt' can be on a five-day suspension without pay. And Solomon, when Petersen is allowed to spar again, you're gonna be the first man in so you can laugh while she messes up *your* face. End of discussion. Dismissed."

Jules is stunned and heartened by the way he'd defended her. She's still embarrassed, but somehow Ramirez telling them off takes the sting out of it. She glances back at Eduardo, laughing and high-fiving the men. Definitely not a good sign.

She looks at her schedule, she is to report to conference room C. She takes the stairs up and enters the room to find the room empty, with stacks of black binders on the table.

She leans in to check the titles. Basic Policy and Procedure: I, II and III. Advance Travel Protocols: I and II. Dress Codes. Black Tie and Celebrity Protocol. Domestic Protocol: Bedminster. Current Hotel Floor Plans. Current Airport Floor Plans. Strategic Driving: I and II. Weapon Protocol: Hand Gun, Automatic Weapon and Long Gun. Disarming: Knife and Gun. Hand-to-Hand Combat. Ballistics Tables. Risk Assessment. Threat Assessment. Threat Assessment Matrices.

Damn. Well, now she knows what she's doing for the next month.

Eduardo strolls in, "You didn't think I was gonna follow you around for the next five days, did ya?"

Jules squints at him, "No, that's the lieutenant's job."

"Hey, you know the boys were just fooling around. They don't mean anything by it. That's how it is when you work with guys."

Jules gives him a fake smile. "Sure. I've worked with guys before. I guess they just had better manners."

Eduardo regards her for a long moment, looking like he wants to say more, then he appears to thinks better of it. "So, you have your schedule. You got three hours of study, two at the range with Junior, lunch break, three more hours study and an hour in the gym with Jorgé, no sparring. Any questions, you call me on my cell. Don't talk to anybody else, any problems, you report to me. Start with policy and procedure. There's a test in two weeks."

"Yes sir."

"Petersen?"

"Yes?"

"You're officially in the grinder now. You and me? We ain't gonna be friends. You got a smart mouth and a hell of a nerve trying to get on this crew. This ain't no tea party. The people that want Williamson want him bad enough to take all of us out trying. You ever get in my way, I'm gonna stomp you. Understand *niña?*"

"Yes sir. Thanks for the encouragement. You're a true gentleman."

He looks her up and down in a way that makes her skin crawl; as if he can't decide whether to backhand her or feel her up. She is relieved when he does neither and leaves, saying something under his breath in Spanish.

'The grinder,' as Eduardo had referred to the training period, has been aptly named. Made to wear the recruit down mentally, physically and emotionally, the average day was ten hours, more or less, depending on the whim of the instructor.

Ramirez, after his five-day trip to Caracas, seemed to return with a renewed energy for the task of breaking down Jules' stamina and confidence, a bit each day. No more inquiries about the state of her health or visits to her home. In fact, it seemed that he hated her with a fresh rancor. It didn't matter; she didn't have the time or energy to ponder the reason. Every day was an exercise in degradation and tedium, punctuated by periods of intense pressure and performance on demand.

The first two weeks, policy and procedure, was a breeze; simple memorization of hundreds of rules. The next two weeks on advance work tapped into her ability to plan, organize and research innumerable details. Jules received tasks such as finding the location of the doctor, pharmacy and dry cleaner closest to a particular hotel. Once she had done that, she was directed to determine their business hours as well as the name of a person who would open at in the middle of the night for the principal, if needed. Jules spent hours on the phone, many with Ramirez listening in. Because he already knew the answer to each question, there was no room for error.

Two weeks of studying hotel and airport schematics followed. Williamson flew his corporate jet, a Gulfstream, out of only one airport, Teterboro in New Jersey. He also arrived and then departed from major hubs including Tokyo, Dulles, Caracas, Miami, Buenos Aires, Dallas-Ft. Worth, O'Hare and San Juan. Knowing the schematics for each was essential in order to provide two routes of travel for each trip. Each itinerary had an A and a B route, meticulously planned out. Route B would be employed in the event of any disturbance, threat or unexpected circumstance, such as a demonstration or security tie-up on Route A.

While the details were complex, the basic model of executive protection was simple. Anytime that the 'principal,' Williamson; was in motion, he was flanked at all times by a certain number and arrangement of security detail members. Depending on whether the environment was high or low risk, the number of men would range from one to as many as twelve. The positioning was simple geometry, either a diamond, box or wedge formation, providing protection in front, to each side and in back of the principal.

In a high-risk city such as Caracas or Mexico City, there would be a lead car, the principal's car, a follow car and a car for any additional staff. The lead car contains the driver, an advance man and two detail members. One of these men is the bagman; armed with a semi-automatic weapon, likely Junior or Tam. The principal's vehicle contains a driver, the personal security officer, Ramirez or Gi, and Williamson, who sits in the back seat.

Williamson was referred to as 'Bird' when he was moving. Mrs. Williamson was 'Bird Two' and the children and dog were 'the Chicks'.

Jules smiles as she reads this, picturing the whole brood moving in a line, ducklings following mama and papa. She wonders idly if Ramirez had come up with the names, maybe he was a closet birdwatcher.

The follow car, carrying a driver, the shift leader and two men, is used as a blocking tool for the principal's vehicle in the event of an attack. Everyone but Williamson is armed with a handgun. Ramirez and Gi are additionally armed with compact knives, in case things get up close and personal.

As she studies, Jules understands that if she ever makes it through probation and gets to be part of the detail, she'll be lucky if she ends up in the staff vehicle. Probably her most dangerous duty will be holding Bird's briefcase or shopping with Bird Two and the Chicks. She sighs, no relief in sight.

Jules is at home on a rare day off from both work and teaching her Krav class. She'd cleaned the house and gone grocery shopping after realizing that every staple in the house was depleted. She reaches up to put a jumbo-sized pack of paper towels into the cabinet over the refrigerator. It only goes halfway in, so Jules pulls a chair over and peers into the back of the cabinet to find out what's in the way. The item in question is a heavy bottle of expensive Irish whiskey, a present to Chris from one of his bosses after he'd settled a half-million dollar lawsuit out of court.

Jules pulls it down from the cabinet, remembering how he'd come home, trench coat over one arm, holding the beribboned bottle aloft. She smiles, thinking of his confident grin and the way he'd said, "Who's your man, Jules?"

She brings the bottle to the sink, intending to dump it, but the scent as she uncorks it makes her pause, remembering the taste of his kiss that night. Julianna sniffs it and takes a swig. It clings to the back of her throat and burns all the way down. "God, how did you drink this?"

She closes her eyes as the taste floods her with memory. Jules grips the edge of the sink and bows her head as if taking a physical blow. A childlike sound escapes from her and she is bent double by the immediacy of fresh grief.

Jules can feel him: young, optimistic, in love with her. The weight of what she's lost is crushing her from the inside; an implosion of rage and sorrow that feels unbearable. She grips the bottle and smashes it against the porcelain sink. It shatters predictably and she's left clutching the jagged neck of the bottle. Instead of letting go, she grips it tighter, letting the sharp edge slice into the palm of her hand until the pain inside of her dulls. She finally lets go and stands, breathing hard, watching her blood drip into the sink, pooling among the broken glass.

"Fuck you Christopher," she whispers, feeling blasphemous. "You left me here alone. Now all I have are those stupid promises you never kept." Jules knows her words are ludicrous, even as she says them. As if he'd made a choice to leave her.

She grabs a kitchen towel and wraps her hand in it. She slides down onto the floor, feeling sick. She gingerly opens the towel. She sees the naked cut for a second before it fills with blood again, it's not as bad as it feels, she can get away without stitches. If she wraps it and keeps it dry, it may take a couple of weeks to heal completely.

She heads into the bathroom for first aid supplies. As Jules works, she catches her reflection in the mirror. She shakes her head at the worn-out-looking girl, "You're an idiot."

After she's plowed through days full of material and pre and post-tests, she learns from Gi that she is scheduled to spend the next two weeks on threat assessment, taught exclusively by the lieutenant.

Oh God. Two weeks in a room with him. Like sleeping in a bed full of rattlesnakes: one wrong move and you're dying a slow, painful death.

She tries not to think about it, but she doesn't sleep the night before. She knows that threat assessment is the foundation of personal protection, more important than weapons or fighting and equally as important as advance work. However, if advance work is geometry, then threat assessment is advanced calculus.

As Jules had learned in the academy, the ability to determine a real threat from an implied one is a relatively new science, created by studying successful and unsuccessful attacks all over the world. The key is not to determine whether the pursuer is a dangerous person, but whether the current threat is likely to escalate into violence.

Twenty years ago, experts in a U.S. security consulting firm and a group of federal marshals had created a methodology which revolutionized the efficacy of threat assessment and management. Essentially, they'd created a software program which leads the assessor through twenty-nine points of inquiry about the threat, how it was conveyed and the person who made it.

As the lieutenant enters the conference room, Jules stands to acknowledge his authority. He motions for her to sit, looking as though he's sitting down in a restaurant that he knows will give him food poisoning.

He regards her with resignation. "All right, the first thing you need to know is that you don't take instruction on threat assessment from anyone but me. This is a critical area, there is no room for mistakes. No guessing, no assumptions, this is only done using the approved matrix. That being said, it will be years before you'll be allowed to do this on your own."

"Yes, of course."

"Now, I know you covered this at your academy, but I don't know what or how they taught you, so I'm going to assume you know nothing. That way there is no risk of any gaps in your education."

"Understood."

He begins to speak, unaware that she has attended an intensive week of training taught by the man who helped design the methodology. She keeps her mouth shut, listens and takes notes, pleased to know that he is reviewing material she already knows. He also has his facts straight, seeming to understand the concept from the ground up.

As he speaks, Jules finds herself studying him, distracted by his mannerisms and voice. He sips coffee from a black mug with 'RSW Geological' stamped on it. He bites his lip as he refers to his notes and outline for the module. She can almost see him translating in his head from English into Spanish. Jules pictures him as a young man, new to the U.S., struggling to learn the language, head bent over a book or newspaper after a full day at the garage.

The image in her head softens her feelings a little, he's worked his ass off to get here, probably ten times harder than she has. She can see the fine lines around his eyes and the gray at his temples. It looks good on him, emphasizing the fact that he's experienced in so many ways that she will never be. She looks down at her paper, embarrassed by her naiveté. She scribbles some notes so he will think she's paying attention.

She looks up at him again, and he is frowning at her. *Damn.*

"You getting this, Petersen?"

"Yes."

"What is the most likely weapon of choice used in U.S. attacks?"

"Firearms, seventy-one percent."

"Handgun or long guns?"

"Handguns, fifty-one percent."

He clears his throat and Jules cannot be sure whether he is pleased or disgruntled that she knows the correct answers.

"What is the most likely point of attack?"

"In or around the principal's vehicle, sixty-four percent of the time."

"Rate of success?"

Her eyes flick skyward trying to recall the statistic, "Ah, seventy-seven percent, I believe."

"Alright so you've proven you're good at memorization, which means nothing."

She nods in resignation, affirming that she is fully aware of her ignorance. This may be the longest two weeks of her life.

After three days of theory, Ramon takes Jules to the computer lab down the hall. He makes a show of giving her a 'temporary' password to access the matrix system, lest she get any big ideas about her tenure here. He sits shoulder to shoulder with her, showing her the keystrokes. She seems to pick them up very quickly. He can smell her, a bright, lemony scent which invades his concentration.

"Are you wearing perfume, Petersen?"

She looks at him in surprise. "No, you said it wasn't allowed."

He leans closer, inhaling. "Then what is that scent?"

"Um," she smells her wrist, nothing. She pulls the tail of her ponytail around to her nose. Ah. "I guess it's my hair. Maybe my shampoo?"

He sighs. He can't exactly tell her not to wash her hair. He feels suddenly foolish. "Well just be aware, I don't want you attracting extra attention," he finishes lamely.

"Yes sir." Her mouth twitches, just the tiniest bit.

Is she amused or annoyed? She'd better not be laughing at him. "Moving on."

He shows her the ins and outs of the program and then gives her several real-life scenarios from the past to work through. As Williamson's profile and wealth had increased, so did the number of intrusions into his business and personal life by would-be stalkers, assassins and those who simply wished to harm him.

He watches as she begins to work the case threats one at a time, making notes and jumping back and forth to the research library screens of the program to review case-related articles and videos.

Jules doesn't seem to be rattled by his proximity, she absently rubs her temple as she reads and seems completely immersed in the material. He, on the other hand, has nothing to do but take her in.

Today she is wearing an ivory button-down shirt, closely fitted and tucked into navy trousers, her waist encircled by a narrow silver chain belt. She has tiny silver hoops in her ears and her hair is slicked back into a low ponytail and secured with a navy ribbon. He has noticed over the last few months that while she has managed to adhere to the rules of dress he'd set forth during their first meeting, she seemed to assert her femininity and personal style in small details he couldn't control.

In the first month of her employment, Williamson had overruled Ramon's edict on skirts for formal occasions only. Said he found it 'dreary' to see a woman in trousers day after day. Petersen in a skirt, even the most conservative cut, was something to behold. The men's sidelong looks of appreciation had only reinforced Ramon's belief that he'd had the right instinct from the beginning. Unfortunately, Williamson trumped the lieutenant on matters of style, as it was his image they were projecting to the public.

Ramon runs a hand back and forth through his quarter-inch crew-cut. He needs a haircut, something he's been putting off due to the increased responsibility of training Petersen. He looks forward to the day she's fully trained, no scratch that, he looks forward to the day she washes out. Though it obviously won't be this module, he thinks maybe they will be able to disqualify her during the moving drills once the weather improves.

He'll have to watch Junior on that module; the Marine is already too fond of her, as half of the men are. Petersen, for all her physical and intellectual intensity, has an easy, affable way with the crew and a cutting sense of humor that the men seem to appreciate.

He glances at her again. She's finishing up her first report, twisting her hair as she waits for it to print. As much as her presence irritates him, she is, if nothing else, very easy on the eyes. He likes the combination of glossy dark hair and pale skin, set off by those eyes and fine-boned face, marred only by the break in her nose.

Ramon looks up from his musing and sees Gi standing in the opposite doorway, watching with a knowing smirk. Ramon frowns at him and Gi winks, inclining his head towards Jules. Gi nods as if to encourage Ramon's daydreaming. Ramon barks out, "*¿Que?*"

Gi shrugs innocently and calls, "We're going to lunch at Martino's. Why don't you bring your student?"

Ramon glances at Petersen, who has not even lifted her head from her report. "She's got work to do." He slides the report from her hands. "I'll check this over lunch. Start on the next scenario."

Gi calls to Petersen, throwing up his hands, "Sorry Jules, I tried." She rolls her eyes as Ramirez walks away.

"No lunch breaks in purgatory, Gi." Ramirez hears her, but decides to deal with her insolence in a more practical way. *She can eat when she gets home tonight.*

For the next week and a half, Jules and Ramirez work side by side. He is a critical, gruff and uncompromising teacher. The gap between what she'd learned at the academy and what he's teaching her is like reading the bible to learn how to be a priest; there is a whole world between theory and things that happen in real life.

Just reading the accounts of the successful assassination of hundreds of people has re-focused her concentration like a laser. The thought of watching something violent happen to Williamson or his family is unacceptable. Jules realizes that there can never be a moment on-duty when she lets her attention lapse.

She has a whole new appreciation for the lieutenant's insistence on perfection. Her respect for him has grown tenfold, though she hasn't come to like him any better. His behavior is a wire brush, rubbing her defenses raw each new day, but at least now she can understand the motivation behind it. At the end of the two-week module, Ramirez administers a five-hour test, on which she scores a ninety-six percent.

His only reaction is to tell her that she'll work a new case scenario each week until the end of her probation and re-test once a month until she can achieve at least a ninety-eight percent.

She thanks him somberly for his time and expertise, knowing that this is as good as it will get. At this point she feels only gratitude that she has another two weeks under her belt.

9

Julianna is standing post in front of the RSW building. She is all the way down at the northwest corner. It is seventeen degrees out, record cold for late March. Ramirez has decided to take advantage of the unusual cold snap by employing it as a training tool. Though she is wearing a long, wool coat over her suit, as well as gloves and a watch cap, Jules feels as exposed as if she were in a bathing suit. A bitter wind whistles in from the northeast.

She furtively checks her watch, 1030. She has been at this post since 0630. She rises up and down on her toes, clenches and unclenches her hands. At this point, nothing helps, she is cold beyond anything she has felt before, trembling all the way to her core. Jules tries to focus her mind and meditate. She stares straight ahead and pictures a glowing ember inside her stomach, burning slowly brighter and hotter. Suddenly Ramirez looms in front of her. She reflexively straightens up.

"You cold, recruit?"

Jules considers the wisdom of telling the truth. He'll probably dump her in a water tank next. "Yes sir."

"You tired, recruit? You need a break?"

"No sir." Screw him, she'll stand here all day and freeze.

"Think I've been hard on you Petersen?"

"No sir."

"It's okay. You can tell me. It's been tough, I've been riding you. How many hours did you work last week?"

"Fifty-five sir." She hates this more than anything; him pretending to give a shit about how she feels. She can feel her anger rising up, she breathes in, attempting to push it back down. The trembling increases.

"Fifty-five. And you taught class how many nights this week?"

"Two."

"Two nights. What time do you get in from that?"

"About 2230." He is really pissing her off.

"And then you still have to eat and wind down a little, so those are pretty late nights for you."

"I've gotten used to it." At least the verbal grilling is taking her mind off the cold.

"Must have taken some getting used to, coming home to an empty house after all those years with your husband."

Her eyes dart, she is slightly panicked, knowing this is dangerous emotional territory. "Yes."

"Lonely."

It is only a word, but it hits its intended mark. She feels the pinprick of tears at the back of her eyes. She is just so tired. Jules gets it now, he's just going to stand here chipping away at whatever strength she has left. "Yes."

"You two were close."

It is not a question. "Yes."

"You must miss him." His voice is soft, empathic.

Damn. How she can get him to stop? She feels her stomach quivering.

"Yes." Her voice is shaky.

"Hard to be on your own?"

"Sometimes." *Don't think, just answer. Don't you dare let him make you cry.*

"Think I should feel sorry for you Petersen?"

Her chin comes up higher. "No sir." She looks at him as though she'd like to take his head off.

He leans in closer. "Brutal, what happened to you," he says softly.

She frowns, blinking rapidly to keep the tears back. His words have hit her in the gut regardless of her intention to protect herself. There is a long pause, during which he studies her intently, head tilted slightly. He looks into her eyes and she looks back with all the hatred she can muster.

He leans away. "Know what? I don't feel sorry for you. You wanted this, Petersen. Remember? You wanted to insinuate yourself into this crew, wanted this more than anything, right?"

"Yes sir."

"Want to go inside, get warmed up and get something to eat?"

"No sir." *Screw him. She'd rather die of hypothermia than let him think she can't take it.*

"You want to stand here all day, recruit? You'd better speak up." His tone has turned cutting.

She hears a hiss of static coming from his earpiece. Gi's voice comes through. "Bird coming your way, Lieutenant."

"Affirmative." Ramirez backs away from Jules and turns. He joins her at post, standing shoulder to shoulder with her, his back to the wall. Jules straightens too, eyes ahead as Gi and Williamson approach on the sidewalk, huddled in their heavy overcoats against the biting wind.

They nod as they pass. "Good morning."

Ramirez and Julianna reply in unison, "Good morning sir."

Williamson and Gi are almost to the door when Williamson stops suddenly and returns to them.

"Lieutenant?"

"Yes sir?"

"Ms. Petersen's lips are blue, Lieutenant."

The lieutenant's head swivels to look at her. "Yes sir. Recruit Petersen is learning to stand post."

Williamson moves to face Jules. "Ms. Petersen, how long have you been here?"

Shit. Jules' eyes flick to Ramirez, who is now standing at Williamson's shoulder facing her. He stares at her impassively, but his gaze carries a warning.

"I'm not sure sir, I've lost track of the time."

Williamson clears his throat.

"What time did you report to duty today, Miss Petersen?"

"0600, sir."

"And what time did you take this post?"

"0630, sir."

Williamson whips around to face Ramirez, his face stiff with anger. "Lieutenant, it is 1045."

"Yes sir." Ramirez does not look the least bit intimidated. Jules is convinced you could spear him in the groin and he'd still give you that stone-faced look.

Williamson turns back to Jules. "Ms. Petersen, go inside."

"Yes sir."

"Lieutenant, a word in my office please," he barks as he sweeps past Ramirez, Gi trotting along behind. Jules goes in, standing just inside the front door. Ramirez lags a stride behind Williamson. As he passes Jules, he hisses in her ear, "Don't you move."

She stands, as miserable as she's ever been. The warmth of the foyer is somehow making the shivering worse. She wishes Williamson hadn't intervened. *It's only going to piss Ramirez off more. Well, at least the interruption saved her from crying in front of him.*

Gi appears again. "Damn, sister, you're in deep. Your lips *are* blue. He really has it in for you. You sure you want to keep going with this?"

She snorts. "I wouldn't quit now if you put a gun to my head. I'm not gonna give him the satisfaction of watching me resign and don't you dare repeat that."

He holds his hands up as if she's going to shoot him. "I don't know nothin'."

"Look Gi, I don't want to be rude, but if he comes back and sees me talking to you, I'm gonna' be outside for the rest of the day."

"All right, I got it. Keep your chin up, Jules." He strolls away, whistling.

Ramirez stands at attention in Williamson's office as the CEO sheds his overcoat. "Sit down Ramon."

He sits.

"All right, Ramon. Please enlighten me. What, pray tell, is the purpose of having her standing out in the bitter cold for four-plus hours?"

"Conditioning, sir."

"Conditioning."

"She has to learn to stand post in any weather condition."

"Did you stand with her?"

"No sir."

"Ramon, I have never interfered with your training methods or with your administration of this detail. However, what I just saw disturbs me. We've had a similar conversation after the incident with the broken nose, have we not?

"Yes sir."

"Tell me, has Ms. Petersen been meeting the training goals?"

"So far."

"Is she being corrected for some transgression that I'm not aware of?"

"No."

"I'll not tell you how to conduct your business Ramon, but I don't want to see her outside again today. Do we understand one another?"

"Yes sir, absolutely."

"Ramon?"

"Sir?"

"I understand that she's a different kind of recruit. I also understand the need to bring her up to speed with the men. However, let us not forget, this is executive protection. This is not Navy SEAL training."

"Understood, thank you."

"You may go."

Ramirez stalks down the hallway and takes the stairs two at a time back down to the foyer of the building. Petersen is standing where he'd left her. The color has returned to her lips, but she is still shivering uncontrollably.

He stands in front of her. "Do not think for one moment that this has changed anything for you. In fact, now you're going to have to make up for our lost training time. Still cold?"

"Yes sir."

"Good. I'm going to go get lunch, you are going to double-time it to the gym, change into PT gear and run laps until I arrive. Let's see if we can't get you warmed up."

"Yes sir."

"Now."

Jules trots into the building and down the steps that lead to the basement. On the way to the gym, she hears the clatter of men moving around the kitchen and smells food being warmed up. Her stomach growls. Oh well, if she's going to run laps for Ramirez's entire lunch break she'll probably throw up whatever she eats anyway. She changes slowly and chugs some water, bringing the bottle out with her.

The gym is deserted. Knowing Ramirez, he's probably happily eating while watching the video monitors, so she starts moving. She paces herself. It actually feels good to move after standing in the cold for so long. However, after twenty minutes she is pouring sweat and getting tired and hungry. She passes another ten minutes by picturing herself breaking *his* nose. She summons all of her rage at him to keep going.

Next, her imagination conjures elbow strikes; then roundhouse kicks to the face. When she is beginning to think she's not going to make it, he finally ambles in from the gym office, coffee in hand.

This means that he has been sitting watching her through the one-way mirror the entire time. *Bastard.* He watches her pant for another eleven minutes. At just about fifty-five minutes, he motions her over.

"Nice stamina. Get down and give me fifty."

Jules drops, glad to be on the floor even for the time it takes to get into proper pushup position. She begins, counting out loud. As she counts, he stands over her, talking.

"So recruit Petersen, what mistake did you make today?"

"Fifteen. I don't know sir, sixteen, seventeen, eighteen."

"You don't know?"

"Twenty-one, no, twenty-two, I'm sorry, twenty-three."

"It was one of the first things I taught you, in the very first week, in fact. I believe it was your third day."

"Twenty-eight, twenty nine, I cannot recall sir. Thirty." She is struggling for air now, fighting to talk and breathe.

"I'll give you a hint, Petersen; it has to do with the interaction with your principal."

"Thirty-five." Her triceps are burning. She tries to remember the conversation with Williamson word-for-word. *Damn! What was it?* Then it hits her. "I told the principal that I had lost track of my time at post. Forty."

"You lied to your principal. You knew exactly how long you'd been at post. Correct?"

"Forty-one, forty-two. Yes sir, I did. Forty-three." She's not going to make it; she is out of breath, her muscles failing.

"And once again, you were trying to cover for me, probie."

"No sir! I thought the matter was best left between you and I. Forty-seven."

"You thought! When did I instruct you to think probie?"

"Forty-nine. You didn't. Fifty." She hesitates, not sure if she should stop.

He barks, "Keep on going probie. You owe me another fifty for thinking."

A week after the push-up incident, Jules is back in the conference room, studying procedure manuals, as she's done most of the day. Her work cell vibrates on her hip. She picks it up, it is Ramirez. "In my office, now."

Damn. She immediately starts reviewing what she's done that day and imagining how she may have screwed up. As she hustles upstairs from the conference room, she is unable to come up with anything, as she's spent most of the day alone in a room with her head buried in manuals. Reaching his door, she knocks briskly.

"Enter."

"Lieutenant."

He is standing, pulling on a black trench coat over his suit. "I need to fly out and pick up Bird Two in Connecticut. "She went to visit her mother, but they had some kind of dispute and she wants to come home tonight. Williamson wants me to handle it personally because she's upset. You're going to drive me to my place so I can get a fresh suit and then take me to Teterboro. I don't want to leave my vehicle at the airport."

"Yes sir."

"Let's go."

They take the elevator to the first level parking garage, where Ramirez's Escalade has a reserved spot, along with the fleet vehicles. He tosses her the keys and she feels a rush of anxiety. *God, can't he drive on the way there so I don't have to drive his precious SUV with him watching?* Though she knows, like everything else, it is another test of her abilities.

She unlocks the doors with the remote and climbs in. The vehicle is immaculate; not new, but it looks and smells that way. She adjusts the mirrors and seat, "Nice vehicle, Lieutenant."

"Another twenty-two years and you can have one too."

She smiles stiffly. *Twenty-two more years of this bullshit and she'll be too damn tired to care about a car.* "Something to shoot for."

He looks sideways at her. "Maybe you should concentrate on getting through the week."

"Right. So how was Caracas?"

"Polluted. Make a left."

It takes about six minutes to get to his apartment, housed in a discreet three-story brick building. This section of town is for the maids and service workers, decent but hardly upscale. She's willing to bet he started out in this place and kept it for its proximity and anonymity.

He directs her to park in a fifteen-minute spot in front of the building.

"You might as well come up; you can help me carry some gear."

She can't believe he's going to let her see his place. Then again, he's seen hers, it seems only fair. As the elevator deposits them on the third floor, he takes his keys back from her and unlocks the door to number thirty-four. Jules makes a mental note, just in case she is ever summoned here again, knowing he will expect her to remember. The place is neat and very clean for a guy's place, she's impressed. The furniture is functional and comfortable-looking, a long upholstered couch, a recliner and a big coffee table.

A dining area outside the small kitchen holds a dinette set with four chairs, she's guessing he doesn't entertain a whole lot. He walks into the bedroom. "There's a black duffel in the hall closet, will you get it?"

"Of course." She hears water running and dresser doors being open and closed. He walks out into the living room as she deposits the insanely heavy duffel onto the coffee table. He is wearing suit pants and a sleeveless undershirt, belt unbuckled. His upper body is amazing, tightly muscled and covered in scars and tattoos. Jules stares a moment too long and then pulls her gaze away from his body. He is holding up two ties, a navy stripe and a pale blue, patterned silk. "If you were really pissed off at your mother, which one would make you happier?"

Jules bursts out laughing. "Definitely that one," she says, pointing to the blue silk. Maybe when he's in his element he's actually human.

"Thanks, never can tell with women. There's a Glock in the duffel, can you get it and load it for me?"

"Sure." She is surprised he would trust her with the task. "I thought you carried a forty-five."

"Not for a gig like this. The only person I may have to shoot is her. I think the Glock can handle that. It's lighter, like you said." He disappears again into the bedroom while she carefully loads and checks the Glock. He reappears in a crisp, white dress shirt, his belt buckled, shirt tucked in neatly. He's wearing the pale blue tie and adjusting a leather shoulder holster into place.

Something about watching him dress makes her stomach flutter. The accidental intimacy of the moment makes her remember being married. She swallows hard, trying to refocus her attention on the weapon. Too late, Ramirez has caught her watching him. He tilts his head, "What?"

"Nothing." She pauses, "That's a very nice suit, Lieutenant."

He studies her for a long moment, frowning. "Thanks. Hand me that weapon, please."

"Yes sir." She shakes off her lapse in attention, trying to regain her equilibrium by using formalities.

He fits the weapon into the holster and shrugs on his suit jacket, buttoning both buttons. The expensive, charcoal wool suit has been impeccably tailored to conceal the bulk of the holstered weapon. Ramirez looks like a very handsome, badass investment banker. He hands Julianna a trench coat.

"You carry this and I'll take the bag. I'm expecting to be back in four hours with her, I'll need you to pick us up in the Lincoln. We'll drop her off at the house and then you can drive me back to the office. Eat dinner with the on-duty crew while you're waiting. I'll call if it's going to be later."

"Yes sir." Jules looks at her watch, it is 1730. So much for getting anything done at home tonight. This is usually Gi's job and she wonders why Ramirez is asking her to do it.

"We're going to start the strategic driving module tomorrow. I thought I'd get you warmed up." Jules feels as if he'd read her thoughts, he probably can. Maybe they teach that in SEAL training.

As she drives him to the airport, Ramon discreetly studies Petersen from the passenger's seat. He's decided to get her driving, see if she has the chops for it. She hasn't tanked on the training yet as he'd hoped, so he figures it is time to up the ante. One of the most important aspects of a protection detail, evasive driving, was a skill that could be learned, but only the best in the business took to it instinctively and immediately.

Ramon has begun to make a tentative backup plan in the unlikely eventuality that Petersen makes it through probation. To have a female driver in the follow car would be low-profile and less threatening to the men than having her in a point position.

He also believes it would please Williamson to have Julianna in a capacity where she might be called on to act aggressively. It would suit his notion of having the firm appear 'modern', yet still allow Ramirez to prevent Petersen from taking a top position on the detail.

She'd seemed nervous in his apartment, at one point he'd noticed a flush in her cheeks. When he'd asked her about it, she'd said something about his suit. He wonders if she'd noticed something about his place that she thought was odd or eccentric. He hadn't really thought it through, her being there amongst his things. There'd been another strange moment when he asked her opinion on the ties, she'd seemed to be staring at him. Maybe she'd been put off by the tattoos or maybe she's just used to younger men. Whatever, it had made him feel self-conscious and old.

At forty-six he has to work a lot harder now at keeping in shape, but he prides himself on being able to keep up with the young men he commands.

As far as bodies go, Petersen's is beyond reproach, every inch of her is long, fluid muscle, punctuated by pleasing curves that seem to draw the eye of every man on the detail. *Damn, why is he back on this subject?*

He looks at her again, she's concentrating on driving the big Escalade through heavy rush-hour traffic. She's doing well, hands relaxed on the wheel, no sudden braking or accelerating. A little tension in the jaw, but that's to be expected while driving the boss' car.

She glances over at him. "Am I doing okay with your baby, Lt?"

"Not bad." Although it pains him to even think it, Petersen might know how to drive.

Protective/Evasive driving begins at 0700 the next morning. Ramirez, Tam and Jules take one of the Escalades from the RSW garage. She knows that Tam, Ramirez and Gi have all been certified as strategic driving instructors. The other men have passed the same training Jules is about to attempt with a proficiency rate of at least eighty percent. Every two years they all have to re-certify; evasive driving, just like shooting, is a perishable skill.

With Tam at the wheel, they head down a small access road which runs behind the main building. They travel approximately half a mile through the woods when the road opens up into a massive paved lot, set up with orange and yellow cones arranged in odd patterns. Jules had no idea that this area even existed. It is completely hidden from sight and enclosed by a chain-link fence topped with razor wire.

At one side of the rectangular lot there is a small wooden booth. Tam drives over to the booth and lets the lieutenant out of the vehicle. Ramirez unlocks the booth and enters, settling into a wheeled chair and putting on a headset. Tam drives the Escalade to the side of the course and motions for Jules to get out. They enter a metal Quonset hut with an open bay door and retrieve a slightly scuffed, armored Mercedes sedan. Jules gets in the passenger side and Tam drives. He puts on his own headset and talks to Ramirez on a wireless connection.

Tam talks to Jules as he maneuvers the car from the shed. "All right, listen up. I'm going to show you how each maneuver is done just twice. You'd better pay attention because then you've got to do it yourself. I won't even be in the vehicle with you. You understand?"

Jules nods, terrified. *You know how to drive Jules. Yeah, I had one day of practice at the academy. Breathe - you can do this. Pay attention and don't fuck it up, Ramirez will be watching.*

"All right. First we're going to do turns and basic braking. You got your threshold braking, J-turn and bootlegger turn. Today's drills will be in this sedan, just to get the feel of the weight and the limitations of the vehicle. Later on, when you know what you're doing, we'll add in the SUVs and drill with a full team. Right now it's going to be you and the cones. Understood?"

"Yes."

"All right, buckle up."

For the next four hours, Tam takes Jules through a series of exercises with the Mercedes. They begin with braking as they approach cones that represent obstacles: a vehicle blocking the lane of travel, an object thrown in the road or a person with a weapon.

Jules is nervous the first few times, but quickly gets the feel of the car and the way its weight and speed affect stopping distances. After the first few exercises, she actually begins to enjoy it. Though the concepts are mathematical, not her strongest area, she is able to see the immediate result of the equations, which makes it easier for her to process.

At the lunch break, Ramirez leaves them and Gi steps in with Jules and Tam. They sit at a picnic table in the shed, eating sandwiches and spend two hours doing classroom work, looking at diagrams and scenarios on a flip chart, learning about turns and reversing maneuvers.

The subject matter is intense, Tam tells Jules real stories about kidnapping and assassination attempts, some of which he was involved in before he came to RSW. Jules learns that he was with a private client in Bogota when their caravan came upon a barricade in the road. The barricade was rigged with C-4, which was detonated as they attempted to reverse out of the kill zone. As they made their evasive turns, three men stepped out from the roadside, armed with AK-47s. Two of the detail's men were killed, including the driver of the follow car, but Tam was able to extricate the principal by driving the armored SUV over a shallow stream and escaping back to the residence.

The story gives her goose-bumps. All she can picture is Williamson's girls in the unarmored BMW that the residential detail uses for school runs and play dates. Once again, she is reminded that the job is about preserving the life of a family, in situations where she needs to be ready before anything occurs. Once you've realized that you are in the weeds, the difference between dying and surviving is measured in tenths of seconds.

They spend the afternoon working on turns and reversing maneuvers. First Tam teaches her the bootlegger turn: accomplished by driving forward, stepping on the emergency brake and turning the steering wheel sharply. If you do it correctly, the car will spin 180 degrees, reversing your direction so you can drive out of the kill zone.

If you screw it up, as Jules does the first two times she tries, the car fishtails and skids, leaving black, smoking tire marks on the pavement. Jules is eternally grateful that Gi is in the booth instead of Ramirez. By the sixth time, she completes the turns expertly.

After the bootlegger turn, Tam introduces Jules to the J-turn, basically the same maneuver, but done while reversing at speed. By the time she gets it right, Jules is sweating bullets and feels as though she's pulled every muscle in her arms and shoulders.

At 0530, Tam pronounces her proficient for now and calls it a day.

Gi punches her in the arm, "Wait 'til mañana girl, you ain't going to be able to lift a pencil."

"Thanks, Gi, you're so supportive."

"Supportive is for jock straps, Jules, I'm just trying to make you feel at home."

"*Gracias señor, eres un príncipe.*"

Gi bows at the waist, displaying his princely behavior. "*De nada.*"

For the next two days, Jules drives, studies diagrams, dodges cones and prays under her breath. Ramirez appears every morning, drinking coffee and watching her silently. Occasionally he will bark a correction to Tam, who then relays it Jules, as if she hadn't heard it the first time. Invariably, if she's going to screw up, it is nearly always with Lieutenant watching. Usually by late afternoon, under the kinder, gentler tutelage of Gi and Tam, she has the skill locked.

The second day is spent working with the Escalade and Tahoe SUVs. Jules learns quickly that the tipping and braking thresholds for these vehicles are infinitely different than the Mercedes. Tam assures Jules that she will continue to practice the drills with both types of vehicles until he feels confident that she can perform in any kind of emergency. In the meantime, she needs to be able to score an eighty percent to move on to the next module.

On day three, Tam and Ramirez bring the Mercedes, two Escalades and six additional men. They create a caravan with an Escalade as the point vehicle, the Mercedes in the middle with Gi in the back seat acting as the principal and the second Escalade as the follow car.

Each vehicle has a driver, a front seat passenger and a man in the back. Everyone except the principal is armed.

Tam gives Jules instructions. She will drive the point, principal and follow vehicle in turn, each in a completely different scenario. Flashing tripod lights will represent muzzle flashes at various points in the course. Various obstacles, such as blocking vehicles, barricades and debris will appear without warning.

In each scenario, Jules is to react, choosing the appropriate maneuver to either block or evade an attack or extricate the principal from a kill zone. Jules' mouth is dry and her heart is pounding. She feels choked by the tension of the situation. Not only is Ramirez going to be in one of the vehicles, but half the crew is watching as well.

She shakes off her doubts and gets in the driver's seat of the point vehicle, praying for grace under pressure. The caravan proceeds rather slowly, about forty mph, as it would in a city or residential area.

They're moving forward through the course when Jules sees an unfamiliar vehicle coming up fast on the left. The vehicle is past her and stopped about twenty yards ahead in less than two seconds.

Her job as the point driver is to put the metal wall of her vehicle between the shooter's and principal's car. This gives the principal's driver and the follow vehicle a few precious seconds to flee the area.

Jules steps on the emergency brake and turns the wheel, sliding to a stop at a ninety-degree angle from the vehicle, as men step out with automatic weapons. The principal and follow cars are already fleeing in the other direction, due to Jules' intervention.

After the first exercise, they regroup and Jules drives the Mercedes in the middle of the caravan. Gi is in the back seat acting as Williamson and Junior is in front with an automatic weapon. Again, they proceed forward at a reasonable pace. Before they've gone two-hundred yards, Jules sees a muzzle flash ahead. At the same time, the point vehicle suddenly careens into cones on the right, simulating a crash as if the driver had been shot.

Jules feels panic rising as she reverses, brakes hard and spins the wheel, attempting a J-turn. She is sloppy, but manages to turn the car about 165 degrees. From that position, she swerves around the follow vehicle and is able to flee the scene, leaving the follow vehicle to block the gunfire.

For the last exercise, she is the driver of the follow vehicle with Ramirez in the front passenger seat and Xavier in the back seat. This time, the caravan takes a circular course around the enclosure. The course is marked by cones and takes them past the garage. The point vehicle leads the caravan and its progress is uneventful. As the principal's Mercedes passes the corner of the shed, an old Impala shoots out from the side of the building and T-bones the sedan, pushing it out the lane of cones.

Jules hesitates for a second, steps on the gas, and slams into the Impala before its driver, presumably a shooter, can exit the vehicle and start killing people.

Once the vehicle comes to a stop, she, Ramirez and Xavier exit and take positions to open fire on the occupants of the Impala.

As Jules had executed her maneuvers, the crippled Mercedes had driven off, now followed by the point vehicle, which would block any further pursuers. At Tam's command, Jules and the men stand down and secure their weapons.

Jules feels like she's going to throw up and her legs wobble beneath her. They were only scenarios, but each and every time, they had felt real. She sees the vehicles coming back to regroup, but has no idea if she's done the right thing. The Impala is totaled and the Escalade has some front end damage, but the principal's car made a clean exit out of the kill zone.

Ramirez walks over to confer with Gi and Tam and Jules shifts nervously from foot to foot while Tam makes marks on a clipboard. There is some discussion, Ramirez turns and looks at the damaged vehicles, Gi and Tam shrug and hold up their hands. Junior and Xavier stand by mutely, looking at the sky. Jules can still smell burnt rubber and exhaust in the air.

Finally the clipboard is handed from Tam to Lieutenant to Gi, who add their signatures to the evaluation. Tam trots over to Jules. He holds out his hand. "Nicely done, Jules, eighty-three percent -- some vehicle damage, no injuries – well, except that fake dead driver on the assailant vehicle, but that had nothing to do with you. We'll keep working on this 'til it's second nature, but you passed this module, so you can proceed to the next. Good luck."

Julianna watches the men disperse, feeling strangely dispirited. *On to the next torment.*

10

Jules is in the computer lab, working on a hotel scenario. The room is silent and she's completely absorbed in the task, relishing the lack of supervision. She works, the computer challenging her with different variables. Errors in judgment cause the program to inform you that your principle is now dead or has been kidnapped. The program is much like a nasty video game, only every scenario is based on a real incident.

From the corner of her eye, she notices Eduardo passing in the hallway. Upon seeing Jules, he backs up and comes in, sitting at the work station next to her.

Jules keeps her eyes on the screen, hoping not to engage him. Eduardo pretends to work at something, but she can feel him glancing at her repeatedly. After a few minutes, he swivels his chair to stare directly at her. Jules keeps typing, but shoots him a warning look. She feels her anger rising. *Jesus, can they ever just leave her alone?* It's obvious that he's come in solely to antagonize her. Finally she can't bear the tension anymore. She swivels to face him, "Help you with something?"

He raises his eyebrows in mock innocence. "I was just wondering. I was in the gym the other day and I heard something about you." He pauses. "Somebody said your old man went down in the towers."

She narrows her eyes at him. "And?"

He shrugs. "It's just interesting, that's all."

"Yeah? What's *interesting* about it?"

"Well, you know," he continues, "I was just thinking, maybe it's true or maybe it's just something you made up so people would feel sorry for you. I mean, Ramirez never hired a newbie with no experience before."

She cannot believe this son of a bitch. In the time since she'd lost Chris, people had said some stupid and insensitive things. But no one had ever suggested that it didn't happen. She feels the coppery taste of adrenaline in her mouth. She knows that Eduardo is baiting her. She knows that she should ignore him or walk away, but everything in her just wants to destroy him. She leans forward in her chair, causing him to lean back, just a little.

"Well, just to put your mind at ease, I'll give you a little insider information. Every person who died that day was assigned a victim number. His was 1137." She stands up, leaning over him. "You got something to say about it, you'd better say it now, because we're never going to discuss this again. You got me?"

"Yeah, or what, tough girl?"

Jules is already heading toward the door. "I don't know Eduardo, maybe I'll call your boyfriend and tell him you're screwing someone else," she says, looking back over her shoulder. She's satisfied to see his ears turn flaming pink.

"I'm married, bitch."

"Yeah, well you know how it is: maybe that's true or maybe you just made it up."

Jules heads to the ladies' room. *Thank God for bathrooms.* She catches a glimpse of herself in the mirror. Her face is drawn and her neck and chest are blotchy. Her hands are shaking. She stares back at her reflection, furious with herself for engaging him. She closes her eyes, trying to picture a time when she was happy, when her stomach didn't hurt, when she didn't have dark circles under her eyes. She tries, but happiness was a whole lifetime ago.

It is Jules' third day of studying ballistics. The first day she'd taken a pre-test and bombed. Tonight after teaching her Krav class, she stays up until 3:00 a.m. studying and catches two hours of sleep before reporting back to work. She then spends four hours studying the new material and takes another test at noon which earns her a seventy-percent, a failing grade.

It's the math that's tripping her up: calculating distance, velocity and variables such as wind and bullet trajectory. Jules had always done well in school, always tested easily and with complete confidence, but the last two days have shaken her. She just can't seem to make her mind work this way. Of course, the lack of sleep isn't helping her concentration either. Last night she'd stayed up again, working out practice problems and trying to figure out how to connect the dots.

She's tried drawing out the problems, flash cards, everything she could think of.

Junior has been trying to instruct her, but as great a shooter as he is, he has no talent for teaching numbers.

So far, Ramirez hasn't gotten involved, but this morning she feels sick to her stomach. She knows that if she can't get this right, he is going to land on her, hard. Ramirez had warned her that he'd find her weakness and exploit it, Jules is afraid that this might be it.

Junior comes in at 0900 with a third test. She has to get at least an eighty-five percent to pass.

"All right, Jules, here we go. Did you study?"

"All night," she nods grimly.

"Okay, I'll let you get to it then." He pauses at the door. "Knock it out this time, Jules. I'll be back in an hour."

"Thanks."

She struggles and sweats over the problems for fifty minutes. Things seem to be making more sense today. At least three-quarters of the problems seem to have clear, workable solutions.

Junior comes in to collect the test. "How was it?"

She shrugs, "Better, I think."

"All right. I'll be back in a few. Try to relax."

She tries, leaning back in her chair and closing her eyes. After about twenty minutes, the conference room door opens and Ramirez stalks in, holding what she can only assume to be her test. *Shit.* Jules scrambles out of her chair to stand at attention.

"Good morning, Lieutenant."

"Not really, Petersen. A *good* morning would be one when my recruit could pass a simple ballistics exam."

"Yes sir."

He is looming over her now, waving the sheaf of papers around. *Goddamnit! How had she failed again?*

"Eighty-three, Petersen. You failed by two points. Three days. Did you study at all?"

"Yes sir! I stayed up until zero-three-hundred the past two nights. I don't know why I'm having such a hard time with this." She is close to tears. Again.

"This is basic firearms training, recruit. Do you know what the normal probationary period for our men is, Petersen?"

"No sir."

"Three months. Shit, I had Gi up to speed in two. We have made a special accommodation for you because of your lack of experience."

"Yes sir."

He is shaking his head. "I could have picked a guy off of the street and had him fully trained in three months." He shakes his head woefully. "You're just not cut out for this, are you?"

"I am. I know I can do it." Even to her, it sounds unconvincing.

"But you haven't done it, have you? It's been three days and you've failed again."

She swallows hard. There is no acceptable response to the question. Jules has always done well at whatever she's attempted. Failure has not been a part of her repertoire. She is drowning and Ramirez is going to throw her a cinderblock.

"Sit down," he says quietly.

She sits, her chair pulled out from the table. He sits on the edge of the conference table, tossing the test aside. He rubs his forehead as if he has a terrible headache. Jules is pretty sure she is the headache.

He sighs, leaning in and lowering his voice. "C'mon Petersen, let's just face facts. This isn't for you."

"I disagree, sir."

"Look, it's not your fault. You're a smart girl, a tough girl, anyone can see that. But this job is not made for women. Do you think your husband would have wanted you to do this job?"

"No, probably not." She feels fatigue settling in upon her, a heavy cloak pressing her further into her chair. She blinks, looking up at the ceiling, trying not to cry. *What is it about him that always reduces her to this state?*

"Then why would you want this? Why do you want to be somewhere that no one wants you?"

The last comment cuts her, she doesn't fully believe him. Most of the men have been great to her. Have they just been humoring her, knowing that she will never make it through the training?

"I really believe I can be good at this."

"Bullshit! I don't buy that 'I just want to be of service' crap. Everybody has a real reason for being here. What's the *real* reason Petersen? Why would a smart, beautiful woman who could do anything else, want *this* job?"

She looks down at the floor. She understands that everything depends upon the integrity of her answer. She looks up at him. "Because this is the only thing I've done in the last three years that's made me feel anything." Her voice is shaking. She has revealed herself to him, made herself vulnerable. Now, as he's been trained to, he will go in for the final strike.

There is a prolonged silence.

"All right, that's an honest answer. Look, I get it. You've proven something to yourself. Fought for something you wanted. You've made it two-and-a-half months, most women wouldn't have made it two days. Why don't you do everyone a favor and call it a day?" His tone is soft and soothing, a doctor with the perfect bedside manner.

The tears are coming, hot and shameful. This is the place she swore she'd never let him take her. Here she is, crying like a girl.

"No." She shakes her head, gritting her teeth. "I'll do this. I'll work harder, I'll pass the next test. I'm only two points away."

"You've *already* studied harder, Petersen. I'll tell you what, let's go up to my office, I'll write you up a nice, fat severance package." He is close to her now, so close she can smell the spice of his aftershave and feel the body heat between them. "Hell, I'll buy you dinner, we'll go get drunk." He has a hand on the arm of her chair. There is no place for her to look but at him. "Sound good, Jules?"

It is the first time he's ever used her nickname. In his eyes there is an explicit invitation. The sudden change in his demeanor confuses her. She can see a tiny glimpse of vulnerability in him. He is so near that she can see the faint dark stubble above his upper lip.

She has a sudden, inexplicable urge to put her mouth on that spot, to feel it under her tongue. A flush creeps into her cheeks.

He holds her gaze. Her cheeks are blazing now.

"It sounds great, Lieutenant, but no thank you," she says softly.

"Are you turning me down, Jules?" Almost a whisper.

A long moment passes, their gazes locked, during which a blatant exchange of attraction takes place. Finally she finds her voice, low and steady, "Sounds tempting, but I'm not interested in your *severance package*, Lieutenant."

His mouth twitches and he rocks back, unable to keep from laughing.

"You're a piece of work, Petersen. *Dios mío*, you really are. Go home and study. You'll test again tomorrow at 0800.'

Jules finally passes the ballistics exam with a score of eighty-seven.

The next evolution in the training is moving firearms drills. First she'll get comfortable on the outside shooting range with Junior as her instructor. Then she'll move into an obstacle course where she'll have to run, find cover and work on target recognition.

At the end of the two-week module, she'll be tested under 'stress fire,' which means that she'll be moving and shooting under the most distracting conditions possible. It will likely be a combination of harassment from the instructors, flash-bangs, sirens and other gunfire. In those conditions, Jules will have to determine which pop-up targets are civilians and which are enemy targets.

Jules does well during her first week. The static shooting is easier now that she knows the ins and outs of ballistics. Running, moving and covering comes easily because of her prior training in Krav, which has made her agile and given her incredibly fast reflexes. Junior trains her using both the Glock and the long gun, an AR-15 rifle, until she's comfortable with both.

Then they begin target recognition. Targets designed like women, children and men are placed in and around the course. Because of the public nature of the job, the skill means Jules has learn to differentiate between a man in a suit (civilian) and a woman in a dress with a weapon (target).

The first day, Jules kills three civilians. Junior, former Marine, yells until he loses his voice. He sends her home, admonishing her to 'get her head on straight.' For the next two days she does better, but on the third day, when he add sirens and increases the speed of the pop-ups, Jules regresses and ends up killing an unarmed teenager dressed in camo.

They are on the outside range in the full June sun. She is dripping sweat and cursing. Junior is standing over her, doing the same. "What the fuck are you doing, probie?"

He's one of the few instructors who've been patient and kind. That demeanor has disappeared and he is in full drill instructor mode, verbally abusing her and doing everything possible to undermine her confidence. Jules is officially the stupidest person on the planet.

She stands at attention and takes it, knowing she has earned it.

He is losing it. "I mean, Jesus, Petersen, you are *three days* away from stress fire testing. If you can't do *this*, how the hell are you going to make your shots when Ramirez and Eduardo are here firing live rounds and kicking dirt in your face?"

Junior shakes his head in utter disappointment. Jules has nothing to say. He looks at her. "You have absolutely no idea, do you Jules? You got a world of hurt coming and you're completely clueless."

She flinches. "Tell me," she manages.

He sighs in exasperation. "I mean, I like you Jules, most of the guys do, but Ramirez was right. You are a complete distraction to the team. You got to know, you are the daily topic of discussion. Maybe people are being polite. Maybe they stop talking when you walk in the room, but everybody's got an opinion on you. Half the guys are betting against you and the other half are watching just for amusement."

Jules feels empty and utterly alone. Junior has just confirmed her worst fears and validated every anxiety in her head. She respects him and knows he's telling a hard truth, not just trying to break her down. "Tell me what to do. I mean, there's got to be some adjustment I can make. Do I have the wrong attitude? Am I not working hard enough? Just tell me how to fix it."

"How you going to fix being a female, Jules? If you were just some useless bitch, the guys would have ignored you from day one. But you ain't useless. You got skills. You got smarts and even worse, you're a nice girl. So the men are going to take an interest, one way or another. There's nothing you can do about it."

She stands, staring at the ground. "What about Gi? Is he betting against me?" *Gi has always been on her side, always encouraged her. Has it been an act? Maybe he hates her too.*

Junior snorts, "Gi never met a pretty girl he didn't like. But he's Lieutenant's second, Jules. Think about it; Gi is holding the keys to the kingdom once Ramirez is gone. Gi's not going to do anything to piss him off and put that at risk."

She cannot think of anything else to say. Junior is right. Every man on the detail has worked hard to secure his spot in the ranks, none of them are going to jeopardize that by aligning themselves with her. She is a leper in a room full of supermodels.

Junior stares at her, aware of the fact that he has completely deflated any drive she'd had left. The Marine in him is not willing to leave a recruit behind. He considers her fate. He sighs. "You still want this, Petersen?"

Jules deliberates. She hadn't come all this way to give up. Though there's a rock in her stomach where her optimism used to be, she's unwilling to believe that this has all been for nothing. "Yes, I still want it."

"All right. Then you and me, we're going to stay here and train until you get this down. When I get through with you, you're gonna be able to do this in your sleep. If we gotta be here 'til midnight, then we're here 'til midnight. You tracking, probie?"

Jules smiles a very small smile "Tracking, sir."

She reloads and begins again.

Five hours later, Ramon calls Junior on his cell. "You still got Petersen? She's supposed to be here for supervision."

Junior raises his hand for Jules to stop. "Yeah, I still got her. Can she skip it today? We're working on some discrete skills, I just need her a little longer."

"Yeah, fine. How's she doing?"

"Doing good."

Ramon hesitates, hearing the lie behind the words. Junior likes to talk. When he's succinct, there's usually a problem. "Right. I'll see you tomorrow."

At 1900, the sun is setting and Junior still has Jules rolling around in the dirt. She is covered in dry, red dust. Her t-shirt is completely soaked with sweat, she is hungry and thirsty, but she has not missed a target in the last three hours. She is elated.

After Junior fails to punch out at his usual time, the lieutenant comes out to the range to satisfy his curiosity. He installs himself at a picnic table littered with empty magazines and unspent rounds and lights a cigar. Junior is holding a stopwatch and working a remote which controls noise effects and the pop-up targets. Petersen is shooting, covering and moving in and out from buildings to vehicles.

It pleases Ramon to watch Petersen struggling and sweating. It pleases him further to know that they've found something that doesn't come naturally to her. He watches, assessing her strengths and weakness. She is fast and accurate with the weapons, but reacts every time there is gunfire or a loud noise, especially close in.

Likely a function of her post-traumatic stress syndrome. Though usually acquired post-combat, Ramon knows that PTSD can happen to anyone who's suffered a traumatic event, causing even the calmest person to develop a hyperactive startle response. He imagines that post-9/11, Petersen has suffered significantly from the syndrome.

He finishes his cigar and motions to Junior to bring Petersen in. Junior waves Jules in and comes over, sitting wearily on the bench. She clears and shoulders her rifle, trudging in off the field. Ramon looks at her, smiling a little.

Jules does not smile back.

"All right Petersen, clean up, clear out and go home. I'm taking Junior out for a beer."

He turns to Junior, "Is this recruit going to be ready for testing on Friday?"

Junior shoots a look at Jules, "Damn straight Lieutenant, she'll be ready or die trying. Right, Jules?"

She forces a smile, "Affirmative."

11

Jules stows her gear and cleans her weapons, then limps to her truck. It is nearly nine p.m. She can't face the idea of driving home, so she grabs her gear bag and heads up to the dorm room. She is too filthy to even sit down, so she grabs her shower kit and makes sure the bathroom is unoccupied. Afterward, she wraps herself in a clean towel and goes back to the room. Locking the door, she lays down on the bed. Everything hurts, from her toes to her eyebrows. She has a massive bruise on her right shoulder where the recoil of the rifle had repeatedly slammed into the soft tissue. She knows she should get some ice, but she can't move.

Her head hurts as much as everything else, so full of information it feels as if it will burst. Jules starts to review the events of the day, but stops herself. She will not think, if she thinks, she'll quit and quitting is not an option. The tears come unwanted, sliding down her cheeks into her ears. She will get through this night and tomorrow she'll wake up and do it again. And again, until the training is over. And then…well. Then it will be just a job. Never a normal job, but something she can be proud of. Something she has done just for herself. Something with no memories attached to it, only forward motion. She will stay in motion until her heart stops hurting.

Four hours later, she wakes up as if she's been electrocuted. She sits up in bed and rakes a hand through her hair, which has dried into a tangle. She feels amazingly alert. She looks at the pile of dusty clothes on the floor and realizes that she is going to have a serious clean clothes shortage tomorrow. She's already awake, she might as well make use of the laundry room. Jules empties her duffel and sorts clothes into two piles. If she's going to have a clean pair of cargos for tomorrow, she'll have to sneak to the laundry room in her skivvies. Jules throws on an XXL t-shirt that comes to her knees, gathers her clothes in a bundle and skulks down the hall.

She flips on the lights to the room. As with everything at RSW, the laundry room is gleaming and state of the art. Jules is doubly grateful that everything is free, no scrounging for quarters or laundry detergent like she'd had to in college. She fills two washers and settles in on a chair next to the metal table used for folding clothes. Jules pulls out her MP3 player and puts her earphones in, queuing up Linkin Park. She turns it up loud to blot out any pesky thoughts.

Jules is startled to see someone appear in the doorway, Jorgé with a canvas bag full of laundry. Jules tugs out her earphones and greets him in Spanish. "¿Qué pasa?"

"*Nada, ropa sucia,*" he replies, gesturing to the dirty clothes.

After what Junior had told her today about the men, Jules feels self-conscious about being here, but she and Jorgé gradually lapse into friendly conversation. If nothing else, it will be good for her Spanish. After a few minutes, they're joined by Saul and Ruben. Both men are on a travel detail tomorrow.

Jules comments that she'd had no idea that the laundry room was such a popular place in the dead of the night. They explain that the fill-in staff have to work their way in before the day-shift men bring their laundry in at 0500. They ask what she's listening to and she passes her player to them. Ruben trots to his room and brings back a small docking speaker so they can all listen.

Saul notices the bruise on Jules' shoulder and asks about her training. She shrugs, saying "Same shit, different day," in Spanish. Saul responds with a filthy expression of his own. Jules asks him to repeat it, so she can use it later.

Jorgé chimes in, telling her that if she really wants to blend in, she should learn how to say cocksucker and motherfucker in Spanish. Jules listens diligently and repeats the words back, serious as a scribe. The men find this hilarious and continue to add words to the list. Soon Jules is laughing so hard she is crying.

As she banters with them, she is conscious of Junior's words. She's guessing that these guys are the ones watching her training for amusement. As Jules moves her laundry to the dryers, she feels a glimmer of hope. If everyone could just relax, she could fit in. It could be okay.

The talk turns to girlfriends and the men start complaining about women. They ask her advice and Jules gives them tips. She tells them the secret to domestic bliss: "Notice her hair, call when you say you're going to call and take out the fucking garbage."

Ruben concedes that Jules may have saved his relationship. As they sort and fold together, Jules feels lighter. She thinks she may be able to sleep a little more. She glances at the clock, almost 0430. She is not back on duty until 0600; maybe she can catnap for an hour. Jules gathers her stack of clothes, saying her goodbyes. The men wish her luck on Friday's testing. She wonders if they mean it.

Jules passes stress-fire testing by the skin of her teeth. She mentally checks off another rung on the ladder to the end of probation. She is exhausted and more than scared, but her training schedule reads "halls and walls" for the next five days. She breathes a sigh of relief when she sees this. 'Halls and walls' means standing post inside a hallway or room, the most tedious and mind-numbing duty for a protection agent. It is a task mainly given to newbies and fuck-ups; if you're on halls and walls, you really need to think about upping your game.

She reports to Ramirez on Monday at 0600. He puts her in the main hallway on the first floor, which runs from reception to the computer and conference room. This is the only public access area, usually for low-level business deals and contractors who are being vetted for service jobs. The long hallway contains two public bathrooms and two doors on each wall. On the left side of the corridor are conference room A and the locked computer lab, on the right is a break room for the men. The doors for the ladies' and men's rooms are on opposite sides of the hallway.

The lieutenant informs Jules that she will stand post in this hallway every other day for the entire week. The shift is eight hours, with a half-hour lunch break. Ramirez addresses her before he takes his leave. "This is one of the most important parts of your day-to-day duties. I don't think I need to tell you that if you make it through probation, you're going to be doing a lot of this. And just because it's tedious doesn't mean you don't have to pay attention. Observe everything, keep your mind active and scan your sectors. Boredom is no excuse for inattention. Got it?"

"Yes Lieutenant." *Shit. Eight hours, one break.* Jules reviews mentally, a sector is a way to break down an area of surveillance: from floor to waist height, waist to eye height and eye to ceiling height. By scanning constantly, you keep the mind engaged and the eyes active, so nothing slips by. Nothing: like the guy who stocks the vending machine in the break room or the little old lady who refills the paper towels in the restrooms.

Four and half hours later, Jules surreptitiously checks her watch. She feels as though she may lose her mind. Her feet are numb; her brain feels like pea soup. Of all the training she has yet endured, this is by far the worst. The guys pass her by, smirking, stone-faced or shaking their heads in sympathy. Her humiliation is complete and public. At 1100, Jules takes her lunch break, wolfing down a sprout and avocado sandwich, gulping a bottle of water and inhaling the strongest cup of coffee she can make. With three minutes left, she speed-walks to the ladies' room and makes it back on post with thirty seconds to spare.

The afternoon looms before her. She meditates, she flexes each muscle in her body, one by one, from the top of her head down to her toes. She tries to recite the alphabet backwards, then the table of elements, then every '80's television show she can remember watching.

More employees pass, back and forth. It is excruciating, she has a blinding headache and everything feels numb again. Jules quietly rises up and down on her toes, trying to flex her feet. She blinks; she turns her head from right to left, stretching her aching neck. *Please God let it be over soon.* As if he'd heard her, God sends the angel of death, Ramirez, down the hall. It is 1358. *How does he know?* Jules wonders. *He must have a chip in his head that beeps whenever it's time to harass her.*

"Petersen. Your shift is over."

"Yes sir."

"You can give me your report verbally if you want."

Jules feels her heart begin to pound. Her report? *Shit. Of course, there is a report, one doesn't stand on post for eight hours and have nothing to report, does one?* "Um, just normal activity sir, employee traffic, a few visitors to conference room A. No incidents." She prays silently, it sounds right.

Ramirez cocks his head at her.

Dammit! Nothing good ever comes of that gesture.

"And these visitors? Can you describe them?"

"Uh yes, of course. Um, two males, mid-thirties. They checked in at reception. They entered the conference room and Gi met with them for about forty minutes, then they left."

"What were they wearing?" His expression is bland, disinterested.

She feels a flutter of panic. She frowns, remembering, "White polo shirts and khakis."

"Eye color? Hair color?"

Oh God, this is bad. "Um, they both had brown hair," she squints, willing the details to come. There is nothing. "I don't think I was able to make out their eye color."

"You don't think?"

"I didn't make note of the eye color sir, I will next time."

"Next time."

"Yes sir."

"Petersen, one of those men was carrying something. What was it?"

She closes her eyes. The men had come in around 0700. At least forty people had passed since then. *Jules, you moron! What the hell were you doing if not noticing what some stranger was carrying?* "A briefcase?"

Ramirez rocks back on his heels. "It was a tool kit." He lets this statement hang in the air between them. "It read, 'ITS Technical Systems' in red. No memory of that, probie?"

"No sir, I'm sorry."

"You're sorry. You had one task for the last eight hours, Petersen."

"I understand."

"On your next shift, you will assign every visitor a number in your head. You will correspond that number to a complete physical description and observation of what that visitor brings in and out of the building. At the end of your shift, you will detail that report on paper. Do you read, Petersen?"

"Yes Lieutenant." *Yes lieutenant, I am a worthless piece of dirt, not fit to be tracked into the building on the bottom of your shoe. Yes lieutenant, I am going to go home now and install that chip in my head with a rusty screwdriver, so I will remember every electrician, janitor and lawyer who passes through this goddamn hallway, down to the color of their tie and the smell of their aftershave. Yes sir.*

Ramirez is making his midnight rounds. Passing the staff lounge, he sees a light on, probably one of the guys watching cable. He pauses at the doorway and sticks his head in. It is Petersen, asleep on one of the leather couches. Ramon remembers that Gi's been fighting with his girlfriend and has temporarily reclaimed his dorm room until the spat blows over. This leaves Petersen homeless whenever she's working overtime, which is daily at this point.

She is curled around a small pillow, partially covered by one of the well-worn throw blankets from the couch, out for the count. Ramirez does a quick calculation in his head; she'd done a 0600 to 1800 shift. A few hours end-of-shift paperwork made about fifteen hours, minus a lunch and dinner break. She was due on again at 0600.

Her bare feet are sticking out of the too-short blanket. Ramon recalls the sleep deprivation of SEAL training, how sleep becomes as precious as money. How one's mind will scheme and plot to steal just a few minutes. He remembers falling asleep on his feet at parade rest.

He leans inside the doorway and turns up thermostat on the room's electric heat. He won't go so far as to cover her up, but at least she won't wake up freezing at 0300. Ramirez watches her sleep for a minute, musing on her training. His goal of eliminating her before the end of probation has not changed, though it's stopped being a personal agenda. Jules has proved herself to be a worthy recruit and a tenacious student, but she has less than two weeks to go before she becomes a permanent part of the team.

He's been steadily increasing her workload, denying her downtime and demanding nothing short of perfection. He knows that the next week will be crucial if he's going to finish her off before probation ends. He'd hoped to be rid of her by now, but every time he'd tested her, she'd pushed back harder. He's far from discouraged, in the last few days he's seen the signs: the smudges under the eyes, a sharpness in the cheekbones, tension in the jaw. Petersen is wired and exhausted. He respects that she's held up this long, displaying an even temperament he hadn't expected from a woman. She'd remained pleasant with the men and held her tongue with him, even when he'd needled her to the point of tears.

He shakes his head, feeling a moment of guilt and then dismissing it. Shame, but business is business. Though she doesn't know it, tomorrow is the first day of hell week for Jules.

Jules' days begin to blur together. It seems she is barely asleep before it's time to wake and begin another endless day. No matter what she eats, she loses weight. Her stomach hurts all the time. Her clothes are getting looser and there is no amount of concealer that can hide the shadows under her eyes.

On Monday night she decides to go home, just to regain some sense of herself. There is nothing in the refrigerator, so she resorts to digging through the pantry and comes up with a box of angel hair pasta. She fixes it plain with butter and salt and wolfs down a huge portion. Maybe the carbs will help her sleep tonight. She pulls on a t-shirt and hunkers down on the couch, flipping channels. She settles on a series of inane sitcoms so she can unplug her mind, but it isn't working.

Jules thinks of her latest mistakes and wonders what level Ramirez will sink to in order to be rid of her before hell week is over. She can't stop puzzling over it, she has performed well enough to finish her probation, but there are four days left and she cannot imagine that Ramirez will allow her to succeed. What's left? She's completed ballistics, advance work, threat assessment, moving combat drills, driving; what else can he bring to the table?

She closes her eyes and tries to remember her Krav testing. For five days, she'd faced a chain of Krav black belts, some whom were her instructors and mentors and others whom she'd never met. She pictures her primary instructor and friend, Lew. A forty-eight-year-old black belt, he'd pushed her to her limit, training her physically, mentally and spiritually to become a completely self-contained fighter. Jules tries to visualize what he'd said to prepare her, but testing was so rigorous, it's hard for her to remember specifics. She remembers only sensations: pain, the trembling frustration of muscle failure, blood, the sting of sweat in her eyes.

The last time she'd seen Lew was at his retirement party. He'd been moving to Scottsdale with his wife and was going to open a new training center. They'd promised to keep in touch, but hadn't.

Jules sits up and looks at the clock, 1930, not too late to call him. Maybe he can help her get her head on straight.

Lew answers on the third ring. After twenty minutes of reminiscing and catching up on each other's lives, Jules explains why she's calling. She describes the lieutenant and the last five months. She outlines what she's facing in the upcoming week and how her fears are getting the best of her.

There is a long silence as Lew considers her situation. Finally he inquires, "Well Jules, am I speaking as your instructor or your friend?"

She hadn't considered this. "I guess I need the advice of my instructor."

"Okay." Another pause. "You're looking at this all wrong."

"Okay. How so?"

"Jules, you're thinking of this guy, this lieutenant, as an opponent. He's not an opponent, he's your teacher. What has he taught you?"

On the other end of the line, Jules frowns in concentration. Ramirez as teacher. The thought had rarely entered her mind, and definitely not lately. She thinks quietly, then answers. "Perseverance."

"Good. What else?"

She considers this. "Humility?"

"Okay. And the last thing, a continual point of correction in your Krav training, if I remember correctly."

This stumps her. What had held her back in Krav training? Then she remembers. Lew yelling, "Do it the way I tell you to do it, not the way *you* want to do it, Jules!"

"Obedience." She hates to even say it out loud.

"Excellent." He laughs. "Obedience is not the same as submission, Jules, you never quite grasped that. You asked this man to teach you, correct?"

"Yes."

"Has he done that?"

"Yes."

"Then whatever you face this week is a function of the education he's providing you. You approach your teacher with humility, perseverance and obedience – nothing else. There is no test. You simply obey the instructions you are given. Clear your thoughts. Thought is the enemy of instinct. There is no fighting, only teaching and learning. Can you accept that?"

"Yes, I can. I understand, Lew. God, I think you just saved my ass."

"Save your own ass Jules, the only thing between you and that job is the noise in your head."

12

On Tuesday morning, Jules notices that the men are making themselves scarce, not a good sign. Instead of her usual 0500 workout in the gym, she goes to her now-familiar utility closet. She lies down on the floor, closes her eyes and clears her mind. She focuses only on her breath. If she can breathe her way through this day, it will be over and she will be on the other side. A day closer to her goal, closer to inclusion.

She'd slept like a baby last night for the first time in months, coming to understand that she has only to yield to Ramirez's experience in order to survive the next four days. She breathes in and out, fueling herself mentally for the day. There is a soft tap at the door. She sits up. "Come in."

It's Gi. "Hey *hermana*, just wanted to wish you luck today." He squats next to her and offers his hand.

Jules takes it. "Thanks Gi. How's the office pool coming?"

He smiles, "Ah you know, lotta money changing hands today. Listen, Jules, stay cool today, okay, no matter what happens. You got the skills, you know what to do, just don't quit on yourself, okay? The only way he can eliminate you now is if he can rattle you. So when it gets ugly, you just think ice. Remember that song, 'Ice, Ice Baby?' That's you today, ice."

Jules bursts into laughter, "Shit Gi. Please don't make me picture that idiot. I'll end up laughing at some crucial moment."

Gi stands up, laughing too. He winks at her. "Ice, baby, that's you."

Jules checks her watch. She is slated to meet Ramirez in conference room B in ten minutes. She decides to go early, so she can be sitting quietly when he arrives. As she enters, it doesn't surprise her that he is already there with a binder open in front of him.

"Morning Petersen." He looks perky, Jules finds it a little unsettling.

"Morning Lieutenant."

"All right, let's begin. You have three evolutions to complete during the next twenty-four hours. You will be presented with clear problems, which you'll solve using the skills you've acquired during your probationary period. The first two will be framed within a specific time period. If you don't complete the task within the allotted time, you lose ten points for every five minutes beyond the allotted finish time. Each evolution is worth 100 points. At the end of this unit, you'll need 270 points to pass. Tracking, Petersen?"

"Yes sir." *Teaching and learning, just like Lew said.*

"The third evolution has no time limit, you'll simply need to accomplish the task if you're capable. When that task is completed, or not, you'll be off-duty until Friday, when we'll recall you to the building. At that time you'll meet with Williamson and me for your final performance evaluation. Are you ready to begin?"

"Yes Lieutenant."

"Okay. First problem: We have received a credible threat that Williamson may be harmed today, this puts us at threat-condition red. Your task is to evacuate him from this building to the residence. However, we have reason to believe that someone on the detail has leaked information to the threatening party, so you may assume that no one but Gi is cleared for knowledge of Bird's movement. I will be observing and Williamson will be cooperative with whatever instructions you give him, but no one else is to know of Bird's whereabouts or see him leaving the building. Because of the imminent threat, the main road is off-limits for egress. You have one hour. Start now."

Ramirez exits the room.

Jules stands. Ludicrous as it is, she hears Gi in her head. 'Ice baby.'

Williamson is in his office on this floor. To exit the building without being seen by the security cameras or any personnel is the primary dilemma. His movements are tracked by the GPS on his cell and every camera in the building. Jules heads to the computer lab on the first floor. Looking at the schedule, she finds that Bruno and Matthew are on the front desk, Eduardo is in the monitoring room and Gi and Jorgé are in the basement, with Gi on range duty and Jorgé in the gym.

Jules thinks for a moment and then types a red-flagged text message from Ramirez asking all personnel, with the exception of Gi and Bruno, to meet immediately in conference room A for a briefing. This will leave only Bruno on reception, watching a random scroll of camera views while the rest of the crew gathers for the briefing. There will be nothing unusual about Julianna being seen with Williamson, it's a daily occurrence. Jules hits send, as far as the reason for the briefing, Ramirez will have to improvise.

Jules exits the computer lab and takes the stairs to the second floor. She enters Williamson's outer office and informs his secretary that Ramirez has asked her to fetch him for a meeting. He stands as she enters his office, buttoning his suit jacket.

"Good morning sir. Have you been briefed by Lieutenant Ramirez about our little adventure?"

"Yes, my dear, and I am at your disposal."

"I have to ask you to turn your cell phone off and leave it in your desk drawer, sir." Williamson frowns, but does as she asks.

"Good sir, let's go, time is of the essence."

Jules smiles at Lauren as they exit. She leads the way to the stairs and hustles Williamson down to the basement level. Checking to see that hallway is clear, she brings him into the equipment locker room. Gi is at the desk.

Jules scrawls a signature on Gi's clipboard. "Going to need my weapon, I'm heading out to the range." Gi retrieves Jules' Glock from the weapon safe and loads it for her. From a locker of extra equipment, Jules extracts a gray hooded sweatshirt and sweatpants, size extra-large. "Sir, I know it's not your color, but if you'd indulge me just this once, suit jacket off and these right on over your clothes."

Williamson smiles as he dons the baggy sweats. Jules takes his suit jacket and stows it in her personal locker. She pulls the hood of the sweatshirt over his head. "Perfect."

She holsters her weapon and throws on a sweatshirt of her own. "Follow me sir."

Gi nods at her as she leads Bird through the doors to the range. They weave past the shooting lanes and out the back door to the outdoor range. Jules checks her watch: seventeen minutes elapsed. At the edge of the outdoor range, there is a large equipment shed. Jules uses her key card to unlock the shed and rolls the door open. Inside she locates a small ignition key and the golf cart it belongs to. "Hop in sir, we're going to take a little ride."

She backs the cart out of the shed and locks it up again. At the north corner of the range, she finds the dirt access road which winds through the woods to the vehicle training course. From that point, there is a secondary road parallel to the driving course that will take them to Williamson's residence, about seven miles away.

Williamson seems compliant, as Ramirez had indicated. Jules looks, but sees no signs of anyone following them. As she drives to the vehicle course, she scans the woods and fields for movement or shapes. She sees nothing.

She breaks it down in her head: there are two major obstacles between here and the residence. One is that she cannot drive the golf cart unnoticed on the road, so she will have to access one of the practice vehicles from the vehicle course. The rub is that the vehicles are locked and garaged.

If she can break into the garage, then she can likely find a spare key. Once that's done, there's the small matter of exiting the driving course, which is surrounded by a razor-wire fence and a locked gate, for which she does not have the code. She'll figure that out when she gets to it.

As they arrive at the garage, Jules jumps out and surveys the building. It is a tin, military-style Quonset hut with sliding double barn doors. The doors are chained and padlocked. Jules inspects the lock, steel and industrial grade. However, the half-inch aluminum chain looped loosely through the door handles looks like a weak point. Ramirez didn't say anything about property damage, did he? Jules runs to the back of the golf cart and digs underneath a toolbox and blankets to find what she's looking for, a small tire iron.

She slides the iron between the chain and the door handles and bears down on it. Nothing. She turns the tire iron clockwise so that the chain doubles back on itself. This time she applies her full body weight to the tire iron. The chain snaps with a dull metallic sound. She pulls the broken chain through the padlock and throws them both to the ground.

She motions for Williamson to follow her inside. There she sees the vehicle she wants, a four-wheel drive black Yukon. It is unlocked, but no keys. She checks the visor, the glove box and the console, nothing. *Think Jules, if I were Tam, where would I hide the keys?* She pictures him, neat and organized. A box, somewhere clean and inconspicuous.

She goes to a work bench where tools are laid out on clean rags. Jules starts pulling open drawers: socket wrenches, drill bits, compressor heads. In the third drawer she sees a small metal box with Thai lettering, some kind of tea container. She pries the lid off and finds them, three sets of keys, neatly labeled, '*Escalade, Durango, Yukon.*' *Bless you, Tam.*

She nods to Williamson, "Okay sir, we're going to upgrade our ride."

She instructs him to sit in the passenger seat of the Yukon, jumps into the drivers' seat, starts the engine and pulls out of the garage. She leaves the vehicle idling, runs to the golf cart and pulls it into the Yukon's empty parking space.

When she swings back up into the Yukon, Williamson is smiling.

"I must confess Julianna, this is all very exciting, you're like a lady MacGyver." Jules raises her eyebrows at him. Somehow she cannot picture Williamson watching network television, but really, what difference does it make?

"Glad you're enjoying yourself, sir."

Jules grabs the broken chain and padlock, closes the garage doors and loops the chains through the handles. From a distance it looks as though the door is still secure. She picks up the tire iron and tosses it in the back seat, checking her watch again. *Shit, forty-nine minutes elapsed.* Jules prays for favorable conditions ahead.

She guns the engine and races the mile-and-a-half to the end of the course, where the gate to Manor Road waits. The gate looms, daunting and immoveable. Jules jumps out again. She inspects the gate, which is reinforced steel, connected to a chain-link fence topped with razor-wire. The gate is not padlocked but automatic, controlled by a coded keypad.

Okay, forget that. The gate is too heavy to knock down, even with the big vehicle. What had she been thinking? But this was the only feasible way to get him off the compound without exposing him or taking him to the main road.

Jules feels panic rising. She closes her eyes and thinks. An evolution is a task, a problem to be solved. The gate cannot be breached. Not the gate, but the fence. She heads to the back of the Yukon and opens the lift gate. Digging under tool boxes and med kits, she finds what she is looking for. Bolt-cutters, kept in every vehicle to create emergency egress; the perfect accessory for every outfit.

Jules pulls on a pair of leather work gloves and lunges at the fence, working as fast as she can, cutting links vertically as high as she can reach. She glances back at the Yukon and forward to the fence, visually estimating the width of the vehicle. She moves about eight feet to the right, repeating the task of cutting the links vertically. She kicks at the bottom of the fence with her boot and it bends forward just a little. It will have to do. Jules throws the tool in the back and hustles back into the driver's seat. *Ready or not.* "Sir, seat belt on please."

Williamson is pale and wide-eyed in a rare moment of speechlessness.

Jules backs the Yukon up about five hundred yards and then steps on the gas. She winces as the vehicle hits the break in the fence. There is a terrible screeching noise as metal meets metal, but the cut fence gives way, scraping over the roof of the Yukon with a horrific noise. Williamson and Jules are both cringing, but they are out on the road and speeding toward the house.

Jules pulls through the back security gate with sixty-two minutes elapsed. She has lost ten points off of her first evolution.

She ushers Williamson into the residence, depositing him in the first floor study. She runs to a powder room to slurp some water out of the faucet. As she finishes, her phone buzzes. It is a text from Ramirez: **"Evacuate BIRD and Chicks from Res. to location B. 1 hour start NOW"**

Okay. Location B is a panic room installed under the generator house, two-and-a-half miles from the main residence. The generator house is deep in the woods, but still in the confines of the family compound. Location B was chosen so that in the event of a bomb threat to the residence, the family could be temporarily placed far enough away to be unharmed by a blast. The generator shed acts a decoy for the steel-walled panic room built underneath.

Jules has been to the shed only once. The terrain is rough; there are no roads, only a path designated by trees bearing scars on the trunks. In the event of a family evacuation, the house detail would take over and transport them in a Jeep kept next to the gardener's shed.

Jules walks swiftly to Williamson. "Sir, we're going to move you and the girls to Location B. I need to go upstairs and collect them, but I'd like you to come so I don't frighten them."

"Of course." Jules opens a concealed panel on the wall, which reveals a screen. The screen has colored dots indicating the location of each family member in the house or on the grounds. Annalise is in her room and Hope is in the playroom, which houses a computer and media system for the children. Jules takes the stairs two at a time, painfully aware of the clock ticking away her future.

She locates Annalise first. Knocking once, but not waiting for an answer, Jules enters Annalise's teenage sanctum. She has headphones on. Jules gestures for her to take them off. She does, frowning. "What?"

Jules changes her demeanor, Annalise is a tough customer in even the most ideal situation. Jules realizes that she going to have to establish her command of this scenario immediately. "Annalise, we have a situation. We think it's not safe for you to be in the house right now, so we're going to move you, Hope and your Dad to another location right on the property. I need you to grab a jacket and get some shoes on, maybe your boots, okay?"

Annalise looks at her father, who has finally caught up. "Daddy? Is she seriously going to make me go out into some shed?"

"Yes, bunny. Now this is very important. Jules is in charge and we need to do just what she says. Quickly now."

Annalise sighs and stomps to her closet.

Well, at least she's moving.

"All right, let's get Hope and then we'll be on our way."

Jules runs ahead to the playroom, while Williamson and Annalise straggle behind. At least Hope won't give her any attitude. "Hey honey."

Hope looks up, brightening. "Hi Jules! Mommy's away at Aunt Louise's. Are you going to stay with us?"

Jules is filled with a sudden surge of affection for Hope. *You're the bunny, Hope. Annalise is just a spoiled little princess.* "Actually, we get to go on an adventure. We're going to have a fire drill to the safe room. Remember that? The one in the woods?"

"Oh cool, do we get to ride in the Jeep?"

"Yup. I need you to get a nice warm jacket and put your sneakers on. Daddy and Annalise are coming too."

Hope jumps up and heads to her room. A surly Annalise and her anxious father wait in the hallway. Jules checks the time: twelve minutes elapsed. Once Hope is geared up, Jules hustles the three of them downstairs and out the back door of the kitchen. It's a quick walk to the gardener's shed. She rolls up the overhead door and heads to the Jeep. As she approaches, her heart lurches, the hood is open and there are torn wires lying across the engine.

Of course, they'd have to throw her a curve, just to make sure nothing went smoothly. It's not enough to shepherd the three bears miles into the woods. *Okay, calm down and think. Two-and-a-half miles. We could walk it, but not in time, plus Hope would end up needing to be carried.* Hope is petite, Jules guesses maybe seventy pounds, but still. Uphill, over rough terrain, Jules is fit, but not strong enough to do that, not in forty minutes.

No motorcycles. They have bikes, but they're not mountain bikes. A thought occurs to her and she smiles. They have horses, lots and lots of strong, fit horses. She turns to her three charges, two generations of expert riders. "Okay guys, change of plans. We're going to ride up there. Sir, Hope, Annalise, will you help me saddle three horses?"

Hope beams, Annalise shrugs. Jules herds Robert and the girls to the stables. "All right, guys, let's see who wins the prize for finishing first." Jules and Williamson start grabbing saddles and tack. Spurred by her competitive spirit, Annalise finishes two horses before Hope can get one done. In six minutes, they have two chestnuts and a Palomino ready to go. "Hope do you want to ride with me or Daddy?"

"Daddy!"

"Okay, off we go then." Jules sends up a silent prayer, thanking her parents for two years of riding lessons when she was in her pre-teen, horse-crazy phase.

She checks her watch, this little detour has cost her precious time. She is at forty-seven minutes. Damn, can she run the horses on that terrain without hurting them? "Sir, how fast can we go through the woods?"

"Anything more than a trot will bring them up lame. As I recall, it's rocky and uneven that way."

"Okay, sir, you lead and set the pace, as fast as possible without anyone getting hurt." The path is due for maintenance, Jules feels briars tug at her pants as they move. The good news is that Annalise appears to be caught up in the urgency of the exercise. She pulls her animal ahead of Robert and takes the lead, "Oh c'mon Daddy, we can go faster than this."

The other horses keep the pace nicely and soon Jules spots the roof of the large generator building ahead. When they reach the building, she gets them off the horses and leads the animals into the shed, dropping the reins to the floor. The horses will be all right for the time being, though she notices that one of the chestnuts has a bloody scratch on his leg.

Jules finds the keypad to the panic room door and enters the numbers Gi had made her memorize. The door buzzes open and Jules breathes an intense sigh of relief. She ushers Robert and the girls down the stairs and settles them in. She checks her watch, knowing that Ramirez will be somewhere doing the same. Sixty-four minutes; another ten points lost, but she's still in the game.

After her time for the second exercise is verified, she escorts everyone back to the residence and calls the resident groom to take care of the horses. Ramirez texts her that she is temporarily off-duty and can go home until she receives instructions for the third task.

The call comes at 0245 Wednesday morning, rousing Jules from a dead sleep. "Report to the gym in PT gear. You have half an hour."

Jules arrives and enters the building, which is dark and quiet, save Junior at reception. He nods, but doesn't make eye contact. She takes the stairs to the basement and approaches the double doors of the gym. Entering, she sees that it is half-lit, inhabited by Ramirez and Eduardo. *Of course, who else would show up in the middle of the night to make sure she fails hell week?* They are in athletic clothes, hands wrapped, barefoot. Jules slips her shoes off at the door and approaches them warily.

Ramirez speaks, "This is your third evolution, Petersen. It is a simple, untimed task. Make it to the north exit door of the gym. If you accomplish that, you've passed."

She looks at the door, in the far corner of the gym. A simple task, except that getting there means getting past these two: a Golden Gloves boxer and a combat veteran.

"Rules?" she inquires.

"No rules."

"Do you have weapons?"

"No weapons."

Jules considers her options, listening to the staccato hammering of her heart. A simple, untimed task. She listens to Lew's voice in her head, "What has he taught you?"

Perseverance.

Jules sits down on the mat. Ramirez and Eduardo, coiled for a fight, look at each other, confounded.

Jules stares at the far wall of the gym and breathes in, assessing the situation. They have probably been here for hours, drinking coffee and gearing up mentally for this moment. Now their adrenaline will kick in as they attempt to eliminate her.

Ramirez has chosen Eduardo because he is the only man in the detail who will not soften towards her in combat. Even his toughest man could hesitate if Jules got hurt. Ramirez knows this and has recruited the sole pitbull on the crew to help him finish her off.

Ramon, staring at Petersen, is rattled. She's taken a passive position on the floor. This means that if they wish to provoke her, they have to attack her as she sits peacefully. It is brilliant, he concedes, but appealing to Eduardo's honor is like asking a pig to say grace before eating; nonsensical.

As Ramon had surmised, Eduardo snorts in exasperation and launches a vicious kick to Petersen's head. She is able to avoid it and grabs him by the foot, twisting it in the wrong direction and torqueing his knee until he goes down. Jules pops up like a surfer coming up on her board and lands a kidney punch in his back. Eduardo twists in pain on the mat.

Jules feels Ramirez coming in behind her as she lands the punch. He grabs her by the hair and begins dragging her backward. The pain and surprise of it renders her helpless until she sees her goal, the exit door, receding. The sight motivates her to act.

Jules grabs the lieutenant's wrist to mitigate the pain in her scalp, his forearm like a piece of rebar. She has to admire the elegance of his solution, he has control and mobility.

She remembers a female Krav fighter who'd advised her after a particularly brutal testing bout. "Fighting is like childbirth. You switch your brain off and release it from the pain. Then, you let the body take over; it knows exactly what to do."

Jules scrambles to get her feet under her, pulling up on his arm to lift herself. The moment she is vertical again, she throws an elbow into the meat of his thigh muscle, creating a Charley-horse effect. Ramirez lets go and goes down on one knee.

Jules twists to face him and uses a hammer fist to the back of his head, stunning him. She takes the opportunity to run, closing some distance between her and the door.

Before she's gotten five yards, Eduardo drives his body into her from the side, tackling her. Jules feels the air leave her lungs as she hits the mat. Somewhere in the animal part of her brain, she understands that she cannot be on the ground with both men on top of her - they will end her.

She scrambles upright and head butts Eduardo in the nose, splitting it. She can see that he is mostly done, but Ramirez, the true obstacle, is behind her again.

Jules understands that there is no substitute for combat experience; Special Forces soldiers like SEALs are trained to ignore pain as well as social impulses toward empathy. She knows that in this moment, Ramirez sees only the task, to be accomplished at any cost.

As Jules straightens, Ramirez takes her in a choke hold from behind. Jules closes her eyes and launches into her *retzev*, a fluid series of deadly, pain-inflicting offensive moves.

Her body knows what to do. She twists, gouges and reaches for soft tissue and joints. She hears popping as his joints lock and threaten to dislocate, feels the slip of blood as she carves a deep gash on his cheekbone with an elbow. The huge silence seems to expand as they both claw for an advantage.

He lands a right to her temple and she staggers, tripping over something. She feels fabric, a nylon windbreaker left on the edge of the mat. She grabs it, twisting the sleeve like a dish towel. Ramirez is bent over, his chest is heaving and he's sucking air. She comes behind him and in one movement, coils the sleeve around his neck, winding and twisting it to strangle him.

He reacts like an enraged bull, throwing his entire weight back on top of her. Jules hears a rib crack but does not release her grip. He punches and elbows her in the ribs, the shoulder and the hip, lunging and rolling. Jules is the pitbull now, she knows if he gets free, it is over. She twists the jacket tighter.

She hears a small huff as he loses consciousness. She waits one more second and scrambles free, stumbling and gasping as she makes it through the north exit door.

The door crashes closed behind her as she tumbles out onto the slippery floor. She slams hard into the painted cinderblock wall and comes to rest in a graceless heap. She is panting and choking on tears, legs splayed in front of her. Jules can feel her body crash as the adrenaline dumps out of her nervous system, leaving her shaking and crying uncontrollably.

She wipes blood and snot on her t-shirt as she tries to pull herself together. *Had she even completed the evolution? Do you get a hundred points for strangling your boss?* In her desperation to survive the encounter, she hadn't even considered the consequence of disfiguring Eduardo and rendering Ramirez unconscious. "Make it to the door," that's what he'd said.

Jules startles violently as the gym door swings open, banging against the wall. Ramirez leans heavily against the door jamb, his face streaked with blood. His eyes are dead black as he assesses her. His voice is raspy and barely audible as he growls, "Go home. You're done."

Jules has no memory of the drive home. She cannot seem to stop leaking tears, even as she showers and patches herself up. Her whole body trembles as she tapes her broken ribs and applies peroxide to her hands. Her knuckles seem grated, her wrist feels sprained and she has an egg-sized lump on her cheekbone where she absorbed Ramon's right hand to the side of her head. The rib is the worst of all, it prevents her from breathing in fully and plagues her with relentless, sickening pain.

She is chilled to the bone, shock, she guesses. She bundles up in clean sweats and guzzles a shot of bourbon, trying to calm herself. Jules shuffles to bed and takes a Percocet, praying for oblivion. In barely lucid defiance, she shuts off her cell phone. If they want something they can leave a message.

Jules sleeps all day Wednesday and Thursday, gulping down painkillers and water haphazardly. Rising only to use the bathroom or look at the clock, she does not look in the mirror, eat or check her phone. Her performance evaluation is at 1300 on Friday, until then, she cannot bear to think of the reality of her situation.

"You're done," he'd said. Coming from Ramirez, that could mean, "Congratulations, you passed," or, "When I get my strength back I'm going to kill you." Jules doesn't care. Until Friday afternoon, she will stay in this safe, soft place where nothing can hurt her.

She comes to about 0600 on Friday. Sitting up introduces her to a new universe of pain. There is nothing that doesn't hurt; no movement without fresh suffering. She turns on her phone, expecting nothing but the worst. There is one text message: **Perf Eval 1300 Friday.**

She wonders how the lieutenant feels this morning. Jules can't seem to shake her anger at him. What had been billed as an exercise had felt like aggravated assault. She supposes that was the point, to break her spirit one final time.

It doesn't matter now. Whatever the outcome, she'd finished her probation, no one could ever take that away from her. Even if she's failed, they won't be able to say that she quit. It will have to be good enough.

Jules arrives at RSW at 1250, no point sitting around letting everyone gawk at her. She's taped her knuckles, covered her bruises with make-up and kept her hair loose, letting it fall forward over her cheekbone. Jules ponders the fact that she has few visible injuries and wonders if they'd avoided hitting her in the face on purpose. Easier to convince Williamson that they'd gone easy on her.

Lauren rises as Jules enters the outer office. "They're ready for you Ms. Petersen," she says, giving Jules a sense of *déja-vu*. Jules enter Williamson's office and he and Ramirez stand formally.

Jules shakes Williamson's hand and nods to Ramirez, afraid to look him fully in the face. From the corner of her eye, she takes in the fact that he has a small row of fine black stitches on his cheek. His left hand is taped and he is holding a thick manila file in his right.

Williamson indicates that she should sit and then starts, clearing his throat. "Well Julianna, this has been quite a week." He hesitates, "Quite a week." He glances at Ramirez, then back at Jules.

"First, let me say how impressed I was by your professionalism during the tasks you completed with me and the girls. You improvised magnificently and managed to engage the girls without frightening them. Hope actually asked me when we could play 'hide from the bad guys' again, so kudos to you. It was obvious to me that the lieutenant has trained you expertly, as I'd hoped he would."

He continues, "The lieutenant and I have reviewed your entire probationary period as well as your test scores on each training module. We also did informal interviews with random members of the detail to get a sense of your demeanor and character over the past five months."

Jules swallows. *Random members of the detail; yeah, I'm sure that was a mixed review.* She imagines Eduardo and the rest, grousing about "the skirt in the ranks."

She frowns in concentration. He hasn't really said anything specific, this is starting to feel like the gentle letdown before they tell you that you don't quite measure up.

Williamson turns to Ramirez, "Lieutenant, I'll turn this over to you so you can elaborate on Julianna's last week of evaluations."

Ramirez swivels his chair to face her, glancing down at the file in his lap. His voice is low and still a bit hoarse, "You had three evolutions to complete. You were over time on the first two, which gave you ninety points for each one. The last task was an untimed directive. You were able to accomplish that directive, though your methods were somewhat unorthodox."

"As Robert indicated, improvisation seems to be an area of strength for you. Your total score on all three was 280, which gives you a pass. However, there is the matter of the significant property damage incurred during the first two exercises."

Ramirez pulls a sheet of paper from the file. He reads, "Replacement of chain link fence section, $3,724. Body work and repaint for Yukon, $5,780.00. Veterinary bills and farrier costs for two horses, $1,057. Total damages: $10,111."

Jules winces at the number. It figures, somehow she'd managed to eke out a passing score and screwed herself on a technicality. She sighs.

Ramirez stares thoughtfully at her. "In fact, if the drill had been real, you would have had the key code to the back gate. And as Robert said, the use of the horses for transport kept the girls calm. Despite your disregard for company property, you used every available resource to protect your principals and complete the objectives."

He extracts a large brown envelope, holding it out to her.

Jules presses her lips together. Okay, so she's getting one last paycheck and maybe a polite letter of recommendation. Better yet, an invoice for ten grand worth of repairs. *Nice effort probie, better luck next time.*

She takes the envelope and opens it. Reaching in, she finds a lanyard attached to a laminated ID badge. She turns it over, it bears a recent photo of her, the RSW logo and the words, 'Julianna Petersen, Personal Protection Agent.'

Ramirez stands and offers his hand. "You're in. We'll see you Monday."

Jules spends the rest of Friday afternoon sitting on her deck, drinking beer and staring at her ID with a sense of disbelief. She periodically shakes her head. She holds her phone. She should call someone, broadcast her news. She tries her brother, he's not home from work yet. She calls Lily on her cell.

"Lil, I got in!"

"What?" she says distractedly. "Oh the job! That's great, Jules we'll have to celebrate. Umm... maybe next weekend, this week is crazy, Jeff's away on business, you know how it gets."

"Okay, great. I just thought I'd let you know."

"Yes! I'm so glad you called. You'll tell me all about it next week, right?"

"Right, we'll catch up."

"Okay Jules, congrats. I'll call you, okay?"

"Okay, Lil, have a good weekend." Julianna presses END. She suddenly feels like crying. Of course it's not Lily's fault, she has a busy life and Jules hasn't exactly been giving her regular updates. She takes another swig of beer and tries to shake it off.

Chris would have been the one to celebrate with her: he would have brought flowers home, would have picked her up and swung her around, kissed her and said "I knew you could do it, baby."

She closes her eyes and lets the tears come. No amount of wishing will give Jules her life back. She needs to live in the present. It's a brave new world and it seems cheerleaders are scarce.

She's on her way to a nice, comfortable buzz when she hears the crunch of gravel in the driveway. Maybe Lil decided to drop by. Jules goes to the front door. She hears car doors slamming. She opens the door to find Gi with a stack of pizzas balanced in one hand. Behind him is Junior, holding a case of beer.

Looking past them, she sees nearly the entire crew, each man holding something, a bottle of liquor, chips, another case of beer. Gi is boisterous, "Let us in Jules! It's party time, *hermana.* You think we forgot about you?" Matthew Lee hands her a bunch of tulips, Tam passes her a DVD, *UFC's Greatest Hits.* "Is it okay, Jules? You don't have company, do you?"

"No, no, of course it's okay. Come in, please."

Each man shakes her hand and makes a comment as he passes. "Nice job, Jules."

"You made it!"

"Hey, nice place."

"You didn't start without us, did you?"

Bruno walks in. "Nice shiner." He winks, whispering, "Y'know, I patched up Eduardo and Lieutenant. They definitely got the short end of the stick in *that* fight. Eduardo took his two weeks of vacation just so no one would see how bad you kicked his ass."

Jules tries unsuccessfully to suppress a grin. She ushers the men in, noticing the distinct absence of Ramirez. The men mill around the kitchen, emptying a bag of ice into her kitchen sink and burying bottles, making an instant cooler.

Jules directs them to the living room with the TV and by the time she walks in there are nine men splayed across her couches and her floor. She smiles broadly, realizing that for the first time in three-and-a-half years, her house is filled with company and laughter.

In his office at RSW, Ramon glances at his watch, 2200. He is working late so the men can welcome Petersen to the detail. He has a sheaf of paperwork in front of him, but has accomplished nothing. He's still eating ibuprofen like candy, hoping that the pain in his back and neck will subside to something manageable.

Jesus Christ, but she had kicked his ass. He'd been so confident going into the exercise, probably overconfident, and Eduardo hadn't exactly performed as he'd hoped either. He'd expected Jules to be exhausted by her last week and figured she'd gas out before she could get past them - what he hadn't expected was her tenacity. She'd fought him like a cornered animal and he'd woken up in a noose fashioned from his own clothing.

Damn, what kind of woman fights like that? He should have remembered the look in her eyes the first time he'd faced her in the ring. Unbelievable, it had felt like a prison fight. When he'd collected himself enough to rise and find her in the hallway, he'd already made up his mind. As humiliated as he'd been, he was forced to concede she'd earned her shot at the position.

There is no turning back now, Petersen is officially a full member of the detail. He reassures himself that time will solve his problem. After all, he is in it for the long haul, Petersen is just a tourist. As his SEAL instructors had taught him: *No plan survives first contact with the enemy.*

13

Jules' first week as a member of the detail is anti-climactic. She's immediately put on the bottom rung of the duty roster, which means she gets to do every tedious task that arises, from sitting at the residence for an eight-hour overnight shift to driving Grace back and forth to her ladies' lunches.

As boring as it is, Jules is grateful for the mental and physical break, especially since her broken rib leaves her in constant, aching pain. As she moves through the corridors of RSW, she takes note of conversations that end when she is within earshot. The men have been gossiping incessantly about her night in the gym with Eduardo and the lieutenant.

Jules is mute on the subject, she's already heard several versions of the story. One says she strangled Ramirez with a jump rope and broke Eduardo's nose with a free weight. Another version has them both kicking her in the head while she sat and cried on the mat. Jules wishes something distracting will happen so that there will be something else for them to talk about.

She gets a memo from Ramirez on Monday morning, her second week. Williamson wants her go to Saks in New York to buy "appropriate clothing" for the upcoming trips to Tokyo, Buenos Aires and San Juan. She'll be driven by one of Williamson's chauffeurs and have the use of a corporate card.

The memo includes a schedule of upcoming events. Grace has thoughtfully prepared a list of things Jules will need. Jules has a budget of approximately $30,000. She does a double take at the number and then checks it a third time to make sure she hasn't read it wrong. The events list reads: cocktail receptions, black-tie dinner, yacht duty, black-tie ball, polo match, breakfast meetings and charity luncheons. This is a part of her training she hadn't prepared for.

Jules is terrified. One of the cardinal rules of personal security is, 'Never out-dress your principal.' She pictures Williamson and Grace dressed in Armani and Prada and the girls in Stella McCartney and Marc Jacobs. *All right, don't panic. You have good taste. If they didn't trust you to do it alone, they would have sent Grace with you.* She doesn't have to compete, just blend in. *Yeah, blend in with a bunch of multi-millionaires.*

Jules decides to keep it to the bare minimum. Just what she needs; nothing more. Simple, classic, refined. *Black. Maybe white for Miami and San Juan. Okay, black and white. Then she'll look like a waitress. Okay, maybe gray. Or navy. Shit.* She decides to call ahead to Saks and beg for help from one of their personal shoppers. She'll take the expense out of the clothing budget.

She arrives at Saks a few days later, feeling like a total imposter in the back of a Lincoln town car. She travels up to the private salon, where her shopper, Kiara, has pulled clothes, shoes and accessories off the rack and assembled them for Jules' purveyance.

Jules declines the complimentary champagne and asks for water. They bring her a bottle of Pellegrino and a Baccarat goblet.

She nervously heads into the dressing room to try on suits. She has e-mailed Kiara the list and event schedule and the shopper seems to know exactly what is required for each occasion. Jules tries on three black suits with skirts. First is a Dior. She glances at the price tag and feels like she needs to sit down. Can you sit down in a skirt that costs $975? She thinks not.

Jules slides the suit on and turns to check it out in the mirror. *Wow.* She has never seen anything so beautiful. She pictures an ancient Parisian seamstress bent over the fabric. On the hanger the suit had looked like an ordinary, well-made piece of clothing, but on her body it does something magical. The cut is perfectly modest, but somehow makes her look as if she were born into money. She is transformed into someone sleek, sexy and knowing. She stares at her reflection. *You're a long way from home, kid.*

Kiara taps once and enters. "So Julianna, how are we doing? Oh." She claps her hands together. "Oh, I knew it! With those legs and that body." She whispers, "Oh honey, you have no idea how many *just embalmed* women I have trying these clothes on. And of course, they're thin as sticks, but you - you have a body for clothes. This is going to be so much fun."

Still in shock, Jules spends the next three hours trying on clothes. Each piece is more exquisite than the next. How will she ever decide? She can't imagine having to do this on a regular basis. She has a new appreciation for Grace's role as the perfect accessory.

Kiara discreetly edits the choices after seeing each piece on Jules, adjusting for her coloring and body type.

Jules ends up with a rack full of mostly Armani, Dior and Prada. She loves the Chanel, but they are much too fabulous. She needs to look perfect but not stand out. Two suits, three day dresses, six blouses, two pair of trousers and a very dressy pair of shorts for yacht duty -- she has spent nearly $11,000. She still has to pick out three cocktail dresses and a long gown for black tie.

Once they have finished with clothing, lunch arrives for Jules and then it is onto shoes and accessories. Jules end up with seven pairs of hideously expensive shoes and an evening wrap. She refuses to purchase jewelry. She knows that she has been acting on Williamson's say-so, but still hears the lieutenant's voice inside her head talking about her being too attractive. This is really going to rub him the wrong way.

Exhausted, she downs another Pellegrino for courage. She hands over the corporate card and wonders how she is going to get this all home. Kiara assures her that they will deliver everything to her home by tomorrow.

Jules shakes her head at the thought of these clothes hanging next to her boring work clothes and casual tops. She gives Kiara a huge cash tip out of her own pocket and a grateful hug. She tries not to allow herself to think of what this money could have been used to accomplish in the real world. She is in a different universe now. She has to adjust her mindset, even if she is just visiting.

In June, Jules is assigned to her first international travel detail. Williamson is going to Tokyo to woo a new client, the Matsuda Drilling Company. A third generation firm, Matsuda has recently become profitable enough for RSW to be interested in pursuing a relationship. The deal could be worth millions to RSW, so every detail needs to be perfect.

RSW has never done substantial travel in Tokyo, so new contacts at the hotel, airports and local police must be managed ahead of time. Ramirez and Yoji Sun, the Japanese translator, have already visited twice to do advance work and grease the palms of the proper officials. Gi has acted as a liaison between Matsuda's security force and the RSW detail, comprised of Ramon, Gi, Yoji, Tam, Matthew, Jules, Xavier and Henry. The rest of the team will stay behind, split between the RSW building and the residence.

Jules is incredibly nervous, the Japanese are fastidious in their business protocol and social customs. In order to make sure that the members of the detail are prepared, Yoji holds a two-hour class detailing the proper way to bow, take a business card, eat and subtly defer to senior members of the group.

Under Yoji's tutelage, Jules had learned that most Japanese men still believed women had a "place." In other words, Jules' presence would be tolerated, but she'd have to be discreet and feminine in manner and dress. Yoji advised Jules to skip the jewelry, pull her hair back and never wear pants. He taught her a phrase, "The nail that sticks up gets hit with a hammer."

Jules had shook her head. *What else is new?* So her objective was to provide constant vigilance as a protection agent and remain virtually invisible. *No sweat, just like Ramirez had said from the beginning: no visible lingerie, no perfume and no jewelry. Perform like a guy, look like a girl and make sure you don't distract anybody in the process.*

14

The five-day trip is scheduled from Sunday to Thursday; two of those days are solid travel. The travel detail, as well as Williamson, his attorney, Christian Devereaux and a male personal assistant, Brian, will fly on the Gulfstream for fourteen hours to Narita airport. Once they've boarded at 1600 on Sunday, everyone but two designated agents, Jules and Tam, eats and falls asleep. After six hours they are relieved by Matthew and Xavier. Seniority has its privileges, Gi and Ramirez sleep until the next morning.

After the flight arrives in Narita, they travel by three-car caravan ninety minutes to the hotel. Williamson is booked at the Tokyo Ritz-Carlton, which has the advantage of being ten blocks from Matsuda's corporate offices. He is scheduled for a 1000 meeting with Matsuda and his team. There will be a security briefing with Matsuda's detail and hotel security at 0900, which gives the detail less than an hour to unpack, shower and change clothes.

The team is split into two shifts. Yoji, Jules, Ramirez and Tam will work first shift until dinner ends and Gi, Xavier, Matthew and Henry will take the after-dinner overnight shift.

Matthew, though Chinese, is multi-lingual and will act as translator for second shift.

The security briefing is short and polite. Bottom line, on Matsuda's turf and in the city at large, his detail will call the shots. At the hotel, Ramirez is in charge but will consult with the hotel's team as needed.

There is a great show of exchanging '*meishi*,' business cards. Yoji has properly instructed them in the art: exchanged by the senior men, offered and received with both hands and carefully stowed in a business card holder, never loose in a pocket.

Jules spends the briefing trying not to gawk at Matsuda's men. They are short, but built like cinderblocks, they look scary as hell and don't make eye contact with her.

She feels jittery and exhausted already, so much at stake and so many ways to screw up, a perfect scenario for her first trip abroad.

The team arrives at the Matsuda offices at 0955. The building is a gleaming glass tower, forty stories high. Matsuda's corporation occupies floors twenty-seven to thirty-nine. As they exit the vehicles and look up, Jules feels queasy. It occurs to her that she has not been in a skyscraper since Chris' death.

They are met at reception by Matsuda's security chief and he leads them into a large elevator. Arriving at the thirty-ninth floor, the elevator opens onto a stunning atrium, complete with Koi fountain, rocks and bamboo. A mirrored chandelier reflects the colors of the planting and the fountain and the sun from a wall of windows behind.

The chief leads them to the right, down a polished hardwood hallway to a conference room. The room is one of the biggest Jules has ever been in, appointed with a teak slab table and leather chairs.

The team stands stiffly until Matsuda and his men appear from a side door. Introductions are made all around, Williamson and Matsuda complete the *meishi* exchange and the players are seated according to seniority.

Yoji is seated to Williamson's right. Williamson's attorney, Devereaux, and his assistant, Brian, are to the left. Ramirez and Tam stand flanking opposite ends of the table. Jules is stationed outside the conference room door with the security chief's second, a massive, sweet-faced guy named Rokuzan.

She and the dark-suited Rokuzan stand at parade rest on opposite sides of the double oak door, watching the hallway. In her case, standing outside is a demotion, in his, it means that he is the guardian of the gate and her babysitter.

Jules scans the hallway and as she does, she can feel Rokuzan's gaze on her. She does not acknowledge him in any way, deciding that this will be the safest tack. Twenty minutes pass and he says in a low tone, "You will help me practice my English please?"

Jules forgets herself and looks at him in surprise. He nods and bows. She does the same, unsure of the protocol. *Are we supposed to be talking? If we weren't, he would know that, right? Shit.* Jules has no choice but to acknowledge the overture.

"Yes okay, quietly? I have to work," she stutters.

"Yes, yes."

She waits. *God help her, what if Ramirez finds her jawing with this guy?* However, she cannot afford to offend anyone at this stage of the game.

He begins. "You come from New York City?"

"Um, close to New York City. New Jersey."

"You know the Yankees?"

Jules frowns and swivels her head, looking behind them to make sure they're not heard. "The baseball team? Um, yes."

"You go to Yankee baseball games?"

"No. I never have."

"Matsuda-san loves the Yankees baseball."

"Oh yes, that's very nice. They're a good team."

Jules scans the hallway, praying that he will get bored and stop.

"You have visit Japan before?"

"No, this is my first visit."

"You are enjoy?"

"Yes, enjoying it very much. It's very beautiful."

"You see Britney Spears in New York City?"

Jules bites the inside of her cheek to keep from smiling. She feels a terminal giggle trying to surface. She chokes a little, suppressing it. "No. I think she lives in California."

"Britney is very popular in Japan."

"Yes." She is starting to understand. *The New York Yankees and Britney Spears, next it will be P. Diddy and the Statue of Liberty.*

"You will say your name and I will say my name?"

"Oh. Okay. Petersen."

"Petersen. I am Tadao Rokuzan."

"Tadao Rokuzan. I'm pleased to meet you."

"Yes. Also am I pleased."

Jules feels as though she should correct him. He did ask her to help him practice. "I am also pleased."

He looks at her, nodding knowingly. "Yes."

Never mind. "Tadao, won't we get in trouble for talking?"

"No, no. Matsuda-san says I must get better English."

"Yes, but my boss, Williamson-san likes me to be very quiet."

"Ah, yes. Then we must be quiet."

"Thank you." She bows, just to seal the deal.

"Thank you, Petersen-san." He bows in return.

The meetings drag on interminably, broken up only by a light lunch and then a late afternoon tea ceremony. Lunch is served in a dining room adjacent to the conference room, prepared by Matsuda's executive chef, in immaculate whites and toque. The businessmen eat first and the crew eats as a second shift, four at a time, so that the principals are never without protection.

The food is exquisite: tempura, vegetables, steamed rice and dumplings made of unrecognizable ingredients which taste heavenly. Jules tries not to wolf her food and to remember everything Yoji has taught her about table manners.

When the meetings finally conclude at 1800, Williamson is whisked back to the hotel and installed in his suite for a shower and costume change, before the 2000 dinner, to be held in a private dining room at the hotel.

The detail will clean up, work the dinner shift and then hand the obligatory post-dinner socializing to Gi, Xavier, Matthew and Henry.

Jules changes into the black Dior suit for the dinner shift. She opts for low heels as instructed, and pulls her hair back, clipping it with a tortoise-shell barrette. She keeps the makeup simple: mascara, nude blush and a rose-brown lipstick. She checks the mirror. No hanging threads, no stray bra straps -- simple, austere femininity, as requested.

She can't help admiring how nice the guys from the crew look in their expensive evening suits. Like deeply polished river stones, they all have a sheen about them tonight, enhanced by military bearing and the slight tension created by the new environment and the formal atmosphere.

Dinner consists of the detail standing post around a long table while the two corporate teams drink sake and wade through nine courses. It lasts a mind-numbing three hours, during which no one so much as drops a fork. When the group assembles for a trip to Matsuda's favorite karaoke bar, the second team step in.

After making the handoff, Ramirez signals his detail to follow him to a dark fusion restaurant on the fortieth floor. Apparently he and Yoji, on their prior visits, have scoped out the best place to eat and drink at the hotel. Though the restaurant officially closes at ten p.m., their little group is accommodated. The hostess escorts them to a reserved table with a skyline view that takes Jules' breath away. Yoji and Ramirez are watching her reaction, smiling, "Not too shabby, huh, Jules?" Yoji asks.

She smiles broadly, "I think you guys just made up for fourteen hours of standing post."

Food and drink begin to arrive immediately: platters of dumplings, pickled salads, sushi, bowls of salty, crunchy edamame and tiny ceramic carafes of warm sake. Jules is the only one uninitiated in the ritual of sake. "I don't know about warm rice wine," she says, hesitating as they pour.

"It's an acquired taste, but once you get used to it, it goes down easy," advises Ramirez. "C'mon Petersen, don't be a girl."

Jules cannot turn down the challenge, though she has a vague feeling that she'll regret this decision later. Tam shows her how to chase each tiny cup of sake with the salty, edamame soybeans. Jules wrinkles her nose, but they refill her cup and by the third one, she is so warm she has to take off her suit jacket.

Yoji makes her eat and drink a bottle of water. His solicitous demeanor makes her happy. As she eats and jokes with the men, she is suffused with a little thrill. She is finally just one of the team, drinking with the men after a hard day. Jules basks in the camaraderie, she's earned this moment.

As she looks around the small table, she catches Ramirez observing her, as always. However, this time his expression is bemused, not critical, and for the first time, she doesn't tense in response to his gaze.

Ramon leans back in the soft leather dining chair, relaxed for the first time in weeks. Off-duty, first uneventful day under his belt, accompanied by a view of the Tokyo skyline and a nice vantage on Petersen as she naively ties on a major sake buzz. While she talks and laughs with the men, he takes in the soft sheen of her shoulders under the sleeveless silk blouse of her expensive suit.

He has to admit, she'd cleaned up nicely in preparation for her first real gig. She hadn't fucked anything up and was presenting an elegant, professional image to the archaic Japanese elders. For all their fuss about manners, he'd noticed every one of them had given Petersen a thorough visual inspection anytime she wasn't looking.

Ramon's reverie is interrupted by Jules asking him a question. "Lieutenant, that Rokuzan guy, the one I was on the door with? He wanted me to help him practice his English. He was asking me all these questions about the states and Britney Spears and I didn't know what to do. If Matsuda's men want to talk, what are we supposed to do? I didn't want to risk offending him."

Ramirez considers this, "Well, obviously the job comes first, but if he wants to pass hall time by speaking with you, you can't exactly say no. 'Course if you were inside, that would be unacceptable. What do you think, Yoji?"

"Yeah, it's a little tricky, he was just being pleasant, right? I'd say accommodate him, especially since he's the chief's second. It's not like he's some flunky, even though he did get stuck on halls and walls with you, Petersen."

She makes a face at Yoji, and sees Tam's face crinkle up around his eyes. Tam is the strong, silent type. He rarely speaks, but he is the guy you want next to you if the shit comes down, plus he has a great sense of humor.

"You can laugh if you want Yoji, but I think I was able to provide old Rokuzan with a broad overview of popular American culture and a deep understanding of the subtle nuances of the English language. Couple more days with me and he might be gunning for your job, sister."

"Ohhh!" There is a collective snicker from around the table.

"You'd better be on your game, Yoji," Ramirez chides.

Yoji smiles and nods, acknowledging that he has been handily smacked down.

She glances at her watch, 0150. "Damn, I have to turn in. I know you guys are used to this kind of schedule, but I'm still getting my sea legs." Jules stands with a barely perceptible wobble. She holds onto the back of her chair with one hand as she slips back into her jacket.

Ramirez notices. "Tam, walk her up," he orders. Tam stands.

"Lieutenant, I don't need to be walked up," Jules protests. "If it was Yoji going to his room, you wouldn't have Tam walk him up."

Ramirez replies drily, "Yeah well, Yoji doesn't look that nice in a skirt, plus he holds his sake a little better. End of discussion."

She bows prettily, "Gentleman, it's been a pleasure. See you bright and early."

Ramon and Yoji watch the pair leave. Yoji looks at Ramon and shrugs, "I do like to watch her go."

Ramon follows his gaze to the slight sway of Julianna's pencil skirt. He lifts his cup to Yoji, "One of the very few perks of having a female on the crew."

Jules wakes the next morning with a dry mouth and crushing headache. After guzzling a bottle of water and taking a shower, she feels marginally better. So much for her international carousing, next time she'll stick to beer.

The day commences the same as the one before, minus the security briefing. Williamson has breakfast in his room with the attorney and assistant, talking business strategy. The gist, as Julianna understands it, is that yesterday was merely a polite, getting-to-know-you scenario. Today they will get down to the task of laying their cards on the table and assuming a negotiating posture. On Wednesday they will hammer out final details, sign contracts and say their formal goodbyes.

Jules has a feeling that it could be a really long day. In addition to the daunting agenda, it is pouring rain. Everyone dons trench coats and secures umbrellas before they head to the vehicles waiting to take them to Matsuda's offices. The city smells like wood smoke, exhaust and fried food.

The entourage enters, shaking coats and umbrellas before handing them off to a group of female attendants. The group ascends *en masse* and reconvenes in the giant board room. Apparently yesterday's arrangement suited everyone, because Jules is placed back out in the hall with Rokuzan. They greet each other warmly.

Though exhausted, Jules feels more relaxed now that she knows she has permission to chat with her co-worker. She decides to turn the tables and asks him to help her learn some Japanese. Jules is painfully aware that the ten words she knows in Japanese are not only inadequate, but that her pronunciation is shameful. She might as well use the hall time to improve her grasp of the language.

Rokuzan appears thrilled by her request and for the next two hours proudly instructs her. At a lull in the instruction, Rokuzan asks that Jules excuse him while he uses the restroom. Jules takes the opportunity to flex her toes and stretch discreetly. She is praying that they will break for lunch soon.

As she waits for Rokuzan to return, she sees a young man enter the hallway. Thin and bookish-looking, he wears wire-rimmed glasses and is carrying a small box gift-wrapped in a traditional *furoshiki*, a silky cloth that ties into a bow. He is wearing a pale linen suit that has apparently been rained on, it looks damp and rumpled.

When she realizes that he is approaching her, Jules stiffens a little, looking past him for any sign of Rokuzan's return. There is nothing about this guy that fits in this environment. Everyone in the building, down to the man that wipes the fingerprints off of the glass doors, is impeccably groomed and dressed in sleek, dark, expensive clothing. Jules tenses. *How the hell did he get past reception?*

He is also missing a visitor's ID, which everyone receives at the front desk downstairs. Before he reaches the door, Jules moves forward, putting a hand up. "Sir, I have to stop you, this is a private area."

The young man looks benignly confused, he bows and smiles obsequiously. Jules holds up her own ID badge. "Sir, you have no badge, you cannot pass." She takes another step forward. She knows that the Japanese value their personal space and hopes she can back him up so she doesn't have to lay her hands on him. She glances around, still no Rokuzan. If this guy makes it through the boardroom door, he is going to be facing a room full of pissed-off security agents.

If he makes it into the room, it will mean that Jules has failed at her one designated task and will be out of a job.

The man bows again and holds out his package. "No, no, please. A gift, for Matsuda-san." He steps toward her again. Jules feels the tingle of adrenaline. *In any confrontation there is a continuum of force, you need only to match your level of force with his.* Inside his jacket, she sees an odd bulkiness, not the shape of a weapon, but something not right.

Screw this, there is too much at stake here for hesitation. Jules steps into him, sweeping the gift to the floor. She puts her left hand in a stiff vee against his chest, moving him firmly back against the wall. "You can't be here sir. What's in your jacket?"

From the corner of her eye, she sees Rokuzan's dark bulk appear. *Thank God.* He is on the young man, speaking softly and harshly in Japanese. Jules doesn't understand the words, but the meaning is unmistakable. Rokuzan turns him around to face the wall and flattens him with one big paw, frisking him. A sheaf of papers slides slowly from under his disheveled jacket, splaying out onto the wood flooring. Jules cocks her head to see what they are.

Glossy color photos of clear-cut forest, dead animals and birds litter the shining hardwood. She makes the connection; an environmental activist, bent on disrupting the multi-million dollar deal that would allow Matsuda's drilling company to do more damage than ever. Jules kicks the papers to the side of the hallway, resisting the impulse to pick them up.

She scans the hallway and the atrium area. People like this are sometimes used as decoys to distract agents from a second wave of men prepped for true violence. Jules radios down to hotel security, she will only contact the team inside as a last resort. To disturb the meeting is to allow Matsuda to lose face, a worst-case scenario for his firm.

She sees no one in the hallway or atrium, so she moves back in front of the boardroom door while Rokuzan grips the sweating interloper and propels him towards a stairwell door. The door opens and a wave of black-suited security agents engulf the unfortunate man. Two agents sweep the foyer and the hallway, volleying quiet commands at each other. Their last act is to pick up the scuffed gift and papers, before they disappear back down the stairs.

Rokuzan rejoins her at the door, leaning heavily against the frame. Jules exhales. She looks sideways at him. "Thank you," she whispers.

He nods solemnly and bows, "No, thank you Petersen-san." He looks pale and stricken.

When the meeting breaks for lunch, Rokuzan heads silently to his chief and fills him in on the incident. The chief glances at Jules, then away. She has a sick feeling that this will somehow end up being her fault. The two men speak to Yoji and Ramirez. Yoji approaches Jules, informing her that she will need to meet with Matsuda's man and the hotel security chief to debrief. Yoji will act as her escort and translator. She looks over at Ramirez, who is bending Williamson's ear, he is stone-faced, but Jules can see the muscles working in his jaw.

Yoji takes her down to the basement-level command room. They are seated at a conference table. From where she sits, Jules can see the hapless activist handcuffed to a steel table. He has been stripped to a t-shirt and looks terrified. *Yeah, I bet Tree-Hugger, Inc. didn't warn you about these guys when they sent you upstairs for your little photo prank. Poor bastard.*

She leans in to Yoji, "What's going to happen to him?"

Yoji replies, "He didn't have a weapon, so when these guys are finished questioning him, he'll be released to the Tokyo P.D. They'll probably slap him with a load of charges: trespassing, criminal mischief, stalking, harassment. If Matsuda knows the magistrate, he could end up with a couple years in jail."

Jules eyes widen, "For that? You've got to be kidding me."

"This isn't the U.S. of A. Jules, we do things differently here, in case you haven't noticed."

She shuts her mouth. Now she's worrying about what's going to happen to her. Or to Rokuzan. The two security chiefs come in. They introduce themselves and explain that they need a detailed account of the 'unfortunate' incident. Jules spends the next fifty minutes going over and over the three-minute intrusion. The investigators hone in on Rokuzan's absence. She minimizes it as best as she can, but knows she cannot lie. They finally seem satisfied and leave to get a digital camera so they can take a photo of her for the file.

Jules whispers to Yoji, "Am I in trouble?"

"*You* didn't do anything wrong Jules. You identified the guy and stopped him. Think about it, we didn't even know anything was going on out there."

They take the photo, have her sign a statement and release her back to duty. Yoji radios the Lieutenant, who reports that Williamson is back in his room getting ready for dinner. Ramirez, of course, would like a word with Petersen. Yoji deposits Jules at the door to Lieutenant's room and takes off.

Jules looks wistfully back at Yoji as he flees to his own room. Ramirez answers the door in his shirtsleeves, a tie draped around his neck. He gestures for Jules to sit at a small table. She's surprised when he sits wearily on the edge of the bed. He rubs the back of his neck repeatedly. Jules has come to recognize this as a bad sign, a gesture reserved for moments when he's at the end of his tether.

"All right tell it again, from the beginning. Don't leave anything out and don't try to cover for your new friend. He fucked up and everybody knows it."

Jules flinches at his words. She tells the story again in detail, leaving nothing out. *Damn it. Things had been going so well and here she is facing off with him again, a bug under a microscope.*

Ramirez sighs, shaking his head. "When he went to the men's room he should have called one of his guys to stand with you. I don't know what the hell he was thinking."

"It was only about three minutes, Lieutenant, maybe four. I didn't think it was a big deal until I saw the guy approach."

"You don't know the language, Petersen, you don't know the building. It's their home turf. He never should have left you there, not for thirty seconds. What if that joker had been armed, what if his little package was C-4, or anthrax? That's the whole point of us coordinating with them, so everyone goes home alive. Jesus!"

Jules sits silently.

Ramirez looks at his watch. "You need to change for dinner." He rises, opening the door, "You handled it, at least. Don't be late, I don't need anyone taking notice of you tonight."

Julianna skulks back to her room. *Great.* She has twenty minutes to shake this off and transform into cocktail-dress Barbie. She takes a two-minute shower and chooses a simple black dress.

She wonders how she could go so quickly from feeling great to utter hopelessness. If her performance is at the mercy of every agent she gets paired with, what's the point of training and working so hard?

Quit your bitching, Jules, you have a job to do and you'd better not make any mistakes tonight.

Tonight's dinner is less convivial, with an increase in Matsuda's detail and Rokuzan conspicuously absent. Jules is posted close to Ramirez and Xavier has been added to the dinner detail. She feels especially paranoid, every time she makes eye contact with anyone, she feels certain that they are judging her. The evening stretches out and by the time they disperse for change of shift, she has a blinding headache and a stiff neck.

Xavier stays on duty with the second shift and Tam, Yoji and Ramirez head toward the elevator to get dinner. They look back for Jules and she waves them off politely, "I'm going to turn in, I'm not really hungry. I'll see you in the morning."

The men hesitate and Ramirez shrugs, "All right, good night."

Jules makes it to her room and slips out of the expensive dress, lying down on the bed. She can't shake her anger. *And what happened to Rokuzan? Had they fired him or just stuck him in an office somewhere? God, what kind of job is this, where taking a piss could end your career?*

She tries to relax, but she's restless and wired, her muscles in knots from standing in one position all day. She wants to hit something. Jules rolls over and looks at the clock.

Almost 2300. Screw it, the gym is supposed to be open twenty-four hours. She changes quickly into a workout top and yoga pants, zipping up a warmup jacket. Time to sweat.

The men are eating dinner at the same place, but the mood has shifted considerably. Jules' absence lends a tension to the dinner and Yoji is clearly exhausted from speaking on behalf of the entire crew. They break things up early.

Ramirez rings Petersen's room to make sure she's gotten in okay. When she doesn't pick up, he is disquieted. He rings her cell and she picks up after several rings. She sounds out of breath. "Where are you?" he demands.

"I'm in the gym. I couldn't wind down, so I thought I'd get loose on something other than sake. Everything okay?"

"Yeah. Listen, I wasn't implying that you did anything wrong today. I was pissed-off, but not at you. I was just hoping that things would go smoothly the first time."

Jules is still trying to get her breath. "I know, me too. Hey, Lieutenant? What happened with Rokuzan? Did you hear anything?"

"No and I could give a shit. As far as I'm concerned, he should be checking coats. Him and whoever let that protester past reception. Besides, Matsuda's people were embarrassed and you know what a sin that is here. They're making like it never happened, so don't go asking any questions. We've got one more day and we're out, so do me a favor and keep your head up and your mouth shut, okay?"

"Got it."

"Get some sleep."

Jules sleeps well and wakes up a new woman. In less than twelve hours, they'll be getting on the plane back to the states. Today's agenda is a morning meeting, a long luncheon and an hour-and-a-half of signing contracts.

The detail has already packed and is scheduled to be in the caravan at 1700. Jules is no longer on the door, now she is in the board room. Xavier and a new man of Matsuda's are in the hall, Rokuzan is still missing. Jules prays he has another vocation to fall back on.

The meeting appears to go smoothly, apparently all of the major details were hammered out yesterday. Today there is a lot of nodding and smiling going on while legalese and numbers are bandied about.

A ridiculously sumptuous luncheon is served and Jules is amazed at how much drinking is done. Everyone appears satisfied, many toasts and speeches ensue in which they assure each other that this will be the beginning of a 'prosperous and honorable' relationship. She can only imagine the scope of it.

After lunch, reams of contracts are signed, sealed and stowed in expensive leather cases. The last ritual to be endured is the exchange of gifts. Williamson's assistant has thoughtfully purchased Hermès leather gloves and business card holders for Matsuda's executives, wrapped in their signature burnt-orange boxes. Because they will not be opened at the exchange, it is important that the packaging be recognizably expensive.

Matsuda himself presents Williamson with a dust covered bottle of what appears to be some ancient liquor, nectar of the samurai, probably. It is understood that this single gift is more costly than all of the gifts Williamson has bestowed.

Matsuda bows deeply to Williamson as he proffers the bottle with both hands. Williamson mirrors him and receives it, but as he straightens, the bottle slips inexplicably from his hands. Without thinking, Jules, at his right, reflexively catches it with her left hand. There is a collective intake of breath as the bottle narrowly misses shattering on the marble floor. Operating on pure instinct, Jules bows deeply and averting her eyes, returns the bottle, with both hands, to Williamson.

Williamson, eternally effervescent, prattles, "Ah, you see, this is precisely why we keep Ms. Petersen close by. One never knows when they'll be in need of a woman's touch, do they?" Yoji translates and there is a delayed ripple of strained laughter.

Jules swallows hard and catches Ramirez' eye, finally daring to breathe. He stares at her for a moment and closes his eyes as if in prayer, shaking his head in disbelief.

15

The summer passes quickly. Jules covers shifts for detail members taking vacations and spends most of her days ferrying the girls to friends' houses, day camps and sports lessons during their break from school.

In early September, Ramirez calls Julianna into his office after lunch. "Sit, Petersen. I wanted to brief you on the travel plans for next week. I'm sure you're well aware that next Friday is September 11th."

Jules shifts in her seat. "Actually, Lieutenant, I was going to make a request for a personal day. I don't think I'll be much use to anyone."

He squints at her. "Request denied. As I was trying to inform you, it appears that Hope has won an essay contest on the topic and the entire family will be attending a memorial service in the city, where she'll read the essay. I need you with Grace and the children."

Jules flinches visibly. "In the city? Not at the *site?*"

"No, Battery Park."

"Sir, with all due respect, isn't there some duty I could perform here?"

"No, we need you with the family, that's your job."

Jules hesitates, picturing herself in a sea of grieving people. She squares her shoulders, "Yes of course, Lieutenant."

He clears his throat. "Look Petersen, I was there, so I get it."

"What do you mean, you were there?"

"A couple days after 9/11, some of my old SEAL teammates assembled a crew. Once I knew that Williamson was secured, I took a leave of absence and worked at the site. At that point we believed it was search-and-rescue, but of course it turned out to be a recovery operation. I spent five days digging through that rubble, so I want you to know that I'm not insensitive to the realities of those days."

He looks steadily into her eyes. There is a softening in his face, and she has her first glimpse of his humanity. She looks away and swallows hard. She had not expected this. *His sympathy?* Somehow it is worse than any insult he's ever thrown at her.

She shifts in her chair. "I appreciate your saying that. I have to keep in mind that I wasn't one of those unlucky people who spent weeks wandering around the city, putting up posters, looking for a missing person. At least I knew he didn't make it out."

She hesitates, wanting to stop, but needing to say it out loud. "He left me a message. I was working…I was in court, and he left me a voicemail. He was above the fire, he knew he wasn't getting out. So I knew, from the first day, that he was dead."

There is a long silence. Ramirez is watching, giving her the space to say more, but she is done. She doesn't meet his gaze.

He passes a hand over his hair. "Did you receive anything, remains or effects?"

She nods. "Much later, about eighteen months after we held the funeral service. They found his wedding ring." Jules can't believe she is having this conversation, with him of all people. She frowns, "I don't ever talk about this. It's just…it doesn't help me, and it makes people uncomfortable." She makes an ineffectual gesture with her hand. "I'll be ready to work on Friday." She stands up, for the first time not caring whether she is dismissed or not.

Ramon stands too, feeling unsettled. He can see her summoning her composure, a tightening in the jaw, a flash of resolve in the eyes. He feels he's crossed a line, either personal or professional, maybe both. He nods. He starts to speak, but decides against it. She closes the door as she leaves.

He sits back down, resting his head in his hands. He'd been trying to convey something to her, but had failed miserably. The five days he'd spent digging at ground zero had altered him. He'd killed men, he'd seen combat, but those days digging through steel and ashes had chilled him to his soul. The hopelessness of finding pieces of people, their watches, an FDNY badge, it had stayed with him. On the last day, he'd looked down to find that he was standing on a woman's ponytail, dusty blonde under his boot. Two hours later, he'd called it quits and went home, wanting only to shower the grit of human beings off his skin.

Friday comes much too quickly. Jules had decided that she must simply focus on the task at hand and detach herself from the proceedings. She's been assigned to Grace and the girls in a very public venue and the situation will require her full attention. No point doing the job half-assed, she'll just have to switch off whatever emotions come up and deal with them later.

The ride into the city is horribly slow, with thousands of people pouring in to attend various memorials around the city. Usually, this is the one day each year Jules gives herself to truly grieve. She always stays at home wearing an old sweatshirt of Chris' and watches the World Trade Center memorial service on TV. She lets herself cry until there is nothing left, drinks a half a bottle of wine and goes to bed early. This year will there will be none of that. Jules supposes this is as good a time as any to move on.

She is in the second vehicle with Grace and the girls. Gi is driving, and Jules is riding shotgun. Grace is immaculate in a white Armani suit, tastefully appointed with beige Prada shoes and matching bag. The girls look like a matched set of china dolls. Annalise wears a powder-blue sheath dress and Hope is in a navy dress with an empire waist and satin sash.

The motorcade has advance clearance for a VIP entrance to the park. They are waived through to a barricaded parking area and at lieutenant's go, they all exit as one unit. The family is whisked to a holding area and Jules accompanies Hope to a cordoned area reserved solely for the guest speakers.

She has a line of sight to Ramirez and the rest of the family and Gi is standing post just outside the ropes in case she needs him. Jules is carrying her Glock in a high hip holster under her suit jacket. The detail had to obtain special carry permits for today's event.

The ceremony begins with a Marine Corps band playing the national anthem. Jules concentrates on scanning the crowd. Hope is next to her, perfectly poised. At the crescendo, Jules feels a wave of tears rising at the back of her throat. She tamps it back down, digging her nails into her palm hard enough to hurt.

The keynote speaker begins. She purposely doesn't listen to the words. If she allows herself to get caught up in the collective emotion of the crowd she will be finished. She is okay, she has to be. Jules concentrates on the agenda for the appearance. Hope is sixth on the list, slated to end the ceremony's speaking portion just before taps is played.

She studies the speaking platform as they wait, looking for stray cables or unsteady construction that could trip Hope up. Hope is wearing her first pair of heels today, so Jules will clear the way and hold her hand until she's safely up the three steps to the stage.

The speakers are long-winded, nearly an hour-and-a-half passes before it is Hope's turn on the program. After her introduction, Jules escorts Hope to the stage, giving her hand a quick squeeze before she lets go. She looks gratefully at Jules.

Jules waits at the base of the steps, watching the crowd at the front of the stage and sweeping her gaze from left to right. Hope begins, her voice quavering just a bit until she finds her confidence and speaks in a clear, true voice.

The beauty and innocence of the young girl has the crowd weeping openly. As Jules watches her, she cannot suppress a flash of resentment. Angelic Hope, who has never experienced loss or likely a moment's discomfort in all of her eight years, speaking knowingly about a tragedy that occurred when she was four years old.

Jules feels immediately ashamed of her bitter thoughts. It is not, of course, Hope's fault that she's been born into privilege. She is merely a thoroughbred, born and bred for one purpose, to accrue noteworthy accomplishments until she is put out to pasture where she will create more beautiful children.

Jules locks gazes with Ramirez, who is watching her intently. She has been aware of his scrutiny all morning, feeling his eyes on her as he grades her choreography of the event. She is determined that she will not fail him or the family. She puts her anger away, reminding herself that there are no emotions that will serve her here, she must be numb today. Hope is finishing her earnest speech to a roar of approval from the crowd. Jules leans across to her and helps her down the steps.

Hope looks to her for approval and Jules whispers, "Great job, sweetheart," realizing that Hope is just a little girl trying to meet the very high expectations of her parents.

Hope smiles. "Really?"

Jules squeezes her hand again as a lone trumpeter begins taps. "Really."

The family and entourage regroup and drive to the W Hotel, where they attend a small luncheon of about eighty dignitaries, including speakers and honorees.

As coffee is being served, another speaker approaches the podium. Jules feels a wave of panic as she realizes that it is the CEO of Cantor Fitzgerald. She is posted against a pillar, near the family's table. The CEO, whom she'd last seen at Chris' memorial service, begins to speak about the enormous losses suffered by the company and its 'families' and the slow rebuilding that followed.

Jules is having trouble getting her breath. Gi appears suddenly at her side. "Hey Jules, I think you're due for a bathroom break. You're looking a little pale, *hermana*. Go ahead and take five, I've got it covered." She looks into his eyes, conveying her gratitude.

She escapes to the ladies' room, finding an empty stall. Thankful that the bathroom is immaculate, she leans her head against the cold steel walls. She fights to compose herself. The luncheon is nearly over, she will be back at RSW in two hours, home in three. Once she is home she can fall apart. Not here. *Not here, Jules.* She presses her hands to her temples, eyes closed tightly. An image of Chris' memorial service comes unbidden.

The CEO, what had he said? 'There are no words, Mrs. Petersen, to convey our sorrow.' She'd thought at the time about the weight of his duties, having to perform that script at every service, how did he remember their names? She'd wondered if his assistant gave him a little cue card to carry in his pocket.

God, what is she doing? Hiding in the bathroom like a teenager at a dance. This is only making things worse. She hears Lieutenant's voice in her head. 'Are you fit for duty or not?' She returns to her post, quietly thanking Gi for his help.

"*De nada*, actually, it was Lieutenant's idea."

She looks over at Ramirez. He is, as always, impassive, his face betraying nothing.

Hours later, Jules is in the RSW parking garage, leaving for home at last. The lieutenant exits the stairwell as she comes out of the elevator, weighted down by her equipment and the cumulative effects of this awful day.

He stops, nodding at her. "Petersen."

She nods back, "Lieutenant."

He regards her for a moment. She waits, expecting criticism. "You did well today."

She looks closely at him, trying to determine if he is being sarcastic. He is not. She blinks, stunned. "Not as well as I would have liked, Lieutenant."

"It was a difficult assignment." He hesitates, "That speaker, he wasn't on the original list, I would have given you a heads up on that." It is not exactly an apology, but an acknowledgement. Coming from him it is a miracle.

She shrugs, "It doesn't matter. It's over."

He notices how pale she is, purple smudges of fatigue under her eyes. "Why don't you take that personal day tomorrow? There's no travel, I'll work out the schedule."

The kindness in his voice disturbs her. She can't be seen as some charity case needing special handling. "I'd rather not Lieutenant, it's probably better if I just keep busy." She is embarrassed, she looks down at the ground, unable to maintain eye contact.

"You sure?"

"Sure."

"All right, get some rest. You look like shit, Petersen."

She smiles. *That's more like it.*

On a Wednesday night after teaching class, Jules has showered and passed out in her bed. She's awakened from an anxious dream of a foreign city by an insistent buzzing. *Please God, it can't be the alarm already.* It turns out to be her phone, set on vibrate. Jules peers at the number: Ramirez, then at the clock, 0142. She answers, "Petersen."

"You're on, Petersen. Grace is having a meltdown and Williamson needs someone at the house immediately. You have twenty minutes to get to the residence." He hangs up on her. *Goddamnit.* She starts moving toward the door, grabbing for clothes. *What does one wear to a meltdown? Something fireproof, I guess.*

Jules makes it to the gate in twenty-two minutes, hoping that Ramirez is already back to sleep. The gate guard checks her ID and lets her drive in, already aware of the situation. The housekeeper is waiting at the door. She silently ushers Jules upstairs to Grace's bedroom, Williamson is nowhere in sight.

Jules takes a deep breath and steps into the bedroom, a fantasy of cream and gold, marred only by Grace's sobbing. Jules approaches her, summoning her old social work skills. She kneels on the carpet next to the bed, so plush it makes Jules wish she could just lie down. "Mrs. Williamson, it's Julianna. What's going on?"

Grace, face down on the silk comforter, rolls over to one side and peers at Jules. Her hair is still perfect, but her eyes are swollen and smeared with runny black makeup. "Oh great," she says, "one of Robert's little toy soldiers. That solves everything. Usually he sends Ramirez." She props herself on one elbow. "Did you lose a coin toss?"

Jules is impressed that Grace is so astute. "No. I just wanted to see if I could help." She looks at the nightstand, littered with jewelry and amber prescription bottles. "Why don't I get you a glass of water?"

Grace looks at her with complete disgust. "Why don't you get the fuck out of here?"

Jules has been in this kind of situation before. Most clever people put you through a hostile little period of testing before they decide whether they can trust you. She settles onto the floor in a cross-legged position, her non-verbal way of telling Grace that she's not going anywhere. "Why don't you tell me what happened tonight? What did Robert do?"

"Robert doesn't *do* anything. Haven't you figured that out by now? I am just the hysterical wife and he is the doting husband, completely innocent."

Jules looks at her with compassion. Grace is like a piece of expensive art, acquired in a moment of passion at an exorbitant price, but probably less loved than the stupid dog. For all of her costly possessions, she must be bored to tears with her life as a decorative object. Jules ventures gently, "Robert's been away a lot. It must be lonely here."

Grace flinches a little. She reaches for a tissue. "You have no idea. I mean, I have friends, but he's just so detached. When he does bother to show up here, it's all about the girls and the dog. I mean you should see him with that dog, it's like one of those romantic movies where the couple runs across a meadow into each other's arms. I could vomit."

Jules bites the inside of her cheek to keep from smiling. Grace is actually growing on her a little. "And do you two get any time alone together?"

Grace rolls her eyes. "He takes me out to these horrifying dinners. Do you know what he talks about? What he ate for dinner in the last country he was in! And then he gives me some little present and tells me what *their* wives were wearing, who got plastic surgery, who's getting divorced. Can you believe it? He gossips like a woman. Here I thought I married this powerful man, but really he's a cross between Isaac Mizrahi and Liz Smith."

Jules nods sympathetically and concentrates on maintaining a serious expression. *This is tricky. How to appear sympathetic without agreeing that Williamson is a vacuous, cardboard-cutout of a man?*

"I guess every marriage has its tradeoffs. All men have shortcomings," she says carefully. "You know, sometimes things that seem awful in the middle of the night aren't so terrible in the light of day. You have this house, two beautiful girls, that's something to be thankful for."

Grace shifts restlessly. Jules can see she doesn't feel like counting her blessings right now. *Okay, different tack.* "Have you eaten anything today? Maybe we could sneak down to the kitchen and have a bite. You might sleep better."

"What makes you think I haven't eaten?" Grace says, narrowing her eyes.

Shit. Jules scrambles for an answer. "Well, it's just, you're so thin, I'm sure you must eat like a bird." She thinks about Grace's call sign, Bird Two.

Grace virtually preens, "You can't imagine."

"So maybe um, just a little fruit and cheese, something like that."

Grace is frowning at her. She pulls up her pajama top to reveal a perfectly flat, tanned belly. "Do you think I keep this by eating dairy?"

"No, I guess not," Jules concedes, suddenly self-conscious about her own body. She can see Grace's ribs. This whole scene is feeling just a little too intimate. She rises from the floor. "So, fruit and crackers and then a good night's sleep."

Grace sighs. "And a nightcap, or I'm not going."

Jules glances at the prescription bottles. Oh well, she's pretty sure this isn't Grace's first party. She probably has the tolerance of a rhino. "You've got a deal."

16

The crew is assembled to celebrate the lieutenant's birthday at Martino's, a Cuban restaurant favored by the men for its amazing food and casual atmosphere. They are regulars at the restaurant and every October, Williamson springs for an all-expenses-paid back room party. Williamson makes an appearance for the first half-hour and then leaves; his presence is only a formality. The real party will begin when he exits.

The men are milling around, getting a second round of drinks, most seated at a very long, crowded table in the center of the room. The private bar, located at the back, is doing a brisk business. Ramon is seated at the table, eating smoked almonds and drinking a glass of whiskey, which is magically refilled every time it gets within an inch of the bottom. Men drop in and out of the seat next to him to chat or drop off small gifts of cigars or imported bottles.

He is waiting for the moment, once Williamson leaves, when they can concentrate on the food and get good and drunk. Gi stops in to talk and hands him a small package wrapped in oiled leather and tied with string. It is a handmade knife, a glorified shank really, long and thin, a five-inch blade made for sinking in deep. Ramon smiles, leave it to Gi to make a present of a killing knife. He slaps Gi on the back, thanking him in Spanish.

Gi is chattering away when a hush ripples through the room. The lieutenant instinctively cranes his head so he can check the entrance of the room. It is Petersen, and he realizes that the silence has nothing to do with danger, but the appearance of Jules in a summer dress, her hair coming down in waves over smooth, white shoulders.

She looks startled, taking in the fact that every man in the room has just shifted his attention on her. She crosses the room, moving toward Ramon's side of the table. Her cheeks flame and she mutters, "Sorry to be late, Lieutenant."

At this, the room is galvanized into noise and action, there is a synchronized scraping back of chairs as the men at the table rise to offer her a seat. Williamson approaches her, kissing Jules on both cheeks in the European manner. "You look lovely Julianna, what a treat to see you off-duty. The dress is marvelous."

The dress *is* marvelous, Ramon concurs in his head: simple, chocolate brown cotton, with thin straps and a neckline that showcases the freckles in her décolletage, but still leaves something to the imagination. She's wearing make-up, enough to emphasize her eyes and cheekbones, but not enough to make it look like she's trying.

Ramon clears his throat and calls out, "Petersen, come sit here." He indicates the now-empty chair beside him, Gi having risen to gawk at Jules like a schoolboy. Ramon growls, "*Cierre la boca, amigo.*" Gi closes his mouth with a snap.

Jules makes her way to the seat, somehow procuring a drink on the way. Gi pulls out the chair for her and she sits, perched on the edge, as though she might flee at any moment. She smiles at Ramon, "Happy birthday, Lieutenant, thanks for inviting me." Ramon glances at Gi, who shrugs noncommittally.

"My pleasure," Ramon replies. It *is* his unexpected pleasure, though he had not invited Petersen. Gi must have sent an agency-wide e-mail. He would not have thought to include her, but now that she's sitting next to him, glowing like a candle, it doesn't seem like much of a hardship to have her at his side while he celebrates.

Williamson makes his way to the head of the table. "Gentlemen, oh and excuse me, lady, a moment please. It is my great pleasure to honor our esteemed lieutenant tonight. We all know I would be lost without his loyal service. Julianna, as you're our newest recruit, perhaps you could raise a toast for the lieutenant?"

Her eyes widen, a deer in the headlights. "Oh…sure, okay. Umm." She bows her head thinking. "*Give me a sec.*"

Finally she lifts her head and raises her glass. "To our lieutenant, who leads by example, commands respect rather than demands it, and inspires us with his excellence. *Salud!*"

"*Salud!*" a deep male roar from the crew, "Ramon!"

He lifts his glass and drains it, "*Gracias.*" He turns to her, stunned. "Did you just make that up?"

"It wasn't too bad, huh?" she says, pleased with herself.

"I'm impressed, it would have taken me weeks to be that eloquent."

"Well, I work best under pressure."

"Yeah, I've noticed that." He sees Williamson discreetly exit the room, leaving them to their celebration.

"Oh, I have a present for you." She reaches into her bag and pulls out a handsomely wrapped rectangle, handing it to him.

"This wasn't necessary." He sips his drink, suddenly nervous. She bought him a present. *It's a gesture, Ramon, a sign of respect. Cool it.*

There is a barely discernible tremor in his hands as he tears off the paper. It's a photograph, a black-and-white group shot of the entire detail. Dressed in their black fatigues, they are leaning against a huge boulder, most smoking a cigar or cigarette, at ease, as if they had just been caught jawing on a break. Every face is crystal clear, the men look relaxed and slightly dangerous, ready to work.

Ramon swallows hard, moved by the deep thoughtfulness of the gift. He looks at her. She is watching his face, smiling tentatively. "It's great," he says, "but you're not in it."

"Someone had to take the picture."

"You took this?" He looks at it again. "I thought it was shot professionally."

"It's not, but I used to shoot a lot, just for fun. I wanted it to look like those World War II Army shots. Do you really like it?"

"I love it." He hesitates, "But you should be in it."

"Well, I know how you feel about female crew members. I didn't want to ruin it for you."

She smiles crookedly at him, there is a long pause, during which they maintain eye contact, sizing each other up.

Jules breaks the silence, "Well, anyway, *feliz cumpleaños.*"

Martino, the owner of the restaurant, is calling to her from the bar. As she gets up, moving to greet him, she moves past Ramon, lightly touching his bicep and kissing his cheek. Without thinking, he turns his head to her, inhaling the soft fragrance of her hair as she slips away.

He finishes his drink in one parched swallow, watching her passage. Every male she comes across turns to her, reaching out a hand, calling out a greeting, making eye contact. She connects with each of them, but keeps moving through the crowd, gracefully deflecting their individual bids for her attention. As she reaches Martino, an old friend, he enfolds her, sweeping her in a circle, exclaiming and fussing over her.

Ramirez watches intently. *Lucky bastard.*

The next few hours pass in a haze of too much food, conversation and alcohol. After dinner, someone turns the music up loud and the men begin calling Jules out to the dance floor. She spends most of her time dancing upbeat salsa with the old man, Martino, knowing that he is a safer bet than the drunken crew members. Gi takes her for a spin, but when the music slows down and he tightens his grip, she deftly extricates herself to sit down next to Ramon.

She leans in to be heard over the music. "Lieutenant, it's a fantastic party, but I have to take off. I have a thing in the morning," she wrinkles her nose, "you know how it is."

Though he'd hoped she would stay, he is slightly relieved that he won't be in charge of defending her honor as the evening degrades. "I'll walk you out."

"Thanks."

He takes her by the elbow and steers her out a side exit. It is an Indian summer night, the air outside warm and soft. She takes a deep breath and looks up at the stars as they walk. "What a great night."

"It is." Ramon is not looking at the stars.

They arrive at her truck. He notes that she has parked underneath a streetlight, always aware of her surroundings, like a good soldier. As she faces him, he notices the spray of freckles across the bridge of her nose. He thinks of all the times he has been in her face, shouting, and never noticed them. *How is that possible?* He tilts his head, studying her face, forgetting for a moment that she is anyone other than a strikingly pretty woman.

She looks back at him, trying to read his expression. "All right," she announces, "I have to go. Are you having a good party?" She scrutinizes him as if the answer really matters to her.

"I'm having a great party," he says softly.

"Good." She hugs him spontaneously, "Happy birthday, Lieutenant."

His reflexes slowed by drink, he reacts too late, wrapping his arms around her as she disengages and grazes his cheek with her lips. He is left standing there awkwardly as she opens the door and climbs in. She rolls down the window, lifting her hair off the back of her neck. She smiles at him.

"Drive carefully." It is all he can manage.

"I will." She points a finger at him. "Have fun. And don't drive yourself home."

She is gone. He walks slowly back to the restaurant, pulling the door open and letting the wave of noise wash over him. The men shout his name, pulling him back into the fray. He takes another drink from Gi, thinking of her bare shoulder under his hand as she hugged him goodbye.

Outside for a smoke half an hour later, Ramon leans against the wall, the stone facade cool against his damp shirt. On an impulse, he dials Petersen's home number on his cell phone.

"Hello?" she sounds tired.

"I just wanted to make sure you got home all right."

"Safe and sound, I'm just locking up now."

"Good."

"Are you still having fun?"

"Yes." He hesitates, drunk and incautious. "You should have stayed."

"Well, I have this family thing, my brother's visiting with his son. I didn't want to be all bleary-eyed."

There is an extended silence. "Thanks for the picture. You must have put some time into that."

"Yeah well, I haven't forgotten that you took a chance on me when you didn't want to. I didn't want to buy you a fucking tie, you know? Besides, you're not as bad as I thought, you're growing on me a little."

Another pause as he processes this. "Yeah?"

"Can't you tell?"

"No. You're a little hard to read." His heart is hammering in his chest. *Is she just playing?* A couple of twenty-something Latino guys walk by. He straightens, nodding at them.

She laughs easily, "I thought you see everything."

"Almost everything."

"Maybe you'd better pay closer attention."

"Guess so."

"Good night, Lieutenant."

"Night." He snaps the phone shut. He closes his eyes and knocks his head against the stone wall: once, twice, three times.

"Ramon! *Hermano!*" It's Jorgé, come to fetch him.

17

One Friday, Jules hears a rumor from the crew that the company is hiring again. She guesses Ramirez has had his fill of women for the time being. She hopes the hiring rumor is true, it would mean that she could finally relinquish her position as the newbie. It'd be nice to let someone else get hammered for a change.

At the Monday morning briefing, Ramirez strides in accompanied by another man. "All right, listen up. This is our new hire, Nate Gunnarson. He is probationary for three months. Four years of Air Force service and two in corporate security. Nate is a former medic and a paramedic. We stole him from a competing firm. It'll be the usual drill, he'll be training with all of us. His training schedule is attached to the briefing notes. Gunnarson, anything you want to add?"

"Just that I'm happy to be here and ready to work."

Jules studies him. Classic Boy Scout, she decides. Just shy of being too good-looking, vaguely Slavic cheekbones, close cut brown hair and clear gray eyes. Nice body, slender but fit. Nothing about him is flashy or overstated: he looks like one of those models in the J. Crew ads, the ones where the guy is always doing something outdoorsy with a beautiful girl and a Labrador. She wonders what he'll be like to work with.

As on her first day, the lieutenant makes the rounds of the table, introducing each crew member. Nate's eyes widen a little when they get to Jules, he seems surprised to find a woman among them.

Ramirez recites her stats. "Julianna Petersen, our last hire before you and our first female crew member. She's a civilian, though she had a stint at the county prosecutor's office. Expert in hand-to-hand combat and our instructor for Krav Maga."

Nate shakes her hand firmly, nodding and giving her a warm smile which reaches to his eyes.

Jules smiles back at him, hoping that he has better luck with Ramirez than she did. She is pretty sure he'll have a much smoother probationary experience. It hadn't escaped her notice that because of his military training, he only has three months of probation until he's a permanent part of the detail. *Must be nice.*

Later in the day, as she's walking back from a stint at the range, he comes trotting up behind her. "Hello, ma'am, I'm recruit Gunnarson, we met this morning in the briefing?"

She stops and turns, offering her hand. "I remember, Nate. And please don't call me ma'am. Everyone calls me Jules."

"Sorry, I grew up in the Midwest, it's sort of a habit. I just wanted to say I'm really looking forward to working with you. I'm really interested in the Krav classes. We did a little bit of that in boot. I do some boxing, too."

"Great, we're starting Friday night classes soon, but we'll be having some one-on-one during your probationary period to get you started. I'm sure you'll do well, you seem very motivated."

"Yes ma'am. Sorry...Jules. And I just wanted to say, I've never worked on a detail with a woman before, I'm happy to have the opportunity."

God, he is a Boy Scout. "Well, Nate, I'll give you a tip, it's exactly the same as working with a man, only I smell a little better."

He laughs. "Well, that's a bonus right there."

She likes him. "Oh and thanks, Nate."

"Thanks for what?"

"Thanks for taking me off of the newbie hook. I hope Lieutenant likes you better than he liked me."

He grimaces and looks around. "Yeah, I was a little worried about him." He lowers his voice. "I heard he gave you a hard time. One of the guys said he broke your nose. That's not really true, is it?" He peers discreetly at the bump in her nose.

She shrugs. "I dropped my hands in a sparring match, you know how it is." That's her story and she's sticking to it.

Nate shakes her hand and retreats. He is not smiling anymore.

Jules comes to Ramirez's office in late January. "Lieutenant, when things were slow at the prosecutor's office, we'd sometimes have a communal meal with the staff. Everybody helped, we'd get together on a Friday night and just hang out. It seemed to be really good for morale."

"Do you think we have a morale problem, Petersen?"

"No, absolutely not. I just thought since most of the men are single or away from their families so much, it might be fun for them to do something other than go to the bar. I'd do all the cooking and shopping, if you'll give me permission to use the staff kitchen."

He frowns at her. "Why the sudden interest in socializing? You trying to get a date, Petersen?"

Jules colors all the way to her ears. "No. Look, if you think it's a bad idea, forget it. It just gets so dreary in winter, I thought it'd be something for the men to look forward to."

He sighs. "I'd have to check with Williamson."

"Of course."

"Is that all?"

"Yes, thank you." Chastened, she leaves, closing the door silently. Out in the hallway, she exhales. *God, why does he have to be such a prick about everything?* She'd thought things were relaxing between them a bit, now he's acting like she'd proposed a group therapy session. *Screw it, bad idea. From now on, she'll keep her team-building ideas to herself. He's probably afraid he'll break down and crack a smile in front of the men. God forbid.*

Three weeks later she receives an e-mail from Ramirez: **Dinner approved. Use company card for groceries. Get a few men to help you. Relay time and date ASAP, so schedules can be arranged.**

Miracles do happen.

That Friday night when Ramirez arrives in the kitchen, things are already in full swing. Gi, Jorgé and Bruno are chopping and prepping, their banter loud and jovial. Jules is at the stove, stirring. Something in the oven smells amazing. She's dressed down in a red sweater and jeans, over which she's tied a thick canvas chef's apron. Tall stools ring the stainless steel worktable, which is littered with knives, cutting boards and bowls. Four pie plates are filled with pastry and their top crusts are laid out neatly on a floured section of the table.

Jules takes note of Ramirez's entrance and smiles at him. "Hey Lieutenant, nice to see you."

He nods. "Looks like you've got this under control."

She looks around. "The guys are doing all the real work, I'm just the foreman."

He takes a stool at the end of the table. "I'm just going to read my paper."

"Okay."

Ramon makes a show of settling in with the *NY Times*, but what he's covertly studying is Jules' ass. It is no small pleasure to watch her hustling around the kitchen in those jeans.

She comes to him with a small plate of sliced apples and cheddar cheese. She also hands him a glass of red wine. "In case you're hungry, Lieutenant. It'll be a while 'til dinner."

"*Gracias.* You're not required to call me Lieutenant tonight."

"Oh. Right. It's sort of a habit now. Enjoy, Ramon."

"Thank you."

Jules heads to the sink, unloading two small bushels of apples. Jorgé washes them and lays them out on dishtowels to drip-dry. Jules and Bruno begin peeling, and then pass them to Gi, who slices them paper-thin with a handmade knife he's brought from home.

They are talking and laughing, lapsing in and out of Spanish. Occasionally Bruno will add a comment in Italian and the others just look and laugh, having no idea what he's just said. The men flirt shamelessly with Jules and she handles it easily, keeping things light.

Ramon eats the food she's given him, trying to remember the last time a woman other than his grandmother fixed a plate for him. He scans the newspaper, imagining for a moment what it would be like to have a woman like Jules in his kitchen, or perhaps, his bed. It's an indulgent, ridiculous thought. Not only is she twelve years his junior, but his employee as well.

He's seen it plenty of times, of course, in the military as well as the private sector. It's bound to happen when you put men and women in such intimate proximity. All that time spent away from home, your crew gets to know you better than your own family.

So far Petersen has been able to maintain a professional distance from the men, as far as he can tell. They like her, that much is plain. He'd be willing to bet if she was offering, they'd be taking numbers. She seems to balance it nicely though, the men's attention and her own sense of self-respect. She manages to remain friendly while conveying the message that she is unavailable. It has given him a grudging regard for her professionalism.

He returns his attention to the paper, an article on global warming. His mind, relaxed by the glass of wine, seems to have its own ideas and wanders around the subject of Petersen a bit longer, kicking at pebbles. Ramon's reverie is interrupted by a sudden burst of laughter, followed by a loud, smacking noise.

It seems that Bruno, in an overzealous attempt at conviviality, has just slapped Jules playfully on her tempting ass. The resounding crack of skin on denim is followed by utter silence.

Ramon leans back, having a thought to rise and cuff him on the ear, but before he can move, Jules is on Bruno. She pulls him into a headlock and begins to strangle him with a purpose.

"What's your combative here, Bruno?" she asks in an even tone.

"What?" He is red and sputtering.

"You were in the military. What's your combative response? You've got about thirty seconds before you run out of air."

"I, I …c'mon Jules!" Bruno is turning a disturbing shade of purple. Jules leans in and says something to him. He is nodding, no longer able to speak. She releases him with a shove. He staggers to a stool and leans over it, coughing until his color returns to normal.

The men are laughing, chiding Bruno for his stupidity. "That's what you get, *hermano*. Don't mess with *that* lady."

Bruno glances uneasily at Jules, not sure whether she is actually angry or just screwing with him.

"Now I gotta go wash my hands," she complains.

Ramon is standing now, having had a moment when he'd thought he would have to intervene. He shoots a look at Bruno and joins Jules at the sink.

"Thought I was going to have to bust that up."

"Nah. We were just doing a little skill-testing." She smiles crookedly at the sink.

"So what did you say to him?" He needs to know.

She glances over her shoulder to where Bruno is gulping a glass of water. "I told him if he ever did that again, I'd break his fingers."

"Remind me never to slap your ass." He turns to go back to his newspaper.

"For you, Lieutenant, I could make an exception," she murmurs softly.

Ramon turns back to her in surprise, not sure he has heard correctly. But Jules is back to washing apples, diligently ignoring him.

Later Ramon excuses himself to make rounds of the building and check in with the active detail. He'd pared down the crew tonight to allow most of the men the chance to attend the dinner.

Finishing his tour on the third floor, he heads up the stairwell to the roof for a smoke before dinner. Keying in his code, he pushes open the heavy steel door which opens onto the cinder-topped roof.

He is surprised to find Petersen there, perched on a low parapet. The sun is still on the horizon, but the night has already turned cold.

"Didn't expect to see *you*. You don't smoke do you?"

"Not lately. I just got hot in that kitchen, I don't know what I was thinking, wearing a sweater. I'm roasting."

"It's a nice sweater," he says lamely.

"Thanks, but I might as well be in the oven with the ham."

Ramirez lights up his usual sweet cigar. He slides a second one from the pack. "Want one?"

She hesitates. "You know, I think I do. I'll probably regret it tomorrow in the gym, but the wine makes me want to smoke."

He hands it to her and leans in to light it.

She takes a deep pull and it catches, glowing in the fading light. Jules takes the first drag into her mouth, closing her eyes. She keeps them shut for a moment, savoring the taste of the smoke. Her lips part as she exhales and she moistens them with the tip of her tongue. "Mmmm," she sighs with pleasure. "Thank you."

Ramon stands transfixed; he has never seen anything so erotic.

She is looking at him curiously, head tilted.

He straightens, realizing he's acting like a twelve-year-old. "*De nada.*"

"You're corrupting me, Lieutenant."

"I'll never tell. Your secret's safe with me."

18

In February, the detail gears up for another trip, this time to Buenos Aires, Argentina. Williamson will be checking in with Armando Figueroa, a long-standing client who has begun making noise about trying to find a younger oil broker with lower commissions.

As in any business, face-time is everything and Williamson is well-schooled in the art of smoothing ruffled feathers. His plan is to swoop in for a couple of days, wine and dine Figueroa within an inch of his life, and remind him that RSW is his conduit of goodwill between the all-powerful oil companies and his successful, but unconnected drilling company.

For the RSW team, Buenos Aires is a routine trip. Williamson has been there many times before and always stays at the Sofitel's Hotel Madero in Puerto Madero. Williamson likes the hotel because it is sleekly modern and has an Argentine-French fusion restaurant. Ramirez approves because it is a short ride from the airport to the hotel, simplifying the route planning and cutting down on the odds that they will encounter any obstacles or major detours.

The Madero also has the advantage of being well-removed from the Plaza de Mayo, which tends to attract anti-government protestors and masses of tourists. Ramirez has deemed the Madero's location to be safe from fallout generated by overzealous citizens and hapless Americans.

Everyone is assembled on the Gulfstream at Teterboro by 0500, Tuesday. The flight is approximately twelve-plus hours. They arrive at Ezeiza airport around 1700, whisk through customs and are on the road by 1720. The detail splits in two, enters the vehicles and heads north to Puerto Madero. The trip is quick and uneventful, in about forty minutes they are unloading at the hotel. Ramon and the big boys, Xavier and Saul, head upstairs with Bird and the luggage, while Jules and Gi take care of check-in.

Williamson will shower and have an early dinner in his suite. This means that half the crew has an easy night in their quarters while Jules, Ramirez, Saul and Henry are on-duty, in and outside the suite.

Wednesday's itinerary includes lunch with one of Williamson's old friends in San Telmo. The lunch is being hosted at his residence, so there will be few worries other than taking a cursory sweep of the grounds and standing post inside the house. The late afternoon will be spent at an art gallery that Williamson frequents on these trips. He has been known to drop a few hundred grand on the gaudy, abstract works of a young artist from Córdoba.

After the gallery, Williamson and the detail will regroup at the hotel while he naps, showers and dresses for a late dinner with Figueroa at the hotel's restaurant. If dinner goes well and drinks and espresso continue into the wee hours, Williamson will hopefully stay put. If it concludes early and he decides to go wandering to a club or bar afterwards, the whole detail will have to shadow.

Departure is scheduled immediately after lunch on Thursday and if everything proceeds smoothly, they'll be back in New Jersey by early Friday morning.

After everyone is checked in, Ramirez holds a quick briefing in Williamson's outer suite to review the agenda. As he is speaking, the entire hotel goes dark. The crew barely responds, temporary power outages are common in South America and the generators almost always kick in after a few minutes.

Ramirez sighs and keeps talking. The lights flicker back on and for a few minutes they listen in relief as the air conditioners power back up. Just as the room is cooling, the hotel goes dark again.

Ramirez orders everyone to stay put and goes downstairs with Gi to check out the situation. Saul and Xavier move to the windows and draw back the curtains to make sure that there is nothing going on outside the hotel. The streets are clear, but the men still look edgy. Jules wonders if she should be worried.

Ramirez returns twenty minutes later, frowning and pissed off. Apparently, there have been "issues" with the power in the city because of an unexpected heat wave. Hotel management was reluctant to convey this to their incoming guests, hoping that the temperatures would return to normal and the hotel would operate as normal. Gi had just exchanged some choice words with the hotel manager. The manager assured him that they expected all would be well in a few hours.

Three days later, the extended heat wave and concurrent blackout have effectively crushed Buenos Aires. The ancient emergency generators bit the dust shortly after the initial power failure. There are no computers, lights, air conditioning or working plumbing. Williamson had fled with Gi, Saul, Bruno and Junior on Wednesday morning, as soon as they could arrange the flight. With a large amount of cash placed into the right hands, they'd managed to receive a special flight approval for a limited number of people just hours before the airport was officially closed.

The rest of the detail, six in total, is stranded at Hotel Madero in the dark and the heat. They've moved from staff quarters into the master suite previously occupied by Williamson. Ramirez wanted to keep the crew together, not trusting the volatility of the situation, a combination of brutal heat and crushing boredom. The local government had put a stop to all but emergency incoming and outgoing flights until order could be restored. It would be at least another forty-eight hours before they could get out.

The men pass the time playing cards, sleeping, smoking and drinking. Because Bird is back at home, they are officially off-duty, so the normal restrictions don't apply to this confinement. Even the pool is closed because there's no electricity to run the filters and the hotel does not want the liability of guests swimming in unclean water.

The ice machines are empty metal husks filled with puddles of evaporating water. The hotel staff is doing everything they can to keep the guests comfortable, but are now running out of towels, linens and fresh food.

Ramirez is in an agitated state, constantly on the phone trying to sort out details both at home and abroad. He's instructed everyone to stay in the hotel and to be available by cell at all times. He's quietly told Jules to remain with at least one member of the crew at all times, not wanting her to wander alone through the darkened hotel. Jules does what she always does in these types of situations, finds a book and stays still, reading.

During the day they close the heavy curtains in the suite against the sun, but the rooms remain stifling. The men commandeer the tables for card playing and the huge sectional couch for sleeping.

Jules finds her own spot in the formal dining room, under a massive, rectangular table made to seat ten. She makes a nest of towels and borrows a pillow from the master bedroom. She drinks warm bottled tea and reads, sleeping when the urge overtakes her, which is often.

Because of his senior status, Ramirez is entitled to sole possession of the king-sized bed in the master bedroom. On the afternoon of the first day, he goes looking for Jules and finds her asleep under the table. She is curled up, wearing men's boxer shorts and a loose, white t-shirt.

The men, playing cards in the adjacent room, are talking quietly and stealing glances at her long legs. Jules' hair is twisted up on top of her head, the humidity having made it into a tangle of curls. The back of her neck is exposed, her t-shirt damp with sweat.

Ramirez takes one look at the situation and realizes that leaving her out here is like throwing a baby seal into a shark tank. He squats down and nudges her awake. She blinks at him like a newborn, groggy with the unbearable heat. "I want you to take the master bedroom."

She shakes her head. "I'm fine here. I made myself a little cave."

He smirks, inclining his head towards the next room, where the men are now busy with their cards. "It's the cavemen I'm worried about, not your comfort. That's an order, Petersen. Move your stuff in there now."

"What about you?"

"I'm not sleeping anyway. I'm alternating coffee and whiskey. I'll be up 'til we can get the hell out of here. Go on."

"Okay, thanks, Lieutenant."

"*De nada.*"

It has been thirty-six hours since the power failed. Everyone is edgy and exhausted, having run out of conversation, appetite and distractions. At 0100, the men are sleeping, sprawled across the living room, the windows open to the balcony to catch any hint of evening breeze, but the city is starting to smell like rotting garbage, so the fresh air is mitigated by the fetid scent. Ramon is out in the hallway talking softly on the phone to Gi, still desperately trying to find a way to get them home.

Jules is dead asleep in the master bedroom, windows and doors open to facilitate the movement of air.

Eduardo, drunk since early afternoon, sits up on the sofa. He looks at the sleeping men and at the open door to the bedroom. He gets up and pads silently over the thick carpeting, listing a bit to the right. Once inside the bedroom, he pulls the door softly closed behind him.

Jules is splayed on her back, legs twisted in the sheets. Eduardo sees the gleam of sweat on her neck and face. Quiet as a killer, he crosses the room and sits on the edge of the bed next to her. He studies her face for a long time. *Beautiful, even with the broken nose. Long,* dark eyelashes, perfect lips. He can see the outline of a breast under the damp t-shirt. Inhibitions long gone, he reaches out and touches her, saying her name.

She starts awake with a jerk, swimming up from unconsciousness to see the dark shape of a man on her bed. She instinctively sits up and pulls back, her hands curling into fists. Eyes adjusting to the dark, she recognizes Eduardo's face. Jules tenses, the muscles in her arms and back twitch, ready to strike.

"Hey easy, easy. It's only me."

"What the fuck do you want?"

"Thought you might be lonely in here, *chica*."

"Yeah? Well I'm not. Get out of here."

He laughs softly, the sound raising the hairs on the back of her neck. "I been thinking. You're always rattling that smart mouth, but I think I got a better use for it. What do you say?" He leans closer, reeking of alcohol. "Don't look so surprised. You think we're all blind? Think we don't notice you? Me and Ramon, we was just the other day talking about you, your fine ass," he slurs the words.

Jules feels her heart begin to pound, her face flaming in the dark. She doesn't believe it. Ramirez can be an asshole, but she doesn't believe he'd stoop to rate her tits and ass with the men.

"Like I said, get the fuck out of here, Eduardo."

"C'mon, *mija*. Look," he grabs her by the wrist, taking her hand and placing it on his erection, "I'm ready to go."

Her reaction is instant and visceral. She yanks her hand away and elbows him in the face, carving a deep, inch-long gash between his eyebrows. "*Now* you're ready to go, asshole."

Eduardo is reeling away from the bed, holding his head and yelling loud enough to wake the entire hotel, letting loose a stream of obscenities in Spanish. Blood is dripping through his fingers.

Ramirez hears the noise from the hallway and as he skids into the suite, lights are coming on and men are stumbling to their feet, some reaching for weapons. Eduardo exits the master bedroom, bleeding and howling. Ramirez takes one look at him and moves past him into the bedroom.

Jules is crouched on the bed, breathing hard. She looks at Ramirez as if he's another assailant. Ramon recognizes that look from the boxing ring. He puts his hands up in a universal calming gesture and moves slowly towards her.

"It's okay, Jules. Take a breath." He inches closer. "What happened?"

Her voice is shrill, her breathing ragged, "He woke me up. He touched me."

"Touched you…how?"

"He grabbed me and put my hand on his dick, okay? He wanted a blowjob."

"All right." *Just what he needs, a hysterical female on top of all this other bullshit.* "Put some clothes on. We'll take a walk and figure this out."

She hesitates, not sure if she trusts him now after what Eduardo had said.

"Do it Petersen, that's an order."

His tone snaps her back into compliance. She throws a shirt and jeans on over her clothes, pulling her hair into a rough ponytail.

They leave the room together, Ramirez positioning himself between her and Eduardo, who is still out of control, spitting curses. Ramirez makes eye contact with Johnson. "Get him cleaned up and under control, I'll be back." Johnson nods unhappily.

Downstairs, the hotel bar is lit only by candles, but still half-full of patrons. Ramirez decides it is as good a place as any to talk Jules down. He orders two whiskeys and finds a booth for them in a dark corner. He slides in close to her and hands her the drink.

She throws back half the drink, washing away the metallic taste of adrenaline which lingers in her mouth. Ramirez pulls out a crushed pack of cigarettes and lights two, handing her one. Jules takes it with a shaking hand. It tastes like salvation.

Ramirez leans back, grateful that in South America you can still smoke in a bar. "All right, start from the beginning."

She looks at him warily. "I fell asleep, I don't know what time it was. I left the door open so I could get some air from the suite. When I woke up, the room was dark and the door was closed. At first I didn't know who it was, I thought maybe it was some stranger. Then my vision adjusted and I could see it was Eduardo. He was drunk, I could smell it coming off him." She pauses to take a drag on the cigarette. "I asked him what he wanted and he said something about wanting to see if I was lonely. I told him no." She hesitates, thinking about how Ramon's name had come up in the conversation. She decides to leave that out for now.

"Anyway, he implied that he wanted me to blow him. I told him to get out. He said he was ready to go and grabbed me by the wrist and put my hand on him. When I pulled my arm away I elbowed him in the face. I didn't really mean to, it was just a reflex."

Ramon sighs, blowing out smoke. "This is exactly why I didn't want to hire a woman. If the men get squirrely, they just have a fistfight. With you around, someone gets an idea in his head and now I have a sexual harassment claim on my hands."

Jules takes another swallow, looking away from him. "I'm not going to file any claim. I just wanted him off me."

"I realize he was wrong, but this kind of shit is going to happen. You're going to have to learn not to go into combat mode every time someone makes a pass at you."

"I woke up to him touching me!" Her voice sounds immature and petulant, even to her. Her throat closes. She feels stupid and defeated, the useless skirt in the ranks, just like Eduardo had said. "He said you two were talking about me."

A shadow of rage crosses Ramirez's features and just as quickly disappears, put away for another time. Jules is impressed by his control.

"Talking about what?"

"My fine ass." It sounds so absurd now, she has to laugh. She shrugs. "I didn't really believe him."

"Jules, I may be a lot of things, but I'm not a misogynist." He registers the surprise on her face. "Yeah, I know what misogynist means. I read books too."

She smiles wryly, embarrassed that he's caught her underestimating him.

"Look. I'll handle him. We go way back, so he thinks he's got an in with me, but everyone knows he's an asshole. I'll make sure nothing like this happens again, but you have to keep your emotions in check if you're going to fit in here."

She nods, crushing out the cigarette in the ashtray. "Can I have another drink? My nerves are shot."

"Yeah, I need one too. This is like being in hell, only in hell I'd be with my friends." He stands up and heads back to the bar. She watches him go, seeing the female heads in the room tracking his progress. He is wearing a black RSW polo shirt and black fatigues and somehow, even after the heat and no showers, managing to look composed and collected. Maybe being Latino has its advantages when it comes to high temperatures.

He returns with the drinks. He notices that Jules' hand is still shaking when she takes her drink. He reaches out his hand "Let me see your wrist. Did he hurt you?"

She holds it out for his inspection. "It's fine. I probably did more damage pulling away."

Ramon can see a faint impression of Eduardo's fingers circling her wrist. He looks her in the eyes, still holding on. "You have a pretty intense attack response, Jules. *Somebody* hurt you, a long time before Eduardo."

She takes her hand back, shifting in her seat. There is a long moment before she speaks. "In college … I was young and stupid." She looks up at him, eyes darkening with an unwanted memory. "I didn't know you have to be careful. It was a date-rape thing. It was over before I even figured out it wasn't consensual. I didn't report it or anything, but it stayed with me."

Ramon lights another cigarette and hands it to her.

She takes a drag. "The thing is, when you're a girl, growing up; your parents, your teachers, they all tell you you're special, you're smart, that you've got unique talents. I mean… that is, if you're lucky enough to be raised in a good place. They tell you that you're in charge of your body and your life and what you do with it. And you believe them."

She takes a long swallow of whiskey. "Only it's all a big lie. You grow up, you go out into the world and you find out the truth. That it's a man's world. And right away, men let you know what you're worth to them, what your real currency is. It doesn't take very long to figure out that all your specialness doesn't mean shit. Half the men you encounter make it clear that *they've* been taught that they have the right to take what they want, when they want it."

"Not all men believe that." Ramon finds himself drawn in, wanting to prove it to her. *You fucking hypocrite, tell me you haven't had the same thoughts as every other guy on the crew.*

She exhales, blowing out smoke. "No, not all men." She realizes she has gone too far, said way too much. *Jesus, if she'd ever wanted to give him ammunition, here it is.* His quiet attention had made her feel safe, but spilling her secrets has surely been a mistake.

"Sorry, I shouldn't have had that second drink. Anyway, learning to fight helped me. It let me walk through the world without being scared all the time." Jules is silent for a moment. "I should try to get back to sleep, it's really late." She stands and Ramon rises with her to walk back to the suite.

"Jules?"

"Yeah?"

"You're on my watch now. I'm not gonna let you get hurt."

She slips her hand into his, squeezing it for a second and then letting go. The contact gives him a jolt. "You're not responsible for my safety, Lieutenant. That's up to me. But thanks for saying it."

19

The crew returns from Buenos Aires ragged and depleted. Jules gives Eduardo a wide berth, but he shoots her scathing looks whenever he gets the chance. The cut she'd given him was healing, but she can feel his suppressed rage and it makes her nervous. She tries to be aware of where he is at all times so she can go in the opposite direction. She knows that eventually he'll corner her somewhere. Though she's sure Lieutenant had read him the riot act and warned him to stay away, Eduardo isn't exactly the honorable type. Besides, he'd been gunning for her since she got here.

The new guy, Nate, seems to be working out well. He's picked up some of the probie duties Jules had been saddled with and seemed to carry out orders efficiently and with good cheer. They'd been stuck together on several early and late shifts and had developed an easy rapport. He was respectful and diligent.

On one particularly endless double shift, Nate volunteers the information that he has custody of his six-year-old son, Beau. Apparently Beau's mother had developed a drug problem while Nate had been on active duty in the military. Nate had come home from a deployment to find his wife addicted to methamphetamine and Beau being left alone for hours at a time. He'd begged her to get help, but after a few failed attempts at rehab, it became apparent that she wasn't going to clean up. Nate filed for divorce and petitioned for full custody of Beau, which the judge granted.

Having seen these painful scenarios played out in court, Jules is immediately sympathetic to Nate's single-parent status. She can't imagine how he does it, especially with this unforgiving schedule. Nate explains that Beau is in school, aftercare and spends the rest of the time with Nate's mom when he is working or traveling. Nate has a girlfriend, Stacy, but says, "She isn't really into the kid thing."

Though Jules and Nate often end up on the same shifts, she offers to help with Beau if Nate ever gets stuck for childcare. The look he gives her is that of a drowning man being thrown a rope.

Jules explains that she has an eight-year-old nephew and knows all the boy games and movies. Nate laughs and says he'll put Jules on speed dial.

Jules feels she can finally ease into a routine at work. Though Ramirez had seemed distant with her since the return from South America, he is even-handed with assignments and has stopped criticizing her every move.

She's more comfortable with the mechanics of the operation and doesn't have to stop to think of the protocol for every step she takes. She buckles down and works as if there is nothing more important than the task at hand. In fact, there isn't: the job is her lifeline, a reason to get up in the morning, a way to beat back the incessant memories of her life with Christopher.

Now that she's escaped the all-consuming stress of training, Jules can feel the grief bubbling up at odd moments, in the grocery store, where she notices couples shopping for the weekend, heads together, consulting a list. She gets another jolt at the bank, when she sees a husband and wife at the ATM, discussing how much money they need for a night out.

She has ways of controlling her emotions so they don't spill over in public. Sometimes she bites the inside of her cheek or makes a fist and digs her fingernails into her palm. These little devices work just long enough for her to push away the thoughts of Chris and the intimacies she's lost.

Jules hopes that eventually the austerity of her single life will kill the longings that plague her. She knows that human beings have an endless ability to adapt, but isn't sure what the timeline is for a thirty-three-year-old widow to stop missing the touch and voice of her husband.

Nate calls Jules from home while she's on Saturday duty. "Hey, Beau and I are going to rent a movie tonight and I thought it might be a good chance for you to meet him in case, you know, you end up sitting for him sometime." He sounds nervous.

Jules hesitates, thinking of her schedule. She is off at 1700, but has been looking forward to a beer and her new book. *Ah well, when does she ever get asked to go anywhere?* "Sure, it sounds like fun, do you want me to pick anything up?"

"No, no. We'll get a pizza and soda. Do you drink beer?"

"Heck, yeah, it's Saturday night." *Well at least she'll get her beer. Maybe she can stay up late and read her book.*

"Great, we'll see you later."

Jules hangs up, wondering about the wisdom of this. *Where is Nate's girlfriend on a Saturday night? Shouldn't she be bonding with the Nate and the kid?* Still, Jules had offered and knows from experience that it is better to get to know a child with the parent present. *Besides, how long has it been since she made a new friend? Other than Ramirez of course.* The thought makes her giggle.

She arrives at Nate's downtown garden apartment a bit after 7:30 p.m. Nate answers the door, looking relaxed in an old pair of jeans and a faded, army brown t-shirt. It's odd to see him this way, Jules is used to the suit-and-tie version of Nate. Here he looks like a young, handsome college kid, except for the wide-eyed little boy clinging to his leg.

Jules tilts her head to look Beau in the eye, "Nate, is this your older brother?"

Beau looks up at his dad, laughing. "Hah, Daddy, she thinks I'm your brother!"

Nate winks at Jules as he lets her in, signaling his gratitude for the icebreaker. "I know it's hard to tell, but this is my son, Beau," he says in a somber voice.

Beau peers at Jules, checking her out in the frank way common to little kids.

Jules meets his gaze, "So Beau, Daddy told me that you can eat three pieces of pizza, but I don't believe him."

"I can too," he shouts, "and I can drink a can of soda in two minutes, I timed myself!"

"No way." Jules frowns at him.

"Yeah and I also have Super Mario and a Star Wars light saber."

"Excellent. Can I see later?"

Nate leans against the doorjamb to the kitchen, smiling.

Beau looks at Nate, "Daddy said we have to let you eat first."

Jules laughs. "Thank goodness, 'cause I'm starving."

Beau takes her by the hand and leads her to the small, neat living room, where the pizza box is waiting. "I bet you can't eat three pieces," he challenges.

"Oh yeah? Just watch me." Jules plunks herself on the couch. "What's the movie tonight?"

"We got *Madagascar Two* and Daddy said I can stay up 'til it's over," he reports breathlessly.

Jules smiles at Beau, feeling her heart expand just a bit. She sighs. Maybe there is something to be said for human contact after all.

Jules is on the bleachers of the RSW gym, watching as the men amble in for their first weekly Krav class. They come in clumps, talking and shouldering gear bags. She watches them as they deposit their bags against the wall and pull off warm-up jackets and sweatshirts. She finds it amusing that, to a man, they are wearing black sweats and white t-shirts, as if they'd been ordered to be in uniform.

Jules knows that the lieutenant is inside the gym office, observing the class from behind the one-way mirror, but she tunes that out and relegates it to the background noise in her head. She hops up and switches on the CD player to signal the beginning of the class. She likes hardcore alternative music for her classes, it has an aggressive beat and tends to get everyone pumped up.

"All right gentlemen, let's get started. On my go I want five laps, one minute of pushups, two minutes of crunches, five more laps, four down-and-back sprints and then two minutes of pushups." Jules hits a stop watch and begins to call out the intervals.

After the first few minutes, they are swearing under their breath and glaring at her. The first fifteen minutes of class are designed to take the men's wind. That means that they'll begin their hand-to-hand combat tired and a little depleted, as they might feel after a long shift or a sudden, disorienting attack.

When the initial drills are complete, she assembles the men in a line facing her. Though they're physically strong, it looks as though most lack the endurance they need for fighting. Jules deliberately provokes them.

"This is what you've got?" She points at the clock on the wall. "We've barely started and half of you are sucking wind."

She stands, hands on hips in full drill instructor mode: "Do you even know why you're here?" No one replies.

"Huh? Because Lieutenant said it was mandatory? Well good for him. The lieutenant, being SEAL-trained, knows a thing or two about close-quarters combat. That's why he doesn't have to come to class. The rest of you..."

She looks around at the collection of men. "You all know how to fight, right? Bad-ass boxers, kick-boxers, martial artists, Marines."

"Gi, you're a boxer. Think you're gonna have room to throw a punch if someone has a gun in Bird's face?" She waits.

Gi, for perhaps the first time in his life, is at a loss for words. He rubs the stubble on his face. "Probably not."

"Mr. Lee, my esteemed colleague. You're a black belt. Room to land a kick?"

"No ma'am." He concedes with a slight nod.

"Okay gentlemen, thank you. Here's what we know: in the U.S., attacks on principals are almost entirely committed by a lone assailant within twenty-five feet. In time-and-distance training, real-time assessment of protector responses shows us that the closer a protector is to the assailant, the better the protector's rate of success."

She looks at the men, they appear to be tuning her out. "Okay let's put this in terms you can all understand. After a few years of executive protection, you are well-oiled machines. Expert shots, hyper-vigilant, detail-oriented machines, right?" She pauses, they are nodding. She's regained their attention by flattering them.

"Wrong. You have been lulled into a false sense of security by body armor, vehicles and weapons. You have skills, but not the right ones to stop a killing. Solomon, come join me, please."

Solomon looks around uneasily, as if she were talking to someone else. He reluctantly joins Jules front and center. Jules pats him on his massive shoulder, "Thank you. Now Solomon, go stand on that piece of tape over there," she points.

"Okay, Solomon, our assailant, is fifteen feet away. At fifteen feet, Solomon has an eighty-two percent success rate. Mine? Eighteen percent. That's what you call the big suck."

The men laugh, finally engaged.

"All right Solomon, step in to the next mark. Now our assailant is at seven feet." The men are focused and listening. "His success rate is now fifty-five percent. Mine is forty-five. Less suck, but not acceptable, 'cause I need better odds. Okay Solomon, come right here to me." Solomon, embarrassed to be so close to Jules, grins like a kid. "Now the assailant is about six inches from me. His odds of success are two percent, mine are ninety-eight percent and I'm a happy agent. Are we clear on this gentleman?"

The men muster a collective "Ma'am yes, ma'am!"

"All right let's get to work. Pair off for combatives."

Julianna and Ramirez are on a routine detail to take Bird to lunch in Bedminster, accompanied by one of his attorneys, with whom he's just had a brief meeting.

"Julianna you remember my attorney, Christian Devereux, from the Tokyo trip, don't you?" Williamson asks.

"Of course." Jules puts her hand out to the young man in front of her. His grip is barely firm, noncommittal. She takes him in: slight build, dark hair cut just a bit longer than most of the attorneys she's known, but perfectly groomed. His suit is flawless, at least two grand worth of silk, finished with a lavender paisley tie. Something about this guy throws her off completely. She has met hundreds of attorneys in her time at the prosecutor's office, young and old, wealthy and struggling. But Devereux just doesn't make sense here.

He is wearing a platinum Rolex, a real one. His shoes are Italian, soft leather, not the sturdy wingtips favored by most of the lawyers she knows. As they head downstairs into the garage, she notices that he seems to be obsessed with fixing his hair, smoothing and patting the back of it repeatedly, even though it is fine. He shoots his cuffs and straightens his tie.

God, it's not as if they just had some three-hour meeting. He was only in there for forty-five minutes, how taxing could it be? Definitely high maintenance. She glances at Ramirez, he looks straight ahead, not seeming to notice anything odd. *Why is Devereux so young?* He can't be more than twenty-six. Big firms like RSW always have old, silver-haired attorneys for the caché and teams of invisible, young associates doing all the real work behind the scenes.

Yet Williamson had said 'my attorney' and she'd heard Devereux's name many times in detail briefings. Before she'd met him, she'd expected that he would be in his fifties. As they reach the vehicle, Ramirez puts Williamson in on the passenger side in the back and Jules opens the back driver's side door for Devereaux.

Devereaux pauses momentarily and looks at Jules, giving her a head-cocked, once-over from head to toe. Jules' eyes widen in surprise. The glance hadn't been the typical eye sweep of a male: face, breasts and legs. It had been the frank, brutal appraisal of a rival female: hair, face, outfit, shoes. She shuts the door and gets in the driver's side, taking a deep breath.

As she drives to the restaurant she connects the dots: Williamson's frequent 'domestic issues,' his intense interest in appearances, his old-fashioned, careful manner of speech. She glances in the rearview at Devereaux, who is surreptitiously applying lip balm.

Williamson is gay.

Jules is completely stunned by the realization.

Why hadn't they told her? Okay, maybe not when she was a probie, but sometime after they gave her the keys to the kingdom. Wouldn't that be a pertinent thing to know about their employer, whom they protect 24/7?

They reach the restaurant and escort the men in. Ramirez sits at the table and she is on the door. Her mind reviews everything from the last fourteen months: Williamson's too-perfect family, right down to the dog. His petulant wife, who has to be pacified with ridiculously expensive baubles. She hears Williamson in her head saying 'Well, I'm not a *saint*, Julianna.'

She watches them from her post. Ramirez is facing her, but absorbed in scanning the room. She notices the proximity of Williamson and Devereux, close, but not too close. Williamson casually drapes his arm around the back of Christian's chair, the way an older man would show possession of a younger, attractive companion.

How had she missed this? Now that she has made the connection, she is astounded by her own stupidity. *Does everyone know but me?* Of course they do, only an outsider like her could have made a misassumption this great.

After lunch, they return to the building and Devereaux exits to his personal vehicle from the garage. She and Ramirez escort Williamson back to his office suite, while he chats lightly about the food and the weather forecast for the weekend. Jules smiles politely and when he has been deposited, she shadows Ramirez back into the hallway.

"A word, Lieutenant?" she asks, gathering her courage.

He stops in the hallway, turning to her.

She hesitates. "In private, please."

He sighs in annoyance. They proceed to his office and he lets her in, closing the heavy door behind them.

"Okay. What is it?"

"Lieutenant, when were you going to tell me that our principal is gay?"

He looks hard at her. "Is he?"

Jules flinches, her heart hammering. *Oh God. Could she be wrong about this?* No, she is absolutely sure. She frowns at him. "Yes, he is."

Ramirez shakes his head. "I believe the correct term is bisexual. He does have two children."

Jules holds her hands up in exasperation. "Okay, Lieutenant, *bisexual*. Did you not think that the information was relevant to my duties here? A month ago I was playing referee with him and his wife at the house. What if I'd made some kind of mistake or said something I shouldn't have?" Her voice is rising in frustration.

"Watch your tone and lower your voice. Okay, you know. Has it changed your objective? To protect the principal?"

"How can I effectively protect him if I don't know who he is? Does she even know?"

"Have a seat and calm down." He leans back in his chair. "She knows he cheats, but she thinks it's with women."

"Have you always known?"

He pauses, weighing the wisdom of giving her the full story. "Not at first. When he was building a reputation, he was very discreet. Later on, he had a situation with some street kid, who decided he could make some money with a small blackmail scheme. Williamson had to come to me and tell the truth so I could handle it."

Jules tries to calm herself. Ramirez looks at her as if he cannot believe the scope of her naiveté. "Look, Petersen. If you think you're going to work in this field and not be employed by someone who's got their own bent or some hidden vice, you're kidding yourself. It doesn't happen. The rule is: you look the other way and keep doing your job. Keep your judgments to yourself."

"I'm not judging him. I don't have a problem with gay people. Or bisexual. Whatever. What I'm saying is, part of our job is to keep him from public embarrassment, yes?"

"Yes, and we do that very well. You've been here over a year, working inside. You didn't know. So I'd say his public persona is intact, correct?"

She sighs in concession. "So what's Devereaux's story? Is he even a real attorney?"

"Of course. He's not experienced enough to handle this enterprise, Williamson's got the usual heavy hitters for that. Devereaux is an accessory, like a Gucci belt. Williamson likes having him around."

"So he keeps him around and when the mood strikes, calls him in for 'a meeting'?" Jules pictures Devereaux straightening his hair and tie, putting on lip balm in the car. *Ick.*

"Correct. He also takes in the local color when we travel out of country."

She rolls her eyes in disbelief. "How does that work? How can you possibly keep him safe?"

"Only two of us handle that aspect of things, that's me and Eduardo. Of course the hustlers know he has money, but they're very well-compensated. We sweep them for weapons, drugs and recording devices before they go in. And having two armed agents outside the room is enough to keep anybody from getting squirrelly. We have it down to a system."

She is not convinced. "But it's so high-risk. What if Grace finds out? What if she decides to divorce him and go to the press?"

He snorts. "Grace signed an ironclad pre-nup. In the case of a divorce, she gets everything she wants on one condition; that she keeps her mouth shut. Otherwise the deal is off and she'll be scraping for every penny. She is well aware of that."

Jules is finally silent.

Ramirez sees that he has exhausted all of her objections. "So, you take a few minutes and wrap your head around this. Once you leave this office, you get the fuck over it and never talk about it again with anyone, not even me. Are we clear on this, Petersen?"

She nods, silent and utterly disillusioned. "Clear, Lieutenant."

20

In late May, the detail organizes for a trip to San Juan, Puerto Rico. Though the trip has a serious agenda, Jules notices that the lieutenant's mood is lighter than usual. She guesses that the prospect of traveling back home is lifting his spirits.

Williamson will be negotiating a huge deal with Fernando Aguilero, a second-generation oil heir who bears the sense of entitlement of a young man who has never worked. Since Aguilero's father died a year ago, the brash young man has decided that his future lies in playing with big oil in the U.S.

Williamson knows a cash cow when he sees one and intends to become indispensable to the young billionaire as he navigates the politically intricate shark tank of U.S oil commerce. The two men have had preliminary meetings in New York and a few getting-to-know-you conference calls, but now Williamson has been deemed trustworthy enough for an invite to *Casa Aguilero.*

The three-day visit will be masked as a social call, but during the visit Aguilero will be making a final decision about whether to entrust his family business to an American outsider. Williamson is salivating at the prospect of adding Aguilero to RSW's growing roster of clients. The detail has been specially briefed that every aspect of the trip is to be checked and re-checked. Williamson is adamant that the image of RSW is to appear impeccable, down to the last shoe-shine.

Williamson himself briefs Jules during the flight to San Juan. It is a two-billion-dollar deal, a high-end shell game.

Her role is to keep Aguilero happy under any circumstance.

"You're my special asset here, Julianna," Williamson says. "I'm counting on you to work your magic."

She nods gravely, but feels compelled to ask the obvious question. "Charming, distracting, entertaining; but all within my own personal level of comfort, yes?"

He looks chagrined. "Julianna, a whore can be found in any country, any hotel, any function. In fact, I'm quite certain Aguilero has a whole stable of them at his disposal. What I want you to do is to illustrate that I have impeccable taste, brilliant employees and only the most elegant women in my company. It will be up to you to discreetly defend your own honor. Only you must promise me, none of that Israeli nonsense you like so much. Try to use your excellent vocabulary instead."

She smiles at that. "Of course, sir, I just want to make sure we're all on the same page." Jules gazes out the window at the amazing view as the pilot announces their descent. As apprehensive as she is, she can't help being excited to see this beautiful island.

They settle into the hotel with a minimum of fuss. Just prior to the dinner hour, Ramirez raps on her hotel room door twice. Jules moves quickly to open it, knowing he will not be kept waiting. He strides in, uninvited.

"Ready?" He turns to look at her and his all-business expression slips. His face changes as he takes her in. She sees his chest fill with a deep breath and her confidence falters. Maybe she has gotten it all wrong, the dress, the makeup, the hair. She squares her shoulders, waiting for the inevitable correction. She still has a couple of minutes to change if she needs to.

He swallows hard, nodding at her, "Very nice."

"Really?"

"Really." There is a trace of a smile, fleeting then gone.

Her dress is jade green, heavy satin that crosses just under the bust and then falls straight to just above the knee. Her legs are bare and glistening with the sheen of coconut oil, ending in three-inch high sandals, which show off her perfectly pedicured silver toenails.

"Wait a second. Are you carrying?" he asks.

"Of course." She opens her silver evening bag and shows him the loaded .22 pistol inside, nestled next to her lipstick.

"All right," he murmurs. *Goddamn.* He suddenly remembers they have a job to do. He looks at his watch. "We're two minutes out, let's move."

During the elevator ride he instructs her again on the evening's protocol. The event is mid-level risk, security at the door checking invites, which means next-to-nothing for the safety of the event. No metal detectors, so anyone and everyone may be carrying. RSW has done its own background checks on the hotel staff. Jules' primary purpose is to stay close to Bird, as well as to provide a charming distraction to their host Aguilero, known for his quick temper and rapacious appetites.

The elevator stops twice on the ride up to Williamson's penthouse, once to admit Gi and Nate and then Xavier and Tam. The response is the same from each pair; they step in, greet the Lieutenant and stop talking abruptly as they spot Jules, their eyes giving her a reflexive up-and-down sweep, mouths falling open.

She looks back at them, trying to convey confidence. Though they'd seen her in a dress at the Lieutenant's birthday party, this is the first time they've witnessed her in full feminine plumage, glossy and upscale from head to toe. The experience appears to take each one of them aback, however, they recover quickly.

All except Gi, who keeps turning around to look just one more time, until Ramirez puts a hand on his neck and growls, "Get your bearing."

The elevator opens to the penthouse floor, where Saul and Henry are on the door. They rap twice and open the double doors to the suite as the entire detail slips inside.

Williamson is a poster-child for effortless affluence in his Armani suit. He rises from a velvet sofa, glass in hand. He greets the lieutenant, "Right on time, Ramon, as always." It is then that he spots Jules.

"Julianna!" he exclaims, his voice filled with the pleasure of a proud father. He hands his glass to Xavier and sweeps across the room to her, grabbing both of her hands and twirling her into an impromptu spin. Jules blushes to her hairline, deeply embarrassed, as every man in the room uses the opportunity to take her in.

"Ah, I knew you were the right woman for the job! You've gotten it just right: elegant, understated, absolute perfection. Of course we may have to peel Aguilero off of you by the end of the night, but you're armed, so there's always that comfort." He laughs, delighted with his own wit.

She is silent, smiling shyly, and then looks to Ramirez for reassurance, startled to find his eyes fixed on her in a moment of raw appreciation. The moment lasts just long enough for both of them to acknowledge the fact of it. She breaks eye contact first, confused by this new development.

"Shall we?" Williamson calls them to action and she realizes that what had seemed like minutes had been merely a fraction of a second.

Seated at the dinner table with Aguilero to her right and Williamson to her left, Jules has a clear view of Ramirez, stationed next to a giant white column. Xavier is at another column behind her, taking in everything beyond her peripheral vision.

Aguilero is aggressively suave, complimenting her dress and her eyes and making a point of leaning in close to whisper his comments.

The restaurant is noisy and crowded, grander than anything she has ever seen. The flatware is gold and there are two plates and two chargers stacked at each place. Jules isn't worried about her table manners, she assumes she can keep up. She'd diligently studied both the business and social etiquette for the region, which helped her understand that Puerto Rican society operates as a formal, structured patriarchy. Women of wealth were valued for their beauty and their ability to produce stunning heirs to their fathers, little more.

Her function as security personnel has obviously been downplayed by Williamson, it appears that Aguilero believes she is there only for his amusement. Jules chats about acceptable light topics: his children, the weather, soccer and the exquisite food. He rests his arm along the back of her chair, 'accidentally' brushing her bare shoulder.

Though Jules had specifically chosen the dress for the way it concealed her tattoo, as she leans forward to hear Williamson, Aguilero spots a fraction of the artwork.

He leans in again. "I see you're decorated," he purrs. "How interesting. What is it?"

"*Es personal, señor.*"

"Perhaps when we're better acquainted, you'll let me see it."

"I'm sure we won't be that well-acquainted. After all, this is a business relationship, *si?*"

"*No, señorita.* My business is with your employer. You, *mi querida*, are merely an exquisite decoration. One which is greatly appreciated, of course."

After Bird is tucked into his suite and the next detail takes its shift, Ramirez rides down in the elevator with Jules. They talk quietly and seriously about the evening and the next day's events and she mentions some minor logistical issues, which will be addressed during the morning's briefing. The doors slide open at their floor and he walks her to the glossy red door of her room. As she extracts the keycard from her bag, he takes it deftly from her, saying "I'll clear the room for you."

Her eyebrows lift in surprise. *Since when has she needed anyone to clear her room?* Nonetheless, she's pleased by his chivalry. He does a walk-through, checking the bathroom, sliding open the curtains and the glass door to the balcony. He turns back to her, "Looks good, you turning in now?"

The question strikes her as odd. The interest he's expressing seems out of character, but then again, his demeanor has been different all evening.

She hesitates. "No, not yet, I'm still pretty wired." She brightens with an idea. "Will you have a drink with me?"

There is a flicker in his dark eyes, there and gone. He shrugs easily, "A drink sounds good."

She crosses to the mini bar, surveying the contents. She inspects the tiny bottles of alcohol and beverages, finally choosing two shot-sized tequilas, a can of ginger ale and a miniature bottle of rum. Jules mixes a light rum and ginger for each of them and ferries those and the tequila outside.

Ramon has already settled on the balcony in a lounge chair, lighting one of his small cigars. He's kicked off his shoes, loosened his tie and ditched the suit jacket. She hands him the tequila shot first and they drink simultaneously, raising a silent *salud* to each other.

Jules hands him a sweating rum and ginger and he passes her the cigar, knowing that she has a weakness for them. She draws on the cigar briefly, holding the sweet smoke in her mouth before exhaling. She hands it back to him and grabs her own drink, settling on the chaise next to his.

She kicks off her sandals, wiggling her toes in blissful freedom. She sighs deeply, relaxed for the first time all day. She closes her eyes to listen to the ocean. The air is a scented mix of frangipani flowers and wood smoke and the humid night breeze is palpable on her skin. "How did you ever leave here? It's so beautiful."

"Duty called. Besides, where I lived didn't look or smell like this."

"Sorry, I didn't think of that. You said you grew up poor."

"We aspired to be poor. In fact, the poor didn't want anything to do with us."

"Bad?" she asks softly.

He shrugs. "You play the hand you're dealt. I moved on and brought my *abuela* to me as soon as I could."

"She's lucky to have you."

"I was lucky to have her. Without her I'd have been buried somewhere on this island by the time I was twenty, like most of my friends."

"What about your mother?"

He pauses. "She was a prostitute. Rumor has it she was beaten to death by a john when she was twenty-one. She dumped me on her mother's doorstep when I was five days old. She showed up a few times, but never stayed more than a week or two. End of story."

She is quiet for a moment. "I'm really sorry, Ramon."

"It's old news, don't worry about it. I have a good life now. That's my revenge."

Jules nods, knowing it is true. Satisfying work, a home of his own and his grandma safe and sound in a place he paid for. Time for a change of subject. "I'd better change out of this dress before I ruin it. It cost more than my mortgage payment, even if it was on the company's dime."

He laughs, "Worth every penny for the privilege of seeing you in it."

She flushes at the unexpected compliment, moving past him with a smile she can't hide. Inside the room, she turns on the bathroom light, leaving the rest of the room in shadow. She removes her weapon from her bag, placing it, still loaded, into the bedside drawer. She straightens, reaching to free the hook and eye on the back of the dress. She struggles, finding that it had been easier to fasten than it is to release. Finally, she sighs with impatience and moves to the balcony door.

"Ramon? This dress has a little hook at the top of the zipper, can you...?" she says, turning her back to him.

He gets up slowly, putting down the drink and the cigar. He is using the delay to think. *Is this an invitation? Possibly, but Jules is no ordinary woman; the man who misreads her could end up having a bad night all around.*

Ramon enters the dim room, still evaluating the situation. Since he entered the room earlier this evening, there has been something tenuous between them, but he isn't completely sure of it.

She lifts her hair, waiting.

He approaches, tentatively, slowing his breathing so his nerves won't betray him. "We'll see how this goes, my hands aren't exactly made for this sort of thing."

"I'm sure you'll do fine."

In order to get at the hook, he has to slide the tips of his fingers just inside the dress. He feels the fine texture of her skin and is suddenly conscious of his rough hands. Ramon struggles briefly with the minute hook, finally freeing it.

Jules can feel the heat of his body behind her and she's breathing in the scent of his spicy cologne. She is suddenly aware of the implications of asking him to touch her, but somehow she's not worried about how he will read the situation. She is tired of toeing the line. *Maybe you need to find out what's on the other side of the line.*

He hesitates once more. "You want me to do the zipper?"

"Yes please."

He unzips the dress discreetly to her waist, exposing a sheer black bra and the edge of her thistle tattoo. He stands poised on the edge of a decision, then leaps.

"I've never seen this up close, can I look?"

"Of course." Jules considers the irony of being asked the same question twice in one night. Yet with Ramon asking, her response is entirely different. She delicately slides one bra strap off her shoulder to reveal the tattoo, demurely holding the rest of her things in place.

"It's beautiful." He reads aloud the words twined through the leaves of the thistle. "**Breathe. Fight. Trust. Be.**"

"I got it after Chris died. I was pretty lost. I guess I felt like I needed a touchstone."

He carefully traces the outline with a fingertip. "It's very well done. Your tattooist liked you."

Now it is her turn to shrug, inclining her head slightly. "I don't know."

"I know." Very deliberately, he places a hand on her hip. She doesn't flinch, doesn't move away. He exerts a small amount of pressure, turning her to face him.

Jules slides the strap back up and lifts her head to look him in the eyes. There is a long beat between them, during which an enormous amount of information is wordlessly exchanged.

Finally he speaks. "You need to tell me this is a really bad idea," he says gruffly.

"It's a spectacularly bad idea." The corner of her mouth lifts. "That's what's going to make it so good."

It is all the invitation he needs. He tells the nagging voice of reason in his head to take a vacation and steps in. Putting a hand on the back of her neck, he draws her into a kiss.

Jules is breathless at his sudden intensity. She'd felt drawn to him at times, but had dismissed those thoughts as juvenile, schoolgirl fantasies. Reading his manner, she'd always assumed that he disapproved of her entirely. Now she drinks him in, the kiss like falling down a well. Everything goes away and there is nothing left but wanting to get closer.

He responds in kind and the kiss becomes its own universe. She can't remember the last time anything felt this good. He slides a hand down to her ass, tugging her nearer. He eases the dress off her shoulders and the heavy satin puddles around her bare feet.

In one graceful movement, she balances by putting a hand on his shoulder and steps out of the circle of fabric. She bends to retrieve the dress, laying it gently over the back of a chair. He follows her, not willing to let the distance between them expand even for a moment. She laughs, feeling the deep pleasure of his attentiveness.

Jules carefully removes his tie, pausing to kiss the edge of his jaw. He breathes in sharply. She begins unbuttoning the elegant starched cotton of his shirt, now slightly rumpled from the heat and her proximity. He is undoing his cufflinks, black enamel with the Navy SEAL trident, a gift from his unit when he left.

As the shirt comes off, he is suddenly conscious of the age difference between them, wondering if his body will please her. He works out hard, but he's not thirty anymore. Despite this momentary insecurity, he refuses to be one of those aging guys, puffing up his chest and sucking in his stomach for her. *It is what it is.*

Jules has seen Ramon in various states of dress and undress, even working out in the gym, but he has always had at least a t-shirt on. She cannot hide the delicious surprise of his body. He is what the guys call 'cut,' his muscles as sharply defined as any of the younger men she knows. His stomach is flat, his biceps and forearms snaked with tattoos, done only in black ink. The head of a rattlesnake curves over one shoulder, fangs open, tail winding around his left bicep. Across his right bicep are the words *Ñeta de Corazon* etched in a flowery script. On the inside of his forearm the ink reads '1.50'.

Jules starts, raising her gaze to him, "You were *Ñeta*." It is a statement, not a question. She knows about *Ñeta* from her time at the prosecutor's office. A Puerto Rican prison gang at its inception, the brotherhood now has chapters all over the states. The numbers 1.50 mean one-hundred-fifty percent, a *Ñeta* slogan.

He gazes evenly at her. "How do you know that?"

"I know lots of things."

"I was a kid. It was before the military took me. I did nine months on auto theft. We were just joyriding. I was seventeen."

She shakes her head. "You never stop unsettling me."

"Good, that's exactly what I want." He lifts her up and throws her unceremoniously onto the bed.

Jules can see that even after all these months of controlling her every move, Ramon still wants to call the shots. She decides that she'll let him, as long as it suits her. Jules watches him strip down to his boxer shorts. She is still in bra and panties.

As he comes to her in the bed, she feels vulnerable. As always, his confidence unnerves her. She is used to younger men, willing to do anything to please her. She wonders, *how many women?* She reviews the history she knows: a teenager running wild on this island, a marriage, prestigious military service all over the world, and twenty-some years of duty around expensive, bored women.

"Wait." She puts a hand on his chest. "You don't have any objection to condoms, do you?"

"No objections, but I don't have any handy. I wasn't exactly planning this."

"I think I have some in my makeup bag." *I pray I do.* She hustles to the bathroom. *Thank God!* She has three at the bottom of her bag and they're not even expired. *The gods are with us.* She tosses them onto the bedside table, climbing back into the bed.

He reaches for her. "You were gone too long." He pulls her down into another kiss. His hands move over her body, full of appreciation for the silky skin over smooth muscle. She is curvy in the hips and ass, the way he likes his women. As he dips his mouth to her collarbone and descends to the well of scent in the soft dip of her cleavage, he silently pronounces her perfect.

He slides the straps of her bra down.

"It opens in the front," she says helpfully. As he takes her nipple gently in his teeth, all conversation ends. She shuts up and gives in, holding onto the back of his head as it moves down her stomach. When he puts his mouth on her, she realizes that she is in way over her head.

Ramon concentrates his focus at the liquid center of her, enjoying her clean ocean smell, the way she tastes. *How long since he wanted a woman this way?* The women he sees are older, slightly worn but comfortable, and available at a moment's notice as he needs them to be. He fucks them by rote, giving them exactly what they require to be satisfied and nothing more. When he is done, he sends them packing with cab fare and a peck on the cheek. Jules does not strike him as a woman who would find that an acceptable sign of post-coital affection.

He feels her moving towards some sort of conclusion and intensifies his efforts, pleased with the result as her feet drum a beat on his shoulders. He grips her by the hips and takes her all the way over the edge, relishing the small animal noises she makes as she comes.

Breathing hard, she looks up at the ceiling and then down at him and his lopsided grin. She shakes her head in awe, unable to speak. Instead, she pushes gently on his shoulder, turning him onto his back.

Ramon relaxes now, wanting to see what she'll do, his question answered as she frees him of his boxers. She spends some time gently nipping the inside of his thighs, arousing him to a point where he can't help grabbing a handful of her silky hair and guiding her to where he needs her.

She takes him in her mouth with slow, expert strokes and in minutes the warm, wet spiral of her tongue forces him to call a halt, pulling her up for another kiss. He reaches for the condom, putting it on with practiced hands. Jules straddles him, looking into his eyes as she pulls him inside.

There is a small noise from each of them as he enters her, pulling her hips down and driving into her, unable to wait any longer. She rocks back on him and he sits up, pulling her to his chest. They find a real rhythm and she bites her lip instead of screaming. He moves her onto her back. She yields easily, assuming that it has been some time since he's been with someone and that he'll finish quickly, whether he wants to or not.

She is dead wrong.

Ramon takes his sweet time, moving deep and slow, touching her face and nuzzling her neck. At some point, he makes a minor adjustment, grabbing her behind the knees, pulling her down an inch or so while he moves up about the same distance. This small repositioning just slightly increases the friction between them and it is as if someone had let out the clutch. She begins to whisper to him in Spanish, urging him to do it harder.

He politely obeys, moving deeper and faster. He replies in Spanish, telling her how beautiful, how perfect she is, how much he's wanted her, thought of her.

Jules feels a disconcerting rush of emotion, he is taking her somewhere she hadn't planned on going.

Ramon is high. High on the acute pitch she has brought him to, on her lemony floral scent, her face, the light in her eyes when she looks at him. He is flooded by something which has been eluding him, a sense of mastery over something so fine, so alive. He'd barely allowed himself to think about her and now they're here, skin to skin, holding nothing back. He is astonished by her fearlessness, her improbable femininity. He lets go, as she does; falling down. All the way down.

Jules is deep in the dark well of sleep when Ramon's voice drags her back to consciousness. She sits up immediately, not fully awake.

"Jules, get up. I have to muster the men in half an hour and I need you to be in that line before I get there."

She is nodding vigorously, unable to act, but wanting him to understand that she is receiving. She takes a deep breath and looks up at him. He is damp, clad only in a towel, a magnificent sight in the half-light coming from the steamy bathroom.

"Good morning," she says hoarsely.

He leans in and kisses her firmly on the mouth, lingering for just a bit. "Good morning. Now move your ass."

Twenty-seven minutes later he strides into the conference room, clean-shaven and sharp, his gaze raking over the crew. He passes sheets from a thick stack of papers. "This is today's itinerary, which you should have memorized last night. If not, do so immediately."

Ramon glances at the list of engagements, pretending to read it over, instead taking in Jules with his peripheral vision.

She is clean and glowing in a pale yellow sheath dress, nearly barefaced but somehow still stunning. Her dark hair is twisted into a sleek knot low on the neck and he swears he can smell her fresh, citrus scent where he stands.

If he hadn't been there in person, he would find it impossible to believe that this was the same girl who had left him in a pool of sweat last night. As he begins to address the detail, he feels an effervescent rush of pleasure in his gut. A giddy, adolescent thought comes unbidden, *'I had her.'*

Jules stands in line with the men, the classic posture, parade rest, eyes fixed ahead on nothing. She had memorized the entire week's itinerary on the flight down, so her mind is free to wander.

She tries to slow her breathing from the mad rush she'd made to get there on time. She'd showered, slipped into her clothes and swiped on blush, mascara and lipstick, twisting her hair back while it was still damp. Jules had managed to slip into line about two-and-a-half minutes before Ramon arrived.

As he addresses the detail, flashes of the previous night come, making her heart pound. The sex had been incendiary. The long, slow burn of attraction had sparked as soon as he put his hands on her. *God, those hands!* She feels a rush of warmth, thinking of the things they'd done, the delicious ferocity of the way they'd been with each other.

She chides herself for her teenage excitement, suspecting that when the endless workday is over, she'll likely be rewarded with a long lecture about how it can never happen again. Jules feels a rush of disappointment, wanting only to be with him again. Well, at least she hadn't embarrassed herself by blurting out confessions of 'feelings.' If nothing else, she'll be spared that little humiliation. Ramon drones on and on, she returns her focus when she hears her name. "As previously discussed, Petersen will be at Bird's table, however she is not point security on this detail. Her primary function is social accessory to the principal, as per his request. Gi and I will be stationed approximately three yards from the table."

As Ramon dismisses them, his gaze flicks to her, but his face is indecipherable.

The day grinds on through breakfast, meetings, luncheon, cocktails and another endless dinner with Aguilero breathing on her. Countless costume changes, as she thinks of them, dresses, shoes, bags.

Her head aches from thinking in two languages. Her neck and shoulders are stiff from holding perfect posture all day. Even her face hurts from the strain of smiling.

Finally off duty at nearly 0100, she sees Xavier in the hallway. She hazards the question, "Have you seen Lieutenant?"

"I think he's in the sit room with Gi, they're changing the route for the trip to the coast tomorrow. Got word that a part of the road crumbled."

"Okay, thanks."

"Night Jules."

She heads to her room. She pictures Gi and Ramon with their heads together, bent over a map. They'll be there for hours, checking and re-checking the new route. She thinks of stopping in, but to say what? 'Hey, when you're finished come by?' She feels foolish. She hadn't had more than a glimpse of Ramon all day, he'd barely looked in her direction. She suddenly feels as though she'd imagined the whole thing, a girl building a whole fantasy relationship around a boy's smile.

Jules showers, bending her head and letting the hot water pound the tension out of her neck. She stays in until she runs out of hot water. She quickly dries her hair, towels off and slips into the cool, clean sheets. Sleep comes like a sledgehammer.

Hours or minutes later, she is awakened by a warm, heavy hand on her naked shoulder. She starts, unsure of who or what is in the room with her. In the dimness, she sees that it is Ramon and breathes a sigh of relief. "How did you get in here?"

"I have a master key."

"Nice. You scared me."

"Sorry. I didn't get a chance to talk to you today."

Here it comes. The lecture.

That thought is interrupted by his kiss, he tastes of sweet tobacco. It takes only a moment for her to catch up, kissing him back with the full intensity of suppressed emotion from the long day. Her hands slide inside his shirt, seeking release in the feel of his skin, the curve of muscle. He sighs deeply, pulling away with reluctance.

"Jules, I can't stay, I have to be up in two hours, I've gotta get some sleep tonight."

"Two hours, what time is it?"

"0320."

"Damn. Stay. Sleep next to me."

He laughs, "You know if I'm next to you we're not gonna be sleeping." He kisses her again and slides a hand over the racing curve of her hip, coming home to rest between her thighs. His hand moves over and into her, causing Jules to breathe in sharply. She tucks her head against his shoulder, submitting like a cat being stroked in its favorite spot.

"I *can* stay long enough to make you come," he whispers.

Once again she is speechless as he increases his speed and friction. She bites him through the perfect white linen of his shirt, struggling to hold back. She is trying to make the moment last, but his skill and her need take over and she is crashing.

He is smiling, exultant that he could bring her there so easily. Already, her body feels familiar.

Jules is breathing hard, trying to catch her breath. "What about you?" she says hopefully.

"Don't you worry, I'll take it out of your hide later. Sleep. That's an order."

She lays back and he kisses her once more for good measure.

"Thank you, Lieutenant."

He grins, "I'll see you in line."

"Yes you will."

Williamson's business with Aguilero goes well, apparently the numbers and terms appeal to both parties and they conclude the deal with a tenuous trust established. The crew hustles Bird back to the airport and they depart for home.

Jules keeps her mouth shut and her eyes on the landscape, aware that despite her transgressions with Ramon, nothing must pull focus from their principal. Ramon spends the entire flight in discussion with Williamson, seemingly engrossed. She wishes he would at least glance her way, so she'll know how to proceed. She wonders if this was just an isolated moment or if he wants to be with her again. The flight seems to take forever and she is grateful when they touch down at Teterboro.

The Mercedes is planeside, Gi and Ramon disembark, survey the tarmac and the activity around the plane before Williamson is allowed to exit. Xavier takes the ramp ahead of Bird and Nate is behind, followed by Jules and the others.

Williamson is driven to the residence by Gi and Ramon. The rest of the crew return to RSW to check in and hand off to the second detail. Grateful to be home, they scatter as soon as possible. Jules knows she has no hope of seeing Ramon before she leaves. Unlocking her front door, she feels exhausted and utterly alone. The house seems emptier than when she left four days ago.

21

Days pass with no contact from Ramon. Jules sees glimpses of him in briefings, but for the most part they are working opposite shifts. Each night she hopes for a call, but the phone remains silent, save for calls from Nate and Lily. Jules instinctively understands that it is not her place to reach out to him. Whatever comes next, even if it's nothing, will have to be his call. She steels herself for either outcome, chiding herself for her impulsivity in Puerto Rico. She returns to her usual routine, working and teaching her Krav classes at the dojo.

On a Wednesday night, Ramon, who has memorized Jules' schedule, sits in his Escalade in the parking lot of her dojo. The studio is brightly lit and flanked by a wall of windows, so he can see her inside, wrapping up the last class of the night. Upon his return from San Juan, he'd resolved to keep a certain distance from Jules and resume their working relationship. After three days of obsessive fantasizing, he'd given in and driven the forty minutes to the dojo. He swats away the intrusive thoughts about how completely inappropriate his actions are, watching her like a stalker.

The class looks to be made up mostly of men and a couple of young women. As the students disperse, he sees Jules putting away equipment, cleaning up and turning off lights. Finally she gathers her gear and steps out the front door, locking up. Ramon watches as one of the male students, who's been lingering outside, approaches her to talk. Ramon can see by his body language that he's hitting on her. Jules stands at a distance from him, nodding and smiling, but making it clear that she's uninterested. Finally she starts to turn away, giving him a dismissive little wave. She heads to her truck, scanning the parking lot like a good agent. Ramon smiles as she spots his vehicle and hesitates, peering at the plates to make sure it's really him.

She can't hide her pleasure at his sudden appearance. She grins as she approaches his door.

He leans out the open window. "In the mood for company?"

She hesitates, not wanting to let him off the hook so easily. "Yeah, about three days ago. What took you so long?"

"I thought if I willed myself to stay away from you for a few days, I might come to my senses, but you can see how that worked out."

She smiles a little, "Follow me home?"

"Right now I'd follow you anywhere."

After a few intoxicating months together, Jules and Ramon find themselves in a routine which maximizes the small amounts of time they can carve out. Any initial hesitation about violating the ethical code which forbids romantic relationships between bosses and underlings had been quickly superseded by their need for each other.

Jules is in the bathroom at her house, washing her face and brushing her teeth. Ramon is waiting in the bedroom. Tonight she feels a rare, leisurely pleasure in her bedtime routine. He is spending the night and they are both off tomorrow. They'll dig in, sleep late and do whatever they want.

"Jules!" he is yelling from the bedroom. "What are you doing?"

She shuts the water off and sticks her head out into the hallway. "I'm washing my face."

"You're taking too long."

She snorts, "You're not in charge *here* lieutenant." She pats her face dry and applies a night cream that promises miracles.

"The hell I'm not," he growls.

She can hear his footsteps coming down the hall. Jules stands, hands on hips, waiting.

He enters the bathroom and picks her up, slinging her over his shoulder in a fireman's carry. "I'm tired of waiting."

She laughs, he carries her as though she's a duffel bag. She is amused by his machismo. No man she's ever been with could carry off a move like this, but it works for Ramon. It even turns her on a little.

He deposits her onto the bed and pins her down with his body. "Now, what were you saying about who's in charge?"

She looks at him fondly, this handsome man, and decides he needs to be taken down a peg or two. "You're not the boss of me," she says teasingly.

He leans on one elbow, studying her. "Okay. Prove it."

Jules complies, pushing him over onto his back. Her smile fades as she becomes intent on her task. With excruciating slowness, she begins at the side of his neck, kissing with a fluttering softness. Occasionally she uses her tongue on parts that she knows are sensitive. She doesn't kiss him on the mouth, but by the time she's to his collarbone, he's breathing heavily and shifting around. His hands come up, but Jules pushes them gently away. She spends some time working her way from his nipples to his rib cage, using teeth and tongue. His hip comes next, then both knees and the tops of his feet.

She glances up at him; his eyes are closed, face flushed. She smiles to herself and pushes his knees apart, working her way to the inner thighs. She lingers there until he is calling her name. She still has not touched him with her hands.

"Jules, okay. You win."

"Shhh. Don't be pushy."

She moves back up to his stomach and unclenches his hand from where it is gripping the sheet. She takes his hand in both of hers, kissing each scarred knuckle like a treasure. Closing her eyes, she takes his thumb into her mouth, letting its wet warmth enfold it. She moves his thumb slowly in and out, her lips soft on his rough skin. Ramon is groaning. Jules opens her eyes. His gaze is locked onto her.

"You're killing me," he says.

"What's that?"

"Jules, seriously, I can't hold out much longer."

"You forgot to say please," she replies absently, kissing the palm of his hand.

"God, okay. Please. Please Jules."

She sits back on her heels grinning. She's pretty sure she's made her point. "With pleasure." Jules gets down to business.

Afterward, as she sleeps, Ramon turns on his side to watch her. She's made him curious. *Why doesn't he know anything about her? This amazing, powerful creature. Where was she before the husband? Did she have other lovers, who and when and where?* It has never occurred to him to ask these questions of any of the women he's been with, because he hadn't cared about the answers. But Jules doesn't fit into any of the categories of women he's been accustomed to: needy girls, easy girls, older women. Jules is so specifically her own person, he feels a need to know what formed her.

She stirs as if she can feel his thoughts. Jules opens her eyes and turns to him. "What? Why are you awake?"

"Just thinking."

"About what?" Her voice is gravelly with sleep.

"Why don't I know anything about you?"

She sighs in exasperation. "Oh, like you didn't get every detail during the six-month background check?"

He frowns at her. "Not that stuff. Before Chris, before you met him."

She looks away, slightly annoyed. "What? Like men?" She hesitates. "He wasn't my first, if that's what you're looking for."

"Jules," he says patiently, "I'm just trying to get to know you."

She studies his face in the dim light from the window. *Why don't they know more about each other? Because they've only been together a few hours at a time, most of which is devoted to decidedly non-verbal activity.*

"I had a high school boyfriend. Dated a few guys in college before Chris."

"I need more information than that."

"Like what? Names, ages, rank?"

"Yes. Please."

She rolls her eyes. "My high school boyfriend was John, an Irish boy, cute, into baseball. Puppy love. I lost my virginity to him when I was seventeen. We lasted until graduation. He was going to school on the west coast."

She pauses, thinking. "Dated um, two, no three, guys in college. One younger guy, a short and sweet relationship, I got bored. One guy, my age, dated maybe six or eight months, Justin. Pre-med, a little arrogant." Now she hesitates, thinking of how to edit the next fact.

"Then, junior year, there was an older guy, early thirties, he was a very successful local contractor. Jack." She stops, not knowing what else to say.

Ramon is listening intently, trying to piece this new information into the puzzle that is Jules.

"Jack was… he was very experienced. I was in over my head. I fell hard for him, only I was too young and too stupid to look before I leapt. He had a couple of other women, which I didn't find out until later. So, I got hurt. Bad. And then I wised up a little." She flinches a bit, Jules doesn't like to think about him, the utter humiliation and the way she'd lost faith in her own judgment. "The next year I met Chris, he was at a neighboring school. We met at a party."

"And?" he prompts.

She hesitates, looking up, trying to recall memories she'd boxed up and put away. "And Chris was a good man. Smart, handsome and decent. And he thought… he thought I was the answer to every prayer and every dream he'd had since he was twelve years old. And that took me exactly where I wanted to go. I got lucky."

Ramon is silent, considering. "And you two, you stayed in love."

"Yes, we really did." She feels suddenly exhausted by the weight of memory. "I'm going back to sleep." She rolls over.

Later that morning as they are having coffee, he thinks about what she'd told him. He had asked, of course, but now he feels the sting of jealousy. Especially about this Jack, who'd broken her heart. He doesn't like it. Where is this guy now? Does she still hear from him? It occurs to Ramon that he knows very little about her private time, other than the fact that she teaches her Krav classes and sees her brother and nephew once in a while. Anyone could be calling her, taking her out. Would he even know?

Finally he thinks of the one question he'd neglected to ask. *Damn, drop it Ramon, she's already annoyed.* He can't, he has to know.

"Jules."

"Mmm?" She isn't good before her second cup of coffee.

"Remember what we were talking about last night?"

"Yeah," she says warily.

"What about after Chris?"

"What do you mean?" Her voice has an edge.

"After Chris died. Before me. Was there someone then?" He can't help himself.

Jules squints at him, obviously aggravated. "Since when did you become this great communicator, Ramon? And what about you? When do I get my Q and A?"

She's right of course. "It might be a long session Jules. I'm twelve years older than you and I've been single most of my adult life, remember? Why can't you just answer the question?"

She takes a swig of the coffee, a shot of courage. She looks him in the face. "It was nothing. One guy. Maybe eighteen, nineteen months after Chris died. I just wanted…I don't know. Something. Not to be alone all the time. He was a cool guy, but then he started to get serious, started to talk about being in love. I wasn't even ready to think about that, let alone feel it. So I broke it off. Looking back, I wasn't very graceful about it. I hurt him. But like I said, he was a decent guy, I still talk to him once in a while. Just friends. Okay? Are you done now?"

"Yeah, I'm done." He searches her face. *Can he trust her?* She could be dating ten guys. How would he know? Ramon pushes the thought away. That is not Jules. She is not a player. "I just needed to know."

A few weeks later, Jules and Ramon are on their way back from the airport in an empty vehicle. Jules is off-shift in half an hour. Ramon checks his watch, "I need to make a stop, do you mind?"

Jules shrugs, "Where are we going?"

"Just a detour, it won't be long. You can come in with me if you want."

"Come in where?" They are pulling into a condominium complex.

"I just need to check on my *abuela*. You want to meet her?"

Jules is stunned. For all of Ramon's casual bluster, she knows how insanely protective he is of his grandmother. The fact that he would bring Jules to meet her is of no small significance.

"Yes, I'd love to. Do I look okay? You should have told me, I look like a Denny's waitress, Ramon." She is wearing black pants and a plain white shirt. Jules frowns into the car mirror, smoothing her bangs.

He laughs tersely, "Jules, you look great, and she has really bad eyesight anyway."

"Yeah, thanks, asshole." She punches him on the arm like a grade-school boy.

"I'm just kidding. Really it's fine. Let's go."

Ramon leads the way to an end unit, its window-box decorated with vivid plastic flowers. He uses his key, knocking twice to let Rosarita know it's him. Jules stands straight, nervously adjusting her clothes.

"Rosarita? *Es Ramon. ¿Tengo una amiga conmigo vale?*" They step in and Jules is enveloped by the specific scents of the home: burnt coffee, Lysol and fried onions. The apartment is overheated and busy with ornate crosses, dusty dried flower arrangements and stacks of magazines. The combination makes Jules nostalgic for her own grandmother, whom she barely remembers.

"Ramon! Why you not call and tell me to expect company? I'm a mess here," Rosarita yells plaintively.

"*Esta bien, abuelita*. It's only Jules, from work."

"Ramon! How you expect me to look nice for your friend? *Estoy muy enfada contigo!*" Ramon smiles and stage whispers, "She's mad at me."

Jules steps up to the chair where Rosarita is fluffing and smoothing her hair. "*Hola Señora, mi nombre es Julianna. Mucho gusto.*" Rosarita takes both of Jules' hands in hers, her sharp brown eyes sliding mischievously to Ramon.

"Ah, Ramon, your work friend, eh? I know this girl, she is the one that's been making you so smiling lately. Come Julianna, you sit with me. Ramon, *hacer café*."

Jules suppresses a giggle, she loves the idea of Ramon being yelled at and told to make the coffee.

Jules asks in Spanish how Rosarita has been, but Rosarita insists, "*In Inglés, por favor*, so I can practice."

"Oh yes, of course. Have you lived here long? Do you miss Puerto Rico?"

"Oh a long time, since Ramon work for that rich man. I miss the food mostly, but I have all my things here, even the Spanish TV, so I don't mind. My home is where Ramon is. He's my only heart, you know."

Jules melts inside. *Yes, I know.*

"So tell me. You work for that man, too? Ramon, what's his name, that rich man?"

"Williamson."

"Yes," replies Jules. "Only for a little while, since last winter."

"Yes, I remember. Oh, Ramon was so mad with you. I told him, didn't I Ramon? A good woman can do anything a man can do. He did not believe me, but now look, how happy. Do you have children?"

"No, no children. I'm a widow." She hates that word, it feels ugly in her mouth.

"Still you're young, plenty of time for babies. You're so pretty! Isn't she beautiful Ramon, such eyes!"

Ramon's head appears in the kitchen doorway, grinning lopsidedly at Jules, "*Sí, es muy guapa.*"

Rosarita leans forward conspiratorially, "He never has brought a girl here for me. That's how I know."

Jules waits for more, smiling self-consciously. When Rosarita keeps nodding knowingly, Jules is compelled to ask. "What do you know, *Señora?*"

Rosarita glances back at the kitchen. "That he is finally in love."

Jules blushes to the roots of her hair. "Did he say that?" she whispers.

Rosarita throws back her head and laughs. "A man in love will never say to anyone, that's how I know. It's what he does, that's what you need to see. And I see him, smiling and bringing you here." She nods again.

Jules feels a giddy flutter in her stomach. *Who knows Ramon better than his abuela?* At that moment, Ramon enters, balancing a tray holding a coffee pot, sugar and cream and three mugs, a domestic scene Jules could never have imagined. *Damn, you never know what a day will bring, do you?*

22

Jules gets a call from Ramon on a Thursday night, after returning from her class.

"Hey it's me. Listen; there's been some scheduling changes. I need you to pack a bag for four days and meet me at the airport tomorrow at 0600."

She hesitates. As far as she knows, there are no trips scheduled for Williamson and Ramon is supposed to have the next three days off. Jules had been looking forward to stealing a couple of late dinners with him after she got off her shifts. "Okay, but what's going on?"

"I have a surprise for you." There is a boyish excitement in his voice.

"What? Ramon, I'm working tomorrow."

"No you're not. You have a family emergency. You'll be away for a few days."

"You're arranging this? At least tell me where we're going."

"Just trust me. Pack for a casual weekend away."

"Hot or cold?"

"Warm in the daytime, cold at night."

"Swimsuit?"

"That's up to you. We might swim, but the suit is optional."

"You're out of your mind. Someone's going to figure it out."

"Who? Williamson? He's in his own world, plus Gi will be on top of whatever happens at RSW. The crew only knows what I tell them to know."

"Okay... I'm game if you are."

"I'll see you in the morning. Don't be late."

"How could I be late for a mystery trip with you? I'm not going to be able to sleep now."

"You can sleep on the plane," he sounds happy, a rare state for Ramon.

Jules packs everything: swimsuit, sweaters, camisoles, jeans, hiking boots, sandals, even a skimpy dinner dress, just in case. Her duffel is so heavy, she can barely lift it. She is stunned by Ramon's spontaneity. For someone who doesn't go out for cigarettes without a plan, he seems pretty cavalier. This new side of him thrills her, makes her feel as though they're in an actual relationship, not just having a secret affair.

She arrives at the airport early and he's there on the tarmac waiting, talking with a pilot. When he sees her, he walks over and grabs her bag from her, kissing her on the mouth. The pilot smiles. Ramon walks her over to the charter plane, a DC-10, and introduces her to the pilot. "Jules this is Manny. He'll be flying us."

Jules, fizzing with excitement, grins at Manny, taking his hand.

"Well Jules, hell must have frozen over today. I've flown this guy lots of times, but this is the first time I've ever seen him take a woman along. You must really be something special."

Jules looks at Ramon, he ducks his head and is suddenly busy stowing her gear in the plane. She smiles, "Don't make him nervous Manny, he might change his mind."

He laughs and winks at Jules, "Right. Well let's get moving then, before he does."

Ramon helps her climb in and get her seatbelt adjusted. He takes the co-pilot spot next to Manny. "All right Jules, just relax, we're driving."

She opens her mouth to protest being left alone in the back, but now they have their headphones on, talking with the tower and fiddling with controls, so she gives up and watches out the window until she falls asleep.

She is woken by Ramon's voice. "Babe, wake up, we're coming in. I want you to see the view."

She straightens up and leans to look out the window. They are over a rocky coastline of black rocks and evergreen forest, the cobalt sea dotted with rocky islands and expensive-looking boats. She looks at her watch and estimates the travel time and mileage. "Oh my God, Ramon, what is this, Maine?"

He swivels in his seat, black eyes sparkling. "Good guess. What do you think? Do you like lobster?"

Her eyes lock with his. She is speechless with happiness. It is a feeling she barely recognizes, it's been so long since she felt it. *He did this for me.*

The plane makes a lazy turn inland and lands at the Bar Harbor airport. They say goodbye to Manny and Ramon leads her to a black Jeep in the parking lot. Twenty minutes of breathtaking scenery later, they travel down a shoreline road and pull into a boatyard. Next to the yard, a two-story gray clapboard sits directly over the water. The front of the house is decking and wall-to-wall windows, looking out onto Southwest Harbor.

Ramon gets out of the Jeep, greeted by a gruff-looking man, midfifties, with stunning blue eyes and a weathered face. The man grips Ramon's hand and claps him on the back. "Son of a bitch. It's about time you got your lazy ass back up here. Thought you died or something." Suddenly he spots Jules coming out of the Jeep, hair thrown up in a wild ponytail, green eyes wide with disbelief.

"Well, what do we have here?" He looks back at Ramon. "You got a daughter I don't know about? 'Cause I know you'd never show up at your hideout with an actual woman."

Ramon clears his throat, "I'm making an exception, just this once. This is Jules."

"Nice to meet you." She feels suddenly shy and a little breathless.

"Hi Jules, Mac. Great to meet *you*. All this time we were thinkin' Ramon was anti-social. Guess you just proved us wrong. Me and this guy go all the way back to SEALs together. He's a mean son of a bitch, but I like him anyway."

He tosses a set of keys to Ramon, "Spare set, in case you forgot yours."

"Thanks, Mac. I'll buy you a beer later." He shepherds Jules to the front door.

"Have fun," Mac calls after them.

They step inside the cool, spacious interior. Ramon shuts the door with an elbow. Jules takes in the room, glass on three sides, a fireplace and clean, well-worn furniture. Then she notices the floor-to-ceiling bookcase and a plaque with a Navy insignia. "Is this place yours?" She is incredulous.

Ramon looks nervous as a bridegroom. "Yeah, it's mine. Bought it with my ten-year bonus, cheap; after some stockbroker lost his wad during the nineties. I fixed it up a little at a time. I come here whenever I can get away. Only no one knows about it, Jules, not Williamson, not even Gi."

She feels tears come up and blinks them back. "And you brought me? Why?"

"I wanted you to see it."

She puts her arms around his neck. "It's incredible. I never saw anything more beautiful."

He holds her for a long time, then pulls back, clearing his throat. "I got tired of sneaking around, I wanted to be able to be with you and actually relax, even if it's just for a couple of days."

She smiles, pleasure radiating from her smile all the way to her eyes. "Thank you *mijo*. Thank you for trusting me with this."

"You're welcome. C'mon, I'll show you the rest."

The upstairs has a master bedroom with an attached bath and a spectacular view of the harbor. There is also a small guest room and another bath in the hall as well as a den under the eaves, filled with books and a computer, printer and fax. 'Mission control,' as he refers to it, so he can be aware of everything that's happening at RSW, even when he's hundreds of miles away.

The main bedroom is almost completely taken up with a king-sized platform bed. There is a chaise in the corner for reading or watching the sun rise over the water. Jules stands at the window, mesmerized by the view: glassy deep blue water broken up by sleek, moored yachts and huge speedboats with names like 'Miss Mandy' and 'Mid-Life Crisis.'

Ramon comes up behind her and locks an arm around her waist. "Like the view?"

"It doesn't even look real, it's so perfect, like you taped a giant postcard over the window."

He laughs. "I did. I didn't want you to be put off by the trailer park and the power plant. If your skin starts glowing green, just disregard it, it'll go away once you're back in Jersey."

"This is so unbelievable. I could just stand here and watch the light change over the water for the next three days."

"That's nice Jules, but how 'bout we make the bed first? We've got to keep track of our priorities."

She likes the way he says 'our priorities.' "Point me to the linen closet; I've got plans for you."

Ramon helps her find sheets, blankets and pillows and heads downstairs to retrieve their bags. Jules makes the bed with care, savoring the clean, soft feel of the worn white sheets and heavy wool trading blankets. Everything smells of cedar from the linen closet and the scent fills Jules with a giddy sense of joy and anticipation for the weekend ahead.

"Jesus, Jules, what's in this bag? I feel like I'm lifting weights here." Ramon fakes a scowl.

"Don't you worry; I have little bit of everything in there. If you're not strong enough, I can give you a hand," she parries.

He drops the bags on the floor and tackles her onto the bed. "You need a demonstration of my strength?" He pins her down.

"Yes please," she replies sweetly.

Ramon wakes a few hours later, momentarily confused as to where he is. Then he sees the stripe of the blanket and Jules' bare shoulder and puts it together. The sun is low on the water and through the open window he can hear the gulls clamoring. He lies back and studies her, curled in a nest of sheets and blankets. He hopes he has made the right call, bringing her here. Her reaction to the place was what he had wished, pure childish delight. He's rolled the dice, trusting that Jules is mature enough to know that a weekend does not mean he's promising her a future together.

Ramon savors the quiet of the house and the decadence of being completely alone with her. He leans into her, smelling her personal perfume, that lemony floral that seems to be a perpetual part of her. This afternoon it's mixed with the crisp cedar aroma of the linens. Ramon inhales, knowing that if he were to smell the same scent thirty years from now, it would take him back to this exact moment.

Jules stirs a little at his touch, turning over to face him. "Mmm. We should bottle this scent," she says, as if reading his mind. "We could make millions."

He kisses her for a long time. "Jules?"

"Hmm?"

"I'm starving. We've got to go eat."

"Damn. I thought you were going to say something romantic."

"Margaritas and *molé* sauce."

"That does it for me. Let me take a shower."

"I'll join you. That way we can get there faster."

"Yeah, I know it's time you're worried about, not being wet and naked with me."

"Don't forget about water conservation."

In half an hour, they are in the car, Jules in an indigo cotton halter dress and strappy sandals, Ramon in dark jeans and a crisp white shirt, open at the neck. His hair is still wet from the shower and he is unshaven, so darkly handsome she can barely stop looking at him.

She takes a deep breath and looks out the window. *Easy there girl, it's three days, don't lose your mind.*

They arrive at a tiny Mexican restaurant, tucked away on a dirt road. If you didn't know it was there, you could have mistaken it for a little ranch house, the porch strung with colored lights. Inside, the tiny place is warm and fragrant with the smell of tortillas and cilantro. The café is dimly lit and each table holds a tall bud vase with a single bloom of the native lupine flower, a purple the color of amethyst.

The hostess is a gorgeous, fifty-something woman with long salt-and-pepper hair and a cascade of silver bracelets on each wrist. When she spies Ramon her hand flies to her breast, "*Dios mío*, Ramon! Where have you been? I have a bottle of tequila I've been saving for you. I was going to drink it myself on my birthday, 'cause I thought you forgot us!"

She spies Jules holding his hand. The hostess looks to Ramon and back at Jules incredulously. "¿*Su esposa*? No, no, *estoy devastado*!" She grasps Julianna's free hand dramatically. "Say it's not true, he didn't marry you, did he? My heart is broken."

Ramon finally speaks up. "Stop scaring her, Michaela." He turns to Jules, giving her hand a squeeze.

"Jules, this is Michaela. She's an actress, in case you didn't pick up on it. Michaela, this is Jules and she's not my wife."

Jules smiles tentatively, unsure of what her role is. 'Not my wife' could mean anything, sister, niece, girlfriend, latest piece of ass. She feels a tremor in her stomach wondering if the beautiful and flamboyant Michaela is just acting or if she and Ramon actually *do* have some kind of history.

She puts out her hand anyway, remembering her manners. "*Mucho gusto*, Michaela."

Michaela gives Jules a motherly pat. "No worries, my beautiful girl, all the women up here have designs on Ramon. It's the long winters, you know, got to keep warm somehow. We keep trying, but he's the elusive type, I'm sure you've noticed," she whispers conspiratorially.

"Actually Ramon and I spend a lot of time together. There's days I can't wait to get rid of him," says Jules wickedly, winking at him.

He nods his head at Jules. "It's true," he says, playing along. "I watch her like a hawk. It drives her crazy."

Michaela arches an elegant eyebrow. "Hmmm, you must tell me your secret, Jules."

She tries to restrain herself, but this woman's proprietary attitude and Jules's own low blood sugar have made her impulsive. She leans in and whispers in Michaela's ear.

Michaela lets out a shriek of laughter and clutches Julianna's shoulder with her long silver nails, "Well then! We better get you both fed. Let me show you to your table." She puts them at a cozy corner table, lit only by a tiny oil lamp. She hands them both menus and retreats, still laughing.

Jules studies the menu intently, avoiding Ramon's laser-like gaze. Behind the menu, she can't stop smiling. She thinks she may lose it completely if Michaela comes back.

He tips down the top of her menu with a finger. "What did you say?" He has his intimidating face on, but for once, Jules holds the cards and is thoroughly enjoying the feeling. Her eyes sparkle.

"What do you mean? We were just making girl talk. You two are obviously close right?"

"Tell me or I'm going to dump you in the harbor after dinner. The water's nice and cold, especially this time of day."

"Well that sounds refreshing. I always enjoy a swim after traveling all day."

He leans in and growls at her unconvincingly, smiling at her audacity.

Jules leans in, pausing for dramatic effect. She looks around to make sure they have their privacy and whispers, "I told her you like it rough."

Ramon leans back in his chair, letting out a deep, genuine belly laugh, the likes of which she's never heard from him. She is elated to see him so relaxed.

Their waitress, a tall blonde, comes over smiling, "You two have to let me in on the joke!"

Ramon has tears coming from the corner of his eyes and doesn't seem capable of speaking at the moment, so Jules translates for him. "Oh, sorry, he has these little episodes every once in a while. It's just his way of relieving stress. Can you bring us two *Especial* margaritas with salt and some salsa and chips? That usually helps settle him down."

Ramon is now doubled over, gasping for air. "Jules, quit it. I can't breathe."

She rubs his shoulder. "It's okay honey, I can always go get your medicine if you need it." She says this loudly enough for the server and the next couple of tables to hear.

It takes Ramon a few minutes to recover himself, just in time for the waitress to arrive with their drinks. "Here you go," she says to Ramon in a soothing voice, looking sympathetically at Jules. And Michaela sent these on the house," she says, setting down two tequila and lime shots. "My name is Lila and I'll give you a few minutes with the menu, okay?"

Ramon chokes out a thank you.

Jules raises her glass and touches the rim to his, "*Salud.*"

"*Salud y estás muerto.*" Cheers and you're dead.

Jules smiles wickedly, "I'm starving, what's good here, babe?"

They order a ton of food: chicken *molé*, roasted corn and avocado salad, crab tamales and cheese enchiladas with *salsa verde*. After the margaritas and the tequila, they order Mexican beer with lime wedges stuffed into the necks of the bottles. They eat ravenously at first, then leisurely, savoring the excellent food and each other's undivided attention.

"So I want you to tell me the story of how a Puerto Rican boy gets all the way to Maine," Jules says. She feels as though they have all the time in the world tonight and is hungry to know everything.

"That would be a very long story," he demurs, reverting to his usual mode of secrecy.

"I've got all night. Spill."

He regards her carefully and begins, telling the tale in his minimalist way, though with each subsequent beer, he seems to relax into it. He speaks of the first hard years in Miami, struggling to learn English and working endless hours in the heat. Then his induction into the Navy and its rigorous culture, which seemed to be just the kind of structure he needed at the time. He tells Jules that his decision to try out for the SEALs was based on an insult from a crew member who'd stated that Ramon 'didn't have the *cojones* to make it past day one.'

His face glows with nostalgia as he describes Basic Underwater Demolition/SEAL training: the intense mental pressure, the physical assault of the cold sea water and wet sand, the degradation by the instructors, all meant to forge them into an unbreakable unit. Jules listens, thinking of how Ramon had translated his own experiences into the training he'd given her. She remembers her silent vows not to allow him to break her. Now look at them.

Ramon reveals that after graduating from BUD/S in Coronado, California and jump school in San Diego, he'd been so cocky and elated that he'd proposed to a local girl he'd been dating for only three months. Lisa was her name, a WASP with long legs and good diction. She'd jumped at the chance to marry a military man, hoping to travel. He confesses that he had believed he could somehow become more 'American' by marrying a beautiful Californian.

Sadly, they'd both miscalculated.

Ramon was immediately put into rotation overseas and Lisa was trapped in base housing with a bunch of pregnant military wives. Only twenty-one, she had no intention of having children yet and tried to pursue an intellectual path until realizing that money was tight and she needed to get a job. She worked at a dress store, catering to matronly officers' wives, growing more despondent each day.

Ramon's grueling schedule kept him away for months at a time and though he wrote and called when allowed, within the year he knew the marriage was in trouble. After fifteen months, he received special permission for a three-day leave to come home for Lisa's birthday. He stopped at the base commissary and bought wine and flowers, wanting to make up for his inability to give her the attention she needed.

Exiting his cab, he was met at the foot of the driveway by his neighbor, a sergeant he barely knew. The sergeant seemed nervous, shaking Ramon's hand and offering to buy him a drink 'over at my place.' Ramon explained that he was anxious to see his wife and when the sergeant winced slightly at that, he suddenly understood why the man was detaining him.

"The thing is, son," he'd said gently. "She's not alone. Hasn't been alone for weeks now. Same guy every afternoon, not military. Tried to get the wife to talk some sense into her, but it's hard on the young ones 'til they get used to how things are. Why don't we go to the club and have that beer and you can call her, let her know you're on your way."

Ramon had stopped hearing him. Suffused with a killing rage, he'd dropped his packages, leaving red wine bleeding into trampled roses. The front door was unlocked and while the sergeant called the base MPs, Ramon was busy peeling a twenty-six-year-old electrician off his wife. Lisa was scared, but screaming, calling Ramon the basest names she could think of, telling him that she needed a man, not a toy soldier who was only going to come around every six months.

Ramon was not listening, he was busy pummeling the electrician into the bedroom carpet, removing teeth and skin in an efficient way. By the time the four MP's arrived, the electrician was curled into a fetal position, while Ramon broke ribs with every blow of his well-shined combat boots.

Ramon was taken to the brig, the electrician went to San Diego Trauma Center and Lisa was discreetly removed from the home and given taxi fare to her parents' home. An official inquiry deemed that the electrician had 'actively provoked a combat-weary soldier, resulting in unanticipated bodily injury.' The electrician was quietly compensated by the Navy for his medical bills and Ramon was suspended without pay for one month. He never saw Lisa again.

Her father came for her clothes and belongings, escorted by an MP. Her father asked to use the bathroom before he left and wrote '*spic loser*' on the bathroom mirror in Lisa's signature pink lipstick.

Ramon signed the divorce papers when they arrived, considering himself well-rid of her and making a silent vow to remain single for the rest of his adult life.

Jules is stunned, taking a swig of her beer while trying to think of what to say.

Ramon shrugs. "You wanted to know. It was more than twenty years ago, I'm over it."

Jules frowns, biting her lip. "Are you? I wouldn't be. God, I'd never trust anyone again."

"Just women, except my *abuela*, of course."

"What about your mom? Did you ever trust her?"

"My mother was a whore too."

Hearing him call his mother a whore shocks her. Jules looks at him intently, wondering what it costs him to talk of her so casually.

He frowns at her. "I know what you're doing. Don't try to psychoanalyze me. It is what it is."

"So your *abuela* hung the moon for you."

"And brought out the sun."

"Finish the story. You're not even to New Jersey yet."

They are minimally interrupted by Michaela, who asks if everything is to their liking, with only the barest hint of a smirk and Lila, who inquires as to whether they would care for dessert and coffee. Both pleasantly drunk by now, they look at one another and answer "Sure," in unison.

Ramon continues, talking of his subsequent tours of duty with the SEALs. Unencumbered by domestic distractions, he easily disappeared into a world of combat and covert missions. He was on a brief leave at home when Williamson called, asking for a meeting. Ramon explains how at first he thought it was a joke, perpetrated by some of his unit members, until he did some research and found out that Williamson was the real deal, using old money to build a new empire.

Williamson flew to California for the meeting. He invited Ramon to the best restaurant in the city and pitched his vision for an elite security squad over steak and thirty-year-old scotch. "I thought he was too soft, I didn't want anything to do with him," he says. "But then he started writing down numbers: for salaries, for the physical plant and fringes. I felt like I'd won the lottery. I was already starting to have physical repercussions from the combat and the training and I was only twenty-eight. I started picturing what I'd feel like after another decade of tours. So I lost a couple of nights sleep and figured it was as good a time as any to get out. When we negotiated the deal, I made him give me full autonomy over the detail. He didn't like it much, but he saw it was a sticking point and finally capitulated. I was in Jersey within the year, supervising the construction of the new RSW building to my specs."

"You were there when it was designed?"

"Who do you think designed it?"

Jules is impressed, more than ever, and better understands why he was so reluctant to let her onto the detail. She looks at him, lazily drinking his coffee and picking at his flan and suddenly wants to take him back to bed. He reads her look and smiles. "Maybe we should walk home and sober up, get the Jeep in the morning. Mac'll drive me over."

"Sounds like a plan. I'm definitely going to need you a little more sober."

"Right. 'Cause now I have my reputation to live up to. Michaela would be so disappointed if I just passed out on you."

"Screw Michaela. What about me? Now that you've been fed, you're going to have to work off some of that meal."

It's a chilly night, clouds skidding across a half moon. He retrieves a jacket from the Jeep and puts it on her. They walk the half-mile back to the house in silence, holding hands, happy for the tonic of the cold and the shivering anticipation of the night to come.

Once inside, she shucks the jacket and the sandals and he slides his hand inside the bodice of her dress. They make it to the couch and she unbuttons his jeans. Kissing him feels like drowning, in the best possible way. She cannot get enough of the smoky taste of him, of his lips. She runs her lips along the stubble on his jawline, biting him gently in her favorite spot just below the earlobe.

He inhales sharply, "Jesus, Jules. You make me fucking crazy." He unknots the tie on her dress, letting the whole thing fall to the floor. She kneels in front of him, unlacing his shoes subserviently. He kicks them off and pulls her up onto his lap, putting his mouth to her nipple, using his teeth on it gently until it's hard as a pebble. She holds onto the back of his neck, feeling as though if she lets go she'll fall. He wraps his arms around her waist and stands up, she instinctively hooks her legs around his waist.

"Upstairs. I need room to maneuver," he says.

"You're doing pretty well so far."

He slings her over his shoulder. "Yeah, but the condoms are in the bedroom."

She sighs, wanting it to be more romantic that that, but truthfully she appreciates his sense of responsibility, as well as the fact that he is strong enough to carry her up two flights of stairs.

In bed, he takes his time, licking her in a maddening, slow rhythm, bringing her right to the edge and then backing off. She tolerates this happily for a time and then grabs his face and brings him up to kiss her, tasting herself on him and begging him to come inside her. Tonight, whether it's the alcohol or the fact that he'd trusted her with his story, she is frantic for him. She cannot get him deep enough and finds herself biting him and digging her nails into him as she comes. He seems intent on taking full possession of her, driving into her even after she has started to relax, gasping out a staccato coda as he too, finally lets go.

Jules wakes, thick-headed and groggy, to an empty bed. She sits up and can see that it's light outside, but the fog is so dense she sees nothing of the view but an occasional gull. She can hear the back-up alarms and busy machinery of the boat yard, already in full swing.

She looks for a clock, it is 7:30 a.m. Beset by a damp chill coming through the open window, she rummages on the floor to find Ramon's shirt, discarded from last night. She pulls it on, buttoning it up. Forcing herself out of bed she runs to the bathroom, gasping at the cold tile on her bare feet. In her duffel she finds her old sheepskin boots and pulls them on. She grabs a wool trading blanket from the bed and wraps it around herself like a cape, venturing downstairs. As she descends, she is deeply grateful for the scent of Ramon's thick, smoky coffee, already made. She grabs a mug and finds him on in an Adirondack chair on the deck, wearing a flannel shirt, heavy sweater and jeans, a black watch cap on his head. He is staring out into the mist, thoroughly absorbed. Not wanting to startle him, Jules whispers, "Hey."

"Hey, you're up. Did you get coffee?"

She raises her full mug in salute, "Thanks, you're a saint. My head feels like a brick."

He looks at her with plain appreciation, a slight smile on his face. "No one would ever know, you look great."

Jules cannot get over this facet of him. After so many months of bracing herself for every confrontation with him, this romantic showing completely disarms her. She is being forced to re-evaluate her entire idea of him.

"What? You don't believe me? Go look in the mirror, you're glowing. I especially like your outfit."

She looks down at her preposterous ensemble and bursts out laughing. "Yeah I got it special for this weekend."

He gets up and pulls another chair close to his. "Sit. Enjoy the view."

"What view?"

"Don't worry, this burns off in about a half-hour and you'll see what I'm talking about."

They sit in companionable silence and his point is proven, the mist clearing minute by minute, revealing first the lines of the masts, then the boats, water, sky and finally the opposite coastline, black with spiky pines and wet-looking boulders.

She sighs, "I feel like I'm going to wake-up to the alarm clock in a minute. It doesn't seem possible that I'm here. With you, no less."

He reaches for her hand. "No alarm clocks here. House rule." After a long pause, he adds, "I feel good too."

It scares her, this new way of being together. It is too powerful and makes her want things she thought she'd given up wanting. Having someone. Someone to talk to, someone to tease. Even as it thrills her, it causes a deep ache inside her. *This will never be, Jules. Don't even let yourself think about it. Just be here, just enjoy the moment.*

Ramon finishes his coffee and stands up, stretching luxuriously. "Mac is going to take me to get the Jeep. When you finish your coffee, take a shower. We'll head into town and get some breakfast and some groceries, then I have a surprise."

She smiles like a child. "Really? What should I wear?"

He squints at her. "Girls, always with the clothes. I don't know, bring warm layers for the day and something you can change into for dinner. Improvise."

"Yes sir." As soon as he's gone she hustles upstairs with her coffee, knowing that no matter what, he'll be back before she's ready. She rummages through her clothes, perplexed. Why couldn't he just tell her what they're doing? She wants to look good for him, but doesn't want to appear as if she's trying too hard. After a quick shower and blow-dry she settles on jeans, hiking boots and a lace camisole topped by a thermal Henley. Into a leather backpack, she throws a fisherman's sweater and a flannel shirt. At the last minute, she adds a pair of sandals, her makeup bag, a hairbrush, a skimpy black tank dress, a bathing suit and a towel. She finishes with a pair of dangling silver earrings. *Never can tell with this one.*

She hears him stomping around downstairs and then he's poking his head into the bedroom. "You ready?" He leans into the closet and extracts a pristine black shirt on a hanger. *So much for his packing dilemma.* She grabs her sunglasses and tube of sunscreen and still feels as if she will be unprepared.

They head to town and grab a quick breakfast at a local café, where of course, everyone greets him like the prodigal son. After breakfast he takes her into an upscale market and instructs her to get 'picnic stuff for lunch' while he goes to the liquor store next door to get a bottle of wine and a six-pack of bottled water.

She gets bread, fruit, hard salami and soft cheese, adding a couple of bars of dark chocolate as an afterthought. He comes in with a paper bag just in time to pay the bill, adding a pack of cinnamon gum and his favorite cigars.

Ramon seems energized, smiling absently to himself. Jules is dazzled, unable to refrain from touching him. He doesn't seem to mind. As they slide into the vehicle, he stops and kisses her until she is breathless.

"All right let's get moving, we're burning daylight."

Jules looks around, expecting that they will go in a different direction, off on some adventure for the day. Instead they head directly back to the house. As he parks, Jules inquires, "Are we having a picnic at the house?"

"C'mon sweetheart, do you really think I'd get you all jazzed and then make you stay at the house? Just trust me. You get my shirt and your bag and I'll get the groceries."

She obeys his instructions and follows him into the noisy boatyard, down onto the main dock. Mac is working beside a gorgeous twenty-five-foot speedboat. He turns and grins at Jules. "Hope you got your sea legs, missy."

"Is this for us?" she asks incredulously. It is then that Jules notices the name emblazoned on the stern of the boat, 'Rosarita'. *God, it's his.* She turns to Ramon, he is smiling like a Cheshire cat. She punches him on the arm, hard.

"Ow. Save the affection for later, you don't want to embarrass Mac, he's delicate."

They load the boat and Mac casts off the lines for them. As Ramon takes the helm, Jules settles in on the padded bench beside him, Mac calls "Don't keep her out too late, it's a school night."

Heading out into the harbor, Jules is lifted by an excitement so strong it brings the sting of tears. She looks away to the horizon, sure that Ramon would not understand. The day is glorious, the sea and sun blinding. She watches, impressed, as Ramon effortlessly negotiates the channel markers and further out, a minefield of lobster buoys, each one marked with its owner's distinctive pattern of colors. As they exit the harbor into deeper water, Jules digs out her flannel shirt and puts it on. Now she understands the mysterious dress code.

She looks at Ramon shyly, feeling intimidated by his command of this new environment. She has, of course, been on boats before, but they were rowboats with outboards, nothing even close to the sleek power of this vessel. Ramon has changed the knitted watch cap for a dark blue baseball cap lettered 'NAVY,' his eyes hidden behind dark aviator glasses. It occurs to her that this is his true home, here on the water, not as she's seen him so many times before, prowling the corridors of RSW, driving its black vehicles and commanding the men.

Jules had always imagined that the tension in him was from the weight of his position, not the fact that he was a seaman at heart, of out his element on land.

Ramon looks over at Jules, her hair whipping around her face, huddling in an oversized flannel shirt. "You cold?" he shouts.

She shakes her head no, smiling.

Good, she's happy too. He'd hoped she wouldn't be the type to be seasick or freezing, though knowing Jules' fortitude it wasn't likely she'd give a voice to either one. He points out some sights to her, naming islands and harbors as they pass them. Once they are out quite far, he cuts the engine. The boat drifts easily, rocking with each swell. Ramon drops the boat's anchor, lights a cigar and digs two bottles of water from the cooler, passing one to her.

Jules moves forward and sprawls out on the triangular, padded bench set into the bow. Without the wind beating at her, the sun is baking, she strips off the flannel and the thermal, baring her shoulders to the delicious heat.

"That's more like it," he says. He joins her at the bow, pulling the strap of her camisole off one shoulder. She pulls off her boots and heavy socks, exposing bright pink toenails.

"Your turn,' she says, kissing him deeply. He takes off his sweater and strips down to a strap undershirt, leaning back against the teak bow railing. He reaches for her and pulls her back against him so they can enjoy the amazing view together.

She leans into him silently, afraid to touch the moment with words. A deep contentment wells up. He strokes her cheek with his thumb, she turns to him so he can kiss her again. He disposes of the cigar in a tin can.

"Look," he says, pointing to an outcropping of rock. She doesn't see what he is pointing at. "Right at the edge of the water, there."

What she thought were only black rocks suddenly reveal themselves to be seals, ten or so, basking in the sun, blending into the boulders perfectly with their gleaming, dark-gray hides.

"Oh my God!" she gasps. At her squeal of delight, the seals move as one, slipping like oil into the water. "Damn, I spooked them," she says, realizing that she's broken the spell.

"No you didn't. Just wait," he advises.

She does, holding her breath. After a minute or two, she hears a small splash portside. A sleek head and a pair of liquid eyes appear at the surface of the water. Seconds later, another pops up starboard and then another behind them.

"See, they're staking us out," he whispers. "Making sure we don't get the jump on them."

Jules presses her hands to her mouth to keep from voicing her enchantment. She feels that the moment has been called up just for them, a gift from the sea.

They watch in awe as two more seals form a perfect perimeter around the boat, bobbing placidly, yet never taking their eyes off the foreigners and establishing their turf in the most primal way.

Jules giggles softly. "They have a perfect five-man detail. I wonder which one's the lieutenant?"

Ramon points back to the rock shelf, where a fat, scarred male lingers on the rocks with the cubs and a few females. "That's him, lounging with the ladies."

She nudges him with her shoulder. "Figures, leaving the close work to the grunts."

"Damn straight, he's the old guy, he earned it." He turns and lays her back onto the bench, moving against her, sliding a hand under her hair. Their kissing becomes an art form. They have all the time in the world and both of them are savoring the taste and texture of each other.

Jules feels her thoughts begin to intrude, *What if? How long?* She forces them away. *Not now. Be here. Be with him.* Losing Chris had taught her that the future is a mirage.

She pushes him off, peels off the rest of her clothes and climbs on top of him, bared to the sun and breeze. She is vaguely aware that someone could happen by in another boat, but doesn't care. Let them look. She wants only this, only him.

Ramon needs no further encouragement than the sight of her naked in the sunlight. He pulls off the rest of his clothes and runs his calloused hands along her smooth skin. He breathes her in, burying his face in her neck, as he slides into her. They use the easy rocking of the boat to find their way.

She closes her eyes, wanting to feel everything and it is better than anything, she feels safe and warm and desired. Though her body is urgently fighting for its own release, she slows down, wanting to make it last.

Ramon is lost in her. Every time he touches Jules, lifts her up and back down onto him, he is on a knife edge of control. At this moment he would give up anything to be with this woman. His career, his reputation, none of it would matter if he could fall asleep with her at the end of each day. He struggles, correcting his breathing, slowing his pace, clearing his mind.

He opens his eyes and looks over her shoulder, seeing the deep shimmer of the sea, his real home. Being here with her is absolutely, essentially right. He finds a new rhythm, faster and more intense. He looks into her eyes again. Her gaze is fierce, a silent dare for him to fall in love with her. The challenge has come too late, he's already there.

Afterward, he stirs and begins getting dressed. Drowsy from the sun and the sex, Jules lazily pulls on her clothes, watching him pull the anchor and start the engine again.

He glances at her, "Okay?"

She nods, unable to speak. She cannot seem to get enough of watching him on the water. He moves effortlessly, with a grace born of a thousand repetitions of the same action. He is barefoot, in jeans and a flannel shirt, open to the waist. He pulls the baseball cap on again, low to block the strong sun. He looks to be exactly what he is, a man in control of everything around him, the waves, the boat and the woman aboard it.

As Jules pulls a shirt on, he tosses out a question. "Wanna go fast?"

She hesitates, knowing that Ramon's brand of fast may be more than she bargained for. Screw it, she can take it. "Bring it on," she says, pulling on a sweater.

"Grab that handhold, I don't want to lose you."

He eases the boat into its natural comfort zone, a speed which makes the bow pound the water as if it were concrete.

The vibration beneath her feels sexual, the wind whips her hair into her eyes and pushes her breath back into her chest. At one point she feels as if the boat will take flight and the thought makes her heart race. She turns to look back at him. He scans the horizon in a 180° arc, arm relaxed on the wheel. He has just the barest hint of a smile at the corner of his mouth. It makes her happy just to look at him. He catches her gaze and winks.

She wonders where they're going. At this pace, they could be in Nova Scotia for dinner.

He throttles the boat back and they come around a rocky peninsula. Seemingly out of nowhere, an imposing wall of sparkling granite cliff rises in front of them, forming a small cove. She feels the wind die immediately and the temperature seems to rise before he has even cut the engine. "Look like a good place for lunch?"

She laughs as he moves to drop the anchor. "It'll do. Do you think we need a reservation?"

"I called ahead."

As he works, she retrieves the groceries, spreading out their lunch and uncorking the wine with a Swiss Army knife from her backpack. He leans over the side of the boat dipping a rag into the seawater. He wipes his hands with it and joins her for their picnic.

She holds up the wine, "We forgot glasses."

"Don't be such a girl, drink it from the bottle."

Back to their usual banter, a place where she feels more comfortable. She takes a swig and passes it to him. She feels its warmth all the way down to her empty stomach. She is unexpectedly ravenous. She grins as she takes a huge bite out of the baguette and passes it to him. She squints, scanning the horizon. "How come there's no one else out here? You own this too?"

"Ha. Nobody owns the water, that's what makes it so great. You have to be an experienced sailor to get this far out. The pleasure boaters stay in near the harbors or by the national park."

"Lucky us."

He regards her thoughtfully. She senses he has something to say, but is afraid to ask. After a few minutes under his direct gaze, she can't take it anymore.

"Okay, what?"

"You're beautiful."

"Thanks, but wrong answer. What is it?"

He shrugs, looking out over the water. "This is new for me."

"What, having sex on a boat? Doubt it."

He laughs. "No, just… being involved."

She regards him solemnly. "You make it sound so ominous."

He smiles again. "No, just different. Dangerous."

Jules thinks about this. He is right, of course. Dangerous for both of them, personally and professionally. She takes another swig of the spicy red wine, grateful for the instant heat. "True. Take your pick; lose your job or get your heart broken. Great choices, no?" She had hoped he would smile but he looks more serious than she'd wished.

"You think I'm going to break your heart?" He asks softly.

"Maybe I'll break *your* heart," she says lightly. *Oh yeah, my heart is definitely fucked.*

"Maybe," he says, standing up, taking off his shirt. "Who knows," he is stripping off his jeans, standing in black boxer briefs, "maybe the planets will align and we'll live happily ever after." With that he steps up onto the running board and dives elegantly off the boat into the black water.

Jules chokes on her wine. She stands up, peering over the side. "Ramon! What the hell are you doing?" At first she sees nothing but a tiny circle of bubbles, then he is breaking the surface, emitting a war whoop.

"Goddamn, that is refreshing! Jules, you gotta try this."

"You're out of your mind," she calls, "that water has to be freezing."

He swims closer to the boat. "Nah, it's perfect. Your body adjusts and then it feels great."

"*Your* body adjusts, you've been trained to be in cold water."

"C'mon, don't you like to swim?"

"I love to swim, but I'm not crazy enough to go in there." She cocks her head watching him. She is tempted, if only by the fact that he is half-naked and slick as an otter.

"C'mon Petersen, I thought you were tough." He is baiting her now.

She narrows her eyes at him. He is grinning from ear to ear, floating on his back. He really does look like he's having fun. She peels off her clothes for the second time today.

He is whooping and yelling, egging her on. "Yeah baby, that's what I'm talking about. ¡*Venga aqui amor!*"

Down to nothing, she stands poised on the edge of the boat. "I have a feeling I'm really going to regret this.

"*No, no es fácil.*"

"Easy for you, crazy bastard." But she is laughing. She has not felt this free in years. She takes a deep breath and dives. As she hits the water, every cell in her body seems to contract. The world is black for a moment and she feels the shock to her heart, lazy and warm from the wine and the sun. She pushes up, breaking the surface, with a shrieking gasp. "Oh my God, I'm going to kill you!" Jules feels all of her appendages going numb. She can't stop gasping. How can he stand it?

Ramon swims to her in three sure strokes. "That's my girl. Are you okay?"

For a moment she savors the sound of his voice saying 'my girl,' but she is interrupted by the chattering of her own teeth. "Okay I did it, but I think I need to get out before I die of hypothermia."

He wraps around her from behind. "Just lay back and float, I'll take you in. Do you hate me?"

Her voice quavering, she replies, "No, but I'm considering kicking your ass a little later."

"Okay, *chica*. You can do it after we get you warmed up."

They are at the ladder. She climbs up, her hands numb and fingers aching. He follows her up into the boat and springs to action, opening a locked hold and retrieving towels and heavy wool blankets. He rubs her down roughly with the towel, stimulating her frozen nerve endings.

"I gotta say, Jules, I'm impressed. I didn't really think you'd do it."

She glares at him. "Oh, c'mon, Ramon. You know me well enough to know the quickest way to get me in there was to say I wasn't tough enough."

He smiles, draping her head with the towel and kissing her on the lips. Jules is amazed, his lips are warm. She burrows into his body, seeking warmth, still quaking. He holds her, rubbing his hands up and down her back. Ramon reaches for a blanket and wraps it around her. He briskly towels himself off and grabs her clothes. He peels his wet boxers off and stands naked, reaching for her clothes before his own. He is magnificent, a racehorse bred just for running.

Ramon leads her to the bench and instructs her, "Curl up, make yourself small." Tenderly, he takes her foot and pulls on her sock.

She watches him, unable to recognize this man as the same one who spent five months brutalizing her. *Everything evolves.* Jules is starting to feel human again, the sun beating down on her. She towels her hair nearly dry and pulls on her clothes as Ramon dresses too.

He comes and joins her on the bench, wrapping them both back up in the blanket. She curls into him as he murmurs further apologies. She is asleep in minutes. Lulled by the motion of the waves and the touch of the sun, he soon follows.

Jules wakes to the static of the radio. Ramon is up and reporting to Mac at the yard, informing him of their location and destination for the evening. Jules sits up, looking out at the horizon, where the sun is already beginning a lazy descent.

"Hey princess. How was your nap?"

"Great, I think. I feel like someone knocked me out. What time is it?"

"About 1630. That's 4:30 your time, civvy."

"I know what 1630 means," she says grouchily. "Y'know, technically you're a civilian now too."

"No, I'm an ex-SEAL. I'll never be a civilian." He moves to pull up anchor. "Listen, we're going to head over to Little Cranberry Island for drinks and dinner, so do whatever you have to do to make yourself feel girly."

Jules laughs. "What, you don't think I'm perfect like this?" she says, shaking her head for effect. She can only imagine how she looks after a dunking in saltwater and a few hours of hibernation.

Ramon considers her, smiling. "You look fine by me. I'll take you anyway I can get you."

She's pleased. "I'll see what I can do," she says, grabbing her backpack and heading into the tiny cabin. There is a miniature sink attached to a tank of desalinated water and a small mirror hung over it. She peers into it and bursts out laughing. "God help me." Her naturally curly hair has dried into corkscrew ringlets, wild around her face. She has dark smudges of mascara under her eyes. She sighs and reaches for her makeup bag and a towel.

She wets the towel and scrubs her face clean. With a light hand, she puts a little gold shimmer on her cheeks and eyes and reapplies her mascara. Her nose, despite her best efforts, is a little sunburned, and her freckles have appeared. She evens her color out with a little blush and dabs on lip balm and a peachy brown gloss. Satisfied with the transformation, she winces again at the hair. There is only one solution. She runs her hands under the water, getting them good and wet, then flips her head over and rakes her hands through the curls, making them looser and even wilder. When she straightens up and shakes her head, she looks like some kind of mermaid at best, Medusa at worst. *Best I can do.*

She strips out of her clothes, sprays on some perfume, slips on fresh panties and a black, racer-back tank dress. She stuffs everything else back into the back pack and stows it, grabbing her sandals and earrings from the outside pocket.

Ramon turns from his work as Julianna emerges from the cabin. She is backlit by the fading sun and glittering sea, looking like some goddess who has hitched a ride. Suddenly he remembers to breathe and lets out a low wolf whistle. "Damn baby, you clean up good."

Her eyes sparkle as she tilts her head to put on her earrings. "Thanks," she says shyly.

He clears his throat. "I guess I have some catching up to do. I'll going to take us out of this cove and then you can drive while I get dressed."

Her heart begins to thud in her chest. "Ramon, I can't drive, I have no idea...."

"Just relax, there are no pots out here and we'll be going very slowly. If you fuck up, I'll be right next to you."

She bristles a little. "I didn't say I was going to fuck up. I just never did this before."

"I've seen you do lots of things you never did before. You're very talented, Jules. I have every confidence. Besides, if you mess up my Rosarita, I'll kill you."

"Very encouraging, Lieutenant, thank you."

"You're welcome." With the anchor stowed, he takes the boat out of the cove. The scenery is spectacular, the gulls clamoring for food and the fishing boats silhouetted against the furthest point of view. "C'mon over and take this. I'll be six minutes washing up."

She smirks at the six minutes. Only Ramon would know exactly how long it will take him to clean up and change. "Okay."

He kisses the top of her head. "See that dark line over there? That's where we're going. If you see anything coming your way, give a shout." He disappears into the cabin with his gear.

Jules grips the wheel as if her life depends on it and in exactly six minutes, Ramon reappears, clean shaven and dressed in his black shirt and jeans. She relinquishes the wheel and moves to pull on her sweater against the biting sea air. Jules inhales the briny air as Ramon pushes the boat to cruising speed. In less than half an hour they're docking on Little Cranberry Island in front of the restaurant. They stow their gear and she peels off her heavy sweater.

The restaurant is little more than a long rectangular bar perched on the end of the dock, but the view is breathtaking. Ramon is greeted by everyone like a lost brother, shouts and backslapping all around. Both the men and the women cast unabashedly appraising looks at Julianna. Ramon and Jules take seats at the bar and don't pay for a drink for the first hour and a half.

Ramon introduces her vaguely, "This is Jules." She is aware that this crowd is intensely curious about her. Though it makes her uncomfortable, their scrutiny helps her to understand that Ramon's word is good. It is obvious that he's never frequented these parts with a woman.

Ramon touches Jules with affectionate pride, possessively draping an arm around the back of her barstool and pausing every once in a while to lean in for a kiss or whisper in her ear. Jules is mostly quiet, taking in the odd island characters and the way Ramon is regarded as one of them, not a tourist. They spin outrageous stories about their exploits fishing, diving and drinking, not necessarily in that order.

As the liquor flows, the men become more boisterous and the women more brazen. When one of the men makes a bawdy remark to Jules, Ramon abruptly decides it is time for them to find a table for two.

They grab a table overlooking the water and peruse the menu, agreeing that lobster, pulled from the sea only hours ago, is the only logical choice. They have a great messy meal with lots of wine and by the end of the night, Jules feels as though she's bathed in the sea-soaked lobster juice. She excuses herself to go to the bathroom to wash up, the bathroom turns out to be located outside of the restaurant, all the way at the beginning of the dock. It is dark and the entryway takes her into a covered hallway, men's to the left and women's to the right.

"Creepy," mutters Jules and she makes a mental note not to linger. She uses the bathroom, washes her hands and face and checks her hair. No point, she thinks, looking at the tangle of curls.

She exits from the brightly lit bathroom into the gloom of the hallway. As her eyes are adjusting to the change in light, she becomes aware of a man at the entrance to the hallway, leaning against the door frame. *Good, it's Ramon.* But then she realizes that the build is different, taller and thinner, one of the men from the bar.

She lifts her chin and proceeds to walk toward the exit. "Hey" she says, nodding casually in his direction, not making eye contact.

"Hey yourself," he replies, moving towards her. "Saw you inside. Great dress."

She makes a split-second assessment in her head. He has followed her from the bar and is testing the waters, catching her in a vulnerable place, far from the crowd. He is also blocking her exit. She draws a breath, consciously relaxing her body. She lifts her hand in a pacifying gesture. "Just using the ladies' room, my date's going to be wondering what took me so long."

She steps to the side, angling her body to slip past him. As she does, he grabs her around the waist with both hands, pushing her towards the wall. Jules lets him, wanting him to think he's in control. She can smell the cloying reek of day-old alcohol and the metallic whiff of his adrenaline.

"Don't worry about your boyfriend, he's just ordering another round. I won't take long, I promise."

"Truth is, friend," she says evenly, "I'm not worried about him, but you should be. He shows up here, you're gonna have a problem."

He puts a hand on her neck. Jules has been trained not to give in to the natural panic that rises when someone has their hand on your throat, but her heart is thumping. She tilts her head seductively and leans in to whisper in his ear, saying one word with utter conviction: *"Don't."*

He jerks his head back in surprise and she uses his moment of hesitation to pluck his hand from her throat. In a smooth arc of motion, she grabs hold of his pinky and breaks it, continuing the movement to bend his elbow against the joint. As he follows his hyper-extended elbow to the floor, a boot comes out of nowhere and settles onto his neck.

"Little help here, *amiga?*" This time it is Ramon. *Thank God.*

"Thanks, but I really could've used you a couple of minutes ago." She lets go of the man, who is now gurgling under Ramon's full weight.

Ramon smiles at her, "I was taking care of the check, you didn't want dessert did you?" he says conversationally.

"I think I lost my appetite. Can we just go?" She is adjusting her dress, trying to catch her breath.

He gestures toward the dock, "After you." Ramon gives a little bounce before stepping off of the man's neck. He growls at him, "Stay down or I'll come back and finish you, *comprendé?*"

They can hear him moaning softly as they walk away.

"Poor bastard," Ramon says. "Wrong place, wrong time."

Jules glances back at her victim, who's cradling his hand in agony. "Shit, I hope he doesn't drive for a living."

The rest of the night is blissfully uneventful and they make the trip home slowly and carefully in the dark. They tumble into bed, too exhausted to do anything but kiss until they fall asleep.

Jules wakes alone again, rousing herself out of sleep to the sound of a driving rain. She looks at the clock, 9:30! She wraps herself up and stumbles downstairs, Ramon is on the couch in front of a roaring fire, talking on his cell phone. He raises a finger and continues for several more minutes.

Jules moves on autopilot to the coffeemaker. She can tell by the content of his conversation that he is checking in with Gi, combing over the details of the last forty-eight hours. As he finishes up, he pauses, "What? Yeah the fishing has been great, raining today though, guess I'll watch the game." He glances at Jules, giving her a lopsided grin. "*Si, si. Bueno.*"

He hangs up as she settles in on the couch next to him. "How are things back at the ranch?"

"Fine. He's got it all handled."

"So, you're going to watch the game?"

"Fuck no. You're the only game that's on today. I plan to keep a very close eye on the score."

She laughs. "You're going to have to let me have some coffee first."

He gently takes the mug from her hand and places it on the table. "*Lo siento*, no can do. I wasted a whole night last night, I've got some catching up to do."

She sighs in pleasure, "I'll have coffee later."

The day passes much too quickly, they make love twice, showering in between. Aware of their impending departure back to the real world, she sends him out to have a beer with Max while she makes a late lunch. Upstairs, gathering some clothes to pack, Jules sits down on the edge of the bed, holding his flannel shirt in her hands.

She brings it to her face, breathing in the smell of him. She sighs, wanting to slow time. Jules wants to burrow into the unmade bed and lay all night listening to the rain with him. Instead they will be flying home. She folds the shirt carefully and tucks it into her duffel, underneath her own things.

Ramon comes back a couple of hours later, relaxed and in a great mood. They eat in front of the fire and then hustle around, straightening and packing. "Don't worry about cleaning, there's a service that comes in, they'll take care of the linens and dishes," he reminds her.

She finishes packing and is looking underneath the bed for any stray belongings when Ramon comes in. "You set?"

She nods. She feels as if she should say something to him, let him know what this has meant to her, but she can't, the words stick in her throat and she feels they might ruin everything.

He holds her hand on the way down the stairs and at the doorway stops her for a long kiss. They drive to the airport and board the waiting plane. She watches out the window as the dark gathers and lets the noise of the plane wash over her as she listens to the pilot talking to Ramon.

As they disembark at Teterboro, she thanks the pilot and walks back to her vehicle with Ramon. He lifts her bag into the truck and turns the key in the ignition, starting it for her. She leans against the door and looks up at him. It is dark and they are alone in the lot, he leans in to kiss her and all of her resolve to be cool disappears. The kiss lasts much longer than it should and they both break away, breathing hard.

"Okay." He kisses her forehead this time.

"Thank you, it was amazing," she says softly. She hesitates, and then adds, "You're amazing."

He laughs softly. "I'll see you tomorrow."

Her heart lifts a little. Of course, she'll see him tomorrow. "Okay."

She watches him go. At about forty yards, he stops and turns. "Hey Jules."

"What?"
"Back to business tomorrow, all right?"
Her heart sinks. "Right."

23

One night Gi asks Jules to drive Williamson home. It is 1830 and Gi needs to write an end of shift report. For safety, the crew tries hard to vary Williamson's routes, especially the mundane daily commutes back and forth from RSW to the house. Though there are only three possible routes, they mix them up as much as possible, varying departure and arrival times. Williamson hates this, but has acceded to Ramon's insistence over the years.

Jules looks at the log to determine which route they drove yesterday and then collects Williamson from his office. He is wearing a brown, glen-plaid suit, a pale green, gingham tie and seems especially ebullient.

"Hello sir, how was your day?"

"My day was exceptionally busy, but very productive, thank you for asking. And you, my dear?"

They are in the elevator now, on their way to the garage. "Similar, busy but productive."

"Julianna I must tell you, I feel absolutely vindicated in my push to bring you into the firm. Even the lieutenant has finally conceded that you're an asset to the team."

"Thank you sir, I'm glad you both feel that way." She shifts a little, imagining what Williamson would have to say if he was aware of their recent transgressions.

Jules escorts him into the back of the Mercedes sedan and gets in the driver's seat. She's finally gotten to a point where she feels comfortable with her driving skills. She'd spent the last several months practicing at least once a week with Tam on the driving course and she finally feels confident with the evasive and protective moves.

She exits the garage and takes a left out of the front entrance. After a half a mile, she makes a right onto the secondary road. As she turns, she notices a vehicle parked on the opposite side of the road.

Bedminster is a posh rural community, characterized by rolling fields and stately houses set far back from the road. Most of the properties are fenced and gated. The upside of this elitism is that the vehicles that travel these roads are of very specific types. The residents drive upscale sedans and SUVs or travel in limousines. The landscaping firms are easily identifiable with their pickups and open trailers full of equipment. Caterers, florists, pet groomers and delivery services drive minivans or step vans marked with large logos.

The vehicle she's looking at is a late-model, brown Suburban. It doesn't fit here. Jules looks closely at the driver as she passes, he is not on the phone or looking at a map. He is staring straight ahead and doesn't turn to glance at them.

Jules pulls a notepad out of the console, the Suburban is marked with a sign that reads 'Apex Construction' but the sign is of the magnetic stick-on type that can be placed and removed quickly. Jules extracts a pen and looks at the license plates, New York plates, but not designated commercial like those on the working vehicles in the area.

Jules scratches the plate numbers onto the pad and speed dials Gi. She relays the info to him, asking him to look up the number. He says he'll get back to her as soon as he has the info.

Jules swings the car into the driveway of the house, stopping at the gate. She swipes her key card and shows her face to the camera. Saul is on the house detail and buzzes her through.

Jules checks the rearview mirror to make sure that the Suburban is not in sight. Her heart is hammering in her chest and she feels a sickening awareness of her inexperience. Intellectually, she knows that she needs to secure Williamson inside the house, but her gut is churning as she imagines dozens of ways that this simple act could go terribly wrong.

If the subject in the Suburban was a spotter, there could be a second man in the tree cover with a weapon trained on the vehicle. Jules pulls the Mercedes around to the back of the house under a portico that accesses the back door of the residence.

"Sir, I'm going to ask you to sit tight for a minute until Saul can come out. I saw an out-of-state vehicle and I just want make sure we have a safe exit."

"Really Julianna, it's five feet to the door, can't we just run in?"

"If you could indulge me, Robert, it'll just be a moment."

Jules calls Saul on her cell. "Can you meet me at the rear portico? I want an extra set of eyes, we're checking a suspicious vehicle on the road."

"Will do."

Jules waits until she sees Saul at the door and then exits. She has parked the car with the driver's side and Williamson next to the door. Saul and Jules make a visual sweep of the immediate area and the property lines. Saul nods to Jules. She escorts Williamson out of the sedan as Saul positions himself in the only sight line between the door and the lawn. Once inside, Jules hustles Williamson upstairs to his study.

"Thank you sir, I'm sure it was nothing, but we want to be alert." Jules wills herself to relax, so he won't see the tension in her posture. "Can I get you a drink?"

"No thank you Julianna, I'm sure you have other things to do. I'd really just like to be alone."

"Have a good night, sir."

Saul is waiting in the hallway. "What's up Jules? You saw something?"

Jules' cell buzzes, "Just a sec, this is probably Gi, he's running the plate for me."

"Petersen."

"Hey Jules, those plates are expired, registration too, back to '98 for an '81 black Chevy Nova; driver probably lifted the plates off some junker. Everything cool there? You see anything else?"

"No. I took Bird in by the back portico and Saul helped me clear."

"All right, come back and fill out an incident report while it's fresh. I'll let Lieutenant know."

Jules hangs up and fills Saul in on the details. She offers to send an extra man to the house, but he declines.

She returns to the Mercedes and pulls down the driveway, pulling in a deep breath. Her hands are shaking on the steering wheel. She drives slowly on the way back to RSW, but sees no sign of the Suburban. *Maybe I'm just being paranoid.* She laughs at herself. *Kind of the whole point of the job isn't it? Finely tuned paranoia.*

Ramon rolls over in bed to find Jules, warm and soft in sleep. No matter how many times he does this, it always feels new, like opening a gift you know will be the very thing you wished for. He'd kept her up for most of the night, unable to get enough of her after only four days apart. It is 0500 now and they're both due at work in an hour.

Jules is curled on her side, prettily tangled in his sheets. He cannot remember ever feeling this way. When he's with her, nothing matters, nothing but touching her, tasting her, pulling her closer. Yet in the back of his mind there is always a nagging headache of reason, reminding him that this is a mistake of epic proportion. Through a fog of denial, Ramon puts the thought away in a box and tucks it away on a shelf, an unpleasant task to be dealt with later.

The women he's known have always required so much. Demanding, controlling, always running some agenda. Jules is a different breed altogether. the smartest woman he's ever known, he has to reach to keep up with her. Every time he sees her, he feels as though he's won a prize, unable to believe that this incredible woman wants him.

Every few days Jules disappears back into her own life to dispatch her responsibilities. She is gone long enough for him to miss her, a first for him. He finds himself calling to ask when he can see her again, something he has never done. He is in deep. He knows it, but cannot stop.

He slides his hand under the sheet to rouse her from sleep. She makes little exasperated noises, not opening her eyes, but rolling over and tucking her head into his chest.

"Please, please, we just went to sleep."

He laughs. "It's 0500 baby, got to get up."

"I can't."

"What do you mean you can't?"

"I just can't, I haven't slept in two days. Can I call out today? I'm serious Ramon, I cannot make myself get up."

He looks at her, stroking her messy hair, smiling indulgently. "All right. Stay in bed, just this once. Call dispatch in half an hour, but make sure you call from your cell. I'll get someone to cover. You can stay here."

"Really?"

"Really. I have to take a shower."

Jules falls back to sleep, burrowing under the covers, thrilled as a child with a snow day. Twenty minutes later, Ramon sits on the edge of the bed, showered, shaved and dressed, looking and smelling delicious.

"All right, I've got to get moving. Don't forget to make that call." He runs his hand over her bare shoulder, wishing he could stay.

She props herself up on one elbow. The tangled, dark hair and sleep-smoky eyes make her look like some old painting.

She looks at him, biting her lip. "Ramon?"

"What?"

She hesitates. "*Te amo.*" There, she's finally said it. She'll take the consequences.

She watches his face change. A flicker of tenderness and then he looks away, considering the weight of her words. They've been on his tongue a hundred times since the first time he'd kissed her, but he's bitten them back, knowing 'I love you' is something that cannot be unsaid.

Jules glances away, shamed. "I just wanted you to know. You don't have to say anything."

He sighs, looking at her with those unfathomable eyes. He puts his hands, so big they make her face look like a child's, on her cheeks. "It's impossible."

She nods, not meeting his gaze.

"But Jules."

"Yeah."

He tips her chin up. "*Te amo. Te amo mucho.*" He plants a kiss on her lips, sealing the contract.

A smile breaks out on her face and retreats just as quickly.

"Really?"

He is nodding, smiling gravely. "Yeah." *What the hell.* He's on the rollercoaster, already strapped in for the ride.

Jules throws her arms around him, saying nothing. He holds her for a moment and disengages.

"Now you made me late."

She is smiling, her eyes sparkling with pleasure. "Sorry."

He kisses her again. "Don't forget that call."

"I won't." She flops back on the bed, staring at the ceiling as she hears the door close. *He loves me. He loves me very much.* Jules pulls the covers over her head.

Two months later, Jules is lounging on the deck of her house on an Indian summer day, having a rare moment alone with Ramon. They are drinking espresso and sitting in a companionable silence.

"So your birthday's coming up."

"Yeah. Did I tell you that my brother's going to come up with Ryan?"

"You did. That's great."

"I'm so excited, they haven't been up here in a while. A long time, actually."

"Since you got the new job?"

"Yeah. I feel guilty. I should have had them up sooner."

"So what do you want for your birthday, *novia*?"

Jules smiles a little sideways smile and glances at him. "I can't say."

"Why not?" He is curious now.

"Because it's something I can't have."

Ramon frowns. "If there's something you want, I'd like to get it for you."

"I want to walk down Main Street holding your hand. But it's not gonna happen."

He considers this for a moment. "It's such a small thing. You should be able to have that." Ramon sighs. His expression is serious. "If that's what you want, you'll have it."

She looks at him skeptically. "How?"

"Well I can't have you walking down the street by yourself. It may not be Main Street Bedminster, but we'll work something out. If someone sees us, I'll tell them you fell down and I'm helping you back to your truck."

She snorts. "Don't worry about it. It's just wishful thinking." She looks at him. "I have everything I want right here."

He gazes out over the lake. "Do you?"

"Of course. A great job, a blind cat, my friends, and a gorgeous man who loves me. What else could a girl want?" Her tone is light, but he hears the sadness, tallying up what's missing.

He bows his head slightly, thinking of her and Chris. "You think about him a lot?" It is a question he's wanted to ask her for a long time, though in his heart he knows the answer.

"Of course." There is a long silence and she speaks in a quieter tone, as though someone might overhear. "You know the thing that bothers me most about it?"

"No." he replies honestly.

"I can't get past the fact of the *way* he died. I think more about that than the way he *lived*. I can't forgive them for that." She pauses, not even wanting to say it out loud. "I could forgive them their religious convictions. I could even forgive them for feeling that there was some kind of honor in what they did. But I can't forgive them for the fact that he was scared when he died."

Her voice breaks, "Chris wasn't some soft, white-collar, rich guy. He grew up poor and knocked around before he found the right path. He worked all through collge. He was tough and could handle himself. But he was so fucking scared in those last minutes, I could hear it." Jules squeezes her eyes closed, remembering his voice on the message.

"Of course he was, Jules, anyone would have been," he says gently.

"I've never said that to anyone." Jules looks at him quickly, as though he may have changed his mind about her. "I always think, he was alone in a room full of people. I think if we would have just been together, it would have been okay. I wouldn't have been afraid to go, even, if we'd just been together when it happened."

"That makes sense. You would have had each other."

"I always feel that I should have known somehow, had some sense that it was going to happen. I mean, how do you wake up next to someone who's going to be dead in four hours and not *feel* that?"

He winces, keenly aware of what she lives with each day. "You're not psychic, are you Jules? It was just an ordinary, beautiful day. No one knew. That's the brutality of it."

She looks at him, grateful for his unsentimental understanding. It is what she loves most about him, that he loves her respectfully. She nods, knowing he's right.

He looks back at her, the hard planes of his face betraying his own painful past. "*Te amo*, Jules. *Esta bien, amor.*"

She closes her eyes, hoping he's right.

24

Several weeks later, Jules is in the computer lab doing advance work for an upcoming trip to Chicago when she hears raised voices down the hall at the front desk. She gets up and opens the door to the hallway. Gi flies past her, muttering under his breath, slamming open the door to the stairwell. Jules walks down to the reception desk, where Junior is standing. He too, is muttering curses under his breath, flipping through the log book they use to record visitors.

He looks at Jules, wild-eyed, shaking his head. "Somebody screwed the pooch, Jules."

"What's going on? Gi looked like he was going to be sick."

"I swear Jules, we've both been on duty since 0600, usual gig, scanning monitors, taking calls. Then Gi looks out at the front door and sees something hanging off it. So he goes out and finds a note that somebody taped to the goddamn glass."

"Shit. What did it say?"

"Look, I can't even talk about this. Gi was headed up to show Lieutenant, so you don't know anything, okay? I'm sure in about five minutes we're all going to be in a briefing, so go back to what you were doing."

"Do you want me to stay here with you? You can't have one person on reception."

"I already got Xavier and Jorgé coming up from the gym. Just make yourself scarce, Jules. Lieutenant is going to be ape-shit that we missed this."

Jules heads back to the lab. She tries to return to her task, but can't stop thinking about the note. Not only had someone gotten into the compound, they'd been right up to the front door without anyone seeing them. Even if they'd done it under the cover of darkness, there were sensors on the compound walls and motion-activated search lights at random points on the lawn. It was an unimaginable breach and Ramon would be losing his mind.

As predicted, within three minutes they are all paged to conference room C and a building-wide lockdown is issued. Williamson is sequestered in a safe room in the basement with Tam and Solomon, both armed with AR-15s.

Everyone in the room looks grim as Ramon and Gi pace at the front of the room. Jules can see the tension in Ramon, now in full tactical mode. The men sit hyper-alert, ready to act upon Lieutenant's command.

Gi is feeding a piece of paper into a scanner and a flat screen in the wall comes to life.

Lieutenant stops pacing, looking around the conference table. "We have received a death threat directed at our principal. We process dozens of these, credible or not, every year, what should be a routine occurrence is now a building breach. This letter was taped to the front entrance door and discovered at 0710."

Out of her peripheral vision, Jules sees Matthew and Nate, who were on night shift, glance at each other. If it had been anyone else, there may have been a suspicion that one of them fell asleep, but Nate and Matthew were both fastidious about doing everything by the book. They never missed a floor check or skipped even the most mundane items on the shift checklist.

Lieutenant's voice lowers to a growl, "What I need to know is how this actor entered my compound, approached the door and left this item, without tripping an alarm, showing up on a screen or being seen by any member of this detail."

There is dead silence. No one moves or breathes.

"Gi! Put it up on the screen so my esteemed colleagues can see what they missed."

Gi enters a few keystrokes and an image of the note comes up on the flat screen:

> **CEO Robert Williamson,**
>
> Allow me to introduce myself. I am the last face you will see before you die. Your greed and carelessness are killing us all. This pandering of earth's precious resources must be stopped. I know what you have done and what you will continue to do if left to your own devices. I have been chosen to end your reign of senseless destruction.
>
> Enjoy your last days Robert, we will meet soon.
>
> **YOUR SAVIOR**

Jules presses her fingernails into her palm, she has goose bumps on her arms.

Ramon is pacing again. "This is the person who has already one-upped our detail. Already walked on your home turf, already been a rifle shot away from your principal. A failure of this magnitude is not a function of the building design, our technology or the system we have spent years fine-tuning. It is a catastrophic loss of focus on the part of each and every member of this detail, including me."

He stands still, Jules can see every muscle in his body vibrating with rage. "This building is locked down until further notice. We will search every floor, every room and every space in this building. Bird is secure: the residence is locked down. No one leaves this compound until every square-inch of these grounds has been scoured. If you find a gum wrapper, a paper clip or a bent blade of grass you will make an immediate report. Gi will divide you into squads and put each squad on a grid. Do you read me?"

The detail responds in one voice. "SIR, YES SIR!"

The entire detail spends the next six-and-a-half hours combing the three-story building, garage and grounds in two-man teams. Ramon and Gi find a scuff in the manicured grass by a side wall of the compound, on the outer wall they find a red thread that looks to be from a climbing rope. Every piece of evidence is bagged and sent by courier to a threat assessment specialist, Dr. Warner Reed, kept on retainer for these special circumstances.

Once the grids have been cleared, Lieutenant lifts the lockdown order and increases the residential and RSW details for the evening. Ramon will remain with Williamson and the family. Gi is put in charge of the compound. Jorgé, Junior and Nate are assigned to scour every vehicle owned by RSW, looking for tracking devices or explosives. They will be up all night.

Jules is assigned to be with Grace and the girls on the second floor of the residence. Ramon tells her to pack a bag - she'll be there indefinitely. Jules sees Williamson leave the RSW building, uncharacteristically silent, escorted by Ramon and Xavier.

The day after the discovery of the note, Ramon sequesters Jules in the monitoring room of the residence, the base of operations for the house detail. He gets right to the point.

"We're going to go over the incident report you filed for the brown Suburban out on the road last month. I want you to give me every detail, minute-by-minute, as it occurred. I don't think I need to explain the relevance."

Jules nods, "Of course."

She tells it again, spotting the conspicuous vehicle, the description of the driver, the magnetic sign, the plates and the steps she took to cover Williamson.

Ramirez grills her for another hour and then dismisses her. "Gi is tracking the vehicle and registered driver for the original '81 Nova, just in case this guy got sloppy and simply switched plates from his prior vehicle. It's not likely, but we have to start somewhere. In the meantime, you're here with the family."

Jules nods again. Nothing personal has passed between them since the building breach. "If there's anything you need, Lieutenant I'm here," she offers awkwardly. He is already out the door.

A full week passes before they receive the report from Dr. Reed. Though the details are not released to the crew, it is announced that the threat condition has been downgraded to from red to orange. All travel plans are temporarily suspended. The details are instructed to return to their normal routines and rosters but are advised to be "hyper-vigilant."

The admonition seems unnecessary, the men are grim and silent. Jules keep her head down and does her job.

Weeks pass with no leads, no further threats and not a hint of unusual activity. The men give Lieutenant a wide berth and double and triple-check every detail of the daily routine. Jules does not reach out to Ramon privately, she senses that there is nothing she can do that will relieve the burden of his responsibilities. He doesn't call, and barely looks at her. Though it stings, Jules knows it has nothing to do with her and that the best thing she can do is quietly wait out the crisis.

After nearly three weeks, he shows up at her door on a Saturday night with a bottle of wine. She wordlessly lets him in. The bottle remains unopened on the kitchen table until Sunday night.

Six weeks out, Williamson resumes his travel schedule and though routines have been tightened, the detail returns to its former state of peaceful efficiency.

Jules is lying on her belly in Ramon's bed, eyes closed, drifting toward sleep. Ramon studies the curve of her shoulder. He loves to see her this way, completely relaxed, so unlike her professional demeanor. Her fingers are open, curving like the edge of a shell. He sighs deeply, knowing that he has postponed this moment for too long.

"Jules."

"Hmm?"

"Jules, we need to have a conversation."

"Can it wait? I was almost asleep."

"No."

She stirs, rolling over to face him, blinking sleepily. "Sounds serious. Am I in trouble?"

He hesitates.

Her smile fades.

"We can't keep going with this." He struggles to find the right words. She watches, a somber expression dawning on her face.

He continues, "That breach woke me up. I let myself get distracted by this and I got sloppy. Luckily no one got hurt, but it made me realize how careless I've been, putting everyone at risk."

"That breach had nothing to do with us. We weren't off playing spin-the-bottle when that joker tagged the building. We were at our posts doing our jobs."

"It doesn't matter. I'm talking about professionalism, about integrity. I never should have let this happen in the first place. We're risking both our careers, Jules. I've got twenty-three years with Williamson. It's only a matter of time until he finds out and when that happens, we'll both be let go."

She sits up, pulling the sheet around her. Her face is clouded with anger, her eyes dark with hurt. Jules feels something clamp closed inside her heart. "Let's not kid ourselves, Ramon. You'll get a slap on the wrist, I'm the one he'll let go."

"Either way, it's unacceptable."

"Since when?"

"Since always. I take responsibility for this, I got caught up and couldn't do what needed to be done. I didn't think I would fall for you like this. I thought it'd be something that would run its course, but it's gone too far and I'm not going to let you tank your career over it."

She is silent now, reaching for her t-shirt and pulling it on, braless. "So it's run its course for you." She finds her jeans and pulls them on, bare-assed. She stuffs her bra and panties into her gear bag.

"You don't have to leave, Jules. It's the middle of the night." He sighs, exasperated at his inability to reason with her. "You know what you mean to me."

"And how would I know that Ramon?" Her voice has a bitter edge. "All those public displays of affection, all the love letters you wrote me? You know what? Never mind. It's my own fault. I knew exactly what I was getting myself into, but I didn't care because I finally felt something that didn't hurt."

She digs her boots out from under the bed and straightens, hoisting her gear bag over her shoulder, boots in hand. She looks him in the eye, opens her mouth to add something and changes her mind. Her posture is defiant, but her face betrays everything, her disappointment in him, in herself for letting her guard down.

She walks out, slamming the door. A picture falls off the wall.

Ramon scrambles out of bed, pulling on a pair of boxers. By the time he opens the front door, she is in the open elevator, barefoot and crying.

"Just come back in, stay here tonight. We'll talk about it."

The elevator doors are closing. She steps back, letting go of the door, turning away from him to push the button.

As the doors close, Jules sits down in the dirty elevator, shoving her feet into her boots, pulling the laces tight and tucking the untied ends inside. She gets up wearily and exits into the lobby, pushing through the main doors. It is cold and damp outside, her jacket forgotten in her vehicle. Her truck is waiting at the curbside and in between is a knot of local boys.

She is jolted back to reality: the time, the location and her vulnerability.

In her head, she berates herself for her stupidity. She maintains her stride and shifts her posture and facial expression into her 'don't even think about fucking with me' mode. As she gets closer, the boys start to make low noises of interest. They call her sister, asking where she's going so late. She takes them in, eyes narrowed, merely nodding.

There are three of them, two skinny ones that she could take and one big scrapper, who would be a definite problem.

She edges past them, regretting that her holstered weapon is at the bottom of her gear bag. The big one comes closer, "Hey, slow down, don't go."

Jules moves away and smiles obsequiously. "Not tonight, *hijo*, I just got my heart broken." With that she is up to her vehicle and in, locking the doors with a click. She throws her bag on the front seat and turns the truck on.

It infuriates her that even now, with all her training and skills, she's still vulnerable to any random bunch of thugs who happen to cross her path.

There is a thud and one of the skinny boys has hoisted himself up on the front bumper, rocking the vehicle up and down. Jules sighs, reaching into her bag and digging for her Glock. To her left, the fat boy is up on the running board. He lifts his shirt and presses his belly up against the window. He has a tattoo that reads *'PELOGROSO,'* dangerous.

She has had enough.

Jules pulls the slide on the Glock, chambers a round and taps it on the window. Surprised, the fat boy jumps down. She keeps an eye on the other two, knowing they likely have weapons of their own. Jules puts the truck in gear and cracks her window a couple of inches. "Tell your boys to get the fuck off my truck or I'm gonna drive over them." She has the pistol pointed at his chest.

The troublemaker has his hands up, laughing nervously. "*Esta bien, hermana.* Take it easy!" He whistles and the men scatter like vermin. She steps on the gas and drives away, shoving the Glock back in the bag. Her hands are shaking, her breathing ragged.

After a couple of blocks she pulls into a parking lot and like those days after training, puts her head on the steering wheel and sobs. She is a total failure, a stupid girl. She has made the classic female mistake and probably ruined the career she'd fought and clawed for.

Two years of training, a year-and-a-half earning the respect of the men and she has flushed it all. *For what? Love? What a joke.*

Once he'd had his fill of her, it was back to business. *What had he said? Twenty-three years with Williamson. As though Williamson would fire Ramon for sleeping with her. He'd probably give him a wink and a pat on the back. 'These things will happen.'*

And guess who'll take the fall, the little protégé who couldn't keep her clothes on. She cries harder. She is, as before, alone.

For the next twenty-four hours, Ramon tries to contact Jules. Her predicament is, as Ramon's subordinate, she must answer his calls. However, once she asks 'What?' and Ramon says they need to talk, Jules feels free to hang up on him.

Ramon is exasperated. Driven by the need to resolve this before they begin their workweek together, he is relentless, calling every half hour. Finally he gets in his vehicle and drives to her house, using his key to let himself in. He finds Jules in full defensive mode, her posture stiff, eyes glittering with rage.

She is backed against the kitchen counter, looking at him like they are back in the boxing ring. Ramon is determined to make her surrender her belief that he is an uncaring bastard who had simply used her for his own entertainment. Though nothing could be further from the truth, he can understand how she'd gotten there. He sighs, unclenching his fists, which had formed instinctively when he'd seen the combative look on her face. Her face softens just a little. He takes the shift as permission to begin.

"What do you want from me Jules?"

Her voice is shaky, "I just want you."

"The men are starting to become aware. Once they know, it's hours 'til it gets to Williamson. So we're about three days from a complete dismantling of both of our careers. You want to trade that for some stolen nights together? C'mon Jules. You knew when we started that there was a limit to how far it could go."

Jules swallows hard, nodding, though it's only partially true. She'd wanted more since the beginning. She is crying again, unable to speak. *What happened to you, Jules? When did you get so weak? You used to able to handle anything. And here you are, crying over a man.*

Ramon, frustrated with his inability to help her cope, tries a different tack. "What did you want me to do? Get married, make babies with you? Look, I know you wanted that with Chris, but it wasn't in the cards. You chose this career, you begged me to make you an agent. Now you want to settle down? You sure as hell can't do both."

She is crying in earnest now, his words as brutal as if he'd slapped her. He is right, of course. She'd wanted this career, knowing what it would cost. Isn't that why she'd taken this on, because she knew it would keep her moving, isolated, safe from any further loss?

His voice softens with regret, "There will be other men, Jules, plenty of them. Plenty of chances for all that, when the time is right. But you've worked hard for this. You put in a few more years at RSW and you'll be able to write your own ticket. You have talent, a genuine talent for this. Don't throw it away." He sighs. "We have to let this be over."

Jules feels her heart, staccato in her chest. She is losing him. She feels a surge of anger and shame. She weighs her words before she speaks, wanting to make him understand. "I know what you're saying and I know that you're right. But here's the thing, Ramon. Growing up, I had this really ordinary life. My parents were together, they worked hard and they loved us. No drama, no abuse. And I was on this path. I was a pretty decent kid, I went to college, got a job, met a great guy and married him. We were trying to have a kid. And then, on what I thought was just another fucking Tuesday, the world changed completely, one minute at a time. By the end of that day, everything I believed in was gone. All that hard work and planning, all of that normalcy, it didn't keep me safe. It didn't mean anything."

He flinches.

"So anymore, I don't really see the point of playing it safe. Because life finds you, Ramon, no matter how good you are or how hard you work. Even in our job. You and I both know that with all that planning and hyper-vigilance, it's only gonna take about thirty seconds for someone to take that whole family out. It's ludicrous, really, what we do. They spend all that time and money on us, just so they can feel better."

He nods. "We play the odds, Jules, we try to stack them in their favor."

"It doesn't matter. Whether you're some high-profile guy like Williamson or some accountant in a cubicle. If some motherfucker decides to fly a jet into your building, odds or no odds, it's over. What if it all goes wrong and you're in between Williamson and the bad guys? You do your job and trade your life for his. Wouldn't you rather have loved me? Wouldn't you rather have loved me than sat alone in your apartment watching some soccer game?"

He is silent for a moment, considering this. He nods again. "Of course, except the odds are that you're going to have a long and happy life. And if that's true, you're going to want to have a career, a job that you love. You'll want to be with someone who can walk down the street and put his arm around you. I can't give you that."

Jules listens, gazing out the window. She tries to imagine ever wanting anyone else. She waits, considering whether she should tell the truth that is demanding its due. She turns to him, "After Christopher, I didn't think I'd ever want anyone again. I was content to be alone and I just assumed that was the way it was going to be for me. But after that first night with you, I felt like I might get a second chance. I felt like I was right where I was supposed to be."

"I know. I did too." He rubs a hand back and forth across his head. "But in the real world you don't get to have it both ways. Us being together means everything you've worked for is out the window. If this comes out, no one's going to hire you again. This business is based on personal reputation. We don't advertise, it's all word-of-mouth. Your next interviewer will know the whole story before you even walk in the door. In fact, he probably won't even call you for an interview. I know I wouldn't."

His last comment stings, though she knows he's telling the truth. She looks at him, trying to find a trace of what he'd felt for her in his eyes. She finds only Lieutenant Ramirez, assuming his thousand-yard stare. She sees the muscles in his jaw clench. She looks away, embarrassed as a child.

Ramon lets the moment be. He's gambling on her independence, her sense of duty. As he'd hoped, her pride kicks in and outweighs her need for him to stay. She crosses to the front door, holding it open.

"You should go, I'm sick of crying in front of you." Her voice is weary.

He leaves, getting in his SUV and pulling away. Nearly half a mile down the road, he is hit by a wave of nausea. He pulls to the side of the road. He sucks in air, trying to quell the rising panic. He has hurt her irrevocably.

It is what the situation requires, but the finality of it leaves him as vulnerable as that boy abandoned in his grandmother's tiny house. He feels now, exactly as he had when he was a small child. When his *abuela* was gone, working all night in the laundry and he'd wake with a start, realizing he was alone in the house; alone in the dark.

Ramon closes his eyes and rests his head on the steering wheel. He's made what he believes to be the right choice, but the cost may prove unbearable. He puts the truck in gear and drives back to his empty apartment.

Jules spends the next month-and-a-half diving back into her life. She quickly realizes that she is out of favor with nearly all of her friends and immediate family. Between the five-month probationary period, the travel and her complete infatuation with Ramon, she has lost months of contact with her social circle and no one is very happy with her.

She has a long, quiet dinner with her best friend Lily, who pours the wine and chides Jules for not confiding in her sooner.

She calls her brother Tim, who invites her to Baltimore for a long overdue visit. Her nephew has turned into a young man overnight and she spends three days watching his soccer games and sharing French fries with the two of them. When she leaves, they both hold on a little longer than usual and she ends up crying most of the way home.

She makes the phone call she has been dreading, to Chris' parents, whom she has not spoken to in months. When she'd taken the job at RSW, they'd subtly let her know that they didn't think it was 'appropriate' for a young widow. It had stung her and she'd been reluctant to call and let them know how she'd been doing.

When Chris' mother answers, Jules offers a heartfelt apology and invites them both to her house for dinner. There is a coldness in her mother-in-law's tone and she replies that they are 'just crazy busy' for at least the next month. Jules makes small talk for a few minutes and then promises to contact them soon. As soon as she gets off the phone she sits down and writes an apologetic letter to them, confessing that she has been remiss and asking them to call and let her know when it is convenient for them to see her.

She'd had a close relationship with Chris' mom and dad when he was alive, but since his death, most of their visits had ended up with his mother sobbing and Jules following suit. They'd begun to stretch the visits out further and further, simply unable to face the pain that never seemed to recede. Jules felt full of regret for this, but didn't know how to fix it.

Nate calls her one Friday night, demanding that she spend the next day with him and Beau at a hockey game. Afterward, they eat out at a chicken place and watch a movie at Nate's apartment until Beau falls asleep on top of Jules. Nate carries him to his bed and returns to Jules to begin his inquisition.

"All right, spill it."

"What?" Jules ask edgily, knowing full well what he is asking.

"You've been in a bad mood for the last six weeks and you haven't said a word about it to anyone, especially not me. So spill it, Petersen."

She looks away. "It's nothing. I really don't want to talk about it."

"Is Ramirez on your case again?"

Jules snorts, "No. Ramirez is definitely *not* on my case."

"So what is it, something outside of work? Family stuff? Just talk to me, you'll feel better."

She would love to talk to Nate about it. And he's right, she would feel better, but it's a risk she isn't willing to take. "I can't talk about it."

"I thought we were friends, Jules." His voice is full of hurt. "What's going on? I don't hear from you for weeks and now that you're finally here, you won't even talk to me."

The cumulative guilt of her lousy behavior spills over. It is wearing her down and the reproach in Nate's puppy-dog eyes doesn't help. "It's nothing. It's just …some guy. It was going well and now it's over. That's all. I just need to move past it."

"What happened? Did you break it off with him?"

Shit. "No, he ended it." She'll tell him as much of the truth as she can. That way she won't have to lie. Again.

"Wait. Just hold that thought." He jumps up and runs to retrieve a beer for each of them.

Settling back down on the couch, he says, "So *he* broke up with *you?* I really don't get that. What was it, the travel thing?"

Jules shifts uneasily, frowning. "Yeah, I guess he didn't think my job was conducive to us having a real relationship."

"That sucks!" He leans back against the couch pondering. "Wait. You said you *couldn't* talk about it. Why would that be?"

There is a long, awkward silence between them. *God, he would make a great detective.*

Nate's eyes suddenly get wide. "Jesus, were you sleeping with one of the crew?"

Damnit! "No! God, Nate." *Ramirez isn't technically one of the crew, right?*

"You were! Unbelievable. It was Gi wasn't it? He's always been after your ass."

"No, Nate, I didn't sleep with Gi! God, he has a girlfriend, she's gorgeous. Haven't you seen her?"

"Oh right, like that would stop him. Well, *you* probably wouldn't do that to her, though."

"Okay, stop it. I'm not doing this. See, this is why I didn't want to talk about it. Shit! I've gotta go, it's late." She gets up, draining the last of her beer. "I'll see you on Monday. Thanks for dinner and tell Beau I said 'bye, okay?"

He puts his beer down and gets up to walk her to the door. "I'll tell him. Listen, I'm sorry, Jules. I just can't believe anyone would break up with you."

She sighs, exhausted from keeping secrets. "I forgive you." She hugs him.

He squints at her. "You know I'm going to find out eventually."

She makes a face. "Okay, good luck with that."

As she walks out into the hallway he calls after her. "Hey Jules."

"What?"

"If I didn't have a girlfriend, I'd break the rules for you too."

She looks at him, nonplussed. "Trust me Nate, it wouldn't be worth it."

25

Ramon is in Williamson's office, hashing over the events of the last few months and trying to formulate a sensible approach to his future travel plans, in light of the recent breach. Williamson has been alternately terrified and dismissive about the situation, depending on his mood.

Ramon parries firmly, "Things will have to change in the way we're handling you, especially when you're traveling. It may be awkward or uncomfortable at first, but our threat level has increased exponentially. We have a credible threat from someone who is expressing religious ideation and extreme grandiosity. He has painted you as a kind of environmental Genghis Khan and is clever enough to have breached the compound at least once that we know of. If he is the same guy that Petersen spotted, and I think we can be confident that he is; then he has been observing you and your routines for months."

Williamson sips his coffee, sets his porcelain cup down and sighs, leaning back in his chair. "Truly Ramon, if I ran scared every time I got a letter from some flower-plucking miscreant, I would be housebound. I simply don't see the difference between this basement-dweller and the other commune inhabitants who routinely decide that I am not a businessman, but someone devoted to wiping out every last earthly resource." He chuckles, waving a hand as if to swat away an imaginary pest. "I mean, why should I alter my lifestyle in response to this person's lonely correspondence? Won't that simply embolden him further?"

Ramon shifts in his chair, willing himself to keep his bearing. Robert doesn't like to be "handled," he has to feel as if he is in a position of superiority at all times. Pushing him only results in fits and ultimatums, as Ramon has learned the hard way over the past two decades. "Robert, you trust me to handle these petty intrusions and dispatch them as quickly and quietly as possible. Your safety is my only objective. But the world is changing very quickly now and the means to access you and yours gets more sophisticated every day. The only way for me to keep up is to re-examine every detail of your daily movements, make changes as necessary and know that I have your full cooperation in doing that."

"Yes, yes, I see your point. I'll make whatever changes you see fit, as always, but no body armor. Ever. Not even if it's Armani."

"Understood. Thank you. I'll get back to you with the changes."

Williamson rolls his eyes, "I can't wait, Lieutenant."

They are in the middle of the morning briefing when Ramirez gets a call on his personal cell. He picks it up, leaving the room to talk, closing the conference room door behind him. They are all surprised, Ramirez never interrupts the briefing, especially not to take a personal call.

Suddenly there is a shout from the hallway and a loud banging noise which reverberates into the conference room. Gi and Nate are on their feet instantly, heading out the door at a run. Jules hesitates, she has been trying to keep her distance from anything regarding Ramon. *Is he hurt?* She stands with several of the other men and goes to the doorway. Ramon is repeatedly punching the steel door to the stairwell. Jules understands immediately: Rosarita. It is the only thing that could provoke this kind of response from him.

Nate and Gi are standing at a respectful distance from him, Gi talking rapidly in Spanish, trying to calm him. Nate turns and ushers everyone back into the room, telling them to sit down and continue the briefing. He closes the door and goes back into the hallway.

Jules is shaking. Surely she should go to Ramon, but doing that will make it unmistakably clear that they've been together. Knowing this is the last thing he'd want, she waits, holding herself in check.

It will kill him. Rosarita is everything to him, his only family.

Minutes pass and Nate finally returns to the conference room. The noise in the hallway subsides and then disappears. Gi must have taken him to his office. Nate stops the briefing to explain to the men what Jules already knows.

"Lieutenant's grandmother has passed. Once arrangements have been made, the entire detail will be expected to attend services. The fill-ins will be used to cover in-house security and any travel will be rescheduled."

The briefing continues for a few minutes and the men disband quietly, none of the usual joking and banter. Nate remains seated while the men file out.

Jules gets up and closes the door after the last man. She turns to Nate.

"Where is he?"

"They're going to her place." He looks at her with something like anger. "You were already upset before I said what happened. How did you know?"

She hesitates. "There's only one thing that would make him react that way. Lieutenant doesn't lose control, you know that," she says defensively.

"You seem to know an awful lot about it."

"It's our job to observe, isn't it?" *Goddamn him, a dog with a bone.*

He is staring at her, shaking his head. "Jesus Christ, Jules."

She feels sick to her stomach. It occurs to Jules that she could lose Nate *and* Beau over this. She'd underestimated Nate's sense of propriety. His Boy Scout sensibilities have been deeply offended by her romantic transgression. Still, she is furious that he's judging her like this. "Let it go, Nate. I'm asking you. Please."

He stands up stiffly. "We have more important things to attend to right now. Just remember what your role is here, can you do that for the next seventy-two hours, Petersen?"

She feels an insane urge to punch him in the head. "Don't talk to me like you're my superior, Gunnarson. You were hired *after* me, remember?"

He looks at her, wounded. "Yes ma'am, that's correct. I'm sure you know exactly what's appropriate. I do apologize." His tone is wooden. He leaves, closing the door a little too hard.

Jules grips the edge of the table with both hands, breathless with rage and worry. *What now?* She sleepwalks through the rest of the workday, hoping she'll hear from Ramon. The news trickles in that Rosarita had been found by a neighbor who'd arrived for their ritual morning coffee date. When she hadn't answered the door, the neighbor had gone back home to retrieve the spare key Ramon had given her for emergencies. She'd entered the condo to find Rosarita lying on the kitchen floor, cold to the touch.

Gi does not reappear for the rest of the day, so at least she knows that Ramon is in good hands. She hangs around after her shift ends, hoping to see one of them, but at 1900 she has to leave to teach her class.

Jules doesn't get home until 2200, disappointed that there are no messages from Ramon. He would, of course, be exhausted, not thinking about anything except his *abuela* and what has to be done.

She thinks about calling Nate, regretting their heated conversation, but doesn't want to wake Beau at this hour.

Jules finally gives up and goes to sleep, vowing that tomorrow she will find some way to be useful to Ramon.

When she arrives at RSW the next morning, the place is hustling to rearrange coverage and organize things for the funeral, which is slated for the next day. She has a message from Williamson, requesting that she see him when she comes in, but first Jules tracks down Gi. She finds him in the equipment room, shining his shoes and polishing a belt buckle with a tin of brass cleaner.

He seems relieved to see Jules. "*¿Como esta, hermana?*" He gives her a quick hug. "You heard about the funeral and everything?"

"Yes. 1100, right?"

"Yeah, we're going to leave here as one detail at 1030."

"Okay. How's he doing?"

He looks at her as if he knows what she's really asking. "He's hurting. You didn't hear from him?" His tone is a bit too casual.

"No. I wanted to call, but …he's so private. I didn't want to disturb him."

Gi looks at her, his eyes kind. "You should call him today, Jules. I'm pretty sure he'd be glad to hear your voice."

She's moved by his unexpected sensitivity. "I'll do that. I'd better go, Williamson wants a meeting. Thanks for staying with him, Gi. He's lucky to have you as a second."

Gi shrugs. "*De nada.* Make that call, Jules."

She looks at him gratefully, "I will."

Williamson asks her to handle flowers, food and liquor for the reception following the funeral, all of which will be paid for by RSW. Though an event like this is usually arranged by his secretary Lauren or an assistant, Williamson asserts that it will have a more personal touch if Jules makes the choices for Ramon and the crew. When she exits the meeting, she slips upstairs to her dorm room and hesitantly dials Ramon's home phone.

He picks up on the second ring. "Ramirez." His voice is weary.

"Ramon, it's me."

"Hey." His tone is gentle.

She wants to tread carefully here. It has been months since they've spoken personally. "I'm so sorry, Ramon. I just wanted to see what I can do. Do you want me to go get the cat or something? I could bring him home with me."

"No, I've got him here. He was beside himself. It took me an hour to get him out from under the couch."

"Have you eaten anything? Can I pick up some groceries or take-out for you?"

"I'm okay. I can't eat. I won't be in today. I have a bunch of stuff to arrange. But I really appreciate the call, *novia*. You'll be there tomorrow?"

"Of course I will. I'd feel better if I could do something for you." She feels helpless.

"You can come tomorrow, that's what you can do. I need to know I'll see you there."

"All right. Call if you think of anything. Kiss Miaow for me."

"No chance, he's got cat food breath."

The funeral is small, there being no other family. There is a tight group of seniors from Rosarita's complex, who come escorted by sons or daughters. The entire RSW detail enters as one, an elegant wave of men dressed in their finest dark suits and Jules in her simplest black dress.

Williamson and his fair-haired family follow, looking like outsiders in the predominantly Latino crowd. The service is conducted in Spanish by a Catholic priest who'd had frequent visits with Rosarita at home. He speaks warmly of her, emphasizing her strength, strong faith and her attachment to Ramon: '*el hijo de la Corazon*,' the son of her heart.

Jules feels that she will suffocate on the thick incense wafting through the church. She does not dare to watch Ramon during the service. It feels unbearable to see his pain, knowing that she can't be with him. She stares at the stained glass murals of Christ and bows her head in prayer.

Nate had slid in next to her just as the service began. She'd taken the act as a silent apology, it has not been their way to be unkind to each other and Jules imagines he is feeling as bad as she. As they pray, he takes her hand gently and squeezes it. She squeezes back, so relieved they might still be friends.

Jules slips out just as the service ends to make sure that everything at the condo association hall is in order. She'd asked Martino's restaurant to cater, wanting Ramon to have the comfort of familiar food. The bar is stocked with the best liquor money can buy, with two bartenders at the ready, so no one will have to wait in line.

Jules had also set up a small tented smoking area outside, stocked with a range of cigars. She'd figured that at this point, nearly everyone would be ready for a drink or a smoke, maybe both.

She dims the overhead lights, checks the buffet tables and the flowers and heads into the bathroom to wash her hands. As she catches herself in the mirror, Jules is taken aback by her reflection. She looks pale and drawn, her hair pulled tightly back from her face, eyes dark with fatigue and sadness. The sight of herself in a funeral dress catapults her into the past, where she remembers her absolute numbness as she buried an empty casket filled with Chris' things in lieu of a body.

She shakes the memory off. *Now is not the time. Today is about Ramon and Rosarita.*

As she comes back into the hall, Ramon is just arriving with Gi. He crosses the room to Jules and holds her tightly by the waist for a moment before anyone else arrives.

Jules keeps her eyes closed and tucks her head into his shoulder, not caring who sees. *They're allowed at least this, aren't they?*

He finally steps back, collecting himself, gesturing at the room, "*Gracias*, Jules. Gi told me you handled this." He has not broken eye contact with her.

She gazes back at him. "*De nada.* I'll get you a drink." She points to the back patio. "Go have a smoke before everyone gets here." He nods in thanks and heads outside.

Gi accompanies Jules to the bar. As they wait for their drinks, Gi bends in and kisses her on the cheek. "Nice job. You know just what he needs."

She looks at Gi. He is handsome and shining in his dark suit. "Same thing everyone needs, a little TLC at the end of the day."

"Amen to that, *chica*." They touch glasses and she goes to the door to usher in the guests.

Late that night, Jules knocks on Ramon's apartment door, waiting self-consciously. He pulls it open. She shifts her weight from one foot to the other, holding up an expensive bottle of tequila she'd cadged from the reception. "If you don't feel like company, I'll just leave the bottle."

He regards her for a moment. "You're the only company I want, bottle or no bottle. Come in." He holds the door open for her. She hands him the bottle as she enters. She shrugs off her jacket, hanging it on the coat rack. Jules feels ridiculous, she stuffs her hands in her pockets, feeling heat rising in her cheeks.

Ramon stands in front of her, still holding the bottle by the neck. He looks exhausted, his face drawn. She can tell by the narrowness of his eyes that he'd continued drinking long after the reception was over.

He leans in and kisses her with a purpose, taking her by surprise. When he is done, he leans back, touching her face. "I don't want to talk about it. I just want to be with you, okay?"

"Okay." *She can give him this, can't she? What had she expected, some big heart-to-heart? She'd decided to come here, offering herself up, why does she feel so conflicted?*

He takes her hand and leads her into the dark bedroom. He uncorks the bottle and takes a long swallow. He offers it to her.

"No thanks."

He plunks the bottle on the bedside table and strips off his sweatshirt.

Jules stands silently, feeling like a hooker he has ordered up. She is an idiot, putting herself here like this. If she feels lousy, it is entirely her own doing.

Finally he seems to notice her ambivalence. He comes to her and gently begins to unbutton her shirt. "Help you with this?" He kisses her neck.

"Okay." Jules begins to relax a little. This is not some stranger. This is the man she has been in love with for more than a year.

Roughly unzipping her jeans, he makes no secret of his need as he urgently undresses her and then himself. Ramon walks her backward to the bed and pushes her down, catching her as she falls.

After kissing her deeply for a minute or two, he dispenses with any pretense of foreplay. He is inside her and it becomes clear to Jules that nothing tonight is about her. She could be anyone, she thinks, as his rhythm becomes nearly frantic. He finishes quickly and brutally with an anguished sound that she has never heard from him before. He bends his head into her shoulder and Jules feels hot tears trickling onto her skin.

Her confusion turns to sadness and she wraps her hand around the back of his neck, rubbing the bristle of his hair. "*Esta bien, novio,*" she whispers.

He emits a strangled noise and wrenches away, pulling abruptly out of her and sitting up on the edge of the bed, his back to her.

She can see by the shaking of his shoulders that he is crying in earnest now. Jules sits up, gently touching his back and silently kissing his bare shoulder. She knows only too well that there is nothing to say, nothing to do.

Ramon takes another draw from the bottle. "Can you just go?" His voice is raw. "Please."

Jules feels the sting of her own tears now. She moves quickly away from him as though she'd touched something hot. She grabs her clothes and takes them into the living room to dress, closing the bedroom door as she goes. He has not even turned his head.

Jules is furious with herself as she scrambles into her clothes. *Hadn't she just played out this same scene a few months ago? Him fucking her and then dismissing her? And you came back for more, like some puppy.*

She grabs her coat and goes, this time closing the door with a soft click.

Ramon doesn't move until he hears the door close, then he lurches to his feet and staggers to the bathroom to throw up. He sits on the floor, leaning against the wall, grateful for the cool tiles. He is disgusted by his own behavior. Jules had come to him as a friend and he'd thrown her out like some streetwalker. *Shit, at least a streetwalker would have been paid for her trouble. And all because you couldn't stand for her to see you cry.*

He pulls himself up and rinses his mouth with water and then mouthwash, deliberately avoiding his image in the mirror. In the living room, he finds his cell phone and calls Jules' home number. He is counting on the fact that she won't be home for another fifteen minutes.

When the answering machine picks up, he attempts to fix what he knows he's broken.

"It's me." He hesitates. "I'm sorry. You didn't deserve that. I was drinking before you came tonight. I drank so much I made myself sick. That's not an excuse, I don't have an excuse. I did want to be with you tonight, I just didn't want you to see me so fucking weak. I love you Jules, I still love you, but I can't talk about her. She was the only person who knew all of me and she's gone…. shit. *Lo siento.* I'm so fucking sorry Jules." He stops, having run out of words for her. She probably hates him now anyway. "Good night baby."

He imagines that she'll call. All weekend he waits.

Finally Sunday night while he's out at the convenience store, she calls and leaves a message, her voice soft, no hint of anger, only sadness. "It's me. I got your message." She sighs wearily. "It's all right. I showed up at your place uninvited. I just wanted to make sure that you weren't alone if you didn't want to be. I hope you're okay." There is a very long pause. "I just…I hope you'll be okay."

On Monday morning Jules sits at the conference room table with the rest of the detail. The mood is still somber. Nate watches her from across the table. Jules is in work mode, her neutral expression betraying nothing.

Ramon enters, passing around the day's itinerary. He glances quickly at Jules. She is dressed beautifully in a skirt and suit jacket, a discreet pearl choker around her neck.

It makes him want her all over again. He'd needed her so badly that night and made such a mess of it. He redirects his thoughts and begins. "Today's itinerary has been revised. The New York lunch meeting detail was me, Gi, Petersen and Nate. However, Petersen will be staying behind to make some changes on the Chicago trip. She's done all of the advance work on that and it has to be handled by end-of-business today."

Jules' gaze flicks to him and then away.

"We have a tentative schedule for next week with changes, so review that carefully. I also wanted to thank you all for coming out last week. It meant a lot." He clears his throat. "Petersen, I'll brief you on the Chicago changes in my office." He stops to chat with Eduardo and Gi for a moment before he leaves.

She is waiting outside his office when he arrives. He swipes his card key and holds the door open for her. She enters, standing stiffly, looking at the desk instead of him. He closes the door.

"Jules, sit, please."

She sits reluctantly.

"You got all dressed up for no reason. Sorry."

"It doesn't matter. What's going on with Chicago?"

"Wait," he begins. "I wanted to say thank you for being there for me, at the funeral, for coming over that night." There is an excruciating silence. "I hurt you. I never meant for that to happen. I was so grateful you showed up."

She looks at him, through him. "It was my mistake. I was trying to be a friend," she shrugs, "you needed something else. I didn't think it through, but it's not your fault." She pauses, taking a deep breath. "I'm done, Ramon. It's just like you said, we have to let it be over. We'll go back to the way it was before, just work, business as usual." She looks at the floor.

He feels a skittering of panic in his belly at her words. She is dismissing him. These past months he has allowed himself the fantasy that he could have her again if he needed to. Being with her the other night had only made him want to start it all over again, no matter the cost. He takes a breath. Jules stands, smoothing her skirt, ready to leave. He studies her face. She is not angry, not anything. "*Te amo, Jules.*"

Ramon's cell begins to buzz.

Jules looks at him impatiently. "Answer it."

He ignores the phone, and eventually it cuts off. "It can wait. You don't have anything to say? I've never known you to be at a loss for words."

She looks at him, frowning. "You say you love me, but it's in your own way, just until you start to feel uncomfortable. I've been loved, Ramon, I know what it feels like. It's not supposed to make you feel like shit. You can e-mail me the Chicago changes, I'll be at my desk." She opens the office door as his phone begins its whine again.

Ramon snatches it up, "What?"

Jules turns, waiting to see if she is part of the summons. It may be Williamson or Gi, looking for her.

Ramon listens and Jules sees his jaw clench. He grabs his key card, heading for the door, "They found another letter... it's in the parking garage."

26

Ramon skids out the door, Jules trotting behind him. They take the stairs and she can barely keep up. At the first-floor landing, they exit into a covered hallway that leads to the garage. Ramon swipes his key card at the fire door that accesses the cavernous space.

Gi, Tam and Bruno are huddled in front of the Mercedes. They all have on blue latex medical gloves, they've been instructed to keep any new evidence pristine. A fingerprint, the brand of tape used to stick the note to the car; anything could help them find this guy before he gets another chance at Williamson.

Jules' heart beats in her throat. *He knows which vehicle Robert rides in. That means it was him on the road that day, watching her take him home.* She feels lightheaded. She leans against the concrete wall. She can't believe this guy has hit them again. *They had decreased the time between routine sweeps of the building. That means that he would have had ... what? Twenty minutes to get in and out without being seen.*

Ramon pulls on gloves and reads the note, his face devoid of expression. Jules is hesitant to approach, but can't help it, she needs to know what it says. She leans in and scans the bold-faced type:

Robert,

Do you sense me closing in on you? Know that your greedy soldiers will not deter me. All the king's horses and all the king's men will not put *you* back together again. As you take your last breath, you will be grateful to me. I am the only one who can redeem your empty life of excess, environmental rape and twisted values. Say your prayers if you know any, Robert. I am coming for you.

YOUR SAVIOR

Jules feels sick. She steps back, looking around the garage. Intellectually, she knows he is long gone, but she can't help moving into fight mode, hands flexing, breathing deep and loose.

Ramon straightens. "I want everyone in, now. I want eight men on these vehicles, Gi, call our mechanics, we are going to strip these cars to the bone. Sweep first for explosives, then look at every circuit, every wire, brakes, all of it."

He looks at Jules, hesitating for a split second. "Petersen, I want you to drive this sample to Dr. Reed, tell him we need everything on this note: prints, provenance of the paper, ink, tape, all of it. If you have to stay there all night, do it, don't come back without the information. I need it by daylight. Then you, Gi and Nate will be on tracking this motherfucker. Use any contacts you have, local, county, state, FBI, NSA, I don't care who it is, call in every favor, get me something."

Jules gloves up and takes the note from him, transferring it into a plastic bag that Gi has provided. She jogs to her truck and programs the GPS on her phone for the Dr.'s residence, forty-five miles away.

The next seventy-two hours are a waking nightmare. RSW is a hive of activity, lights blaze in every corner of the building, men jog stone-faced to and from every routine task. Williamson and the family are locked down in the residence with a detail of fill-ins and the travel muscle.

Jules waits all night for Dr. Reed to perform his analysis. She drives him to a forensic lab at one in the morning so that he can sit shoulder-to shoulder with the technicians, telling them specifically what he needs. Jules sleeps in the vehicle until Reed raps on her window around 0600. She takes him back to the house, where he spends the next couple of hours calling stores and manufacturers to check batch numbers, retail sales logs and cash register records. Reed spends another hour typing up his findings and burning them onto a CD. He also e-mails them to Ramirez.

Jules conveys RSW's undying thanks and drives back to Bedminster, guzzling coffee and downing a bran muffin she grabs on the way.

She tracks Ramirez down in the computer lab where he is standing over Nate and Gi. Nate is on the phone with a state police contact while he types inquiries into the computer. Gi is taking a different tack, calling every street boss and aspiring criminal he knows, giving the description and identifiers of the vehicle Jules saw on the road, offering large cash rewards for the first person who comes up with information leading to Williamson's stalker.

Jules touches Ramon on the elbow and holds her manila envelope aloft. He takes it and moves to a work table in the corner of the room. He carefully spreads out the lab results and the report and begins to read. When he is done, he rubs the back of his head viciously and looks up at the ceiling as if seeking guidance.

He barks at Nate and Gi to join them at the table. "Reed did his job, but this information is essentially useless. The paper is from a ream sold in Delaware, last year. The tape was purchased in Ohio three months ago. The ink is of a common type, untraceable to a specific manufacturer. The font type is available on every word-processing program sold in the last eight years. No finger prints, a wool fiber, probably from this guy's garment, no discernible DNA on the fiber."

The Lieutenant clears his throat. "So what we know is we have a guy operating generally on the east coast, moving around. From the looks of it, he is careful about prints, and may have had a bead on Bird for at least a year, maybe more."

There is silence around the table. No one dares to ask what their next move is.

They cannot keep Williamson and his family locked up indefinitely, business will eventually have to resume and Williamson is the only one who can conduct that business.

In eight days, he is scheduled to be the keynote speaker at the annual Global Energy and Power Conference, a two-day event to be held at the Ritz-Carlton in Chicago.

Williamson has attended the conference as a panel member for the last twelve years. The conference is essential to making new contacts and maintaining old ones, and its organizers have singled him out this year as a shining example of the future of global oil commerce.

Ramirez finally speaks. "So. You three will stay put and keep hunting for anything we can use. I'll brief the rest of the men here and on the residential detail, as well as Williamson. No one goes home. Grab sleep if you need it, but keep moving. We have eight days to try to trip this asshole up. If he makes no further contact, we're going to have to do Chicago like a military operation: in-and-out, full tactical readiness. If this guy knows Bird's movements like we suspect he does, then he knows about this trip and the conference agenda, all easily accessible public information. This person has engaged us twice. Our only goals are to find him before he engages a third time or ensure that he fails to complete his objective. Let's move."

Three days pass with no viable leads. The family has been allowed restricted movement, to and from RSW for Williamson and school for the girls. Grace has been restricted to the residence and is taking full advantage of the fact by staying intoxicated at all times and spending enormous amounts of money shopping online.

Jules is at her desk working on the changes to the Chicago trip. Originally, the event was planned for 450 attendees utilizing three event rooms on the twelfth floor of the hotel. Due to a last-minute surge in reservations, attendance is now at 830 people, utilizing all six event rooms on the twelfth floor. The advance had already been done for the hotel and the three event rooms, but now Williamson's speech will be held in the 9,000 square-foot Diamond Ballroom, which has an adjacent lounge. Those rooms had not been vetted, so Jules is studying schematics and talking with hotel security. Ramon and several men will need to fly into Chicago two days before to assess everything in microscopic detail.

She is utterly exhausted. Her neck aches from typing and sleeping on the couch in the crew lounge. She enlisted the help of a neighbor to care for her cat Helen until she is back from Chicago. She has not spoken to anyone else, though she's typed a few furtive text messages to her brother and her friend Lily, just so they won't think she's gone missing.

As she tries to refocus on her task, Eduardo pokes his head around the corner. Jules tenses further, though it's been months since the incident in Buenos Aires, she still can't stand being in the same room with him. She suspects the feeling is mutual. He lifts his chin at her, "Lieutenant wants to see you in his office."

"Right." He disappears from sight. Jules takes the stairs to the second floor in order to stretch her legs, she's stiff from sitting at the computer day and night.

Jules raps on the lieutenant's door, she hears a gruff, "In."

"Sit." Ramon has shadows under his eyes and though groomed and shaven, has a rumpled look, unusual for him.

"I wanted to check on your progress with the hotel advance. I'm heading out in three days with Yoji, Tam, Solomon and Nate. We'll go over everything with Lou, the hotel's security chief. You, Gi, Matthew, Eduardo and Junior will be on detail here and the rest at the residence until departure. Tell me what you've got on the conference agenda and hotel advance."

Jules explains in detail the shift in the number of attendees and conference layout. She concludes, "As far as I can tell without being on-site, our three vulnerable points are arrival, departure and his keynote speech. We'll take him from the airport and in through the side entrance of the hotel, that's North Michigan, a one-way. Once he's safely in his suite, we have a good plan for any movement inside the hotel. As for the main event, hotel security will work with us on securing the ballroom and sweeping all participants and wait staff before they enter. Lou said he can have a metal detector at the ballroom entrance or just hand-wand them, whatever you want to do. These suits are used to the security procedures, so nobody's feathers will be ruffled."

Jules hesitates, not wanting to give Ramon any more bad news. "Departure is a little sketchy. Normally, we'd take him through the kitchen and out the side entrance, right to the alley and into the vehicle. The problem is, the hotel has a huge PR event taking place that evening, so they're going to have refrigerated trucks bringing in food all day. So the side entrance is no longer a viable exit. We'll need to have our vehicles out front and take Bird out through the lobby."

Ramirez considers this. "There's no other egress that's less public?"

Jules is prepared for his question. "Not unless we take him through the basement parking, but that would mean we'd have to sweep the elevator before we put him in it, because the stairs don't go all the way down to parking level. For the extra time we'd lose doing that, it ends up being much quicker and safer to take our chances hustling him through the lobby."

Ramon rubs his head. Jules watches him as she tries to stay detached. Not a word of personal communication has passed between them since the arrival of the note and she knows it will continue that way until Ramon is certain Williamson is out of harm's way. She's resigned to the fact that whatever they'd had has been boxed up and put away for good.

She reminds herself that it had been her choice to restore their relationship to business-only. *Don't lose your focus, the two of you are better off keeping things simple. Besides, he's already over it. Might as well follow his example.*

The RSW crew spends the next five days turning over stones, finding nothing and growing increasingly tense. Ramirez and his detail leave for Chicago as scheduled, Gi is in charge in his absence. Gi, Jules, Matthew, Junior and Eduardo focus on tying up loose ends and prepping for Williamson's departure.

Once Williamson is in the air, part of the house detail will form a skeleton crew at the RSW building and the rest will stay with Grace and the girls at the residence.

Finally Friday morning comes and the detail, as well as Saul, Xavier and Henry, shepherd Williamson onto the jet at Teterboro, going over the plane, the flight staff and the area with due diligence. The flight and arrival proceed without incident and Ramirez and Solomon are waiting at the airport to escort them to the hotel. Once they've ensconced Bird in his palatial suite overlooking the Miracle Mile, everyone begins to breathe again.

Williamson and the ridiculously large detail move cautiously through the scheduled events: cocktail reception, opening remarks, a senior panelist breakfast, seminars, Q & A sessions, lunch and finally, Saturday evening's black-tie dinner in the ballroom.

Half the detail is unseen, moving around the perimeter of the room, watching wait staff and moving in and out of the hallway, lounge and bathrooms. At last it is time for Williamson's speech. Thankfully, there is no stage, just a podium which comes up to Robert's chest, offering a solid, though not bullet-proof, obstacle.

Ramirez and Solomon stand post on either side of him, merely feet away, though they'd like to be right on top of him. Xavier has been seated at a dining table full of attendees, directly in front of the podium.

Jules is slated to escort Bird to and from the podium. Because of her close-combat skills, Ramon has selected Julianna to be near Bird at all times when he is moving from location to location.

Even the unflappable Williamson seems slightly anxious as the event organizer gives him the go to begin his speech. Jules gives him a half-smile and he takes his place at the podium. She scans the room as Robert delivers a flawless address. She's not entirely sure of what she is looking for, but believes that if their adversary is in the room, she will be able to spot him.

Before she knows it, Williamson concludes to great applause and Jules is meeting him as he exits the podium. Trusting that the men have her back and seeing Ramirez directly ahead, she whisks Robert out of the room, down the hall and down the stairwell to his floor.

Once inside the suite, there is a general feeling of relief and a widespread loosening of ties among the crew. Jules discreetly slips off her heels and grabs a bottle of water. She feels as if she's been carrying a hundred-pound weight and just been allowed to set it down.

Ramirez addresses the detail, "All right, well done, but we've got tonight and tomorrow's departure to handle before Bird is home safe, so don't get complacent. You all have your assignments for the night and we'll do a quick briefing here at 0700 before we leave. Night crew, wake me with anything out of the ordinary and I mean anything, an odd phone call, a maid at the door, anything. I'm one door down. The rest of you, sleep well, you've earned it."

27

The lobby is crowded, but it can't be helped. To compensate for the higher-visibility exit, they've increased the first detail to six men; second detail is two men in a follow vehicle and four of the men have gone ahead to the airport to secure the plane and make sure the space around it is cleared for Bird's arrival.

First detail is positioned in a classic diamond formation. Julianna is on point, slightly in front of Williamson, who is flanked by Ramirez and Gi at three yards. Nate is directly in back of Williamson. Saul is behind Nate, his nine millimeter unholstered underneath his overcoat.

Henry is waiting outside in the vehicle and Xavier, their biggest man, is already at the door. Because of the threats, all of them except Williamson have body armor on. Williamson had refused to wear a vest, despite the lieutenant's further efforts to convince him. He hadn't wanted to ruin the line of his suit.

They are moving in an efficient way through the crowd. Jules is in front, clearing, using her body and left arm to gently part the individuals in their way. Scanning left to right and back again, she is making eye contact, reading body language. To her, most of the crowd appears faceless: they are hassled, distracted and clutching coffee cups like life preservers.

At four yards, Julianna sees a face coming toward them that pulls her attention into sharp focus. Male, late thirties, non-descript, but there is a tension in his face and body. He looks at Jules and then quickly looks away. His suit is okay, but his hair is wrong, chopped rather than cut, glaringly odd in this sea of exceptionally well-groomed businessmen and upscale tourists. Jules forces herself to look away, not wanting to alert him to her attention just yet.

She speaks to Ramirez on her wrist mic. "Lieutenant I have a possible at eleven o'clock, three yards and closing, gray suit, bad haircut, you see him?"

"Got him. Nate get closer on Bird. Jules, I'm at your nine, I'll head him off, slow the pace. Saul, in front of Bird."

By the time he finishes his sentence, it is happening and there is no time. Jules sees the man reaching, moves toward him, breathing efficiently and loosening her hands. She deftly unsnaps the holster underneath her jacket, but there is no time to draw or shoot.

In the same moment, there is the dark glint of steel coming into the light. Maybe a .38.

"Weapon." No shouting as in the movies. The goal is to de-escalate, minimize the confrontation, and eliminate the threat. There is no logical thought process taking place now. They are all moving forward by instinct.

Their adversary is upon them, aiming stiffly, focused only on his target. Jules, as planned, is first in, gripping his shooting wrist with her left hand, driving his arm back and up toward the ceiling. At the same moment she hooks her right leg around the back of his left knee and drives her full weight forward, taking both of them to the floor in a slow arc. When she feels the impact of the floor, she begins using her right elbow to strike the bony parts of his face: cheekbone, nose and chin.

She simultaneously brings her left knee into his groin. Bleeding and growling, he pulls into a fetal position and hits her hard in the lower abdomen with a left.

Ramirez and Gi are there now - Ramirez breaks the man's fingers, taking the weapon from his hand. Gi plunges into the fray and knocks him out with a vicious right. Saul has his weapon out and he, Nate and Xavier are sweeping Bird to the vehicle.

As Gi cuffs the shooter, Jules rocks back into a kneeling position. She feels a deep, sickening tug in her gut as she does. *Tore a groin muscle.* She takes a deep breath and there is a sudden wetness underneath her trousers. *Oh God, did she pee herself?* She knows this happens in combat sometimes.

"Jules!" Gi's voice is sharp, urgent among the staccato commands flying in Spanish. She looks over; Gi is holding a stubby hunting knife. It has blood on it.

It takes a long, dull moment for her to make the connection. By the time she looks down at herself, blood is seeping through her navy pants in a widening black stain. Her heart begins thumping hard in her chest.

"Ramon." He is only three feet away, barking orders over the radio. Hotel security and police have begun to arrive, trying to herd the stampeding civilians from the mess on the slick marble floor. "Bird to location B. ETA eleven minutes."

"Ramon!" Her voice turns shrill, she's beginning to panic. Gi, unable to leave the prisoner, shouts in his command voice, "Ramon! *¡Venga pronto!*"

His head swivels to Gi, who's motioning to Jules. She is bending like a sapling under the searing pain pulling at her insides. Ramon is to her in an instant, his hand curling under her neck as she slides sideways onto the floor.

He catches her on his lap. "Get Nate, get him back in here. Call the squad, get them rolling." His voice is hard, propelling the men with his tone.

Trying to convince Ramon as well as herself, Jules says shakily, "It's all right. I'm okay. It's okay." The shock kicks in, making the pain distant, but it pulls her down and away from him, making the situation seem unreal. She is scared, really scared for the first time in years. Ramon rips away her jacket, her once-white blouse, the Kevlar vest underneath.

The pain of taking off the body armor brings her fully back to consciousness and she grips his bicep hard, telling him to stop. He peels her off and finishes the task. When the armor comes off, a well of blood is released from the wound in her lower left abdomen - a deep diagonal slash, a professional's cut, aiming upward for maximum damage.

Ramon is grim-faced, pulling off his suit jacket and using it to apply direct pressure, which makes her curse him again. He is still calling for Nate, who arrives out of nowhere, kneeling with his trauma kit. "Keep the pressure, Ramon, just bear down."

"Don't you need to look at it?"

Nate shoots him a look, shaking his head vehemently. "Describe it to me."

Ramon does, his voice quavering. Then he lowers his voice, "It's fucking deep, Nate."

Nate nods. "We need to move, where's the squad?"

Ramon barks to a local police sergeant, "Sergeant, what's the ETA on our ambulance?"

"Uhhh, twelve minutes, Lieutenant, they're fighting cross-town traffic."

Nate responds, "Twelve minutes? That is unacceptable, Sgt." Nate draws himself into full military bearing. "Northwestern is four blocks from the hotel. Ramon, we're taking her. We can get her there faster if we go."

Ramon is back on the radio with the second detail, who are waiting outside in the follow vehicle. "Junior, Henry, I want your vehicle in front in ninety seconds, you read?"

"Lieutenant it's impossible, they got the whole block taped off already," Junior responds.

"Junior, put that fucking vehicle up on the sidewalk in ninety. I'm sending out a Sgt. Wolf, he's gonna get you there. Copy?"

"Affirmative."

Nate bends to Jules, speaking to her in a low, soothing voice. "All right Jules, we're gonna take you in our vehicle, get you to the hospital quick as we can, understand?"

She nods, speaking seems an effort which would cost too much.

"I know you're tired, but I need you to focus now. The sleepiness is the shock and you've got to fight that, it can kill you, understand?"

"I'm scared, Nate."

"Of course you are, sweetheart. We're all right here. Everything's going to be okay. You just focus on me, okay? We'll do this together."

She nods again, curling into herself as another wave of pain pulls her under. She is gasping, cold and sweating at the same time. Now Ramon is behind her, wrapping his arms around her. His warmth and scent feel like salvation. "Time to move, baby. I'm just gonna pick you up and take you to the car. You hold onto me, okay?"

"Ramon, it feels bad."

"I know, *esta bien*. Help is close. Four miles, couple minutes. Don't fade on me, I need you right here, *comprende?*

"Okay."

Ramon sweeps Jules up off the floor. Nate is running alongside, keeping pressure on the wound. All Jules sees are staring, wide-eyed faces. Police, hotel employees - all shouting directions, attempting to keep chaos at bay.

As she fights the drowsiness, her thoughts drift. She wonders why she had wanted this; to be the lone woman in a world run by men. She'd mistakenly believed that it would be an escape from getting too close to anyone. And yet, the connections she'd made had proved even more intimate, each relationship as unique as a fingerprint. They'd each needed something different: Ramon, a lover, Gi, a comrade, and Nate, a best friend.

In this moment, she no longer feels equal to them. Their perseverance in the face of fear and disorder is unwavering - she has only faltered and fallen. With complete clarity, she finally understands that these men are not soldiers, simply human beings, absolutely true in their respect and affection for her. She can do nothing but place her faith in them with awe and gratitude.

Jules lets go. She has spent years struggling, grieving, fighting, training, working and now she gives in to the weight of the world. She is cold, shaking and utterly exhausted. She slips down into the warm, deep quiet. It is so easy; she wonders why she'd fought so hard for so long.

Ramon is driving, Junior is in the front seat and Henry had stayed back at the hotel. The Escalade weaves through the streets toward the hospital. Confronted with unmoving obstacles, Ramon finds each new route of escape and slips through.

Nate, in the backseat with Jules, feels her lose consciousness. "Goddammit! We're gonna lose her. How far?"

"Half a mile. Jules, don't you fucking leave me!"

"Get us there *now*. She's going."

"Talk to her, Nate. Is she breathing?"

"She's down. No respiration, no pulse. Shut the fuck up and get us there."

Nate works on Jules as best he can in the backseat, doing CPR and watching desperately for a sign of life. Ramon puts the vehicle sideways into the ambulance bay. The hospital, already alerted to the arrival, has a team waiting. Nate barks out vitals as they transfer Jules to a stretcher. He reluctantly lets her go. He and Ramon follow the hospital team. Ramon continues with Jules and the trauma team into an elevator, while Nate stays behind to give her information to the admitting nurse.

Finished with the nurse, Nate walks to an empty hallway filled with vending machines. He sits on a decrepit vinyl chair, puts his head in his hands and begins to pray. He prays for the tenacious girl who'd never wavered in her fight to find her place on the detail. For the woman who'd read bedtime stories to his son, who'd mothered the hardest men on the crew, who'd made the lieutenant fall in love. Nate prays for Jules as he has never prayed for a fallen brother: prays for the impossible, for her to come back to those who need her.

Ramon is leaning against the wall of a different hallway, having been gently shoved aside as they took Jules into an operating room. His earpiece is squawking with urgent voices and he rips it off, for the first time resentful of the needs of those on the other end. *Let them work it out for once. Gi will handle it.*

He feels the effects of the adrenaline dump, his legs suddenly shaky. Ramon slides down the wall to a sitting position. He bends his head and feels a rush of emotion. He has cried once in his adult life, the night he buried his *abuela*. He is helpless to suppress it now. He has watched other men weep post-combat, knows it is unavoidable, but at this moment it feels nearly unbearable.

It floods him and he is gulping air, his face cleansed of sweat and grit by a torrent of tears.

Passerby cannot help but stare at this grown man, hunched over and sobbing, his white shirt covered in blood. Not one of them fails to be moved by the sight, by the palpable sense of his pain.

Nate enters the hallway from an elevator and stops in his tracks. Though he understands what he is seeing, he cannot imagine what he should do. *Would the Lieutenant be furious to be seen this way? Should he go to him, comfort him like a brother-in-arms?*

In Nate's universe the lieutenant is mythical, a man who doesn't falter, never fails. But of course, in this moment, he is simply a man who may lose the thing dearest to him; something so valuable it can never be replaced.

Nate backs away, choosing privacy over intervention. As he turns away, he can hear the lieutenant praying in Spanish. Nate does not hear what he expects: a prayer for Jules' recovery. Ramon is praying to be forgiven for failing in his duty, for failing to protect her.

Three hours pass. Nate gives Ramon a half-hour of privacy and then brings him a steaming cup of coffee from the cafeteria. Ramon takes it gratefully, drinking while he paces the hallway waiting for some word on Jules. Nate retreats to the stairwell, fielding frantic calls from Gi and Williamson who are at location B, downtown. He tries to pass the phone to the lieutenant a couple of times, but Ramon waves him away saying, "Handle it."

Finally a surgeon and a resident emerge. A nurse directs the surgeon to Ramon.

"I'm Dr. Singh. Ms. Petersen is your wife?"

Ramon hesitates, "No... my girlfriend." He has never said it out loud.

The doctor nods. "I understand you were with her at the scene."

"Yes, I'm Lieutenant Ramirez."

"Yes, so you're aware that the damage was extensive. What we found was that the knife sliced through the abdominal wall, the bladder and a fallopian tube behind it. We thought at one point it was beyond our capabilities to repair the bladder, but we were able to resection it and suture it back together. The fallopian tube was easier, but I'm sorry to say we had to take the ovary. A very delicate organ, you understand."

Ramon nods, though his knowledge of a woman's internal anatomy is basic at best.

Dr. Singh continues, "At this point she's in recovery, but we're by no means out of the woods, as they say. We've been able to stabilize her, but the blood loss was massive. The good news is that she's fit and healthy, however, we can't know what was introduced by the cutting. At this point, infection is our primary concern. She's on IV antibiotics, but the next forty-eight to seventy-two hours will tell the tale. Do you have any questions?"

Ramon is no stranger to tending the wounded, but this situation feels entirely foreign to him. "How long until I can see her?"

"She'll be out of recovery in about ninety minutes, however, I've ordered her heavily sedated, she may not be fully conscious until tomorrow." He hesitates. "She's going to have a lot of pain. If she survives, it will be a long recovery."

Ramon nods again. *If she survives*. He understands that the phrase is not uttered lightly. "Thank you, doctor."

The surgeon walks away. He stops, glances back at Ramon and returns, inclining his head close to Ramon, speaking very softly. "Lieutenant, I don't typically give advice on personal matters, but... if there's anything you need to say to this young lady, you may want to say it now, even if she doesn't seem to be awake." He pauses, "It may be a comfort to you later."

Ramon meets his eyes and sees what is unspoken. "Yes, I'll do that."

"Also if she has family, you should get them here, let them see her."

"Yes, thank you." The weight of Jules' prognosis settles upon him. He watches the doctor pass through the door. Nate is at his shoulder. "What did he say?"

Ramon looks at him expressionlessly. "Get her brother on a plane."

28

In the dimly lit intensive-care cubicle, Ramon holds Jules' hand. There is a spot of dried blood on her fingernail, he rubs it away with his thumb. The rhythmic swish of respirators and distant beeping of monitors surrounds them in a cocoon of white noise.

He takes a breath and pushes it back out with a concentrated effort. "Jules," he begins, his voice just above a whisper, "I've got some things I need to say. If I know you, you're still listening, even if you're not awake." He pauses, waiting for the right words to come. "I did everything wrong. *Everything*. I put you on point, it was too high-risk. I didn't get to you in time…" his voice breaks.

"I should've kept you with me, no matter what. No matter what happened with my job or yours. It doesn't mean anything without you. I never…. I never loved anyone like I loved you. Right from the first day, God, you were under my skin and I didn't want it, any of it. I didn't want to be attracted to you, I didn't want to like you or respect you. But you just did what you do - you stayed true to yourself. And I didn't. Even after I was crazy in love with you, I wasn't true to myself. I didn't do what I wanted to do; I did what I thought I was supposed to do…to protect you." Ramon rubs his forehead, as if it will bring the truth.

"And you got hurt anyway. I fucked it all up. I need you to forgive me. All the ways I pushed you away, all the ways I hurt you.

I always felt like you still loved me, that was the strangest thing. Like you still wanted what was best for me, no matter what." Ramon struggles, searching for the grace to earn another chance. "I can fix this, Jules. I know I can. If you have any choice here, if you have any say, come back to me. I can make it right. But you have to try, you have to fight. I can't do it by myself. You still have your will. I know you're tired and scared, but I'm right here. All you have to do is come back, Jules."

He waits, as if expecting a reply. "I'm just gonna stay here. And I'm praying. Can you believe that? I'm Catholic, the one thing we know how to do is pray. Rosarita believed it was her full-time job. I'm asking her to pray for you too, she can do her part. I bet she's got some pull up there. So just stay baby, please. I'm not good at this, asking for help, but stay with me and I promise I'll make it right." Ramon rests his head on her hand, thinking there must be some way to reach her, but he finds only one thought left. "*Te amo.*"

Williamson, safely back in Jersey, is barking into the phone, "I need you back here *immediately* Ramon. We are in a complete lockdown situation."

"I'm aware of that sir, I ordered the lockdown. Everything is in place, everything is taken care of."

"Yes, everything except that my lieutenant is four states away from my operation and my family, immediately following an attempt on my life." His voice is edging toward hysteria.

Ramon closes his eyes, attempting to control the rage that is rising in him. *You bastard, you didn't get as much as a wrinkle in your suit and Jules is dying as we speak.* "Gi is handling it. I can't leave her here by herself."

"Nate can stay in Chicago with her. Julianna is not the one who's been threatened."

Ramon rubs his forehead, biting back to the urge to tell Williamson that he'll kill him personally if he doesn't stop his whining. "I won't leave her here. She's in critical condition, her brother had to get his kid back home, he's not even here right now." *Not that I'll be leaving when he gets back.*

"This is a matter of prioritizing, Ramon. Julianna is an *employee*. I cannot believe that I have to spell this out for you."

"She's a member of my detail and she got wounded on my watch. Robert, listen to me. We're not even sure she's going to make it. I'm not coming back right now."

"I would think, Ramon, that after more than twenty years of service, you'd show me some loyalty." His tone is prissy and indignant.

Ramon's tolerance for his employer's histrionics had reached its limit several minutes ago. "I've never been anything but loyal to you sir." His tone is a warning.

"You didn't even want Julianna on the detail, Ramon. Now you're going to choose *her* over the safety of my family?"

"You, as well as your family, are safe, Robert. Perhaps you should keep in mind that without Jules, you and I wouldn't be having this conversation. Everything I've done has been to one end: keeping you alive. Jules is part of my crew now."

"Julianna is an infatuation, Ramon. Do you think I haven't noticed? You are making a career decision here. I want you to be entirely aware of that." Williamson has regained his imperious bearing.

"Yes sir." Ramon's replies crisply.

"Then I'll be promoting Gi immediately."

"Gi will do an excellent job for you, sir."

"So you're certain." His voice is incredulous.

"I'm certain."

"Fine. You can see the attorney about your severance package when you get back."

"Yes." Ramon's tone is emotionless.

"Ramon?"

"What?"

"You're making a terrible mistake."

Ramon lets a long moment pass, thinking this over. "It won't be my first *or* my last."

"Yes, well enjoy that sense of confidence while it lasts, Ramon. In the cold light of day things may not seem so romantic."

"Yes sir, I'd imagine you know all about that. I'll give Jules your best."

Williamson sighs heavily, at least slightly chagrined. "Yes, do that. Have her speak with the attorney when she's up to it, he'll draw up her separation package. She'll be well-compensated."

There is a long silence, something Ramon didn't think Williamson was capable of. "Take care of yourself, Ramon," he says wearily. "Take care of Julianna."

"I'll do my best." Ramon is left with a dial tone.

Jules opens her eyes, blinking away a gray stickiness. The hospital room gradually comes into focus. *This is bad: I'm in the hospital.* There is a man slouched in a recliner at the far edge of the room. Jules blinks again several times, trying to clear her muddy vision. It's Ramon, with a stubbly beard and clothes that look like they have not been changed in days. She tries to lift up on her elbows, but she has an IV line in one hand and sitting up makes her feel like her guts are being torn in half. She gives up and lies back down.

"Ramon?" Her voice is a barely audible croak. She tries again. "Ramon!"

He starts from sleep, coming to his feet like a colt finding its legs. "Jules!" He is beaming, a beautiful, winning smile she has never seen before.

She is smiling now too. "God, you're okay. I heard you talking in my dream, Ramon, I thought you died." She feels a wave of relief.

"*I'm* fine, you're the one that's been hurt." His voice softens, "It was bad."

Her smile fades. "Where's Williamson?" She feels a constriction of panic in her chest. "Did he get hurt?"

Ramon frowns slightly, his tone turns bitter. "No, he didn't get hurt. Safe at home. You saved his ass, Jules. Don't you remember?"

She thinks about it, looking up toward the ceiling, as if it holds the answer. She shakes her head. "The last thing I remember is that creep pulling a weapon. What about him? Did we get him?"

"Yes, we got him. You took him down, only he had a knife you never saw." Ramon looks grim. "He cut you bad, up under the vest."

Jules frowns at him. The whole thing seems surreal. Still, she knows Ramon isn't prone to exaggeration. "How long have I been in here?" She feels afraid of the answer.

"Eighteen days." He hesitates, not wanting to upset her. "You lost part of your bladder and an ovary. Then you had a bad infection. We almost lost you."

Jules feels disoriented, close to tears. She closes her eyes. *Goddammit. Why is she still here? She could have been with Chris.* She feels suddenly bereft again and very alone. She grips the sheet in her fingers. She feels his hand, heavy on her head.

"Baby. I know, it's a lot to take in. It's okay. Everything's going to be okay, I promise."

She looks up at him, "I don't even know where I am. Are we in Chicago still?"

"Yeah, just you and me. Everyone else went back."

"You stayed with me."

"Of course I did." He looks at her, half-smiling.

"How did you swing that with Williamson?"

"I didn't." He laughs.

"What? I hope you're kidding." She is frowning again.

"Nope."

She shakes her head, denying what he's telling her. "You'll go home now, he'll change his mind," she says firmly. "He needs you."

Ramon is shaking his head patiently, still smiling that half-smile. "Good news and bad news. Which do you want first?"

She squints suspiciously at him. *What possible good could come of this?* "I guess the good first."

"Good news is you've got me. That is, if you even still want me."

She leans forward, touching his stubbled face, more handsome than ever, his eyes soft with a humor new to him.

"Yes, I still want you. What's the bad news?"

"You're fired."

She breaks into a smile and then erupts into harsh, disbelieving laughter, which leads to tears. "He fired me? For saving his life?"

He shakes his head, still smiling. "No, he fired you for making me fall in love with you. It just happened to be after you saved his life."

Jules looks out the window, running a shaky hand through tangled hair. Ramon takes the hand as her tears fall, the gravity of the situation settling in upon them both. She leans against his shoulder, drawing a breath to steady herself. Suddenly she lifts her head, leaning back to look at him, her eyes sparkling.

Ramon meets her gaze with curiosity, amazed that she is here with him; alive, her moods shifting like storm clouds.

She grins crookedly, "You know what?" She leans toward him in conspiracy.

"What?" He really wants to know.

"It's gonna make a really great story."

He nods, the corners of his mouth turning up. *Yes it is.*

The End

ACKNOWLEGEMENTS

This book started as a kernel of an idea. It is a work of fiction, liberally woven with standard methods and practices in the field of personal protection. As many writers do, I took artistic license with the facts for dramatic effect. Any errors are entirely my own.

My initial research focused on the non-fiction works of three highly respected individuals, each with their own area of expertise.

First, international security expert, Gavin de Becker of Gavin de Becker and Associates. Author of four books, including the New York Times bestseller, "The Gift of Fear," Mr. de Becker and his firm serve as consultants to corporations, individuals and presidential administrations. Mr. de Becker and his firm designed the threat assessment system, MOSAIC, now used globally as the standard for assessing threats both personal and terroristic.

Second, Dr. Richard W. Kobetz, Executive Director of the Executive Protection Institute in Berryville, Virginia. Dr. Kobetz is the author of "Providing Executive Protection Volumes I and II," as well as four other books on security. Many thanks to Dr. Kobetz and his staff, who afforded me the opportunity to attend his seminar: "So You Want to Be a Personal Protection Specialist?" where I was treated with incredible courtesy and made many valuable contacts within the protection community.

Third, Lieutenant Colonel Dave Grossman, author of the groundbreaking books, "On Killing," "On Combat," and "Stop Teaching Our Kids to Kill." Colonel Grossman is a former West Point psychology professor, Army Ranger and a nationally renowned lecturer on violence and the science of combat and killing.

Though I centered my research on the works of these teachers, my novel could not have come to life without the real-life experiences and wisdom of those on the ground, who were kind enough speak and correspond with me personally.

Special thanks to Jerry Heying, CEO and president of the International Protection Group, who offered both his time and patience to a civilian. Jerry, your kindness has not gone unappreciated.

Thanks also to John Negus, VP of Protective Operations for International Protection Group, and Thomas Stark III, of Northern Duchess Paramedics EMS for encouragement, recommendations and contacts.

Invaluable assistance was given by Ana Alfonso, security driver, who helped me understand both the mechanics and intentions behind evasive driving skills.

Tony Scotti and Joseph Autera, of Tony Scotti's Vehicle Dynamics Institute, Driving Academy, helped me overcome a major literary hurdle in the area of strategic driving, unselfishly sharing knowledge with a layperson.

To the families and loved ones of the victims of September 11th: I hope to honor the ongoing struggles that you face daily. Through Jules' story I wanted to illustrate that there is no 'getting over' such a trauma, only the day-to-day rebuilding of lives that pay tribute to those taken from us. We will never forget the enduring sorrow of what was lost on that day.

Thanks to my first readers: Luke, Peter, Ron, Nancy, Donna, Fran, Phil, Jen, Julie, Mom, Lynn, Chal, Anne, Debbie, Jill and others, for their notes, observations and gentle encouragement. Lynn, you are deeply missed.

To John Monteith, author of 'Good Doggie,' whose tough love kept me working when I was slogging through the hard parts. What would life be without coffee, dogs and books?

To Mom, for a lifetime of love and support.

To my beloved friends and family, who kept asking "How's the book?"

To my husband, Luke, who has always facilitated my dream to write and loved me through the dark places.

And to my son, Evan, you are and always will be, the light of my life.

AUTHOR BIOGRAPHY

Like her heroine, Kathleen Gasior studies and practices boxing and Krav Maga.

Gasior has written for EHow.com, Livestrong.com, and Tyra Banks's Type F. She is currently working on the second book in the Skirt in the Ranks trilogy and her third novel, *Scrapper*.

Gasior received her bachelor's degree in social work from Monmouth University. She lives with her husband and son in New Jersey.

Made in the USA
Middletown, DE
24 June 2017